Three Days of
DARKNESS

Book 3 in the Ross 128 First Contact Trilogy

DAVID ALLAN HAMILTON

DeeBee

For information contact :

davidallanhamilton00@gmail.com

http://www.davidallanhamilton.com

ISBN: 9781896794341

First Edition: August 2020

10 9 8 7 6 5 4 3 2 1

For my Dad

Truly the light is sweet, and a pleasant thing it is for the eyes to behold the sun: But if a man live many years, and rejoice in them all; yet let him remember the days of darkness; for they shall be many.

    Ecclesiastes 11:7 – 8

Historical Note

IN THE FALL OF 2085, City College professor Jim Atteberry detects the first tap code signal originating from the Ross 128 star system. At this time, North America is entrenched in a cold war between the Northern Democratic Union and the United Confederate States of America.

Several years later, in 2092, Kate Braddock and Jim's daughter Mary uncover anomalous geophysical readings on Luna that lead to the discovery of the Rossian alien ship. Clayton Carter, CEO of Titanius Space Resources, and Dr. Esther Tyrone, head of Space Operations and the Search for Extra-Terrestrial Intelligence at the Terran Science Academy in San Francisco, join Jim and the crew of the *Echo* to rescue Kate and Mary. But Carter's other intention is to secure the alien's faster-than-light technology, and he's not afraid to do anything necessary to claim it.

The *Echo* does not go unnoticed by other powerful nations and corporations operating in space, and in no time, a flotilla of ships gives chase, including weaponized heavy cruisers from the Prussian Consortium used to protect the mineral runs to Mars and the outer planets. The alien Keechik transfers its knowledge to Mary—for it is the last of its kind—after which she is rescued; however, Kate remains aboard the vessel and departs Luna with the creature. Before they leave, Keechik fires a crippling shock blast at the *Echo* to hasten their escape.

This story begins immediately following the departure of the Rossian ship from the Moon.

ONE

Mare Marginis, Luna

Atteberry

THE IMPACT FROM THE ALIEN SHIP RUMBLED through the bones of the *Echo*, ripping the corvette from Luna's surface and slamming her down on her starboard side. Jim Atteberry and his teenage daughter Mary tumbled over each other in the prep area aft of the flight seats amid the crush of voices, screaming klaxons and the deafening ring in Atteberry's ears. As he lay against the ship's bulkhead, disoriented, the pungent tang of burnt circuitry assaulted his nostrils. He turned his head and found Mary sitting upright, gripping the back of a misaligned seat. Lights throughout the vessel flickered, then died, replaced by emergency runners. Silence enveloped the *Echo*. The only exception was the sporadic clicks and the buzz of electrical shorts.

When Atteberry's senses returned, he saw the shadowy figures of the crew on the bridge struggling to find their balance on the rotated craft. He recognized Captain Powell's calm voice, and the deep baritone of Titanius CEO Clayton Carter—owner of the ship— sputtering words and bewilderment. Emergency lights continued blinking on and in the hard shadows cast by their glow, Mary spoke to him but the ringing in his ears persisted and he didn't catch what she said. Instead, he reached out, took her hand, and shifted his weight closer until he could hear.

"Where's Kate?" she asked. "Did she make it out?"

Atteberry grunted. "No, but she could still be on the surface, or . . ."

An amber and green glow shot up from the bridge. Two of the operations crew, Ishani and Dub, clambered over and around him from the stern cargo area, making their way toward the light. Esther's voice cut through the mumbled din.

"We've got power restored in navigation, Captain," she said.

"Thank you, Doctor."

The viewing screens remained dark, so they were all blind to whatever had happened—whatever was happening—on the Moon's surface. Atteberry recalled the moments before the shock blast hit. He, Dub and Ishani had brought Mary in to the *Echo* after she'd appeared on the surface from within the alien ship. They waited a few more minutes outside the vessel for Kate to do the same, but she hadn't come. The captain finally ordered them to return as a Prussian heavy approached, running hot. They passed through the airlock and removed their helmets when the wave struck.

The klaxon ceased its shrill siren, but the flashing red alert continued. Momentarily, the ship's systems coming back online vibrated through Atteberry's envirosuit, and one by one, the main lighting and viewscreens blinked to life. Each of them, except for the primary viewer on the bridge, showed nothing but multi-colored static. The images remained at ninety-degree angles, murky with dust, hissing at them.

Captain Powell's voice resounded over the intercom. "Secure yourselves in the flight seats as best you can. We'll fire up the engines and right this ship, and it might get a little rough. Stand by."

Mary, already holding the back of a seat, wriggled around and strapped herself in. Atteberry climbed over another and fell into it, buckling the harness. He reached over and squeezed Mary's hand. "Thank God you're alive, Mares." She struggled to return a smile. The ordeal of nearly perishing on the Moon, only to be saved by the Rossian alien, had taken its toll. Large black shadows surrounded her eyes, and her skin had become grey. She'd aged several years since he'd last seen her only a few weeks ago.

Powell continued issuing orders to the crew, and then Carter, Esther, Ishani and Dub climbed back toward the flight seats and buckled in. Carter sat across from Mary and studied her with a calculating, guilty sneer. This latest turn had shaken his confidence and Atteberry could smell his shame at threatening to destroy the alien vessel with her on it so he could grab its advanced tech. He dropped his gaze.

"Stand by, crew. Firing starboard thruster engines in three … two … one …"

A fresh, deep groan churned through the ship as the *Echo* tilted and jolted from the bounds of Luna's grey surface. Several seconds passed before she reoriented herself along the horizontal axis, then descended to the dust in an upright position. The viewscreens flickered again and now they all showed Luna's relief on the primary viewer. They remained buckled in.

Esther nodded to Mary as she nervously fingered her harness like a trapped animal. "She's exhausted, Jim."

"Yeah, I can't imagine what she and Kate went through these past few days."

Esther's gaze shifted to a viewscreen. "Look at that."

Atteberry twisted his neck toward the screen. The Moon's surface across the entire *Mare Marginis* was carved in lines as if some massive creature had dragged a giant trowel across it. Dust continued floating through the vacuum, but there was no mistaking the chunks of crust lying in heaps, and a new ditch-like crater snaking from the *Echo*'s old position to where the alien ship used to be.

The vessel itself had disappeared.

Atteberry scanned the area, hoping, praying to find Kate out there, but there was no sign of anyone or anything else inhabiting the gloomy landscape. Both she and the Rossian ship were gone.

"We've got company, y'all. I don't know how the Prussians repaired all them systems so quickly, but the *Sara Waltz* is moving in on us fast!"

Atteberry recognized Quigg's drawl rising out of the noise from the comms station.

"Dammit!" Carter hollered.

"Remain calm, folks," Captain Powell said. "Mr. Jenson, take us up and initiate evasive maneuvers. We need time to repair our ship before we think about tackling that cruiser."

"Aye, sir."

The *Echo* thundered to life and pulled away from Luna's surface. Her primary engines engaged, and she blasted off, but before the defensive flight pattern took effect, the *Sara Waltz* fired a salvo of rail guns toward them. The first shots missed wide, but the second volley found their target and flung the ship aside. More sparks burst from the command deck and the shrill klaxon sounded anew. Mary bolted up, restrained by her harness.

"What's happening, Dad?"

"We're under attack by one of those ships. The *Sara Waltz*."

Her eyes widened, and she scanned the ship's layout.

"Status, Mr. Jenson," the captain said, and Atteberry detected a note of concern in his voice.

Elin Jenson, the co-pilot, shouted. "Main engines out of commission . . . nav thrusters still operational . . . weapons offline, sir!"

"Shields?"

"Primaries are holding," she said, "but hardshields are down." She turned to face him. "They hit us bad, Captain."

Atteberry held his breath and reached out to Mary, but she ignored him, fumbling with her harness instead. He grabbed her arm. "Mares, what are you doing?"

"I can fix this, Dad."

"What are you talking about?"

"The *Echo* is broken. I can fix her." A short reassuring smile spread over her lips. "Trust me."

He glanced at Esther for support, but she was in her own world of disbelief, hands gripping the armrests.

"They're coming again, Captain!"

Atteberry threw a cursory look at the viewer. The *Sara Waltz*, at least ten times larger than the *Echo*, had swung around and was closing in fast for another run.

"Dad, let me go before it's too late."

Atteberry swallowed hard, staring at his daughter, unable to move. She pulled his hand off her arm and jumped from the flight seat. A secondary comms hub near Esther glowed, and she raced to it.

"They're firing another round of rail gun missiles."

"Evasive action, Jenson!"

She maneuvered the nav console and shook her head. "Sir, there's no time. They've locked on. We're dead in the water."

Mary reached out to the panel, spread her fingers wide and touched it. A misty blue glow enveloped her hands, and Atteberry witnessed faint threads of energy sparking off in all directions, as if following the ship's internal circuitry through the bulwark.

"Stand by for impact!"

"Mares . . ." He reached out for her.

The primary viewer flashed in a brilliant display of orange and white as the missiles rained down on the stricken ship.

Atteberry squeezed his body into the flight seat. He held his breath, and . . .

They missed?

TWO

Atteberry

CONFUSION SPREAD ACROSS ESTHER'S FACE. The blue glow dissipated from Mary's hands and she drew them away from the panel before collapsing against the ship's bulkhead. A howling scream from deep within exploded out of her mouth and, clutching her temples, she tumbled hard to the metal deck.

As Mary fell, Atteberry unbuckled his harness and jumped to her aid. He held her head up and winced at the intense heat radiating from her skin, as if a fever tore through her body. Esther checked her pupils, then her pulse. They unlatched the envirosuit, struggled with it, and freed her. She was soaked with sweat. Esther squeezed her arms and legs and inspected her glands.

"Let's get her back in the flight seat," she said.

Atteberry lifted her and settled her in, adjusting the headrest to keep her neck straight. He placed his hand on her forehead and overheard more commotion on the bridge.

"What the hell just happened?" Carter bellowed from his position behind the captain's command chair.

"Uncertain, sir," Jenson replied. "The Prussians had us locked in their sites." She continued checking her nav display. "I'm running system-wide diagnostics now."

"This is weird and all, y'all," Quigg mused. "The entire comms network is down. No operating channels or open frequencies. It's like we've been unplugged."

Carter shouted again. "Why aren't we dead, John?" He voiced the question they were all thinking.

"I can't say. Somehow that last salvo passed right *through* us. No doubt they had us, but then . . . it's a mystery." Powell returned his attention to the *Sara Waltz*. "Mr. Jenson, set a course for the far side of Luna."

"That could take a while on nav thrusters only, sir."

"I understand. Do what you can."

"Aye, sir."

The ship limped toward the dark side of the Moon. Meanwhile, the heavy cruiser broke off her attack, paused several minutes, and established a 3-D elliptical flight pattern.

Captain Powell tracked her movements. Staring at their adversary's path, he asked, "What do you make of that, Mr. Jenson?"

She studied the ship's position for a moment, then said, "It's as if they can't see us, sir. She's following a standard search routine used for any lost vessel that's gone dark."

"Agreed. So does this mean their sensors have malfunctioned?" Powell stood and approached the main viewer, watching the Prussian cruiser sweep through the area. "Whatever's keeping us hidden, I'd like to take full advantage of it. Mr. Jenson, how far to the shadow zone?"

"Ten minutes, sir."

He threw Carter a concerned look. "Clayton, we're not out of danger yet." Then, to everyone else, "Stay alert, folks. Be prepared for anything."

Esther peered at Atteberry. "We better strap her in." They harnessed Mary's body and covered her with a blanket as the captain strode toward them.

"You okay back here?"

Atteberry clipped in one of the harness buckles, wondering how to answer. He wiped a drop of sweat from his forehead. "Yes, a bit shaken up from the near miss, and my daughter's burning up and needs medical attention, but we're alive."

"We'll do our best to get you all home. Any idea what happened to Kate Braddock?

Atteberry tugged on Mary's straps to ensure she was secure, then shook his head.

"If we get an opportunity to investigate further, we will. I haven't lost a crew member in 18 years of space flight, and I'd like to keep that record intact."

"Thank you, Captain."

He squeezed Atteberry's shoulder reassuringly and returned to the bridge. Once he'd gone, Atteberry pulled Esther aside.

"We both saw what she did here, Es. Something strange happened to my girl on that alien ship, and did you hear what she said about being able to fix the *Echo*?"

She glanced around nervously. "I did, and yes, this doesn't feel right. How did she seem to you on the surface?"

"Fine, all considered. Maybe quieter than normal, but I figured she was in shock from her alien experience." He narrowed his gaze. "Why do you ask?"

"Whatever happened, she's changed. Look Jim, she obviously acquired some kind of power on that ship and used it to save us and the *Echo*, but you can see the consequence of it. She's not well."

Mary's lips moved as if speaking, and her body twitched in the flight seat.

8

"We'd better find out the truth." Esther leaned over to the seat and brushed her cheek with the back of her hand. She stirred, and then awakened.

"What happened?" Mary asked, her voice thick and cracking.

Atteberry answered. "You touched the comms panel. A rail gun blast narrowly missed us, and now . . ." he peered toward the bridge, "we're chugging away from that nasty cruiser that wants to finish us."

"They won't . . . can't. The *Echo* is safe, at least for a while." She seemed disoriented, her gaze flitting around the vessel, her body shivering.

He held her shoulders. "Mares, please, look at me."

"Hm?"

"What happened to you on that ship?"

Mary leaned forward in the flight seat and Esther and Atteberry gathered in. She said, "Short answer is the alien, Keechik, transferred copies—no, more like echoes—of its memories and experiences and knowledge to me. It's the last of its kind and needed me to preserve its entire history, its culture, its people." She touched his hand. "Dad, you were right all along. The creature only wanted to be remembered." She waved away a yawn, closed her eyes and her mouth fell open.

"And what about—"

"Jim," Esther intervened, "not now. Let her rest." She stroked his back and guided him a little farther aft toward the galley. There, she drew in close and whispered, "This isn't good, not at all."

"What do you mean?"

"If what Mary says is true, and she's gained all the knowledge of this *Keechik* thing and its civilization, then consider the repercussions."

Atteberry played it out in his mind. At first, he focused on the historical and cultural aspects of this first alien contact, learning about a new society, it's location, beliefs, abilities. Then he came around to space travel and how the alien used faster-than-light technology to not only communicate on subspace frequencies, but also to travel almost 11 light years from the Ross 128 system to Earth in a matter of years, or perhaps months. Who knew how long that ship had remained on Luna's surface, observing the Earth?

A wave of panic rose from his gut. "Wait a second. If Mary has all this new knowledge, then she might know how to build the technology needed to travel across space."

Esther ran her fingers through her hair. "It seems she also knows how to cloak the *Echo*."

"Which means we don't even need to find that ship. She has everything that Carter, the Chinese and the Prussians and . . ." He paused and released a lengthy breath. "Sweet Jesus, Es. If the others discover this, they'll want her too." His mind collapsed around scientists, politicians, and foreign governments all conspiring to exploit her new abilities for their own purposes. Although he prided himself on sharing all information with all people all the time, his experience rescuing Mary and now losing Kate had soured that belief. Perhaps Esther had been right all along: it doesn't pay to be so transparent.

"We can't let the others know," he said.

"Agreed. We'll have to spin a yarn." She looked toward the bridge. "Come on, let's see what's up."

Jim removed his jacket and draped it over Mary's chest. The flight seat was equipped with a built-in bio-sensor, and her vital signs appeared at the bottom of the nearest viewscreen. Her heart beat stabilized, and her fever hovered at 39 degrees Celsius. Chills continued shaking her body, so Atteberry didn't follow Esther to the bridge. Instead, he fell back to keep a close watch on his ailing daughter.

Captain Powell swung his command chair around when she approached and said, "How's the girl?"

"Exhausted. She's been through such an ordeal these past few days, and I think her functions are shutting down for repairs. We've got to get her home and have a doctor check her out." She paused. "It still hasn't hit me yet, Captain."

"What's that?"

"That young woman struggling back there was the first human being to contact an alien life form."

"That we know of," he grinned, and a ghost of a smile appeared on Esther's face.

Powell motioned to the screen showing the *Sara Waltz* continuing its methodical pattern. "Doctor, as a scientist, what do you think happened here a few minutes ago?"

Atteberry, overhearing their conversation, wondered how she'd handle this question. He watched Carter, the man's enormous arms folded across his chest, head bowed, move closer to her.

Esther shrugged, choosing her words carefully. "It must have something to do with that alien ship's departure when it blasted off at light speed. Tell me, is there any sign of it on your long-range scanners?"

Jenson punched a couple of buttons on her display, then turned. "Negative. It's disappeared from our solar system."

"Say, I'm no expert on faster-than-light space travel, but what we might be experiencing is a distortion in the space-time fabric caused by the alien's sudden disappearance. Since we were so close to it when the vessel took off, we may be caught in that distortion now. Like flotsam in an eddy."

Quigg leapt from his station and joined them. "That makes sense. It would explain the sudden loss of comms and our apparent invisibility if we're out of phase with space-time prime."

Atteberry drifted in closer to the conversation. Although he didn't follow the science being discussed, he wanted to encourage this focus on the Rossian ship and away from Mary. He chimed in. "This is beyond my understanding. What is this distortion?"

Everyone turned to Esther. She cleared her throat and explained, "Think of it as the exhaust signature from a conventional ship's engine, or carbon monoxide from an old fossil fuel car. It's a residual cloud, but powerful enough to distort the space around it, causing the *Echo* to be out of phase with space-time prime, that is, what's real for us."

He worked it through. "If it's like an exhaust plume, then at some point it must dissipate."

"Yes. I have no idea when," Esther said, waving her hand in the air, "but if the distortion is akin to a ripple on the water's surface, which the research seems to suggest, eventually the wave loses its energy and the water returns to normal."

Captain Powell glanced at the main viewscreen. The *Sara Waltz* had broken off its search pattern and appeared to ease away from the Moon. "Mr. Jenson, ETA to the far side shadow?"

"Thirty seconds, sir."

"Thanks." Then turning to the other crew members, he said, "Ish, you and Dub head aft to Ops and get those primary engines repaired."

They doubled it off the bridge.

"Mr. Quigg, you and Esther run the science on space-time disruptions. I understand there's not much data to go on, but I want a better sense of how long we'll remain out of phase from prime, if in fact that's what happened."

Atteberry said, "Is there anything you need me for, Captain? If not, I'd like to stay with my daughter."

"Go ahead. As soon as she's up for it, I want to know more about her experience on that ship."

He stole a glance at Esther who now stood beside Quigg at the comms station. She caught his eye, then snapped her attention to the analysis at hand. As Atteberry marched away, Carter watched him, his gaze narrowing.

THE *ECHO* DRIFTED THROUGH THE DARK SHADOW ZONE on Luna's far side, firing a second or two of thrusters to keep her close to the lunar surface. The viewscreen over the flight seats showed the Moon's dim, craggy relief below in grey, and the billions of stars around it shimmered like layered satin in a gentle breeze. Atteberry, sitting next to Mary, fought waves of sleep while the rest of the crew effected repairs to the ship.

Two hours had passed since the *Sara Waltz*'s attack. Ishani, the operations tech, took a brief spacewalk to replace damaged tiles on one of the nacelles, Jenson had most of the piloting functions back online, and Esther produced a few space-time disruption models that she and Quigg pored over with the captain and Carter.

Mary's condition deteriorated. Her face had turned an ashen color and her tongue flicked over cracked, dry lips. Atteberry kept a moist towelette close by to wipe the sweat from her forehead, telling himself they'd soon be home, god willing, and to a hospital. Every few minutes, she hallucinated, speaking gibberish and other incoherent words. As Esther left her work with Quigg and walked toward the flight seats, a thought struck him: she knew the truth about Mary and what she did, too, and although she spun a believable theory about how the *Echo* survived the attack, linking it to the alien vessel's supposed jump to light speed, fear continued to dog him.

Just how far can I trust her to keep my daughter safe?

"How is she now?" she said, her voice soft and alluring in that sleepy way of hers.

Atteberry stood and joined her a few feet from where Mary rested. "Her fever's stable. It's a little over 38 degrees, but she has these bouts of hallucinations or dreams or something. Scares me a bit, you know?"

"But she was lucid before the attack, right?"

"Yeah. This only happened after she . . . well, after she touched the comms panel and we became invisible to the *Sara Waltz*." He scratched his beard. "How soon until they repair the engines?"

"Almost there, Jim, and just in time, too. Quigg and I put together some models, and if the math is right, the distortion will disappear any minute." She sighed and looked at Mary asleep on the flight seat. "Are you still okay keeping what she did a secret?"

He bit his lip and straightened his shoulders. That sense of distrust oozed into his veins. "I don't see any other alternative if I'm going to protect her."

A commotion ensued on the bridge and Carter bellowed, "Esther, I need you at navigation."

She didn't move, fixing her gaze on Atteberry.

"You'd better go, Es. His Highness beckons." No love was lost between him and Clayton Carter. If he'd had a little more courage when they confronted each other on Luna, he'd have dropped the bastard instead of backing down. But Mary and Kate's lives were at stake, so he capitulated under Carter's bluster. Still, he itched to return to Earth and be done with this self-important fool.

Esther frowned and pulled herself away. "Can you join us?"

"Sure, I'll be right up."

A FEW MINUTES PASSED, AND THE SUDDEN BURST of the primary engines roaring to life pierced the relative silence of the craft. The bridge crew cheered and they all patted Jenson on the back. She sat taller, basking in the moment, then quickly returned to her station. Dub and Ishani raced past Atteberry on their way from the engine room to the flight deck. When they arrived, handshakes and fist pumps greeted them.

Atteberry breathed a sigh of relief. One step closer to home. He wandered up to join the others and positioned himself near Quigg.

"How's your baby girl doin'?" the comms officer asked without looking up from his console.

"Stable for now, but I'll feel better once she's checked out by a doctor, thanks."

"Well," he said, turning to face him, "it won't be long. Jenzie's worked her magic and the ship's fixed up good enough to fly. They're running through the pre-flight protocols."

Atteberry glanced across the bridge where Captain Powell and the co-pilot ticked through their checklist. Carter chatted with Esther in low voices over at navs.

"How long's the trip home?"

"A couple hours is all, if we get through clean," he said.

"What's that mean?"

"Well, we all have to assume we'll run into that flotilla of ships that followed us up here, and the Prussian cruiser won't be too far away either. She could be waitin' on the other side."

Atteberry furrowed his brow. "Aren't we still invisible?"

"Dr. Tyrone doesn't think so, and I agree. Our models show the space-time disruption has likely dissipated by now, so we're buck naked again, know what I mean? And if'n we are, well then, that's a whole lotta *what the hell* and all we'll be in."

He liked Quigg. Always cheerful and relaxed no matter the circumstances. Atteberry moved closer to the captain. He and Jenson were finishing their pre-flight check and the tension in the air, although reduced while they repaired the ship, grew thick again.

Esther must have briefed them and the others on the return to, what was it they called it? *Space-time prime.*

Captain Powell acknowledged Atteberry and invited him to sit. "Your daughter's been through a lot. I bet she's exhausted."

"Yeah, I can't wait to get home."

"Oh?" he asked, "Is there something more going on with her?"

Atteberry wondered about how much to share with this fellow. He didn't strike him as a selfish narcissist like Carter, but he wasn't exactly warm either. Reading people, other than his students who lied about assignments, proved challenging, but since the Ross 128 adventure began, he'd been learning.

"She's running a fever and who knows what else she might have picked up on that ship? So I just want to make sure she's okay."

"Of course." Then to the co-pilot, "What's the satellite relay showing, Mr. Jenson?"

She brought the long-range scan up on the monitor, displaying a dozen icons floating in the space between Luna and Earth. She said, "The *Sara Waltz* is maintaining her position over the Moon. Our own cruiser, the *Malevolent*, is dancing with the *Volmar*, and the *Edelgard* is close to joining them. Those other smaller craft are aligning themselves in formation."

"What about the alien ship?"

Jenson flicked through additional long-range scanning parameters. "Nowhere to be found, sir."

Atteberry asked, "Are there any life signs on the Moon?"

"Negative."

Captain Powell frowned. "She remains on that Rossian vessel then."

"Or lying dead on the surface."

Powell studied the ships on the viewscreen, then said, "Lay in a course for home, Mr. Jenson, the military base at Shearwater."

"Aye, sir."

Carter faced the bridge crew and said, "Folks, we're not out of the woods yet. There are hostiles between us and Earth, and we must fight our way through if we want to see home again." He went through the room, eyeing each person. "Time to buckle up. Prepare to accelerate."

The captain glared at Carter, then repeated the order.

Quigg and Jenson pulled on their harnesses. Atteberry and the rest scrambled to the aft flight seats. Once they'd secured themselves, the *Echo* burst forward in a shock of force that pounded him into the back of his chair, and he experienced that mix of fear and excitement that he first felt when they'd left the Earth several days ago. He caught a viewscreen and watched the Moon swing hard to starboard, replaced with a flash of sunlight and the marbled Earth as the vessel increased speed.

"HOW ARE YOU HOLDING UP?"

Esther's question dragged him away from his focus on the diminishing acceleration forces as the *Echo* reached cruising velocity. He turned toward her. "I've got a million questions, Es. Not sure where to begin." He glanced at Carter sitting across from him, lost in his own world. Dub and Ishani were already releasing their harnesses. "Mary's health, of course," he said, "but I'm worried about Kate, too. She was supposed to leave that alien vessel right after Mares, but apparently never did." He leaned in, lowering his voice. "Maybe that ship held her against her will."

Esther cocked her head. "Anything's possible. Until we . . . or you talk to Mary about what happened, whatever I say is pure speculation. Still, remember that Kate's a former Spacer. She's worked in crazy situations her entire life. Something tells me that if she's on board the Rossian vessel, and alive, she'll find her way home."

He leaned back and reflected on the past decade: his teaching job at City College, raising his daughter by himself after Janet the mercenary left them, his deep friendship with Kate, and his failed relationship with Esther. As he finally relaxed in the flight seat and the heaviness of fatigue engulfed him, Atteberry wondered if he could have somehow changed the course of events since he first detected that Ross 128 signal.

His ex-wife Janet Chamberlain, whom he'd loved and married, Mary's mother, turned out to be an operative with the Northern Democratic Union. Perhaps because her assignment with him finished, she disappeared without a trace only to resurface when all the crap with the mysterious tap code was going down in '85. He still hadn't gotten over her years later when Esther arrived in the picture, and because of that and her cover up of the alien signal, their romance died and a permanent distance grew between them despite working closely together on this rescue mission. *Besides, she's changed, becoming cynical.* At least, that's the impression she gave him.

And, there was Kate. It took this mission to find her and Mary and prevent their deaths on Luna for him to realize he cared immensely for her. Yet, she remained a mystery, aloof, hurting. He had to admit that being with her, despite her broken, sick body, appealed to him. And Mary loved her as much as anyone, but something kept holding him back. He was an open book. Kate wasn't. Perhaps that was it.

Carter unbuckled his harness, grunted, and returned to the bridge as the *Echo* blazed homeward. He and Esther remained in their flight seats with Mary nearby.

"I've been mulling something over," he said, staring at Carter's empty seat across from him. "I think we're cursed." He smirked and looked at her.

"How so?"

"Oh, not just me and you. The whole human race." He rubbed his neck. "For example, speaking selfishly for a moment, everyone I've ever loved, however that's defined, abandons me. Except Mary, but she will too once she's off doing her own thing. She's 17 and already eager to leave home. And that happens to everyone."

Esther's mouth opened to say something, then thought better of it.

"What is it?" he asked.

She hesitated. "Well I don't know about the rest of us, but your wife turned out to be a mercenary, so her commitment was elsewhere. And our time together in '85 was doomed to fail for several reasons."

He frowned at that.

"And Kate's gone, too. So, yeah, I understand how you'd think that. But cursed? Maybe more a reflection of our natural human state of suffering."

He studied her face. Even though Esther was a decade older than him, plain and bright, there was something about her that kindled his soul. He asked, "What about you? Never married, no kids . . . we never did talk about that, other than the stalker you threw in jail once."

She snorted. "Well, not much there either, I'm afraid." She leaned back against the head rest and stared at the ceiling. "I've always loved my work, but never believed it ever got in my way of other pursuits. I'd have given it all up for the right relationship, I suppose. All of it. But I can't recall anyone I truly fell in love with, you know, *that* way." She paused, turning to him, her eyes piercing the depth of his soul. "Clayton, despite his bluster, came close. But not as close as you." Silence filled the space between them and Atteberry dared not breathe as an ancient hunger nudged in his gut. "Anyway, I woke up one day to find I'd grown old and missed a bunch of life I'd counted on. I regret nothing, mind you," she added, "except for what happened to us. You infuriated me, you know." Her face was made of stone.

"Likewise," he managed. He returned his gaze to Carter's empty seat. "Funny, isn't it?"

"What's that?"

"Well, like I said, everyone I've loved or had feelings for left. Some, I helped along with that. But you've got no one either. Carter doesn't. Don't know about Jan. So what do we do for the rest of our lives? We work, I guess."

The thrum of the engines filled the cabin for several minutes before he continued. "Tragic."

"Hm?"

"It's tragic, Es. We float through life doing meaningless things, aching to be in relationships that someday will ultimately fail us, too. Even if you find someone to spend the rest of your days with, one of you dies first and abandons the other. What does that get you?"

"When you put it that way, life doesn't make a whole lot of sense. I didn't peg you as a nihilist," she said.

"I've grown more cynical lately. Maybe there's nothing more, but perhaps there's something wonderful in the interim... magical in between birth and death."

"If so, it's temporary. The outcome is the same. You will still die alone, Jim. And so will I."

She unbuckled her harness and pushed herself up, swinging her legs over the side of the flight seat, and paused. "Makes me wonder if we're looking for something that can never be found, never attained. Know what I mean?" She stood and caught her balance, then stretched and glanced at Mary. "I'm heading up to the bridge. See if I can lend a hand. You coming?"

He released the harness and touched Mary's forehead, then checked her bio-signs on the viewscreen. Her temperature had returned to normal, and color filled her cheeks again. "I'd like to be here when she wakes up."

Esther stroked his cheek, lingering on it for a moment, then left.

Mary

ALTHOUGH MARY HAD NEVER EXPERIENCED one in any actual sense, the thoughts creeping through her mind could only be described as a violation. Consciousness was something she now yearned for to take her out of this mental dreamscape *cum* nightmare, sharing her thoughts and memories with the alien creature Keechik (*was it real or a simulacrum? No matter*). Wave after wave of mystery, of natural science, bombarded her, that she had no hope of understanding (yet now understood) and a civilization near the Ross 128 dwarf star system that she knew nothing about (except now she knew exactly where it spun in a lazy galaxy, and exactly how long it would take her to arrive traveling 1.4 times the speed of light).

She remained Mary. But she was also Keechik. Both, yet separate. Merged, yet distinct. This allowed her to plumb the inner depths of the creature's memories, to understand the principles of matter manipulation, to allow her to save the ship by shifting space-time.

But more.

Something far more . . .

Mm . . . we cannot continue like this, Mary.

I know.

I will kill you. Soon. Mm . . . my people's history is too much.

I know.

19

She studied the deep blue and black of her formless, mental surroundings. He floated with her. Orienting herself proved impossible in the void. A shiver ran through her as the memories of Keechik's world – as fresh as if they'd just occurred – assaulted her mind. She saw it all. Relived it all. The sudden cries and death of millions of creatures, as if the oxygen they breathed had vanished. Yet, no panic. Only peace and curiosity. Like when she was a child and someone left the back door to the shed open. In the morning, garbage littered the entranceway. Her dad was angry at himself for not closing it, but she wondered about the animal that got in. Why would it eat garbage? Was it afraid? Apparently not. Where did it go after? How curious!

And the little one Keechik, alone in his ship, unable to help his people.

Am I speaking with you? The living you? Or a simulacrum?

I am Keechik's memories. The Keechik has gone.

Flashes of spindly-legged creatures and cities built of obsidian and glass, of a civilization unknown to her, played in her mind. Emotional impressions from Keechik's thoughts tickled the edges of her own, producing in her at once a rich tapestry of fully-realized feelings. And fear. The beauty of his world and depth of understanding crushed her.

If I'm dying, then the record of your civilization dies with me?

Yes.

Is there nothing we can do? Someone else who could be the keeper of your history?

No.

There are so many of us on Earth. We could find another, or something to—

No, the Friend Mary.

My dad mustn't know that I'm dying, Keechik.

Mm...

20

THREE

Atteberry

"EVASIVE MANOEUVRES, JENSON!"

The *Echo* pitched and rolled away from the incoming rail gun blast delivered by the *Sara Waltz*. The Prussian heavy cruiser continued firing on the smaller, nimble corvette while she chased them toward Earth.

"That was too close for comfort, John," Carter bellowed. "What's our situation?"

The primary viewer displayed all the ships in the Earth-Moon sector. It was a formidable arrangement of everything imaginable: small science vessels, intermediate cargo boats, escorts, right up to the heavy cruisers. Carter's own security ship from the mineral runs, the *Malevolent,* faced off with the *Volmar and Edelgard*, two Prussian Braadenton class cruisers. Although the *Echo* could outrun any ship built to date, she remained vulnerable to attack and her hardshields, effective for routine encounters, were nothing like the armored heavies.

Captain Powell released his grip on the command seat's armrests as the *Echo* pulled out of a tight spiral. "Half of those vessels are onlookers and don't pose a threat, but since the *Malevolent* destroyed that ship a couple days ago, we're in the Prussians' sites. They've got their two heavies, the *Edelgard* and the *Volmar*, and three weaponized frigates near Earth waiting for us. Plus, even though she's crippled and flying on fumes, the *Sara Waltz* is on our ass and as you can tell, there's nothing wrong with her weapons."

"What the hell," Carter said. "Is it all out war now?"

Powell didn't answer. He glanced at him and then returned his attention to Jenson and plotting various courses around and through the flotilla.

Atteberry heard all the bridge commotion from his place on the deck, and watched the action unfold on the nearby viewscreen. Mary, still harnessed in the aft flight seat, awakened and stretched against the constraints of the buckles.

"Dad?"

"We're on our way home, but there's a skirmish with some other ships."

"She punched the release on the harness and sat up. "The Rossian?"

"No, honey, the Prussians. It seems Clayton Carter picked a fight with the wrong crowd and stirred up a hornet's nest."

An explosion burst port side, sending ripples across the ship as she screamed through the cluster. Someone on the bridge shouted, "Calypso mines!" and the *Echo* lurched and heaved again. Mary swung her legs over the seat. "I can help, Dad."

"Not a chance. Last time you did that, you passed out, remember?"

Her eyes narrowed and her tongue darted over her cracked lips. "Yeah, I remember." She pulled herself up and caught her balance by holding on to his arm.

"Stay here, Mares. Wait until your strength returns."

A scraping metallic sound shrieked from the Ops room, causing the onboard lights to blink. The *Echo* shuddered but maintained velocity. Carter's voice continued rising over the commands of the bridge crew. Dub raced by them toward Ops.

"Mares, tell me more about what happened to you on that ship. I have to know what they did."

She pulled a water gel packet from the seat stores and gulped it down, then answered. "The only alien was a creature named Keechik. It transferred all its knowledge and memories and experiences to me, so I could be the holder of its entire history."

"But what does that mean?"

"Dad," she said, reaching for a protein bar and brushing back her blond hair, "it means everything that Keechik ever experienced, all it knows—including its home world and technology—is all in here." She tapped the side of her head. "I haven't processed it yet, and I've got this massive headache, but that's how I hid the *Echo* from the Prussians a while ago. I shifted our space-time and put us out of phase. Pretty nova, don't you think?" She grinned.

Atteberry exhaled, relieved to hear her speak like old times. The black circles under her eyes and dishevelled hair reminded him how close she and Kate had come to dying on the Moon's surface and thinking of that brought a lump to his throat. He buried it.

The *Echo* banked hard and the two Atteberrys held on to their flight seats. Esther said, "The *Malevolent*'s got the cruisers on the run!" and Quigg whooped before the gravity forces on the ship eased.

Atteberry searched his daughter's face. "Mares, Es and I were wondering something."

"What is it?"

"If you have all this alien knowledge, and you're the only one who saw the creature—"

"Kate did, too. You should see what Keechik did to her."

Atteberry swallowed, imagining the worst. "Well, I'm worried others will want to literally pick your brain, collect that knowledge. I'm not talking historians and sociologists."

Mary chuckled. "Yeah, all those crazy scientists."

23

He took her hand. "Not them either. I'm thinking more of those nastier people that your mother runs with."

"I'll be careful."

He continued. "And if anyone ever finds out how you made this ship invisible . . ."

"I got it, Dad. Safety first." She pretended to zip her lips.

Dread and frustration mounted in him. He kept seeing his little girl, not the independent woman she was becoming, and wondered how long it would be until he became irrelevant to her.

Esther arrived from the bridge and greeted Mary.

"What's it like up there?" Atteberry asked.

"We've cleared the flotilla. Those ships weren't sufficiently quick to pose any threat, and the three cruisers are playing cat and mouse with each other. No more mines or shots fired, so I hope that's that for a while." She turned to Mary. "Feeling better?"

"Yeah, thanks. My head hurts, and I'm tired and hungry but otherwise okay."

"Wonderful. Unless we run into something else along the way, we'll be landing in Nova Scotia in about an hour."

"Sweet!"

THE ECHO'S APPROACH VECTOR TO THE TARMAC at the Canadian Air Force Base Shearwater was steeper than most ships returning to Earth could manage. The hardshields and cooling tiles, one of many innovations Carter and his team developed, allowed for faster descents—a definite strategic advantage.

Their flight path took them over the Arctic, across the North American east coast, and into Shearwater. When they attained an elevation of 50 meters, the ship hovered a moment, then descended using nav thrusters on her belly to touch down.

It was late afternoon. When the airlock opened, the heat and humidity and salty ocean breeze hammered Atteberry. He inhaled and helped walk Mary down the ramp to the tarmac. Esther and Carter followed them, leaving the crew onboard to assess any needed repairs. A Titanius employee in a jump suit met them.

"Mr. Atteberry . . . Esther . . . there's a heli-jet standing by to take you home to San Francisco, If you'd like to follow me?" He motioned them toward a large, cerulean blue aircraft on the apron. Atteberry smiled at his daughter, who clung on to his arm as she staggered across the asphalt.

A commotion behind caused him to look around. Quigg raced down the ramp from the *Echo* and jogged up to Carter who spoke on his indie-comm, marching toward the hangar. Ishani and Dub also joined them.

"I wonder what that's all about?" Esther asked.

Atteberry's intuition unsettled his brain. *This isn't right.* "Come on, let's keep moving." He quickened his pace toward the heli-jet.

As they approached the aircraft, he glanced back and saw Carter studying Quigg's data slate, then they both raised their heads. Quigg waved and yelled, "Mr. Atteberry!"

"Jim?"

"Ignore him, Es. Let's get out of here."

Then Carter bellowed. "Stop right there!" Dub raced toward them at full speed.

Their escort stopped and turned around. "Hang on. They must have forgotten something."

Dub arrived first, scowling, with Carter falling in behind. "Please," he said, catching his breath, "I know you're concerned about Mary's health and I wonder if she shouldn't get checked out by a doctor here before heading to the coast. We can be in New York City in no time, and they've got the best doctors in the NDU if not the world." He looked at Mary.

Atteberry desperately wanted to escape, but needed to play it cool. "Her own doctor is pretty good, too."

"Of course," he said, "but these are special circumstances. I feel a huge responsibility to make sure one of my Titanius family members is a hundred per cent." He took a step forward and reached out his hand. "Come. We'll leave for the hospital on my personal heli-jet immediately."

Mary gazed up at her dad and shrugged. "I'd rather see someone now, Dad. My head feels like it's gonna explode."

Atteberry clenched his jaw, smouldering. His instincts screamed to grab his daughter and run like hell, get as far away from these assholes and this nightmare as possible. Instead, he exhaled, recognizing that Carter was probably right. "Thank you for the offer, Clayton. Let's go to this hospital."

FOUR

Esther

THE FLOOD OF REPORTS AND DEMANDS from the TSA Director, Keiran Kapoor, disturbed her. They'd worked together for years at the Academy, held each other in great esteem, and she'd never been the target of the boss's wrath in all that time. Until now.

"How could you . . ."

"The audacity . . ."

" . . . reputation of our fine institution in tatters . . ."

She snapped the indie-comm off and stared out the window as the heli-jet tore through the darkening sky toward Gotham Medical on Manhattan Island. The madness spiralled out of control. Kieran briefed her on the skirmishes flaring up between the NDU and the

Confederates along the southeastern border, and how the California Congressional government was on high alert. He sent her a photo of republican guards posted on the Academy's campus, the only caption he'd written beside it was an exclamation mark. Interspersed in these updates were his own opinions on how her actions—or lack of leadership, as he claimed—now jeopardized the safety and security of the TSA and its work.

How she managed to do all that, he didn't elaborate. Nevertheless, she'd been on the *Echo* test-driving a possible partnership with Titanius (*who ever dreamed such a thing imaginable!*). Her student nearly died on the internship with them (*the height of irresponsibility!*). She came within a hair's breadth of first contact but instead, took a back seat to the others (*that's not leadership, Esther*). The only positive in all this was her connection with the Atteberrys, and even that dragged up echoes from the past of the Mount Sutro disaster and subsequent Ross 128 cover up.

Moreover, media reports of ship movements in Europe also trickled in. Not only did the Prussian Consortium ramp up its rhetoric over the live fire in space and the destruction of one of its ships, the science vessel *Nachtfalke*, but the Russians too had launched several of their own gunships from Baikonur to patrol the upper atmosphere over their territory.

She sat with Jim—Mary dozing between them, her head leaning on Esther's shoulder—and wondered how much Carter had figured out about the cloaked ship story. Quigg suspected something. Perhaps their recorders picked up Mary's interface with the comms panel before the *Echo* vanished from space-time prime. Or, they have fresh evidence on the alien vessel and wanted to keep the group together for debriefing. Either way, he was right about New York having the best medical professionals in the world and, given Mary's condition, who knows what kind of infection or disease the creature gave her? Better to have her checked out sooner rather than later and quarantine them all if necessary.

Jim faced forward, protective headphones askew, lost in his own thoughts. But then he turned to check Mary, placed his hand on her forehead in a moving act of tenderness, and she caught his eye. The last few days wiped them out. His usual messy hair now looked like he hadn't run a comb through it in years, and his drawn face portrayed the deep worry and fright of a parent nearly losing his daughter.

I imagine I don't look much better, especially with these ear things on.

He lingered on her a moment longer, then she turned away and resumed her watch out the window, mind racing with the sudden labor pains of a terrible and beautiful idea. *All will be forgiven if Mary shares her alien abilities with the TSA, and the way to do that is to regain Jim's trust.* The bonus? Extra leverage over Carter and securing his fleet for future space exploration.

She closed her eyes, listening to the thrum of the heli-jet, and for the first time since the madness began, she fell into a deep sleep.

Atteberry

THE BRILLIANT FIERY SUN DROPPED LOW on the horizon as the Titanius heli-jet descended on the rooftop pad of Gotham Medical Center in downtown Manhattan. The pilot reviewed the disembarking procedures again and checked that they all understood. Dub would go with them into the hospital and keep Carter apprised. The Titanius boss himself would return to his office on the other side of town and check in with his second-in-command, Ed Mitchell, and deliver the recovered data tubes from their destroyed lunar habitat to his team.

Atteberry didn't see the need to have this Dub character stay with them, but Esther convinced him it was standard protocol involving corporate interests, something about liability blah blah. "The authorities will debrief us at some point too, Jim," she said as the aircraft settled on the pad.

Several nurses and hospital workers greeted them at the base of the heli-jet. They helped Mary onto an antigrav gurney and rushed her into an elevator. Esther, Dub and Atteberry followed. As soon as they cleared the area, the jet lifted off and ripped eastward into the dying light.

By the time Mary arrived in the emergency room, an IV drip of saline solution hung from her along with an active bio-signs monitor. Once she transferred to a bed, the in situ sensors and scanners hummed to life. An on-duty doctor with greying hair pushed everyone out except for Atteberry and a nurse, then studied Mary's vital signs: pulse, heart rate, VO2, organ scans, and a myriad of other measures. Then she flashed an optical sensor at her pupils.

"My name's Dr. Hamid," she offered cheerily. "How are you feeling?"

Mary grimaced. "I'm beat and my head is . . . well, I can't stand this headache, and I want to go home as soon as possible."

Turning to Atteberry, she asked, "So you're part of the crew who rescued her from Luna, yes?"

"Yeah, and her father," he replied. "I don't think any of us have slept for a week. But Doctor, from what Mary told me, she hasn't eaten or had much to drink at all. Just a protein bar on the ship when we returned."

Hamid changed screens on the monitor and multiple scans of her brain tissue appeared. She cycled through numerous views, toggling back and forth, and the humor dropped from her face. She flicked between various angles.

"What is it?" Atteberry asked.

The doctor ignored him. Instead, she instructed the nurse to give Mary a shot of painkiller for her headache, then motioned for Atteberry to follow her. "Mary," she said before leaving, "I'll be back in a moment. I'm calling in our neuro-specialist. He's much better equipped for this sort of head trauma than am I."

"Will I be okay?"

Hamid sighed. "Your vital signs are satisfactory. I'm concerned something's happened to your brain, and that's why you've got the headache, so when Dr. Angelis has a look, we'll know what we're dealing with." Then to the nurse, "If there's any change in her condition, ring me."

Atteberry glanced at his daughter, then followed the doctor to a tiny consultation room off the primary nursing station. Once inside, Hamid turned on a wall monitor and linked up Mary's bio-signs.

Atteberry sat in front of the screen. "How is she, Dr. Hamid? Please, tell me straight up."

She studied the brain scans again and, without looking at him, said, "I don't wish to speculate, but to be honest, I've seen nothing like this in all my years . . ."

HALF AN HOUR LATER, DR. DARIO ANGELIS arrived in Emergency and joined Hamid and Atteberry outside Mary's room. She'd fallen asleep shortly after the nurse administered the painkiller. Angelis was a short, stocky man with thinning hair and a slight limp, but he also possessed an engaging smile and put Atteberry at ease. After their introductions, the neuro-specialist referred to his data slate and, keeping his voice low, said, "Your daughter has gone through an extraordinary ordeal, and if the reports are correct, it's no wonder her body's slowing down for repairs." Then his brow furrowed. "But I'm concerned with these scans, and I need to ask some questions."

Hamid found an empty room where the three of them could speak. Dr. Angelis flipped through the data slate again before placing it on the table in front of them.

"What happened to your daughter on Luna, Mr. Atteberry?"

He cleared his throat, gauging how much information he should reveal. "Mary worked there with a former Spacer on a summer internship. Something destroyed their habitat, so they traveled to an old mine site and survived there for a while before the *Echo* rescued her."

Dr. Angelis studied him. "There's more to the story, isn't there?"

"I don't think so," he answered, but his voice quivered and he couldn't maintain eye contact.

"Dr. Hamid, can you give us a few minutes alone please?"

"Certainly, Doctor." She darted out of the room and closed the door.

"Now then, what exactly happened? You know," he said leaning back, "there's a rumour going around that your Spacer person was abducted by aliens." He grinned. "Pretty outrageous, isn't it?"

Atteberry's remained unfazed. He shook his head and sighed. "If others knew, my daughter could be in grave danger. Please," he said, "if I tell you what I know, promise me you'll keep it to yourself."

Angelis leaned forward across the table. "I will protect whatever you say as part of my doctor-patient confidentiality. You have my word. Now, if I'm going to help Mary, what happened?"

Atteberry spoke slowly, deliberately at first, detailing the events of the rescue mission, including the discovery of the alien ship at the *Mare Marginis*, Mary and Kate being taken aboard the Rossian vessel, and what she told him on the way home. Angelis watched him, taking no notes, but asking clarifying questions from time to time.

"And this creature, this alien, transferred its knowledge to her brain?"

"Yes."

"Did she say how?"

"Apparently, it used some kind of fibre optic head cover. That's how she explained it. And it penetrated her brain directly."

The doctor grew silent for a moment, twirling a stylus between his fingers.

Atteberry said, "There's one more thing."

He raised an eyebrow.

"On the way home, she touched part of the *Echo* and, well, something happened. Esther Tyrone—she's waiting outside—said the ship had been knocked out of phase with space-time. Something like that, anyway. But Mary . . . well, she passed out right after and a fever kicked in and she was sick for a while."

The doctor studied the scans again for several minutes, zooming in on certain parts of her tissue right down to the micrometer level. Then he folded his hands and said, "I'll run more tests, but if I had to offer an early diagnosis now, I'd say the reason your daughter has these headaches is that her brain is overwhelmed by the alien's material. See here." He pointed to an image. "In a normal scan, this area would register as yellow on the screen, showing the brain's healthy and functioning well. But Mary's is such a deep crimson . . . almost black. It's like if you had a litre jar and normally kept it half full, then someone came along and tried to cram an extra full litre into it.

The jar couldn't hold it all and the excess would spill over. Except in Mary's case, there is no place for all this extra alien knowledge to go so it simply floods the neurons."

"But you can do something about that, right?"

Dr. Angelis frowned. "We don't have the technology to, er, siphon off the surplus matter from her mind without jeopardizing her normal brain. This isn't a typical procedure. We'd have to get in to the neurons themselves and extract the alien memories on a molecular level." He exhaled. "And what I can tell you, Mr. Atteberry, is that Mary's brain— hell, any human brain—isn't equipped to assimilate all this information, and there's nothing I can do about it."

Atteberry slumped in stunned silence and he fought back the howl that formed in this throat, avoiding the question he already knew the answer to.

"What are you saying, Doctor?"

"Mary won't recover."

He laughed nervously, "What do you mean, like, she's going to die from this or something?"

Dr. Angelis, his face grey and stoic, said, "Based on what I see on her scans, I give her a week, maybe two."

"No . . ."

"Less if she does, well, whatever she did to render the *Echo* invisible. From what you told me, that drained a significant amount of energy from her and her ability to recover will deteriorate if she does it again."

A rush of conflicting emotions surged through him, swirling from anger and fear to a deep sense of impending loss and helplessness. The doctor's hand touched his shoulder.

"There must be something, Doctor. A drug treatment or . . . or nanosurgery . . ."

"I'm afraid not. Mary's condition is unlike anything I've ever seen."

"What about those treatments for multiple personality disorders? I've met students who are cured."

"Unfortunately, that's entirely different. Personality disorders are psycho-chemical. Mary isn't suffering from a personality issue.

She's literally got some other creature's mind trying to occupy a limited space in her brain. There's no—" Angelis bolted upright.

"What is it?"

"Hm, probably nothing. Never mind."

The room began spinning. "Doctor, tell me!"

"I could be mistaken, but I recall hearing of a medical researcher at last year's national neurology convention, an odd fellow who was experimenting with memory transference in mice. Hang on a second." He punched the data slate and pulled up some fresh pages. "Yes, here it is. Dr. Robert Elliot. He's published some of his work. Some encouraging preliminary results."

"Transference . . . like moving memories in and out of the brain, right? That's good, isn't it? Maybe he can extract this alien consciousness without damaging her."

Angelis grimaced. "Let's not get our hopes up too high, Mr. Atteberry. Dr. Elliot's research is on mice, not humans. It's extremely experimental and years away from application to humans."

"Still, he may be able to help."

"Perhaps, but there's another even more serious problem." He wiped his forehead. "Elliot is based in New Houston, deep in the Confederate Republic. If the last 48 hours are any indication, it would be far too dangerous to travel there now as a foreign citizen. Plus, one can only assume his politics are aligned with the southerners."

"I don't care. I'll go anywhere to help my girl."

"Of course, but by doing so, you may put Mary's life in genuine danger. She's the only person, as far as we know, who has encountered a sentient, advanced alien. There are doctors, among others, who would stop at nothing to scrape her mind and extract the information in it."

Atteberry bit his lip and sighed. Scraping referred to human data gathering and was a popular procedure with the militia, correctional agencies, and spies—a method in which the victim being scraped rarely survived and if they did, it reduced them to a vegetative state. He clenched his fist.

"And they won't care if she lives or dies."

FIVE

Space Research, Intelligence Division, Prussian Consortium
Berlin, Germany

Winter

BENEDIKT WINTER RE-READ THE INITIAL REPORTS from the *Volmar* and the *Sara Waltz* under a single lamp in his musty basement office in Kladow, the southernmost area of Berlin's Spandau Borough. The antique clock on his bookcase chimed midnight. He checked his indie-comm, noticed the old wind-up ran a couple minutes fast, and made a note to have that adjusted in the morning.

As Head of Intelligence in the Prussian Consortium's Space Research ministry, he often worked through the night, catching naps whenever and wherever he could, undertaking the important tasks assigned to him by the Chancellor. To wit, ensuring the Consortium remained at the forefront of space research. It was an objective that grew more challenging, what with the Terran Science Academy in California attracting the brightest minds away from the continental conflict, and Titanius Space Resources beating them in ship engine technology and AI computational design. Moreover, the damn British kept turning his agents and the Indian educational factories overwhelmed their own institutions with the number of engineers and scientists. The Chinese influenced all progress in the Asian theatre and were building their own conventional fleet of heavy cruisers in advance of pursuing exploration in the outer planets, and again, what they may have lacked in innovation they made up for in numbers. Intel estimated ships in the thousands.

Thousands.

But he loved it.

The minor firefight between his vessels and the *Echo* were easy to dismiss. Most of the world's leaders were clueless about what happened in space, anyway. They sullied their minds with mundane issues like economic performance and invented human rights. What a joke. However, when Titanius' *Malevolent* destroyed the *Nachtfalke* and sent over a dozen crew members to their deaths in the Earth-Moon system, that was problematic and demanded a response. If Clayton Carter thought the maverick style of leadership he used here could work out there, he was in for a surprise. The Prussians would see to that.

Winter replayed the personal vid transmission from Captain Krause of the *Sara Waltz* and sipped his dandelion tea, letting the delicate, bitter brew settle on his tongue before swallowing. On the monitor, the veteran officer of years in space spoke from his private cabin. Evidence of the run-in with the *Echo* showed in the cracked bulkhead and non-operational view screens surrounding him.

"Benedikt, I hate to admit, but the *Echo* outmaneuvered us when she hit our energy transfer hubs and brought us to a standstill. That's on me, not the crew, and I understand I shall answer for that when I return even though we inflicted our own damage on her. My ship requires extensive repairs and we'll be putting in at the space dock over New Houston." He lowered his voice and continued. "However, what I must inform you about is what happened after we'd patched her up and got our engines online."

The screen flashed to a recording of the ship's running log.

"The *Echo* could have destroyed us after she hit the hubs, and I expected her to, but her crew seemed more interested in what lay on the Moon's surface. Yes, there were survivors from the Titanius Lab malfunction and I recognize the need to rescue them. But what were they doing on the eastern limb, hundreds of kilometers from their lab site? What was so special about the *Mare Marginis*?"

Krause digressed into speculation about the mineral potential on the Moon's edge, the presence of highly volatile magnetic fields there, and a general history of exploration in that area. Winter fast forwarded through a series of lunar maps, then picked up when the captain's face reappeared.

" . . . a clear disruption in the space-time fabric. What you'll see here is nothing more than a flash, like the glare of sunlight off metal. But my scientists have slowed the motion down to just before the light explosion takes place." The view shifted from the captain to an image of the *Mare Marginis*. "This was taken from an orbiting satellite and from our own recorders, so I'm confident it's accurate. Stand by . . ."

Winter leaned in closer to the screen and set his cup down on its matching saucer.

The angle from the *Sara Waltz* showed a grainy image of the Moon's shadowed limb under night vision. The outline of two ships appeared on the surface. One, he recognized as the *Echo*. His operatives had provided him with files of intel—incomplete, it turned out—but there was no mistaking her sleek, compact design. The second ship, well, that was the big mystery.

The craft were near each other. On the vid, in real-time, the *Echo* fired two rail gun warning blasts over the second. Then the latter shot what appeared to be a sonic wave through the Moon's crust toward the *Echo*, knocking her over on her side. The recording paused at that point.

"Now I'll show you the next sequence, slowed down."

The mystery ship rose from the surface and vanished in a pool of blue light. The video repeated several times, both from the satellite imagery and from the *Sara Waltz*'s own cameras, before the captain's face returned on screen.

"We have studied this over and over, Ben. She was not destroyed. We detected no debris, no residual vapour trail, no radiation cloud. Plus, no record of any other ship being on Luna exists, and the way she simply vanished leads my science team to suggest the unbelievable." The captain frowned, pursed his lips and hesitated before speaking. "This must be the alien vessel we heard about several years ago . . . the one from Ross 128. And assuming it is, then the vessel possesses faster-than-light engines which would explain her sudden disappearance."

Winter stopped the recording there. He scanned the other reports on his screen again but the elusive Rossian ship had vanished, undetected by any of the terran tracking networks in the solar system. Captain Krause's assessment appeared to be correct. He resumed the video.

"We also noted someone leaving that alien ship prior to the firefight and can only conclude it was one of the Titanius workers from the destroyed lab. The second worker never came out. Perhaps she succumbed to the environment. Nevertheless, when my crew confronted the *Echo* in lunar orbit, the corvette disappeared before we could avenge the *Nachtfalke*. That's when we discovered a second disturbance in space-time prime. It lasted long enough for the *Echo* to escape and return to her base on Earth. My crew put up a valiant chase once we found her again, despite our damaged systems, but to no avail."

The Prussian operative embedded at that military compound in Shearwater later informed him of the *Echo*'s return and, according to the mole, the ship required extensive repairs. He also confirmed the survivor was Mary Atteberry, the *fraulein* on a summer internship, and that an awaiting heli-jet flew them to a hospital in New York. The girl was the key and had to be secured. And questioned. Whatever happened to her on that alien ship, she must have helped the *Echo* evade the *Sara Waltz* with a technology that to date had remained a theoretical exercise for the long-haired professors in the Berlin Mathematics Research Center, something for amusing and challenging their unbathed students.

But now, the technology seemingly existed. This alone would mitigate the thousands of Chinese cruisers coming into service in the next few years. This alone would allow the Consortium to establish itself as the de facto leader in space and, by extension, on Earth. And this alone would propel him further into a position of influence in the inevitable, future Prussian world government. His pulse quickened.

As a precautionary measure, he ordered the cruiser *Edelgard* to abandon the stand-off with the *Malevolent* and return to Luna's vicinity and continue investigating the *Mare Marginis* where the alien ship had landed, and more importantly, to ensure no other terran ships poked around in their business. He regretted leaving the *Volmar* alone to deal with the Titanius heavy, but she had a fine crew and would hold the line until reinforcements arrived.

Yes, the girl was the key.

Fraulein Mary . . . I look forward to meeting you.

For the fourth time, he reviewed the cadre of assets he controlled in and around New York City. So many to choose from, yet he needed someone at this point to simply watch the Atteberry girl and track her movements and note who came to see her. An operative, Anna Gottlieb, worked at the Gotham Medical Center where the fraulein was being treated. Winter established a secure link through his computer, rang her up, and gave her the assignment. Then, to avoid the suspicion of his own enemies both outside the Consortium and within, he booked a commercial flight to New York leaving early the next morning, instead of ordering a special accommodation. Routine business. With that done, he returned to the *Sara Waltz*'s logs, sipped his tea, and watched the captain's vid again.

Atteberry

ESTHER SAT UPRIGHT IN A WAITING AREA, sipping burned coffee, across from Dub who had fallen asleep. She stood when Atteberry arrived and followed him to a quiet space where he briefed her on the doctor's discussion. When he told her Mary only had a couple of weeks at most to live, Esther steadied herself on the back of a nearby chair.

"But there's a doctor who could help separate her mind, a fellow in New Houston who's been researching this."

"New Houston? Oh, that's not good, Jim. I've been catching up on the news reports and the cold war is heating up terribly since the incident in space. Terrorist bombings at key military installations on both sides, and the NDU has closed its southern borders."

He nodded. "The doctor said as much, too. He also wants to keep Mary here for a couple of days at least to monitor her condition, but I'd rather take her home."

A young nurse with short-cropped sandy hair entered the waiting area carrying a medical kit and data slate. She stopped and tapped something on her screen, scanning the room. Atteberry watched her for a moment. She didn't look right to him.

"I don't think it's safe here."

"Agreed, but after all we've been through, we could use a day or two of rest and some solid food ourselves. Perhaps the doctor knows best."

Atteberry lowered his voice. "Maybe, but consider this. Why is Dub here? Do you honestly think it's because Carter's concerned for Mary's well-being or some stupid liability thing, or is it because he's watching us? Guarding us?"

The nurse wandered to the sitting area and sat down facing them, glancing up from time to time, busy with her slate. Atteberry wasn't fooled.

"That short woman over there, the one who just came in, she's also following us."

Esther glanced around. "Now you're being paranoid," she said. "This is a hospital."

He had an idea. "Come on, follow me." He led her down the hall toward Mary's room in Emergency and as they arrived, the nurse from the waiting area turned the corner and stopped at an info-desk.

"Paranoid?"

Esther pursed her lips and worked her jaw. "What are you thinking of doing?"

"I want to sneak Mary out of here and return to San Francisco on the next hyper-jet. Get her settled back in her own bed and away from the conflict going on between the NDU and Confederate States. Then, I gotta see this other doctor in New Houston. If we can't go there, maybe he can meet us in California."

"There's no way she's leaving unnoticed, Jim."

He scanned the floor. Security cameras and patient tag detectors dotted the place. Esther was right. A nurse who helped Mary on arrival walked by. He recognized her blue cardigan and hardened features. Atteberry said, "Excuse me, Is Dr. Angelis around?"

She said, "He's checking his other patients. May I help?"

"Yeah, I was wondering when my daughter might get moved to another room. He wanted to keep her under observation for a couple of days."

The nurse checked her data slate. "We're keeping her in Emerg overnight, then she'll go to the first available bed in the morning." She tucked the slate under her arm."

"Thank you."

The nurse continued on her rounds.

Atteberry put his hands in his pockets and swept the floor with his shoe. Then he whispered to Esther, "We'll need a diversion to get that one down the hall out of the way and to make sure Dub stays asleep. I can take Mary out on an antigrav gurney, then we'll head to the airport."

Esther's eyes widened. "Okay," she said, "but what about Mary's tag? It'll alert the nursing station if there's an unauthorized movement."

Dammit.

"If I remove it without being noticed and hide it in the room, no one's the wiser."

She grimaced. "I'll take care of that strange nurse and Dub in the waiting area. You'll know when to run. Then we can meet outside the main Emergency entrance and grab a hover-cab from there."

Atteberry ducked inside Mary's room. It was quiet and gloomy. Mary continued sleeping under heavy sedation, and he glanced at her bio-signs on the overhead monitor. He didn't understand half the numbers and images floating by, but he understood pulse and heart rate, and they both showed green.

The patient tag dangled off her wrist and the locking clasp was one of those tamper-proof mechanisms used to prevent any mix-up and for tracking movements. However, since most patients had no reason to remove them while in hospital, the mechanism was easy to manipulate. Nurses relied on dedicated magnetic keys and Atteberry noticed one hanging outside at the nearby station. He snuck out to get it.

Esther, meanwhile, had disappeared and so had the curious short-haired nurse. When no one paid any attention to him, he pinched the mag key sitting by a series of data slates, returned to Mary's room, and released the tag from her wrist. Then, he wrapped it around an equipment arm attached to the wall, lifted Mary onto the antigrav gurney in the corner, removed various tubes and monitoring patches, and covered her under a sheet. A pile of extra gowns and smocks lay on a shelf. He grabbed one, pulled it on, and waited.

Come on, Es, any time now . . .

A scream followed by loud crashes echoed from the waiting area. He recognized Esther's voice and poked his head outside Mary's room. Half a dozen nurses and orderlies ran toward the commotion. He pushed the gurney out the door and, trying not to run, floated Mary down an opposite hall to a bank of elevators. It took forever for the carriage doors to open, and when they did, two doctors inside who had been talking, stopped, looked at him, then resumed their conversation. He moved the gurney in and hit the main level button.

On the ground floor, paramedics, doctors and nurses, cops and concerned families milled about. Some people were in wheelchairs, others on gurneys or sitting in bio-chairs. Atteberry pushed Mary toward the double set of sliding doors leading outside. Night had fallen, and the glare of overhead lamps cast shadows around the entrance. He waited while a team of paramedics brought a patient in on a gurney, and before the doors *whooshed* closed, he ducked into the night.

"You at the gate. Tall man with the gurney. Stop!"

He stepped into the cool night air, lifted Mary in his arms and loped through the shadows and bushes around the corner. She felt light and fragile. A hovercab stood at the edge and he raced toward it. He helped Mary inside first then tumbled in after her.

The cab AI said in its metallic voice, "What is your destination?"

"Get us out of here!"

"Incomplete information. What is your destination?"

"Hard around the block!"

The cab rose from its parking skids and glided into the dark. It passed the main entrance where a handful of orderlies and paramedics stood arguing with each other. Another ambulance floated up, and the group went back inside.

"Pull off the road and wait for a moment."

Esther appeared at the doors and marched away from the entrance. Atteberry lowered his window and shouted. She looked, saw him, and raced toward the hovercab. He opened the door, and she scrambled in.

"Daly City. Go! Go!"

As the cab pulled aside and flew into the night, Atteberry glimpsed Dub scrambling out the door, shouting into his indie-comm, running a hand over his bald head.

SIX

Seattle
Independent Republic of Washington

Janet

THE EARLY EVENING SKY HEAVED AND ROLLED IN SHEETS of grey that began over the Pacific Ocean and continued undisturbed into the mountains, covering them like cotton blankets against a rare cold spell in June. Janet Chamberlain stood in front of the bay window in a three-story walk-up, tumbler of vodka in hand, gazing into the heart of this ugly suburban setting, fighting the spider.

One won't do. We know that.

No lights shone in the dirty apartment. Only the glow from her computer on the kitchen table provided any comfort. That and the alcohol. The reports from NDU operatives associated with Titanius, the *Echo*, the Prussian Consortium and various related agencies like the TSA all outlined, in moderate consistency, the unfurling of events over the past week. The open run and gun battles that occurred in near space were inevitable. Her group had been predicting these clashes for a couple of years, so she brushed the recent skirmishes off.

However, hostilities developing between the NDU and the United Confederate States was a surprise. When America split into the various republics a decade ago, leading to a fresh cold war between north and south, the general feeling was that neither side wanted any more fighting. How many once-impressive cities lay in ruin? Still, for those in the espionage game, wars never truly ended. This was simply the latest chapter in an eternal story.

Janet paid more attention to these reports once she learned Mary's life was in danger, and Jim had wedged himself into the *Echo*'s crew. The fact Esther Tyrone was also part of the rescue effort on Luna was expected, so nothing about her presence raised an eyebrow. But the video of an alien ship disappearing in a flash of light and the *Echo* somehow evading capture on her return to Earth was remarkable.

And disturbing.

Let's make a night of it, Jan.

Her indie-comm pinged and she pulled herself away from the window, cleared her throat and refocused.

"Chamberlain."

"Yueng here, ma'am. Update on the target. She's left Gotham hospital, causing quite a disturbance. She's with her dad and the scientist."

"Where are they headed?"

"I'm tracking them to the airport, ma'am."

"Okay, get some agents on them and make sure they all get there in one piece."

She put herself in Atteberry's shoes and, knowing him the way she did, figured he'd want to take her home to San Francisco, back to his own personal safehouse. He remained so predictable. And careless.

"Do you have intel on their house? I'm interested whether the premises are clean. I recall Braddock, the Spacer, embedded various devices."

"Correct. They're still functional, but out-dated. Minimal effectiveness."

"Understood. Anything else, Agent Yueng?"

"Negative, ma'am."

She killed the connection and flopped in front of her screen and sighed. The glow of the machine caught her reflection in a glass of water beside it, reminding her that now she'd hit her early forties, the scars of over 25 years of missions showed. She traced the line across her chin and combed her fingers through her sandy-colored, shoulder-length hair replete with ever more streaks of grey.

For the past six months, holed up in this safehouse with only sporadic forays into the world, she'd spent considerable time wondering whether her career in the Operations theatre neared an end. The physical demands she could handle: she was as fit today as she was when they first recruited her as a seventeen-year-old in university. But the mental pressure overwhelmed her. Unlike in her earlier days, killing other human beings now tore into her soul like a cancer. When the change in attitude occurred remained unclear but that's when *it*—the *spider*—appeared. Possibly that failed mission in Atlanta where she lost five of her own squad. Perhaps the assassination of a professor suspected of selling top secret engineering plans to the Confederates (turned out he was nothing more than a gentle, beloved teacher).

No matter. The important conclusion was that her days in the field were ending, and for the first time in decades she didn't know what to do.

Quit ignoring me. Punch out. Let's do this right.

She shifted her gaze to the screen and pulled up satellite images of Atteberry's home in Frisco. Her old home. It had changed little. He'd painted the garage a fresh color since she was last there in 2085, but nothing else was noteworthy.

A gust of rain pattered against the window, streaking it like a Monet impression. Janet half-heartedly toggled through the screens, then rubbed her face. Part of her missed the action and adrenaline of field work. Being a caretaker in a safehouse was hardly an inspiring occupation.

If Jim and Mary were heading home to recover from the ordeal on Luna, then she'd post some agents around their house to keep them safe, at least until the world's interest in the events on the Moon waned or got displaced by the next disaster. That's one thing she could do, one thing she could still authorize.

A message flashed up from her operative in New York City with an urgent flag on it. She bolted upright and opened the encrypted communique. The note was a brief update on Mary's health from an undercover operative at Gotham MC: *Target in critical condition. Problem with the brain after alien encounter. Not expected to live beyond two weeks. Hospital crawling with agents, others. Titanius implicated.*

She read it again then sent it to the fire bin. This information changed her approach. Years ago, when Jim asked how to reach her in case of trouble, she said, "I'll know, and I'll come to you." If there was ever a time where she needed to live up to that promise, this was it. Her only child, even if estranged, held a deep, visceral connection for her.

Could she meet them in San Fran and be there for Mary's last days?

Oh, that would be a splendid occasion. Get drunk with Jim, like the old college times.

She pulled up the page outlining the various arrest warrants and contracts out on her. The California Republican Forces sought her on charges of murder and terrorism, all related to the Mount Sutro incident. Not a big deal. There were dozens of similar charges around the world for her. The contracts were a different matter. These were not official in any capacity at all.

She scrolled down the list and tallied in her head the new total this week, then smirked bitterly at the $30.2 million. *Not enough for the kind of damage I've done.* The Prussian Consortium released the largest contract, one that had been around for a couple of years. Many had tried to collect, and she or her colleagues had taken them out thanks to a superior intelligence network and her own NDU doubling the contractual value for every would-be assassin her agents removed.

Still, she lived today because she'd been careful, and sojourning in California, hanging out with her former family – if they'd have her – was reckless by any accounting standard. She'd have to approach this like an active field assignment: get the right team in place. Sabotage the CCR infrastructure in key areas and stay one step ahead of whoever sniffed around Jim's door.

Janet realized how dark the apartment had become, so she crossed the floor and drew the blackout curtains before turning on a couple of lights. Then, after checking in with her op cell boss, she opened the page where recent assignments were posted and initiated Project Family Time. *Cute name.* Her colleagues would chuckle at that. She completed the form, approved it under her own authority, and launched it on the network. Within minutes, several agents responded expressing their desire to work with her on this. She selected those she knew, either by reputation or from working with her in the past, and sent the request for final approval to her director.

So perhaps she'd lost a step or two on the high-profile operational missions. Maybe she'd have to resign from that kind of field work by the end of the summer. For now, though, she leaned back and wondered: *am I up for one more mission?*

SEVEN

Titanius Space Resources Headquarters
New York City, Northern Democratic Union

Carter

CLAYTON CARTER SHOWERED IN HIS PRIVATE BATHROOM, put on a crisp set of clothes, and settled onto the couch in his 43rd floor office. The *Echo*'s video log that Quigg handed to him on the tarmac at Shearwater played on his data tablet in a loop. He'd already watched it a dozen times and still couldn't believe what he saw: Mary Atteberry, standing at the comms panel by the flight seats, placing her hands on the unit like nobody's business, and then the glow of blue light appearing. Milliseconds later, as Quigg pointed out, the salvo from the *Sara Waltz* apparently passed right through the ship. But that's impossible. And yet, the evidence didn't lie. Since he was alive on Earth proved that.

Despite surviving the Prussian cruiser's attack, Carter was anything but pleased. The past forty-eight hours in space haunted him like childhood guilt. He'd over-reacted, intoxicated with the idea of grabbing this alien technology for himself, for his own ambition, his own desire to help humankind reach new goals and improve their own quality of life. His tough upbringing in the Heights continued to inform his decisions, his actions today, even though he had nothing to prove to anyone. A successful man by any measure, he still wanted more for his fellow humans and for himself. He craved recognition.

But at what price? Carter shook his head as he recalled firing warning shots over the Rossian vessel on the Moon's surface, then threatening Jim Atteberry's life, and pissing off Esther, the one woman who could hold her own with him scientifically. The resentment forming toward John Powell, captain and friend, when Powell took charge on the *Echo* was ridiculous, but real. Still, despite these bothersome emotions, he remained the leader and would ensure the captain understood his place in the Titanius hierarchy. Fucking fly-boy.

A gentle knock interrupted his reverie.

Carter's Director of Operations and overall fixer of things, Ed Mitchell, stepped in and shook his hand. "Welcome home." He'd arrived from the Technical Ops Center in the building's basement with a handful of documents, photographs, and charts. He smiled pleasantly as he sat down in the Queen Anne chair across from Carter.

"It's good to see you again, Ed. Thanks for all your effort these past few days."

Mitchell caught the video on the tablet. "That log is something, hm?"

"What can you tell me about it?"

Mitchell tugged on his shirt collar. "We've reviewed all the *Echo*'s data from before and after that event, and Rich Patel and his science team have concluded the space-time that *Echo* occupied shifted out of phase. That made her invisible to all observers in space-time prime." He adjusted his glasses, one of only a handful in the corporation who had yet to have his eyesight corrected.

"Well that explains why we weren't destroyed, but what's the correlation between the phase shift and this video of Mary at the comms panel? She seems to be the cause of it, but how could that be?"

Mitchell took a swig from a bottle of water he'd brought with him. "Uncertain, but it's clear to me and Patel that she initiated the shift. How it happened, that is, the mechanism she used, is anyone's guess."

"But Esther said the departing alien ship caused it."

"She did."

Mitchell remained silent a moment, but his face suggested he didn't buy Esther's explanation. "What do we know about the girl, Ed, other than her dad being the man who first heard the Rossian signal?"

"Very little. Brilliant as all hell. Her application and background info she submitted for the summer internship indicates she's strong academically, good at sports, psychologically sound. A lot of high achieving typical teenage stuff. What's more curious is that she's eidetic."

"What does that mean?"

"She has a photographic memory."

Carter rubbed the side of his face, fighting his own fatigue, his lack of sleep and proper food. He'd stop at Zito's for a steak dinner on his way home once he received an update on the girl's condition.

"Is it possible she learned something on the alien ship, something she could apply?"

Mitchell said, "Anything's possible. Until we speak with her, debrief her, we don't understand what the aliens did. But one thing's for sure," he paused, cocking his head, "if she picked up this alien . . . technique, that makes her a valuable asset. Imagine how we could use her knowledge to further mineral exploration." His indie-comm pinged, and he glanced at the screen. "It's Dub Wojtek." He opened the line and spoke in low tones, concern spreading across his face. He ended the call and sighed.

"What is it?"

"Mary and the others disappeared from the medical center."

"What? How?"

Mitchell frowned. "Mix up in Emergency. Her dad snuck her out."

"Dammit, Ed, where are they now?"

Mitchell's indie-comm pinged again as multiple messages arrived. He scanned the information. "It seems they're on their way to San Francisco. Wojtek got held up at the hospital with the cops and internal security, but I have other contacts in play, and they say all three of them—the Atteberry's and Esther Tyrone—boarded a commercial hypersonic flight to the coast." He continued reviewing his messages and frowned.

"Now what?"

"It seems we're not the only ones interested in what happened to Mary on that ship. A handful of unidentified operatives ran interference on my guys at the airport, allowing them to board unimpeded."

"The hell? Is it the Chinese?"

"Don't know, Clayton. These days, it could be anyone."

Carter leapt from the sofa and fumed in front of the massive picture window overlooking the East River. A hint of blue from the end of daylight lingered on the western horizon. He placed his huge palms against the pane.

Who else knows about the Echo's *escape and what Mary did?*

He ran down the list of competitors and enemies. Mitchell was correct: as a large, leading corporation with extensive space resource operations and its own fleet of ships, including the fastest spacecraft around, Titanius had always been a corporate target, and many organizations could be tracking the girl.

How many of them knew what happened on Luna?

No, not the Chinese or the Indians. Only one group bubbled up: the Prussian Consortium. They understood what transpired and their ships have the scars to prove it.

Mitchell interrupted his thoughts. "I've got more info on those agents running interference."

"Tell me."

"Well, it wasn't the Chinese."

"The Prussians, then."

"That would make sense, but no. My guys recognized one agent as being from NDU Special Intelligence."

"Our own government? But how are they involved? And what are they doing protecting foreigners from California? It doesn't add up, Ed."

Mitchell joined him at the picture window. "Someone other than the Prussians or the usual suspects is behind this extra level of protection. But there's a larger problem here. We must assume the Consortium operatives are doing their homework, reviewing their own logs and concluding that Mary Atteberry's abilities, her experience, are an asset too. But NDU involvement suggests we've got spies among us, and log leaks, and who knows what other breaches."

Carter clenched his jaw and scowled.

"There could be at least five other organizations who know exactly what we know: that Mary's a mineable asset. And if our competitors or, god forbid, enemies get to her first, we could lose our competitive position."

The prospect of suffering defeat to anyone tasked him, but if Mary had learned how to render a ship invisible, what more could she do? If her knowledge led to developing faster-than-light technology, and she fell into the wrong hands, then not only would Titanius be finished, but those wanting to use that knowledge to serve their own purposes could enslave the entire world.

He had to run her down first, learn whatever she knew, and protect that information. Fortunately, he already had an in. Then, as if reading his mind, Mitchell cleared his throat. "How well did you and Esther Tyrone get along in space, by the way?"

EIGHT

Atteberry

MARY'S SEDATION HAD WORN OFF BY THE TIME SHE, Atteberry and Esther arrived at the airport and booked seats on the next commercial hyper-jet flight to San Francisco. During the hovercab ride from the medical center, Esther dressed Mary in her proper clothes, and tossed the hospital gown out the window. She still needed help walking but her laugh had returned and Atteberry helped her into the window seat and covered her in a blanket. The meds the doctor provided helped manage her headache.

During the flight through the Earth's lower atmosphere, Atteberry filled Esther in on what the neurological specialist said. It sounded completely unbelievable, like something out of a nightmare. He sat beside Mary; Esther across the aisle. He leaned over the open space and whispered, "I don't know if this is the right thing to do or not, Es, but if this other doctor in New Houston can help, I've got to find him."

She smiled without a hint of humor. "These are dangerous times. Have you seen the latest news?"

"No, I've been too preoccupied with Mary."

"Well, it's not good between the two big republics. Reports of open firefights along the border. I don't think you can just go to New Houston even as a California Republican and expect a warm welcome."

Atteberry brushed her off. "Whatever. I'll find a way somehow."

She raised her eyebrows and faced forward again. He squelched his rising frustration with her negativity and turned toward Mary, brushing the golden strands of hair off her face. Unexpected feelings of impotency rankled him, but he wouldn't give in to them. Instead, he focused on his own next steps: get her home, help her regain some strength, and find this Confederate doctor. All the others could roast in hell.

A hand touched his arm, and he raised his head to see Esther leaning toward him.

"There's something I've been meaning to tell you for a while and I've either been sidetracked by events or I lost the courage. But I have it now, so here goes."

He assumed a wry, intrigued look on his face.

"Back on Luna," she began, "when you were on the surface with Clayton, and they were trying to cut into the alien ship . . ."

"Yes?"

"I admired the way you stood up to him."

He sat in silence, expecting something more to it that didn't come.

"That's all I wanted to say." She sighed and looked down.

Atteberry asked her, "What is it between you two, Es? As long as we're being open here, that one question has nagged me ever since we boarded the *Echo* for the rescue mission."

She frowned and remained silent.

He lowered his voice. "I understand the politics going on, the need for your organization to secure a fleet of ships for an expanded exploration program. And he probably wants access to your expertise in return. So that part's business. But are you lovers, too?"

Esther blushed and turned away.

"Okay," he said, "I think I'm getting it."

"Really?" she snorted, "If you do, let me know please, because I'm drowning in everything that's happened this past week. All I want is to help you and Mary."

Atteberry studied her face now filled with an incongruous mix of hope and defeat. "You're exhausted," he offered. "We all are. But you're smart and confident. I have no doubt you'll figure it out." He paused. "You don't need me to tell you that."

"I'm not as confident as you are, but thanks," she sneered, with an odd squint that caused him to flinch. He'd seen that look before on her but couldn't quite place when or where. No matter, his intuition screamed at him that something wasn't right. He wondered again how much he could trust her, and whether he'd already said too much. There was one way to find out.

"Esther, I have to ask you this."

"Anything."

"I've always been completely honest with you, even when I couldn't find the words to express what was going on inside, you know?"

"Yes, and that's one of those traits I admire about you."

Atteberry grimaced. "Sure, but what about you? I appreciate your help with Mares. Causing a scene in that damn hospital was amazing, but I gotta understand why you're doing it? It's not for any loyalty to me, not when you and Carter are .. you know. So what is it? When you say you just want to help, is that the only reason?"

Her face flushed, and she blinked rapidly. Esther muttered some words, but he didn't hear them. He already had the answer he sought.

THEY SPENT THE REST OF THE BRIEF FLIGHT IN SILENCE, Atteberry caring for his daughter and Esther catching up on her work. Despite their fatigue, neither could sleep. The hyper-jet landed as the sun dipped below the western horizon over the Pacific. The moment Atteberry stepped off the aircraft, helping Mary by linking her arm, he smelled the thick, familiar coastal air.

Outside the airport, they said goodbye. Before hopping into a hovercab, Esther added, "Let me know how I can help, okay?"

Atteberry remained silent. He was certain she wanted more than simply to support them out of the goodness of her heart. Esther was many things, but she never struck him as altruistic. Still, perhaps he misjudged her. The possibility that she'd felt some measure of guilt or concern over Mary's well-being was real. After all, she was the one who'd recruited Mary for the summer internship under Kate's guidance on Luna. And, she'd hinted that her own boss was not too happy with the past week's events. Still, he wasn't prepared yet to give her the benefit of the doubt. There was even more wending its way through her actions, her cynical talk, and he was determined to find out exactly what.

Mary, it seemed, had caught her second wind upon their return to San Francisco. On the cab ride home, she stared out the window, prattling on about all kinds of things: friends she knew in this neighborhood; interesting projects going on in that corner; passing the apartment building where Kate used to live. Atteberry wondered for a moment if she might pull through on her own and that Dr. What's-his-name in New York had overreacted. But when a streetlight shone on Mary's face and he detected the strain in it, the sunken eyes and sallow skin, he lost that optimism.

After the cab dropped them off, he helped Mary stagger up the path and opened the door. She flicked on the hallway light and they wandered to her bedroom.

"Dad," she said, outside her door. "Thank you for everything you did. I love you."

"Love you too, Mares." He hugged her until she broke away and flopped on the bed, not even bothering to change.

He padded out to the living room and found the sofa. It would be so easy to fall asleep but an urge pushed him on to learn more about this New Houston doctor doing research into memory transfer and extraction. He hauled himself up again after a moment, and headed toward the basement stairs. That's when he heard the gentle rapping on the front door. For some odd reason, he considered that Esther had followed him home and wished to talk some more. Then he wondered if this night visitor wanted a piece of Mary's brain. He grabbed a baseball bat from the closet.

Atteberry opened the door and peered around the crack. He recognized the curt, hard smile, the living, wild eyes, and his heart leapt.

Damn it.

San Francisco
California Congressional Republic

Janet

BEFORE JIM COULD SAY A WORD, Janet put a finger to her lips, and broke past him to enter the house. She withdrew the sniffer from her jacket pocket and waved it around in the hallway. A couple of red lights glowed. She punched a keypad on the unit and they turned green. Then, after repeating the same procedure—this time no red lights appeared—she tucked it away.

"Your house is clean, Jim."

"I—I don't believe it. What are *you* doing here?"

She flashed a warm smile and reached out to touch his face, but he recoiled. She dropped her hand to her side. "I've been following the rescue and had to see you and Mary." She took in the environment and, other than some new furniture here and there, noted it had changed little since the last time she was here. She stared hard. "Where is she?"

"Mary's gone to bed," he said, his voice full of defiance. "Why, have you come to take her away again?" A phantom of the sharp pain when Janet had taken her to a safehouse in '85 still haunted her, but it was the right call despite his protective instincts and protestations.

She didn't answer. Instead, she peered down the gloomy hall toward Mary's bedroom. "I've read the doctor's report, his prognosis for her."

Jim's jaw dropped. "How did—?" He shook his head. "Let's chat in the kitchen." His voice softened. "Can I get you something to drink?"

He's into it, Jan. He's into you. Let's go!

She followed him. "A glass of water would be great, thanks."

Atteberry pulled a tumbler from the cupboard, and filled it. They sat across from each other at the breakfast table in the same seats they'd occupied as husband and wife, father and mother. She studied him in the dim glow of the corner lamp. He'd aged since the last time she appeared in '85 with a team of operatives. His hair had thinned on top, and flecks of grey sprinkled his beard. Black circles fell from his eyes and the wrinkles around his mouth were more pronounced. He looked at her the same way.

"Your hair's shorter.

"It's easier this way," she said. "If you look closely, you'll see a few grey streaks layered throughout too. This growing old thing creeps up, hm?"

He appeared nervous and beaten.

"How've you been, anyway?" she asked.

Atteberry shrugged, his guard up. "Getting by, other than the past few days." He watched her nervously. "You?"

Janet sipped her drink, fighting the spider, then folded her hands together on the table. "Slowing down now. My time in the field is ending, but I've still got a project or two to keep me going." She paused, checking the hour. "Jim, I'm concerned about our daughter."

"That's a first," he scoffed.

She ignored the bitter comment, and his face reddened.

"Sorry."

"Never mind. Look, I recognize she only has a week or two before her brain explodes, and there's nothing anyone can do about it. But that doesn't mean she's safe." She took another sip. "Your friends on the *Echo* want to know what she knows, and my intel suggests the Prussians are mobilizing agents, too." She scrutinized him. "They're not in town to enjoy the Pacific Coast weather. These people will stop at nothing to pull whatever they can from her head, and they don't care if the process kills her."

Atteberry tapped a thumb on the table. "Are you here to scrape her mind, too, for your own side?" She ignored the question, and he continued. "Because this looks like you're no different than any of the others. Take that Titanius asshole Carter. He's only interested in using Mary for his own gain, but at least he's honest and upfront about it. At least I know where I stand with him. But you," he added, "I can't trust you at all."

She pursed her lips, and the spider whispered in her ear. She sighed, reached into her jacket pocket, removed the flask and pulled on it hard.

"Maybe you'd better leave us alone. Neither of us needs to be saved by you or anyone else."

Some things about him hadn't changed over the years. His innate defensiveness, for instance, and the way he studied her now with those innocent eyes across the space between them.

"I deserved that, but hear me out and then I'll piss off if you want me to." She set the flask on the table. He folded his arms across his chest. "Your house is being watched by your own government's special forces. Has been ever since you first heard the alien signal."

"I know that. It's for our own protection."

"Sure, that's what they tell you." The cynicism in her voice was unmistakable. "Others are watching you and Mary, too. The Chinese, Brazilians, Indians, three para-military factions, Russians . . . shall I go on?"

His brow furrowed. He had no idea.

"Whether or not you like it or think it's unfair is irrelevant." She finished the rest of her water in one gulp, poured a shot of vodka, and checked her indie-comm. "We don't have a lot of time, so I'll bottom line this. You're not safe here, Jim. I figure in about ten minutes your own goddamn CCR special forces will appear. They may not suspect I'm jamming their surveillance, but if they find me here, and since I'm wanted for murder—"

"Murder?"

She dismissed the outburst and continued. "Put it this way. They'll arrive on the doorstep, take me away, arrest you for aiding a known terrorist, and then interrogate Mary and discover she's not a typical teenager. If they're feeling generous, they'll kill her before her knowledge falls into someone else's hands. If not, they'll sell her to the highest bidder."

His face turned ghostly white. He placed his palms on the table, leaning back as if trying to distance himself from her words.

"What I propose is that we take off right now to a safehouse. If Mary's gonna die anyway, let's make her brief time a safe one, hm?"

Atteberry had nothing to say. He remained quiet and pensive.

The spider wriggled inside her head, screaming for attention.

"Jim, we have to leave."

His jaw fell as if to speak, but no words came. Then a noise from the hall caused them both to turn. Mary stood in the shadows of the kitchen doorway, eyelids heavy, clothing disheveled. Horror scarred her face.

Janet rose from the table, quickly tucking the flask into a pocket, fighting back a hint of shame. Mary watched, not missing a beat.

"Hi Mares. Remember me?"

NINE

Esther

SLEEP WOULD NOT COME TONIGHT.

Esther threw off the covers and sat on the edge of her bed in darkness. A sliver of light cut through her curtains and grazed the chair by the closet, dropping glints of moonlight crumbs across the room. The past few days in space rescuing Mary, the near encounter she had with the alien, and the escape from the New York hospital played in her mind like one of those childhood memories she almost remembered but wasn't sure about: distant and surreal.

The bedside clock blinked 11:08, and she stood, wide awake.

No use sitting around here on a perfect night.

She threw on some comfortable clothes, grabbed her data tablet, stepped out from the apartment, then commanded her hovercar to drive to the TSA. En route, she mapped out her observation plan for the next few hours. Luna, of course. Her old telescope was too limited to resolve any surface details of the events they'd been through, but she wanted to explore the various mares and in particular, the Aristoteles Crater in the north. Then some of the constellations. The Perseid showers wouldn't begin for several more weeks, so those were out. She explored the Calnet in the car for other planets making appearances in the midnight sky.

The hovercar stopped at the main entrance to the TSA off John F. Kennedy Boulevard. Two soldiers on night duty flagged her down. The smaller one approached while the second held his weapon pointing at the ground, finger along the trigger.

"This is a restricted site, ma'am. Do you have clearance to enter?"

Esther, surprised by the CCR military on campus, flashed the soldier her ID on her indie-comm. The man inspected it, waved his scanner, and returned the device to her. Then she remembered what Dr. Kapoor had told her about all hell breaking loose and the need for extra security.

"Thank you, Dr. Tyrone. How long do you expect to stay tonight?"

"A few hours. I want to observe the sky."

"Very well. Please be careful and keep an eye out for anything strange. Call me if you see anything. I've linked our emergency number on your indie-comm." He stepped back, nodded to his colleague, and waved her through.

Inside the main lobby of the TSA, the familiar commissionaire welcomed Esther from her trip to space. She hurried past him and rode the escalator to her office on the third floor overlooking the Pacific Ocean. To develop her night vision, she closed the door and punched up the red light on her data tablet before setting up the old telescope and opening one of the enormous picture windows.

This will help unearth the problem.

The ocean lolled tonight, almost as smooth as glass, and no fog had developed yet. After rolling the desk chair over, she sat down at her scope, guiding it toward the eastern limb, the *Mare Marginis*, where the Rossian ship had been. The extremity was in shadows and because of the brightness of the sun's reflection on Luna's surface, she discerned little. So from there, she turned west, over the *Mare Crisium*, studying the distinct shades of grey and white. Her heart settled down as she picked up the familiar rhythm of stargazing, something she'd done throughout her life, and that always brought peace and comfort to her.

As she positioned the telescope toward the north, her indie-comm pinged. She ignored it until the noise stopped. But a moment later it resumed, and she wondered if it might be Jim. She returned the chair to her desk and picked up the device.

It wasn't Jim Atteberry.

It was *him*.

Esther didn't want to explain to Clayton Carter why they left New York when they did, and sure as hell didn't want to talk about Mary's rescue or anything else related to the partnership negotiations. All that could wait. The indie-comm timed out and she switched the device to silent mode before rolling back to the stars.

There's something bubbling up . . . don't rush it.

As she studied Luna's features and took solace in them, her mind drifted to the game she now played with Jim and what she hoped to achieve: Mary's knowledge, not to put too fine a point on it, but to what end? To repair the relationship with Kapoor and gain leverage over Clayton? Here, in her office, while the stars and planets danced overhead, that seemed like a petty reason, and one she had trouble accepting.

Yet, that's the way they had always played the corporate game. She'd avoided engaging in that madness throughout most of her career, but there comes a time when scientific skill and competence isn't enough, and the reality of politics sets in. Advancement, achievement became less and less based on what you did, and depended more and more on who you pleased.

She surveyed the Aristoteles Crater and expanded her field of view to include the abandoned strip-mining site, even though it was far too small to be distinguishable. She knew where it was, and on a cloudless night when the atmosphere was stable, she had seen the kilometers of trenches running along the mine fields and wondered if others on Earth with more powerful telescopes had watched the rescue operation unfold in real time. No matter.

It's close now.

He said he'd investigate this medical researcher in New Houston before taking any action. He said he'd talk to her about it too, and she believed he would. If Mary survived and they extracted the knowledge she carried, the impact on the world would be enormous, like discovering another entire civilization all at once instead of over decades. As long as that wisdom remained in the right hands. But who among us could be trusted as a civilization's guardian? If history taught anything, it's that human behaviour was consistently self-serving. With that much power, someone would use it.

That assumed she'd live.

The other frightening aspects of her case centered on the more likely outcome that she would die. Esther shuddered at the possibility. She had known Mary for the past six or seven years and picturing her dying at such an early age tested her ability to think and act with objectivity. She shifted her attention from the Moon and gazed across the ocean. Running lights from massive cargo ships shimmered in the distance, and lines of aircraft filled the sky. These scientific and technological advancements had come in fits and starts. What was it Kuhn said? Sudden leaps in understanding followed by seasons of mundane, routine work. A quantum-like model of experimental development. The knowledge Mary held in her brain would trigger the next leap, and what a an upsurge that would be! It was her duty to—

Even closer now.

She returned to the eyepiece and traveled along the boundary between light and dark where the rusty brown colors lived. The doubts, the uncertainties crept into her mind. How does one weigh the value one human life against the immediate and profound advancement of the species? Surely the sacrifice of one life must be worth the gains. If it had been someone else, Kate Braddock perhaps, who carried this knowledge, she wouldn't struggle with her decision. Mary made it harder.

And what was that decision? Had she even made one?

Without saying the words, her actions reminded her that, yes, she knew what she was doing and why: this was an example of the needs of all humanity outweighing the needs of a single person. The beauty was, no one had to wrestle with the selection of whom to sacrifice: the alien already had when it dumped its intelligence into her brain. So now, the question became more practical than ethical. Who will retrieve that knowledge?

She will.

And how will she accomplish that?

By getting involved with Jim's plan to protect his daughter. Without telling him. By pretending to put Mary's interests first so Jim would trust her. Then, when the time was right, she'd convince him that harvesting Mary's brain would be something Mary would want.

That was the worm under the rock.

It made perfect sense. Rational, logical.

Perfect sense . . .

Esther leapt from her chair and raced to the washroom down the hall where she didn't quite make it. She threw up on the tiled floor near the sink and wept.

Atteberry

THE HOVERCAR JANET PRE-ARRANGED WITH HER AGENTS waited for them around the block from his house. Without saying a word or making any noise, the trio slipped out and crept along the edge of shadows toward the car. The second she clicked the door closed behind her, the vehicle rose off the asphalt and flew, stealth mode, out of the neighborhood. She entered the coordinates of the mystery destination, then checked her indie-comm and relaxed.

Atteberry studied her movements, still unsure whether he'd made the right decision to take Mary to this safehouse, but Janet insisted and the last time she appeared in his life, she'd saved him, Esther and Kate, and kept their daughter—who was 10 at the time— protected. Despite the marriage betrayal, he admitted he trusted her with their safety.

Mary leaned into him, a little closer than she normally had as a teenager, and remained quiet.

The route they followed meandered through various sections of town, diverse boroughs—some neglected, others in the grip of gentrification—slowing, speeding up, until they hit the open road toward Redwood City. More sideroads, more neighborhoods, and soon the hovercar pulled into a bland suburban community near Santa Clara. She entered a code in her indie-comm and a double-car garage door opened a few houses in front of them. She manually guided the vehicle inside, the door closed, and they grounded.

"Follow me." She hopped out and entered the house.

Atteberry helped Mary, who remained groggy and quiet. Inside the modest home, Janet pointed to a bedroom and Mary crawled into the bed. Atteberry kissed her on the forehead and joined his ex in the living room. She sat in front of a panel rising out of a coffee table, studied distinct images on a monitor, then turned to him.

"We're good."

"Okay." He yawned and rubbed the back of his neck. Then, falling in a chair, he said, "How long do we have to stick around here?"

"As long as we're secure, we'll remain here until Mary dies and make her as comfortable as possible."

He gulped. "You say that so matter-of-factly, Janet, like she's a package of meat. Mary's as much your daughter as . . ."

Awkward silence passed between them.

"I'm sorry," she whispered, "you're right. The truth is, since I saw her again in your kitchen, I'm fighting my emotions." She walked to a cabinet and pulled a bottle of scotch and a couple of glasses from it. She poured out two good measures, downed hers and refilled it. Then handed the other glass to him.

"When did you start drinking?"

"Like this? A few years back. Long story. I lost one of my agents in a firefight with Russian operatives in Vancouver. Died in my arms." She took another large swallow. "She had beautiful green eyes . . . I can still see them begging me to help, but there was nothing left of her."

"I guess you've seen a lot of death in your line of work."

She gazed into the distance.

Atteberry sipped his drink, grimaced, put the glass down and leaned forward. "Janet, there's a doctor who might be able to help her."

"Hm?"

"The specialist at the hospital said there's a guy who's done memory transfer experiments and could separate the alien mind from Mary's."

"Where is he?"

"New Houston."

She grinned ruefully. "Perfect."

"I want Mary to see him. If there's a chance to save her, to keep her alive, I've gotta try." He picked up his drink again, sipped, feeling the burn down the back of his throat. "Maybe you could come with me?"

"If I enter Confederate territory, I'd be committing suicide. Hell, if the soldiers or cops in California discover me, I may as well kill myself." She narrowed her gaze. "You don't know what you're asking."

"Actually, I do. I'm seeking your help to give Mary a shot at a full life. And if that means going to New Houston and whatever danger that represents, well, I'm prepared to do that for no other reason than I love her." He finished his drink. "So, I'm going anyway."

"Jim, you don't get it. Even if the border is still open, the minute she steps off a plane, Confederate agents will be all over her. Or maybe Prussian or Brazilian operatives find her first. Anyone who suspects she gained some powers, some abilities from that Rossian ship will want to scrape her brain. Hell, they'll scrape her whether she's alive or not." She reached across the table and took his hand. "To you, Mary's your daughter. In my world, she's an intelligence asset of the highest magnitude. She has the potential to change the political map of the world forever."

He stared at her as a lump formed in his throat. "I can't just sit around and watch her die."

Janet looked away.

"What . . . what is it?"

"I'm afraid we need to do more than keep her comfortable for the next week or two."

"What are you talking about?"

"Thing is, these mind-scraping techniques work on both the living and the dead. Once she dies, her body remains an asset. Others will want to study her brain and, where possible, mine it for its chemistry." She looked at him but Atteberry didn't follow.

The room began spinning. "Are you saying we have to . . . destroy her body?"

"Yes. Would you entrust anyone with what she holds?"

He groaned and stood up, running his fingers across his head. "I couldn't possibly do that, Janet."

She slammed the rest of her drink away and joined him, wrapping her arms around his shoulders. "I'll do it."

"That's not helping."

"The consequences of Mary's knowledge falling into our enemies' grasp are far too great." She guided him over to the sofa and sat beside him, holding his hand.

After several minutes of silence, he mumbled. "And there's no chance of sneaking into New Houston unseen? Like, we travel down there and talk to this guy without alerting these other creeps?"

"No."

"We could in theory, right?"

She hesitated and pursed her lips. "It's not that simple."

"But still possible?"

"Jim, you don't understand the risks—"

He shifted his weight to face her. "But if you absolutely had to, you'd find a way."

"Yes, but the chances of getting caught are far too high. Mary's on their radar and so am I, and they'd discover us in no time."

Atteberry detected a trace of panic in her voice, but in his mind, the way forward was clear.

"Please, Janet, let's do this. Get down there, see if this doctor can do anything, then return. We'd be gone, what, a day or two?"

She lowered her head, pulled her hand away, reached for her indie-comm and punched it, scanning maps and images, entering codes and names. After several minutes, she tossed the device on a cushion beside her and threw him a solemn look.

"All right, I'll do this. But let's be clear on what might happen. If we're outed, no matter where we end up, they will torture and kill us. I hate to think what those animals would do to Mary before they scrape her brain, but whatever your worst nightmare is, count on someone doing it. You understand that, Jim?"

He hated her for being so cold and calculating, but he had to try saving Mary no matter the risk. She was everything he lived for. "Yes, I understand."

Janet dipped her head and smacked her lips. "Okay, leave it with me. You need sleep and there's a spare room down the hall." They stood. "We'll move out before dawn."

As they faced each other, relief washed over him and he reflected a moment, thrilled for the help that Janet would bring, yet wary of her true motives. Was she doing this as Mary's mother, or as an NDU agent protecting an asset? Before he knew it, several seconds passed, and she remained standing close in front of him, a thin smile on her face, and an old memory gripped him, pushing him to lean forward and kiss her. Instead, he fought the urge and mumbled, "Good night."

Janet refilled her glass. "Sleep well."

TEN

Berlin

Winter

LINING UP TO BOARD THE HYPERSONIC FLIGht to New York City like a commoner was unfortunate but necessary to cover his actions under a blanket of normalcy. Still, there was nothing routine about his objective: find, detain, and mindscrape Mary Atteberry.

The restless woman in front of him, struggling with too many bags and junk dangling off her wrists, turned and asked, "Do you know if the flight is leaving on time?"

He sneered at her with disdain. "Madam," he said, "the craft is on the tarmac right there, you see? So, yes, there's every reason to believe it's on schedule." He regarded her with ice in his eyes, picturing her being rendered into glue like the old nag she was, and his disposition improved.

The indie-comm in his jacket pocket pinged just as the line of passengers shuffled forward. He pulled it out and checked the message.

Target no longer in NYC. Now in SF, CCR.

Interesting. They must have released the girl from hospital and sent her home to the west coast. Good for her. Flight information flashed on his device showing the next three departures to San Francisco. A direct one was scheduled to leave in 40 minutes. Perfect. He wished the woman in front of him a pleasant journey, then hoisted his carry on and left the queue.

THE FOUR-HOUR HYPERSONIC FLIGHT unfurled with no surprises. He enjoyed the low orbit view of Earth, read some engineering reports on emerging technology, and worked on mind puzzles. When he arrived a little after 7:00 in the morning local time, two of his operatives met him and drove to a small breakfast café near the downtown core. During the trip, they briefed him on the whereabouts of Mary Atteberry, her father, and the mysterious security person with them.

"Do you have information about who this woman is aligned with? Is she California Republican Special Forces?"

Hanks, the younger op who did most of the talking, said, "Unlikely, sir. Our contacts in the CalRep Forces have detected no traffic in that regard. They seem to either have little interest in the girl, or they're unaware of her importance."

"I suspect the latter. These Californians are lazy."

"Yes, sir."

He unwrapped a breath mint and popped it in his mouth. "I wonder who she is? Have you monitored the other networks?"

Hanks hesitated. "To the extent possible, yes."

"What does that mean, Agent?"

"Well sir, we have a limited organization here on the coast. It's just me and George, I mean, Agent Mirsky. We've checked the Chinese and Indian hubs, and the Confederate network. There's no knowledge of, or activity around, the target."

That was a surprise. Winter understood that one agency may be behind the others in its intel, but that many? Something didn't add up. The Atteberry girl was far too important and public to fly this low under the radar.

"Any chance she could be NDU?"

"Unlikely, sir. They're not much of a player out here."

Winter glared at the young op. "Do you know this, or are you guessing?"

The agent tugged at his collar. "Ah, I'm ah . . . well, I'll check in with our contacts and confirm it, sir."

"How long have you been with us, Agent Hanks?"

"Three years, sir."

"Three years. Agent, may I offer you some advice?"

The man shifted his weight in the small hovercar. "Please, I mean, I don't mind and I'd love to—"

"Yes, yes. In our business, people die if the intel is incomplete or missing or based on speculation rather than on the facts. Governments fall, businesses go bankrupt, spaceships engage in firefights . . ." He leaned forward, invading the agent's personal space by going eye to eye. "So let me be clear. Never, ever *guess*, Agent Hanks. You must be sure of what you know. Understand?"

"Yes sir, it won't happen again."

The car dropped them off at the Coffee Nook and they blended in with the cosmopolitan crowd eating their eggs and toasted poppers. The café smelled rich and inviting, the way summer sunlight does in the morning. Hanks excused himself and made a couple of phone calls before joining Winter and Mirsky at a small table in the back. A pretty, tall girl, red hair pulled in a ponytail, arrived with three espressos.

"They're on the move, Dr. Winter."

Winter sipped his demi-tasse. *Of course, they are.* He studied the jittery agent and said, "How long ago did they leave their safehouse?"

"Sometime in the middle of the night or early dawn. I kept the house under remote surveillance, tracking any comings and goings. There were none. But my eyes in the field did a morning drive by and suspected the place was empty. She then confirmed it."

"A few hours is a long time in our world. They could be anywhere by now."

Hanks grinned nervously. "Yes, but we have independents stationed at all the key border crossings, airports, train stations. A family fitting their description booked a private heli-jet."

Winter took another sip and grimaced as the bitter drink went down. "I don't understand what you mean by *fitting their description*. Was it them or not?"

"The probability it's them is high." Hanks referred to his indie-comm. "Tall, bearded middle-aged man. Blond-haired teenage daughter. Trim, short-haired woman. And the daughter had trouble with her balance."

"Interesting. What do we know about her hospital visit in New York?"

Hanks flipped through various screens. "Here's the briefing from Anna Gottlieb. She's undercover as a nurse."

"I know who she is, Agent."

"Yes, sorry. She says information is sketchy and incomplete. The doctor wanted to keep her there for another couple of days, but she, her dad, and that TSA scientist disappeared." He scrolled through again. "Here's something more, sir. The specialist who treated her was a neurological surgeon." Hanks looked up. "Concussion?"

"Perhaps. What else does Anna say?"

"That's all. She'll speak with this specialist when he's in later today and will send an update then."

"What about the scientist, Dr. Tyrone? Where is she?"

"One of our independents followed her home. She remained a couple hours, then traveled to the TSA in the middle of the night. She's back at her apartment now."

"Excellent."

The constant stream of customers through the café caused Winter's anxiety level to rise. Too many ears. He leaned across the table. "Where was this heli-jet going? It must have filed a flight path, no?"

Hanks touched his screen. He scanned the device and then his jaw dropped.

"What is it, agent?"

"Sir, I don't understand." He scrolled through more pages.

"What is it?"

Hanks looked up. "They're en route to New Houston. Are they defecting?"

Winter furrowed his brow and stroked his chin. This was a surprising development. If these travelers were the Atteberrys, what could they possibly want in New Houston? He dismissed the idea of a defection for the moment, since that made no sense. But he set the notion aside to revisit later if more information became available.

Since the end of the second civil war, New Houston emerged from the rubble of the fighting and had mushroomed into a top-rate scientific community. Not only were they leaders in satellite and tracking systems, but they also owned one of the few space elevators in the world, allowing them to shuttle more goods and people to and from space dock without rockets or crystal technology. What else . . . universities and colleges, regional health centers, pharmacology, medical research . . . Perhaps the fraulein needed to see a specialist there?

"Oh shit, you won't believe this, sir."

Winter cringed. "Hanks, you know my rule about cursing. I don't care for it."

"Sorry, sir, it's just that . . . well, we've learned the identity of the security woman."

"Who is she?"

"It's . . . she's the girl's mother. NDU Agent Janet Chamberlain. Special Ops."

Winter bolted up, his wrought-iron chair tumbling behind him, scraping against the terracotta flooring, creating enough of a scene that several heads turned. He apologized to the other patrons, then said to Hanks and Mirsky, *sotto voce*, "Time to go. We're on our way to New Houston."

Janet

JIM DIDN'T NEED TO KNOW ABOUT THE non-descript hovercar, parked at the end of the street, protected by a high frequency EM cloud, a clear indicator that whoever remained in it had only one function: to watch the safehouse.

She first noticed the vehicle during a routine security audit of the premises, shortly after he went to bed. The house itself remained clean, a relief given the conversation they'd had about traveling to New Houston, but when she ran a SAT check followed by the EM sniffer, that's when she realized the hovercar must have tailed them.

At 4:30 in the morning, she woke him and Mary and motioned for them to follow her through an escape tunnel built under the freezer in the garage. At first, he complained but one look from her shut him up. They'd agreed that if she would join them and fly into hostile territory, she would be in charge. He hadn't argued. *No surprise there.* Often, there were times during their marriage when she implored him to fight back, to present a counter-argument or just be pissed off with her, but he rarely ever did. Jim had his own gentler way, which she still found attractive despite driving her crazy.

Didn't matter now.

Mary struggled with the steel barred ladder descending from the garage floor into the tunnel, but once she was down, her orientation and strength improved. Janet led them through the 500 meters of darkness, under the subdivision, arriving at a faux conduit exit leading out to a small meadow. The eastern sky hinted at morning. She pushed them to keep going and they quick-marched across the dew-laden field, sticking to the shadows of arbitrary trees whenever they could.

On the other side, near an abandoned transformer station, a hovercar waited for them. She'd already arranged for a flight into New Houston but had to do it outside the regular NDU network. In this environment, she recognized her bosses wouldn't have the authority to approve that, but any pilot and any machine could be had for a price, and she located a dated but reliable heli-jet with a young aviator on the outskirts of Oakland who needed cash and didn't ask questions.

Once they'd crossed the Golden Gate Bridge, she relaxed. It was a short-lived reprieve when she saw the tired craft at the municipal airport. Her name was *Relic*, and, yes, that's exactly what this heap of shit looked like. Still, once she'd checked the engine, rotors and thrusters herself, she was satisfied the machine could fly, and the pilot, Sam Castillo, had plenty of hours under his belt flying through the California hills and along the coast, and that was good enough for her. They boarded and within moments, the heli-jet was airborne. Forty minutes later, they passed over the Mexican border.

Afterward, as they screamed over northern Mexico toward the Gulf, she focused on Jim and Mary. The brief sleep last night brought Jim back to life, and Mary seemed comfortable enough, although the headaches continued to plague her. Janet gave her an inhalant with pseudophine to manage the pain which also caused her to doze off and on.

"Mares, pay attention. This is important." Janet ran through their new identities on the data tablet again. "Know these answers in case we're questioned by anyone."

She fussed. "I'm ready. My name is Alison Bates and I'm from Reno, Nevada, going to school in New Houston in the fall."

"What program are you taking?"

"Mechanical engineering."

"What's the purpose of your visit to the city?"

"Check out the campus and do some sightseeing."

Janet turned to Jim. "And your name?"

"Vernon Bates."

"Occupation?"

"English teacher at Reno Central High."

"Favourite sport?"

Jim paused. This wasn't in the briefing package. "I, er, that is . . . basketball, I guess?"

Janet snorted. "Is it? I thought baseball was your game."

"It is, but you caught me off-guard."

"Look, if you don't remember, just say what you normally would. If it's basketball, you'd better know something about it if a border agent wants to talk hoops. Got it?"

Jim sulked and leaned back. He was the wild card here and getting him to focus was a challenge. Mary enjoyed acting and had no difficulty integrating into her character, but Jim never liked falsehoods and secrets.

We're a secret too, aren't we, Jim?

Castillo interrupted their preparation, announcing they'd be over the Gulf of Mexico in about ten minutes. The flight path from there would swing around to the north into Confederate space over what used to be Galveston.

Jim said, "Keep asking me questions. I need to get this."

Mary giggled. "Dad, you're such a loser. I'll help you."

THIS SECTION OF GULF COAST LINE from Port Arthur, south toward Corpus Christi still showed the destruction from the civil war. Atteberry gazed out his window at the remains of Galveston, which had been completely abandoned after the conflict, since every building, port and bridge had been flattened to dust. According to Janet's intel reports, only squatters and feral dogs lived there now.

When the Confederate leaders built New Houston instead of resurrecting the old, destroyed city, they picked a location west of the original, near the town of Brookshire. A lot of work remained, but the infrastructure itself came together faster than most could have believed. It was easier to build from scratch than to clear all the rubble.

Air Traffic Control gave the *Relic* the green light to land, and the heli-jet followed standard approach procedures, changing elevation when directed, then hovering over the tarmac and landing. Before the engines had shut down, two guards wearing sunglasses and carrying automatic weapons approached and waited for them to disembark. Janet stepped from the jet and caught her breath in the sudden shock of heat and humidity.

"Good afternoon, gentlemen," Sam said. His cheery disposition could come in handy at a time like this. Janet stood guard in front of Mary and Jim. The warm steel of her knife along her thigh instilled confidence, and she placed her hand close to it.

"Are you the pilot?"

"Yes sir. How can I help?"

"Seems your flight path wasn't registered. What's your place of origin?"

Sam hesitated and shot a glance at Janet. "Well, I'm from Oakland. I got my ID right here if you want to check it out."

The guard took his card and scanned it. "Sam Castillo, hm? He handed it back. What are you doing here, Sam Castillo?"

Janet stepped forward and flashed her best smile. "I'm afraid I'm responsible for that, Officer . . .?"

"Wendell, ma'am."

"See, Officer Wendell, we're from Reno and wanted to tour the campus and see the sights for a couple days. My daughter here, Alison, well she's planning on studying here in the fall and the only flight we could charter quickly was Mr. Castillo here. I hope that's all right."

Wendell turned his attention to her. "May I see your ID ma'am?"

"Certainly."

They all pulled out their fake IDs and Wendell scanned them. Then, he showed the results on his device to the other guard, who threw a cursory glance at her.

This is taking too long.

She dropped her hand again and touched the blade, feeling a surge of adrenalin course through her veins.

Wendell studied the scanner again, then handed the cards back and said, "Sorry for the confusion, ma'am. Everyone's a little bit on edge what with the conflict heating up and all."

"Understood, Officer. Are we okay to carry on with our visit?"

"Yes ma'am. Enjoy your stay." Then, turning to the pilot, he said, "If you can come with us for a few minutes Mr. Castillo, we'll get the flight path documentation sorted out." Sam grabbed his bag and followed the two guards into the hangar.

Janet's intuition, born out of years of subterfuge and deceit, screamed they'd never see Sam the pilot again. She broke out in a cold sweat. "Come on," she said, "Let's get the hell out of here."

New Houston Research Hospital

New Houston
Union of Confederate States of America

Atteberry

THE FIRST SHOCK TO ATTEBERRY'S SYSTEM was the cornucopia of smells that assaulted him when they walked through the main entrance of the medical research hospital. The mix of food and coffee, soiled linens, the pungent wafts of cleanser and decay melded together in such a way as to cause his stomach to lurch. The odors juxtaposed sharply against the gleaming chrome and mirrors of the lobby.

Mary noticed it, too and scrunched up her nose. "What are we doing here, Dad?"

"We need to find this neuro-specialist and see if he can help you." He reached out to take her hand but she swiped it away. An info board showed them where Dr. Elliot undertook his research.

After following multi-colored stripes along the corridors and riding an elevator to the seventh floor, they found the Neurological Research Unit and presented themselves at a reception desk that looked like any other office in any other corporate building. Atteberry strolled forward and asked, "Excuse me, is Dr. Robert Elliot available?"

The young receptionist, dressed in professional garb and wearing a medical smock, peered up from her charts and said, "Oh, do y'all have an appointment?" She glanced at Janet and Mary, then returned her gaze to Atteberry.

"Afraid not. My daughter here," he motioned to Mary, "has a complicated neurological condition and the other specialist we saw in New York couldn't help her. He suggested Dr. Elliot might be able to do something."

"What's the problem, honey?"

Mary grabbed her head. "My brain's overflowing."

"I see . . ." She scrolled through various screens on her computer. "Well, the doctor is primarily a research doctor. He doesn't actually have patients. I can send y'all down to Emerg and they'll be happy to check you out." She picked up her comms device and was about to speak into it when Janet grabbed her hand.

"Hey, you're hurting me!"

Janet squeezed a pressure point in her wrist and, in a cool voice, said, "We've been down that road, miss. My daughter is dying, and conventional medicine can't do a damn thing. We're desperate, and your guy Elliot may hold the key to her survival. We only want to discuss her case with him, then we'll go, so you'd be wise to accommodate us." She dropped her hand.

The receptionist rubbed it and anger filled her eyes. "Just a minute." She checked her screen and, without looking at them, said, "Dr. Elliot isn't here at the moment."

Janet clenched her jaw and glared at the young woman. "If you're playing with me—"

"No, no, I'm not! He's been at a meeting at the university all morning."

Atteberry exhaled and checked the clock on the wall. "It's afternoon now, so when will he return?"

"He's reserved the lab for 2:00, so he should definitely be in by then." She paused. "I'll send him a message that y'all are here and need to speak with him."

Atteberry watched Janet. Her stone face hadn't changed.

"Thank you, that would help a lot. And I'm sorry about getting upset, but we're running out of options. My daughter's, well . . ."

The receptionist softened. "There's a family area by the elevators where you came in if you'd like to wait there." *They-ah.*

Atteberry thanked her and headed to the lounge. He noticed the absence of walls on this floor, everything being open concept with portable barriers and overflowing potted plants here and there, dividing the various labs and workstations. Near the elevator bank, they came across a series of oversized, soft chairs and sofas, interspersed with side tables, lamps and video screens. An older woman in a lab coat, hovering over a data slate, occupied one of the seats, and a callow man—an intern or research assistant—head back, mouth agape, papers falling from his outstretched arm, slumped in another.

Atteberry and Mary sat together across from Janet. She read and punched her indie-comm, scowling. Mary watched her with probing intensity, studying her face, her movements. Janet looked up. "Where's Esther Tyrone?"

He shrugged his shoulders. "When we arrived at the airport last night, she was going home. I haven't been in touch with her since."

Mary piped up. "I like her."

Janet flashed a rare grin at Atteberry. "What do you like about her?"

"Esther's smart and brave and totally nova. Keeps that egomaniac Clayton Carter in his place."

Janet smirked and returned her focus to the indie-comm.

"Why do you ask?" Atteberry said.

Without looking up, she said, "Oh, curious I suppose. I'm following up on the intel and there're soldiers posted at the TSA. I assume she knows about Mary's condition?"

"Yes. Is that important?"

"Could be." She put her device down and leaned forward. "Do you trust her, Jim?"

He quelled his first reaction, a defensive *how dare you ask me* response clamoring to be heard. Instead, he counted to ten, calmed himself, and said, "To the extent that I can trust anyone these days, yes. She knows about the alien memories in Mary's head. I told her all about that. And I honestly feel she has our best interest at heart."

"You realize if she got hold of Mary's knowledge, the TSA would become the most powerful scientific organization in the world, don't you?"

He pursed his lips. "Of course, but she wouldn't do that."

"Because she's infallible?"

"No, because she's actually loyal to Mary." The bitterness of his past relationship with his ex-wife churned, so he took some deep breaths, and continued. "And to me."

Janet shrugged. "Perhaps you're right. As long as we're having this conversation, I admit the concept of loyalty to another person is not something I'm familiar with."

Atteberry shifted in his seat.

82

"No need for drama, Jim. We've both moved on from those past days. We can be grown-ups."

He reached over and stroked Mary's hair. "Yes, I suppose."

"So tell me, are you and Esther in a relationship?"

"No, just friends, and I'm not even sure how far that friendship extends but running alongside her on the *Echo* felt good." He paused. "When we're together on a project, we get along better than when we think about an *us*. On the way home yesterday she tried convincing me that any relationship is a waste of time, because one will always betray the other. And even if you stay together for years, one dies first, abandoning the other." He grimaced. "I think she saw them as unnecessary and preferred to focus on the tangible nature of work."

"I understand that. Make no mistake, I've missed you terribly, but my over-riding loyalty is to the work I do to preserve democratic values. It always has, and this," she waved at the hospital, "changes nothing. So I'm not here because I have any residual feelings for you and Mary: I'm here to protect an asset that can help solidify our beliefs." Her face became sad, distant. Mary pretended not to listen.

"What is it, Jan?"

"Oh, just that I'm not getting any younger and I'll need to transition into something new before too long that doesn't require as much physical stress. These old bones are creaking and it's got me down." She checked her indie-comm. "I wish that doctor would hurry up. This place makes me nervous."

Atteberry reached across the space between them and stroked the top of her hand, aware of her gnarled knuckles and how rough her skin had become. "Perhaps this won't mean anything to you, but I've missed you. We both have."

Mary turned and watched him like a lawyer.

She thanked him and said, "You always were a lot more sentimental about such things."

At that point, a middle-aged, balding man carrying a lab coat over his arm stepped off the elevator and paused when he saw Mary leaning back on the sofa. Atteberry stood as the fellow approached and extended his hand.

"You must be Dr. Elliot."

ELEVEN

New York City
Northern Democratic Union

Carter

THE LAST OF THE INVESTIGATORS PACKED UP his data tablet and scraps of notes, brushed his balding head, and followed Carter's assistant Marla Sullivan out of the office. She returned a moment later with a bottle of cold water.

"Are we done for the day?" he sighed.

"Yes, but you've got more meetings tomorrow and for the next few days you'll have to prepare for."

He yawned, thanked Marla for the drink, and flopped into the sofa near his personal boardroom. She sat facing him, crossing her legs, her back ramrod straight.

"Who knew there'd be this much trouble over a simple . . . misunderstanding with the Prussian fleet."

"Yes, Mr. Carter. The repercussions have been far reaching."

"What's on tomorrow's agenda?"

"NDU Intelligence at 9:00, Space Workers Association at 10:00, Gotham Medical officials over lunch, one of the UN Science directors in the afternoon, then the—"

He waved his arm. "Enough, Marla. Can you reschedule any of those?"

"Afraid not. Some of these characters blame Titanius for starting a new global war."

The madness continued. Self-important, fear-riddled bureaucrats stoking the embers of conflict to promote their own goals, and secure their mind-numbing, unimportant jobs for another few years.

"I don't have time for this."

"No, sir."

He paused, took a swig of water and relished the cool liquid flowing down his throat. "I'd better touch base with Esther Tyrone. Compare notes and such."

Marla stood. "I'll put in a call right now, sir."

"No, wait a second." He rose and, in a lowered voice, asked, "Have you heard from Ed or the others about Mary Atteberry?"

She shrugged. "Nothing since their flight to the coast last night."

"Okay, I can ask Esther about that too."

Sullivan sauntered out, and as he admired her well-kept form, he stretched before returning to his desk and poking through Captain Powell's report. It would take several days—if not weeks—to get the *Echo* repaired. The good news was, no major structural problems. Just a lot of minor fixes, systems checks, and they still needed to finish work on some of the primary elements they hadn't completed before they launched the ship on her first lunar flight. The medical bay, secondary airlocks, and inventory of tools for the workshop, for example. His mind drifted back to what happened on Luna, and he scowled. Something had changed within him, and he didn't like it.

He chewed his bottom lip. Marla poked her head in the doorway touching her earpiece, and said, "That's Dr. Tyrone on line one."

Carter punched the connection on his desk comms and Esther's face appeared on the tele-screen. Shadows scarred her face, and her hair flew up and off to the side more than usual, but she still radiated warmth and comfort. Perhaps she was the source of his dis-ease.

"Hello, Esther, thank you for taking my call. I hope all is well."

"Couldn't be better," she announced in mock enthusiasm. "Seems everyone wants to talk to me about the rescue and . . ." Her voice drifted away.

"Same here. Tell me, how is Mary doing? You left unexpectedly last night, and I worry about my people."

She shook her head absently. "Yes, sorry about that. I'd rather not discuss it over this link, but I hope we'll go over it thoroughly soon. In fact," she added, "there's a lot of things we should talk about, don't you think?"

Carter clenched his jaw. Somehow, she knew. Sending Dub with the Atteberrys to the hospital likely tipped them off. *Should've included Ish. More likeable.* He wouldn't underestimate her, or Atteberry, again. "Perhaps by the end of the week? I have another full day of debriefings tomorrow, but then I hope our operations will return more or less to normal."

Esther sipped from a Styrofoam cup. "And the Prussian Consortium? The *Echo* destroyed one of their observer vessels, after all."

"A known spy ship. Let's not tumble into a vortex of sympathy over a gang of thugs. I'll have my comms folks deal with it, and the NDU diplomats. I have little concern about them."

She looked off screen and asked, "What can I do for you today, Clayton?"

He narrowed his gaze. "I wanted to discuss our partnership negotiations." She opened her mouth to speak but Carter cut her off. "Now, now, I understand the timing may not be the best, but time is one thing that runs out quickly if it's not managed." He leaned forward

86

toward the screen. "So let me say I thought we made a skilled team. Notwithstanding the conflicts with the Prussians and others, our crew performed well, and your knowledge of science and space operations was extremely helpful."

"I agree there appeared to be some positive synergy that, frankly, I hadn't expected."

"Good! Then I assume you'd be open to completing our discussions."

"Look, it's far too soon for that. I haven't even briefed Dr. Kapoor on what's been going on these last two weeks. He's coming by in a while for a full discussion, and I can't commit to anything just yet."

This may be the right time to play the card.

"Of course, I understand. But please appreciate my position as it relates to our future together." He tented his fingers under his chin. "I want access to your researchers and all that state-of-the-art equipment you have sitting in your Ops Lab, especially that quantum computer and deep space sounding technology."

"And I need a reliable fleet of exploration ships, and security to ensure the safety of their crews while on missions for the TSA. Our positions haven't changed."

"See?" he smiled confidently, "We are made for each other. Let's not allow the skirmish in space to interfere with all the good we can do together."

"And I told you, Clayton, it's too soon to commit to a full-on partnership with Titanius. Far too soon now, given the interest around Luna and Mary, and the *Echo*." She shrugged half-heartedly. "Is there anything more?"

Time for the ace in the sleeve.

"Well there is, yes. I will have this partnership with the TSA, Esther. It's not a question of if: it's only a question of when. And I feel the sooner we solidify our work together, the better for everyone. Especially for Mary Atteberry."

She furrowed her brow and folded her arms across her chest. "What are you talking about?"

"Oh, I don't think I need to remind you what we both know about young Mary . . . how she manipulated space-time fabric to evade the

Sara Waltz . . . how she must have gleaned some alien power or knowledge while she was on that ship. It would be awful, simply awful, if what she learned fell into the wrong hands. I can only imagine how her father would react to that."

She bristled. "Is this a threat? Are you so evil and selfish that you'd harm Mary if, say, we don't enter into a partnership?"

"I could never hurt her."

"Bullshit."

"Your lack of judgment about me is confusing, especially after we spent that evening together, making love and chatting about the Rossian signal . . . and how you buried the evidence and claimed there was no such tap code? Can you imagine how the world would treat the TSA?"

She scoffed. "Your word against mine, so good luck with that."

Carter took no pleasure in performing what he had to do next. No pleasure at all. He didn't smile or frown, after all, this was simply business. He pressed the button on his data tablet and her recorded voice filled the space between them. The evening she opened up to him about the truth behind that initial signal in 2085, how it led to murder and terrorism at the Mount Sutro Tower. The evening she came clean about her role in the cover-up. The evening she asked him to stay.

"Asshole . . ." she whispered.

He stopped the playback and stared into her down-turned face. "To be clear, I have no desire to share this with anyone. However, I want what I want. And right now, that's full, unfettered access to all your assets. And that includes Mary Atteberry."

"She is not an asset. Besides, I have no sway with her."

"But you do with Jim Atteberry." He paused. "Look, I don't care how you do it, but I suggest it's in your best interest and mine to make sure Mary is safe and on the right team, if you catch my drift. One way or another, I'll have what she knows. We can either work together cooperatively, like true partners, or I end your career with this audio file. You'll be lucky to teach high school physics in some backwater town."

Esther remained silent and still. Then, she looked at the camera and muttered, "All right, you win. I'll see what I can do about Mary."

Terran Science Academy
San Francisco, CCR

Esther

ESTHER SANK INTO HER OFFICE CHAIR, wallowing in the depths to which Clayton Carter threatened to go in his quest for technological dominance in space. She'd taken an enormous risk opening up to him about the truth of Mount Sutro and her decision to eliminate all related data to protect the Academy. Colossal mistake in hindsight. Sleeping with him was another, but whatever. Still, there was something about him that awakened her deeply.

Note the roosting chickens on the doorstep, Esther.

She swivelled back and forth at her desk, forgetting Kapoor's imminent arrival for a full briefing on what happened over the last few days. Mary knew the truth about the alien memories dumped in her brain and the bio-physical problems emanating from that. She understood and admired Jim's need to protect her from the vultures like Carter—hell, even herself—who wouldn't think twice about extracting her knowledge no matter what shape the mindscraping left her in.

And now this. Of course, he recorded every word she said regarding the truth around the Mount Sutro incident. That shouldn't have come as a surprise to her and yet it weighed heavily on her shoulders now as a disappointment and a reminder of her own need to keep others out, not let them close to her thoughts or feelings. Not trust anyone. Not anymore.

Could she blame Carter for doing what anyone else in his position would do? The only person she pointed a finger at now was herself for being so naïve, so cocky to think she could do business differently. And he was right. If he sent a copy of her words to Kapoor, her career would end instantly. She shook her head.

Her assistant appeared in the doorway and cleared his throat. "Excuse me, ma'am. Dr. Kapoor is on his way down for your meeting."

She organized the papers and folders on her desk and asked, "What kind of mood is he in?"

"Hard to tell since he's consumed with this rescue and the *Echo*."

He entered the office and placed bottles of ice water on the side table at the sitting area. Esther thanked him and stood, arching her back, fatigue penetrating her bones.

A good stiff drink and a dreamless sleep would fix me up.

She heard Keiran Kapoor chatting in the hall long before he showed up at her door. One of his habits—something she admired—was the attention he paid to every employee, asking them how they were, what they worked on, the kids, the spouses, and on and on. An extrovert to the core. No wonder he'd been the TSA's director forever and was accomplished and respected in that role. When she pictured him listening to her explain the nuts and bolts of the Mount Sutro cover-up on Carter's recording, shame filled her pores. Her cheeks flushed.

"Dr. Tyrone," he said warmly, loud enough for the outer office staff to hear. "Again, welcome home and congratulations on rescuing that young girl." He closed the door behind him, and turning to face her, his disposition hardened. "I'm afraid I don't have a lot of time, Esther. Come, let's talk." He sat on the sofa and opened a bottle of water.

She joined him, choosing her straight-backed chair to his side. In situations with her boss like this, when his anxiety permeated the room, she took charge of the conversation, steered its direction, focused on what she wanted him to take away. This afternoon, she needed him to feel relief and confidence.

"Allow me to begin this briefing by going back a couple of weeks to the status of the partnership negotiations with Titanius."

He sipped his water.

"The talks spun around and the minions on both sides were in a feeding frenzy over what I considered irrelevant or minor issues . . .

like who would head the joint project office, and how resource levels would be ascribed and monitored, financial codings . . . Kieran, these are subjects the managers can work out once we have an agreement-in-principle, would you agree?"

"He leaned back, picking his teeth with his tongue. "Yes, of course. Foster or Wu should handle those things. Go on."

She swallowed. "When the crisis hit on Luna, I was already in New York to meet with Clayton Carter one on one, to cut through all the crap and agree on the fundamental points. He had to manage the immediate problem with his workers up there—one of whom was Mary we hired for the internship program—and I offered to help any way I could."

He studied her with his warm, hazel eyes. A mental note-taker. No audit trail to leave behind.

"As you know, I joined the *Echo* and from there, provided navigation and analytical expertise wherever possible. I think Carter and the crew appreciated that, and in the end, my involvement in the rescue mission showed how well our two organizations work together, hinting at a wonderful, exciting future as partners."

"But it wasn't just a rescue mission."

She stopped, her mind upended and scattering. "What do you mean, Kieran?"

He leaned in closer to her, as if the office itself had prying ears, with a sly, knowing look on his face. "I want to learn about the alien ship, and why I'm only finding out about this now when, apparently, you've known the truth about it for several years."

A cold sweat broke out on her forehead and, although she fought to maintain eye contact with him, her feelings betrayed her, and she turned away. She focused on breathing, then wrestled to regain control of the discussion. "How much do you know already?"

"Oh, come now, Esther. We're both grown-ups."

Her shoulders relaxed. This was not a simple briefing on a routine project. He knew what happened. Anyone in his position would have private, secondary channels of communication to supplement the official ones. Perhaps he'd known about the Ross 128 signal back in

'85 when it first appeared, and kept it to himself until the time was right, until he needed to use it.

Game theory suggested she had no choice but to tell the complete truth now, since she had little idea how much he knew. Withholding information would only make the discussion worse if he already understood the reality.

"Esther, I have no desire to pick a fight with you, and I'm not angry you destroyed all the data associated with Ross 128 years ago. Why, I'd probably have done the same thing if I were in your shoes, if I were a little younger." His gaze burned into her, and she wanted to crawl into a hole.

He knows everything.

"But I am disappointed, no question about it. I'm hurt you couldn't come to me with that information back then, and I'm surprised you didn't tell me immediately about the alien ship and the firefight and how this girl somehow tricked a fucking heavy cruiser to let the *Echo* pass unnoticed."

"But that's—"

He raised a finger. "I appreciate everything you've done for this Academy. Working alongside Marshall Whitt couldn't have been easy, and merging Space Operations with your own SETI directorate took much finesse given the unique cultures of those groups. I congratulate you on doing that."

Her cheeks burned.

He lowered his voice. "But the dishonesty, Esther . . . I simply cannot abide dishonesty. Yes, you tell me most things, but keeping alien contact from your boss is unacceptable. Embarrassing, actually."

Silence filled the room and Esther was vaguely aware of the wind whistling around her large windows. She stared at the poster of Titan on the back of her office door, waiting for the shoe to drop. She didn't have long to wait.

"I'm taking Space Ops away from you and giving it to Mark Jefferson. I need someone in that position who won't keep secrets from me, and he's performed well for such a young man. Knows the importance of sharing information with his superiors. Understands the complexity of this file."

That traitor! The only person at the TSA who could implicate me in the Ross 128 madness, who I trusted to have my back. The bastard must have told him everything.

"I should fire you, don't you think?"

She remained silent.

"Hm?" He intercepted her gazing at Titan. "But I won't. I need you to complete these negotiations with Titanius and land us a space fleet. And I want you to keep leading the SETI directorate, at least short term until this attention dissipates." His voice was almost a whisper now. "But make no mistake, Dr. Tyrone. I expect you to tell me everything that goes on, even if you don't believe it's relevant. Because if I ever smell deception or lies of omission, I guarantee you'll never work in this field again. Understand?"

Esther fought the shame and rising tears and couldn't wait for him to leave. When he finally excused himself and closed the office door behind him, she clenched her fists with only one goal on her mind now: destroy Mark Jefferson.

TWELVE

Medical Research Center
New Houston, United Confederate States of America

Janet

DR. ROBERT ELLIOT'S OFFICE REMINDED HER of an organizational, cubicle-driven, standard-issue bureaucratic hell-hole, the kind she'd probably end up in over the next few months. Portable five-foot high sound-deadening barriers served as walls. A desk, a thin workstation with sterile overhead lights, and a couple of hard-back chairs filled the sparse area. Jim brought an extra chair in from an adjoining unit.

Somewhere in her life, she came to believe that doctors at the forefront of medical breakthroughs were all built like Adonis. This fellow, with a coffee stain on his tie and smelling of cooked cabbage, looked like he'd stumbled out of an accounting office. *What a fucking mess.*

"The receptionist tells me Dario Angelis at Gotham Medical referred you here?"

Mary sat in between her and Jim, quiet, apparently off in another world.

Jim spoke first. "I won't waste your time, Doc. Do you know about the events on Luna this past week?"

"I have heard the reports."

"What you may not know is we encountered an alien, that is, Mary did, and this creature somehow dumped all of its memories into her brain."

Mary snapped to attention and quickly added, "They're parsed, Dr. Elliot. I carry all the experiences: its culture, knowledge, feelings, belief systems . . . in short, the creature's life is part of me."

"Fascinating," he whispered, leaning forward.

"It's all too much, though. I can't integrate all this nova information. Some of it, sure, but it's overwhelming." She grasped her head in her hands. "It hurts."

"We need your help," Jim said. "Dr. Angelis examined her, did brain scans, and doesn't think she'll live past a couple weeks unless we find a way to extricate the alien's memories from her brain. He told us you're the only one he's heard of who might understand what to do."

The doctor rose from his desk and faced Mary. He examined her eyes, her ears. He applied pressure to her temples and the back of her head. Mary flinched when he touched the neck area.

He returned to his chair. "Traditionally, mindscraping is the technique used to remove information from the brain, but it can't be done without seriously harming the patient. It's only practiced as a last resort."

"Or torture," Janet added.

The doctor continued. "There's no known case of someone making a full recovery from that barbaric process, no."

Janet said, "But you have another procedure. Mind transference, I understand. So unlike the others, you can actually help."

"No, I don't think so."

Atteberry interrupted. "Why not?"

"Mr. Atteberry, my research into memory extraction and transference is at a basic, fundamental level. I work with lab mice, not human beings. Granted, we're getting close to solving some aspects of this problem, but there's a decade of research to do before we ever begin trials on primates or humans."

"Tell me, doctor," Janet said, "why exactly are you interested in this?"

Let's get this over with. I'm thirsty, and I'll make your life a living hell if we don't finish here soon.

He paused a moment, evaluating her. "Well, there are things we'd like to do as a profession to address challenges such as multiple personality disorder, as one example. Imagine if you had a dozen voices in your mind, all fighting with each other. My research, fingers crossed, will eventually allow a patient to choose just one and eliminate all the others. Of course, there are instances where we might need to extract information from a single personality patient for a number of other reasons: eliminating horrible acts that they endured in the past, or other traumatizing events. Honestly, Mrs. Atteberry, the applications are numerous."

Janet glanced at Jim, but his focus remained on the doctor.

Mary groaned and held her head again.

"But never mind all that. Let's get your daughter into an observation room and run some scans. I'd like to understand the extent of the problem better, and perhaps then I can give her something to ease the headaches."

They exited the cubicle and followed Elliot through an open space containing several more blue and white work stalls, high-powered computing hubs, enclosed bio labs and nursing stations that had been converted into technical work areas. The equipment sparkled. Janet scoped out cover positions, scrutinized the other workers, looking for anomalies.

He held the door open for them at a lab tucked away in the corner of the floor. Mary entered, followed by Jim and Janet. There were two beds like she'd seen at various hospitals in the NDU, with bio-readers and assorted medical equipment hovering nearby. Several massive screens covered the walls, and another workstation with computers squatted against the far wall.

"Come, Mary, lie down and we'll take some pictures."

She rested on the edge of the bed and the doctor swung her legs on it, then flipped the machines on. The moment she placed her head near the sensory pillow, the bio-reader above sprang to life. Her pulse and heart rate displayed prominently. Other bio-physical information populated a table at the side of the screen. Elliot studied the data, muttering to himself and occasionally hiking up his pants.

"There are marginal discrepancies in vital signs compared to the norm for your age, Mary, but still you're well within the normal despite needing sleep."

"It's my brain, Doctor."

"Yes, yes. Let's have a look at that."

He punched some buttons on the screen and cycled through various pages, stopping on one and inputting different parameters. Blue light hummed around her and the bed, and images of her brain appeared on a screen on the facing wall.

"Sweet Mother of God . . ."

"What is it, doctor? What do you see?" Janet spoke in a low hard voice, shifting her gaze between the scanned images and Mary on the bed.

"I'm sorry, I've just never seen anything like this. Not even in our test subjects."

"Out with it, doc." The strain in Jim's voice caused him to speak a bit too loudly.

"It's remarkable. See this?" He walked to the screen and pointed to an area of the brain that, at least with this color scheme, appeared blue against a grey background. "The dark part is her normal brain function containing both recent and stored memories. The blue is, presumably, what the alien left behind since it represents the anomaly. Note how it moves, almost like flowing water?"

"Yes, but what does it mean?" Atteberry asked.

"I'm speculating, but I believe what it means is exactly the way Mary explained it: there's too much information vying for too little space." He turned to face them. "We use an expression around here when someone drones on and on about a topic by including all kinds of superfluous material. We call people like that Verbal Overflowers. What I think is going on in Mary's head is the alien—still hard to believe I'm saying that word—the creature's memories far exceed the capacity of her brain to store it all. A Mental Overflower, if you will."

Jim muttered, "The New York physician said something similar."

Elliot continued studying the scan, putting his face right up close to the screen and making clucking noises with his tongue.

"I'm speculating, but it appears this knowledge is being cycled in and out of her brain, as if the memories themselves are sharing her mental capacity so that none are permanently lost. If we can . . ." He stopped and shook his head.

Janet grabbed his arm. "If you can *what*, doc?"

He worked his mouth, and she released her grip. "I was going to say that if we could somehow intercept that flow and guide it into a bio-mechanical storage unit, then we may be able to extract this knowledge without scraping. It's not quite the transference we're working on, but if I set up the precise conditions, the correct pressure differentials, perhaps we can transfer all the alien experiences from her body and leave Mary's normal brain untouched."

His eyes narrowed, and his jaw clenched. "But no one has ever attempted this before. As a thought experiment, it's a curiosity, but . . ." He looked at both Atteberry and Janet, then to Mary resting on the bed. "I honestly don't feel I could risk it. I'd have to rethink and scale all my procedures, and there'd be no time for thorough testing in the week—"

"Actually," Janet said, "we don't have that much time. You may have guessed we're not from these parts."

"Not even a week? Impossible, then."

He returned to the screen and traced the flow of blue matter through the brain tissue.

"Doc, please . . ." Atteberry's voice cracked, full of desperation.

The doctor paced around the room, stopping to examine Mary's vital signs and other health markers as he worked through what to do next.

Finally, he turned to both Janet and Jim. "I wish I had more time. I'm convinced I could help your daughter if I only had a few months to develop and test the procedures."

"Doctor, she's going to die, anyway. If there's even a remote chance . . . please."

Mary raised her head from the pillow. "We can—I mean, I can establish the protocols, Dr. Elliot. I understand how to do it. I mean, the alien does, or . . . well, I do too."

Elliot worked his jaw muscles, flipped through some additional scans, then said, "Suppose that's true, even if the creature's knowledge is trustworthy, I can't guarantee the procedure will work. The only assurance I can offer is, well, to perform an *experiment*. If you accept the risks, I'll pull a team together right away, determine with Mary's help the proper sequencing to use, and operate first thing in the morning as long as I find the equipment and people."

Janet felt a wave of relief flood through her, and a deep thirst that no soda could slake. The mother she might have been wanted to hug the foul-smelling doctor. The mercenary she was didn't give a shit. And the spider waited patiently on the sidelines. Jim grabbed the side of Mary's bed to steady himself, his mouth agape.

"She'll have to stay here overnight so we can work with her to crack this nut. I'm assuming that's fine with you?"

Atteberry looked at Janet.

Janet said, "Forget it. We can figure out a way for the two of you to discuss the procedure, but she doesn't leave our sight."

"But—"

"Don't fight me on this, doc. She stays with us. Now, is there anything else you need?"

The doctor shook his head. She gave him her encrypted contact coordinates while Jim helped Mary off the bed, and they hurried toward the bank of elevators, Janet in the lead. On the way out, various workers in lab coats watched them in silence. Janet made a point of staring each one of them down.

Winter

He read the intel on his indie-comm for the tenth time, a habit he developed in his early espionage days when posted in Dublin. The action reminded him of his father's advice: measure twice, cut once.

Benedikt Winter stretched his back in the hovercar, watching the entrance to the medical center like a patient bird of prey. The agent inside the hospital had tracked the Atteberrys to one of the floors that focused on research, in this case, Dr. Elliot's lab specializing in experimental neurology. Made sense, given the girl's apparent ability to alter matter with the touch of her hands.

A flurry of nurses and other workers blew out of the central entrance. Shift change, he surmised, and checked the intel again.

When the message pinged on his device, the sound shocked him. It read: *Targets exiting now, main door. Closed meeting. No details yet.*

Winter acknowledged the report, drew the gun from underneath a hat beside him, and waited. This would be simple, no need for backup or support. Two bullets, one for each adult. Then scoop the fraulein. He watched for them to appear, but when they did, they were cloaked in a group of workers moving en masse toward public transportation or the hovercar depot. His pulse quickened as he recognized Janet Chamberlain from the network intel. Before he knew it, a cab whirred up to the doors, and the Atteberrys disappeared inside. There'd be no clean shot today, not yet at any rate.

He commanded his car to follow theirs, but at a distance, stealth mode.

Acknowledged.

As he swung out of the parking depot and onto the freeway, he'd completely lost track of their cab, but the car's AI tracked it as an icon on the map screen. Chamberlain may suspect she was being followed, but she'd never guess it was him.

The cab dropped them off in a busy market area in downtown New Houston. Minutes later, Winter's car pulled over on its skids a couple of blocks away. He stepped out, surveyed the streetscape, and wandered toward the spot where they had been. A minute can be a decade in this business, and he'd just inadvertently given them a lifetime to disappear.

He checked his indie-comm again, re-reading the message from the ward agent.

A neurological unit? Second opinion?

Although the desire to kill had locked itself in his brain, the delay caused by the confusion at the hospital entrance cooled him off. As he considered his options, he wanted to know what they were doing, and why here—a potentially deadly place for Chamberlain.

Any new info about their meeting? He waited a moment for the response.

Negative, but lots of activity. Surg sked in the am. Talk of bio-mech specialist bn called in.

It didn't add up. Bio-mechanics were nothing original. Limb replacement tech had been around for years. Hardly warranted going to a neurology researcher if the girl needed a new arm or leg. He considered the question longer. Could this be a brain transplant?

Winter meandered along the street, looking in windows, watching people go by, but the Atteberrys were nowhere to be seen. He concluded they were either picked up by a second cab, or they'd gone into hiding. One of the coffee shops he passed had outdoor seating, so he purchased a dandelion tea and sat in the shade of a struggling oak tree near the pristine sidewalk.

New Houston was as beautiful as other agents had reported. Nothing older than twenty years, well-planned, well-maintained. He admired their commitment to clean lines and clean streets, an ordered assortment of shops, and traffic signals that made sense. The people, too, appeared happy. Mind you, warm weather year round could be responsible for that. Spend a winter in Berlin, and the damp cold there would kick the joy from the happiest soul.

Why would the girl need a brain operation? And why perform it here?

The questions refused to disappear. He sipped his tea, relishing the familiar tang, and he knew exactly what to do.

After punching the indie-comm, he held the device to his ear and waited for the other party to connect. A man's grim voice scratched out of the speaker. He heard the telltale encryption alerts ping.

"Yes?"

"This is Winter. Interested in a contract?"

The voice on the other end remained the same, no fluctuation in tone or intensity. "Go on."

"First, tell me, are you in New Houston?"

"Yes."

"Good. I have a favor to ask, as part of the contract. I need information from the Medical Research Hospital. Can you gain access to their files?"

The man paused a moment, then said, "That's a Level Six security framework there. Hack-proof. What are you looking for? Maybe I can perform an on-site search."

Winter explained what he wanted: a full understanding of an operation scheduled for the next morning involving patient Mary Atteberry in the experimental neurology research unit. It was the extent of his knowledge.

"What do you need me for? You must have operatives in the hospital to assist, no?"

Winter hesitated, sipped his tea, covered his free ear to better hear. "I may, but I require someone who knows how to extract information from reluctant persons of interest. This doctor who's performing the operation tomorrow, for example. I suspect he's in bed with the Confederate States, but where do his loyalties lie? I must know."

"Understood. I'll be in the hospital within half an hour."

"Perfect."

"Now what's in it for me? I haven't taken a shake down contract in years. My expertise is removing human scum from the genetic pool."

Winter clucked his tongue, watched a pretty mother and her young son cross the street. "You do this for me, get all the goods on Atteberry's operation, and I'll deliver you Janet Chamberlain."

The pause on the connection was palpable. Winter, relishing the defining moment of the conversation, continued watching the people stroll by in the late afternoon sunshine.

"Chamberlain's been off-grid for years. Her whereabouts are one of the best-kept secrets in the profession. How may I be sure you know where she is?"

"Because if I'm lying, you'll kill me. Look," he added, "how much is the contract on her worth right now?"

"Thirty-eight, thirty-nine million Confederate dollars."

"I will double that amount for you, if you get me what I need by midnight."

"Consider it done."

The man disconnected, and Winter placed the device on the small wooden table in front of him, arranging it just so beside his tea cup.

I may not know where Janet Chamberlain is at this moment, but I know where she'll be in the morning. If I were the assassin interested in collecting on a kill contract, I'd be at that hospital at sunrise, waiting.

For now, all Winter had to do was relax. With the plan set, he prepared to enjoy the rest of his drink in peace, and allowed himself a smug grin.

AT 11:30 THAT EVENING, HIS INDIE-COMM PINGED on an encrypted channel in the darkness of a downtown hotel room.

"The doctor, Robert Elliot, was most cooperative when he understood the importance of my interest in the girl. She's scheduled for surgery at 7:30, and it will take place on the eighth floor, where his research lab is located. A bio-mech surgeon is flying in later tonight to assist. The operation is risky, he says, and the patient may not survive, but she'll die either way, so . . . "

"What kind of operation is it?"

"An experimental scheme designed to siphon off foreign memory data that somehow lodged in her brain and is killing her. The doctor plans to drain this into a bio-mech device to save the girl."

"Perfect."

"Now . . . where is Chamberlain?"

"You'll find her at the hospital tomorrow morning for the surgery."

"Why there?"

"She is the child's mother, and I suspect in her old age she's feeling somewhat sentimental."

Janet

JIM STIRRED IN THE LIVING ROOM OF THE NEW HOUSTON SAFEHOUSE, and hauled himself into a sitting position, working at the kink in his shoulders. Outside, the rolling grey sky threatened to rain. Janet, still in form-fitting sleeping gear, sat at the two-person table in the kitchen, studying her indie-comm. She'd already been up a couple of hours. She'd already had a drink to soften the pain.

The downtown safehouse proved to be a blessing. Located above a clothing boutique, it was almost invisible from the street . . . just another flashy apartment among many in the area. Janet entered the living room, extending a coffee, and sat beside him. "Big day ahead of us."

Jim yawned, nursing the mug in his hands. "Yeah. Say, you didn't sleep much."

"Fighting demons. What can I say?"

He watched her cautiously.

"Don't look at me that way, Jim. It's nothing you don't already know about. Besides, I wanted to keep an eye on things. New town, new situation. I'll feel a whole lot better once we're out of this place."

He took a sip. "Mary sure was busy on the comms last night, talking about the procedure with the surgeon, but I suppose that's a benefit of being filled with all that knowledge."

"It takes a lot out of her."

Janet wondered if Mary's gaunt look and grey skin had simply been from the lighting in this apartment. She hoped that's all it was, but Jim reminded her of how sick their girl was. An odd, instinctual wave of dread rose within her, and she struggled to remain professional.

"If they're right about the surgery taking several hours, do we have any idea how soon she'll be able to travel after?"

Janet shrugged, her gaze darting around the room. "Since its non-invasive in the traditional sense, she could be ready to move in a couple days, I imagine. At least, that's what Mary told me last night." She hesitated. "There's another potential problem to consider."

"What's that?"

"Transportation out of Confederate territory." She looked at him with a renewed cold, detached concern on her face. "Sam Castillo, our pilot, is incommunicado. Haven't talked with him since he followed those airport cops into the hangar after we landed."

"That's a grave sign." His mouth shifted into a hard pout, the way she remembered when he mulled over a problem in his mind.

"I had a funny feeling about those guards," she said. "Should've intervened at the time, but we needed to see that doctor. Besides, there are few friendly agents in the area, and intel is sporadic." She stood, working her jaw muscles. "I'll figure something out once Mary's in surgery." The wall clock flashed five-thirty in the morning. "Come on, let's wake her and get ready."

THE HOVERCAB'S ROUTE WOULD CARRY THEM to the medical center's main entrance, but as they hummed on to the campus, Janet commanded the AI to continue to the far end of the building and drop them at a service bay. Her caution and aversion to risks increased Jim's anxiety, which added to the palpable concern about Mary's operation.

Janet . . . ?

Mary floated in and out of lucidity.

"How's she doing?" Janet asked. Perhaps because she'd already faced death on the Moon, she remained quiet and pensive. In fact, she had said little since she shifted space-time on the *Echo*'s return trip, other than the muted conversations with the doctor last night.

Jim didn't answer.

After they'd hopped out of the cab, Janet scanned the neighborhood, and motioned for them to follow her. They entered a delivery bay, much to the surprise of the workers hauling crates and other supplies. She waved at them and continued marching toward the common area as if this was an everyday occurrence. Mary had difficulty keeping her balance again and leaned on Jim as they proceeded down a marble-tiled floor toward a bank of elevators. Janet kept her right hand close to her side where her gun was holstered and, when they'd dressed an hour earlier, she caught him staring at her in her underclothes, and all the weapons she'd strapped on her body. Two knives, pocket-shocker, thin stiletto nails, and a garrotte just in case. He called her a perfect, dangerous stranger.

Oh my Stranger, don't ignore me.

"How are you, Jim?" The last thing she needed was his emotions running amok. Mary could be dead in a few hours, never mind the real and present danger of the cloak and dagger world Janet moved in. And she was particularly skittish this morning too, as if she half-expected trouble any moment.

"Okay, you?"

She said over her shoulder. "Same, but I despise this goddamn place. Keep a watch out for anything that looks suspicious."

"In a hospital?"

She glared at him, and the stare he returned was that of a too-familiar lover. Mary held her gaze down, oblivious to the surroundings, mouthing silent words. The grey pallor worsened under neon lights, and her tongue darted across her lips like that of a lizard.

They rode the elevator to the eighth floor, then presented themselves at the receptionist's desk where the same young woman from yesterday met them. Her name was Sal, and she looked worried and preoccupied.

"Hello, Mary." She called a nurse over. "Margaret will take you to the prep station, honey."

Mary grinned, and followed the nurse around a corner.

Janet, observing everything going on around them, asked, "Where's Doctor Elliot?"

"Oh, he's here somewhere. Probably reviewing notes in his office."

As if on cue, Elliot's head bobbed over the portable walls of his cubicle. He wore blue scrubs with a matching cap. Janet noticed how hairy his arms were, and muscled, yet his fingers were long and thin like delicate instruments themselves. He greeted them, then in a monotone voice asked the receptionist, "Is the patient being prepped?"

"Yes, Margaret took her down a minute ago."

He motioned to Jim and Janet to follow him to a quieter corner on the floor, surrounded by padded chairs and tall, lush plants. His expression showed signs of muted concern, perhaps lack of sleep, and he scratched his forehead with his thumbnail.

"You know, Mary and I talked a lot last night about this procedure."

"Yes, she was adamant that she could help you," Jim said.

He drew his bottom lip into his mouth. "It was much more than that, Mr. Atteberry. Quite remarkable, yes, quite. She knows an incredible amount about the brain, its functions, neurological pathways. I've rarely come across anyone like her, never mind that she's a teenager."

Atteberry suppressed a grin and gazed around the floor. "She is eidetic, did she tell you that?"

Elliot stared in silence.

"She'll watch a vid or read textbooks and recall pretty much everything."

Three techs stepped off the elevator, laughing, carrying coffee, and flirting with the receptionist as they passed her.

Janet studied them over the doctor's shoulder. A tall man in a navy lab coat followed them out, a coat that looked just a bit too small on him. He carried a leather bag. The shoes he wore were hardly comfortable enough for a real practitioner.

Trouble.

Adrenaline raced through her body.

"Are you confident about today's operation, Doctor? You seem nervous," she said, maintaining a locked gaze on the stranger with the bag.

He swallowed hard. "I am, yes, I am. See, I've never attempted this before. Well, on mice perhaps, although the parameters—" He paused, regrouped. "Mary gave me an extraordinary amount of step-by-step protocols to help with the memory extraction—ideas and techniques I'd never even considered. Anyway, it's exciting and risky, which is I why I wanted to check in with you one last time and ask again whether you accept the risks, including that she may not survive."

"Yes," they said in unison. Jim noticed the tall man, too, who kept glancing at Janet.

"Very well. I expect it will take several hours and I'll provide updates whenever I can during the procedure." He shook Jim's hand and turned to Janet, but she'd caught an odd movement in her peripheral vision and before she reacted, Jim drove her down before a muffled shot rang out. She crashed hard on the ground, then rolled out into a crouched position, her weapon drawn, squeezing off rounds in the would-be assassin's direction. Screams echoed across the floor and workers ducked and dropped behind anything they could. A shrill alarm sounded. The shooter stole away.

"Stay here and don't move," Janet whispered.

"But Mary . . .?"

"First things first." She crept away, around furniture and benches, following the tall man. After lifting her head to peek around a corner, a shot whistled past her ear.

Gotcha!

The toe of his shoe poked out from behind a stack of linen and food trays. She pictured the assailant crouching there, waiting in ambush for her to make her next move. Two key targets filled her mind: the heart and the head. Then, she fired a couple shots in quick succession: *pop . . . pop*. The floor grew silent for a moment, save for the alarm, then the tall man's body slumped out of the trays, blood pooling under him, his weapon skittering across the tile.

Janet raced back and knelt down beside Jim, weapon still drawn, her eyes scanning the area. "Come on, we have to find Mary and leave."

"What about—?"

"Taken care of." She ceased all movement, eyes widening. "Oh, shit."

Jim couldn't stand, and his breathing was labored. "What is it?" He raised himself onto his knees, inhaled, and followed Janet's glacial stare to the corner.

Dr. Elliot lay in a puddle of blood, half his face splattered like a Jackson Pollock drip painting against the chairs and wall.

THIRTEEN

Janet

"LET IT ALL OUT, JIM, BUT HURRY."

Atteberry heaved again, spilling the remaining contents of his stomach across the floor where he knelt. Janet rubbed his back while she scanned the area.

He must've been working alone. There's still a chance.

She pulled him to his feet, clutching the weapon in her other hand. "Come on, we've gotta bail." Her voice was soothing and firm. "Get your shit together, Jim. Don't hold me up." She took off at a half-run through the cubicle offices, past workstations and shocked lab techs and nurses peering around tables and plants.

"Stay down and shut up!"

Jim stumbled after her, the stench of his vomit clinging to his shirt. She wished sometimes he wasn't so damn weak. When they reached the operating room—the same room where Mary's tests had been—the staff had barricaded the door. Janet gestured for them to clear it away, and within a few seconds, she burst into the theatre. They'd hidden Mary underneath the surgical table. A burly man in scrubs lay in front of her. Mary crawled out, her face strained and disoriented, and she staggered to her feet. Jim hugged her and held her by the shoulders. "Come on, Mares, we've gotta go."

"But, Dad. The surgery . . . it'll work, we know it."

"Not now, not today. They found us."

The man who'd been protecting her said, "What the hell is going on here?"

"Who are you?" Janet demanded.

"Lewis Palmer. I'm the surgeon helping Dr. Elliot with the procedure."

Janet positioned herself by the door, scanning the room. The nurses and surgical team stood around like confused statues. "There won't be any operation today, Doctor."

"Well I didn't sneak into this country for the hell of it. Where's Bob?"

"Dad, please. It'll work."

Jim sighed. "Dr. Elliot's been shot."

Tears welled up and her lips trembled. "No . . ."

"Come on, Mares, we'll find another way. There's always hope, remember?"

The trio left the surgical unit and marched toward the elevator banks. Janet swapped a fresh magazine into the gun and held it out in front. Jim and Mary struggled to keep up. When they arrived at the receptionist desk, Sal scurried out from underneath her workstation.

"Is the danger over?"

"Yes, for now." Janet helped her up, then turned. "Jim, you and Mary get to the elevator. I'll catch up in a second. Stay alert." He pushed Mary along. As they passed the doctor's body, Mary gasped and held his arm tighter.

"Is Bobby, I mean, Dr. Elliot okay?"

"He's dead. There's another body around the corner. Grab a couple of nurses and get that mess cleaned up."

Sal was in shock, then snapped out of it and said, "Wait, before you go." She wrote on a piece of paper and handed it to Janet, and burst out crying. Janet stuffed the note in her pocket and raced toward the elevator where they descended together.

They rode the car to the ground floor in silence. Janet holstered the gun. As the doors whooshed open, shouts and more alarms filled the air. Security guards were busy evacuating the hospital, assault rifles drawn. The Atteberrys melted into a stream of panicked workers, patients and families all pushing toward the main entrance. Jim kept his head down, helping Mary. Janet walked ahead, adopting a similar look of shock as the others.

Outside, rain fell hard and most of the evacuees huddled under the massive awning of the building or under the canopies of a nearby stand of trees. Janet pushed along the side wall until the crowd thinned. Then she stopped, waiting for Jim and Mary.

"You still good to walk, Mares?"

She nodded. Rain streaked down her face, matting her golden hair. Her eyes were red with tears.

"Listen carefully. We need to go to ground until I get intel on who's behind this. As soon as possible, we'll return to San Francisco." Mary protested, but Janet stared hard into her eyes. "It'll be okay, Mares. I'll protect you." Then, looking around, Janet pointed out several hovercabs parked at a recharging station. A squad of police officers—possibly soldiers—worked their way through the crowd as if searching for someone.

"Come on," she added, and marched off to the stand.

AFTER FIFTEEN MINUTES IN A HOVERCAB tacking across the city, retracing routes and zig-zagging over flight paths, Jim relaxed and gathered himself.

"Who was that guy?"

"Not sure. Either a contract killer or confederate agent. Could be any number of mercenaries. Good news is he worked alone."

"Why would anyone want to kill the doctor?"

She cocked her head and smirked. "The surgeon wasn't the target, Jim."

"But if not him, then . . ." Cold realization dawned on his face. "You . . . I saw a flash, a laser tag. You're the target and talk like you're reading some boring policy paper, while I'm about to blow crap in my pants." He stared out the window, vomit stench lingering on his shirt. "Where are we going, anyway?"

"We can't return to the safehouse. We got made somewhere along the line, and I've no doubt whoever's behind the attempt to kill me has other agents watching that house."

"Where do we go, then?"

Janet worked her jaw. "I know a place in the country. It's never been a safehouse, and I only had to use it once before. Not even sure it's still there, but we'll check it and sort out this business. The worst thing to do at this point is panic, so stay cool, Jim."

Mary had gone inside herself again, the shock and strain of the morning's events darkened her face. Her father held her hand.

"Before we leave, I want to stop in at the doctor's house and look around. I need to know how he's involved in this. Nothing showed up on a search I did before we came here, but I gotta be sure. If he is, there could be trouble waiting for us, but if not, maybe there's something there to help us get the goddamn drop on them."

They flew through a well-manicured, well-ordered suburb and floated to a stop in front of Dr. Elliot's home. Janet surveyed the area, referring to her indie-comm for signs of bugs or other spyware in the vicinity. "Looks like we're in luck." She hopped out and said, "Stay right here. I'll only be a minute. If you see anything odd, get the hell out of here, okay?"

Jim nodded and gripped the seat, then Janet ran up to the house, used her anti-mag key to play with the lock, sprung it open and ducked into the shadows. It took no time to find what she'd come for: Elliot's personal work station. It was poorly encrypted and Janet quickly broke past the thin security layers. She skipped through various folders until she found the one labelled "Transference Projects". She pulled a data stick from her pocket, slammed it into the computer, and downloaded the contents of the folder. As soon as the transfer was complete, her indie-comm pinged with an alert from her network. *Time to book.* She licked her lips and stole a glance around the room. *Where does he keep it?* There was no cabinet, no stand. She checked the other rooms, landing in the kitchen, and flipped open the cupboards. Above the sink, she discovered the object of her desire. She snatched two bottles and worked them awkwardly in her pockets.

Seconds later, Janet trotted out to the cab, hopped in and gave the AI fresh coordinates. Confidence surged through her body. She pulled the flask from her inside pocket and took two large swallows, one right after the other, then grabbed a bottle of bourbon and refilled it.

Jim said nothing, but watched her with sadness in his face.

Screw him and his judgement.

He asked, "Find something?"

"Yeah, the doctor's computer logs and main data tabs. The files are all protected, but I downloaded them and I'll hack my way in once we go to ground." She exhaled deeply, savouring the familiar burn down her throat, putting the flask back in her pocket.

Don't stop now, Janet, you deserve more.

"We're heading to that safe place now?" Jim asked.

"Yeah. It'll take a while to arrive. I need to discover what's in his files, and I want to call Castillo to pick us up there." She looked around. "Far too dangerous here. Maybe you should get some sleep."

"Sleep? Not a chance." But with Mary leaning against his shoulder, he soon settled back into the seat as his body relaxed. Despite her attempts to remain objective, Janet felt something new, something other. Among the fears surrounding Mary's health, the shooting and uncertainty around what to do next, another idea surfaced, one she hadn't recognized in years: being with Jim and Mary seemed *right*, regardless of what she'd done to them in the past. However deeply buried in the recesses of her mind, her feelings for him kindled. And they wouldn't be ignored.

FOURTEEN

Janet

THE LATE-MODEL HOVERCAR SLICED THROUGH the driving rain, over highways and abandoned back roads, deeper into Confederate territory. Within half an hour, oncoming traffic had all but disappeared. Jim and Mary dozed across from her in the cab, and Janet fought the urge to do the same when her indie-comm pinged on an encrypted channel. She held the device to her ear and spoke in a whisper.

"What've you got, Eli?" Encryption codes beeped, varying the operating frequency to avoid detection.

"You were right to clear that doctor's house. The place is crawling with confederate agents and the hospital remains under lockdown."

"Any sign they're onto us?"

Eli paused. "No, ma'am, not from the confeds. They've identified the assassin's body but haven't put any clues together at this point. The man you killed was Austin Keul, an independent."

"Running into these guys isn't unusual," she said.

"No ma'am, but there's more." He cleared his throat. "We picked up routine chatter last night . . . thought it was random but now makes sense. Keul was hired by Benedikt Winter."

"Winter? Who was the target?"

"You were, ma'am."

"You're sure it wasn't Mary."

"Positive, but Winter is after your daugh—I mean, after her too, ma'am."

She played with the plastic trim on the edge of the car seat. "Where is he now?"

"Apparently in New Houston. He traveled to San Francisco early yesterday, then on to NH. Lying low at the moment. Off the grid."

She rubbed the back of her neck, massaging the area where aches and stiffness settled in. "Anything else, Eli?"

"Just a heads up that you're on the Prussian radar and causing a stir in the assassin community. Chatter's picked up significantly over the past 12 hours and, as you know, we have few agents on the ground in the UCSA. The ones still there are running silent given the military flare-ups, so they won't be able to help you." Eli paused at the other end. "Ms. Chamberlain, there's more."

"Go on."

"That pilot of yours, Castillo? He's being held in a cage at the airport, undergoing interrogation and who knows what else."

"What about the heli-jet?"

"Still on the tarmac with 24-hour guards on it."

She frowned. Although she could fly some aircraft, the heli-jet was not one of them. Castillo's detention wasn't much of a surprise, but it added an extra wrinkle to her plans.

"Thanks. Anything else?"

"No ma'am, but do you know when you'll be returning north?"

The fact Eli didn't indicate NDU or Washington or California wasn't lost on her.

"No, I'm disappearing for a while. You understand I can't tell you where, though, in case they've cracked the encryption. Talk soon."

She ended the call and flipped screens to various satellite images showing the city and their destination north of the abandoned town of Montgomery near the Sam Houston Confederate Forest. Several homes in that area had long since been abandoned from the civil war days, and she hoped to find one where they could take cover for a few hours, perhaps a day. Peterson Road, where she'd hidden in the past, appeared to be their best bet.

She raised her head to find Jim studying her silently. She offered him a perfunctory smile. "Should be there in another forty minutes."

He shifted his weight.

It shouldn't be this difficult talking to him, but so much between them remained unresolved. She couldn't have explained anything ten years ago when the NDU pulled her cover and sent her on missions around the world. He was sweet and naïve, thinking that moral democracy just sorted itself out as a natural, rational occurrence, not realizing for a minute the amount of behind-the-scenes energy required to keep it functional. During the Mount Sutro event when she'd taken Mary into hiding, whatever remnant of trust remaining between her and Jim up to that point had disappeared. She and her team saved them, destroyed the only subspace transmitter in the world, and set in motion a series of events culminating in Esther Tyrone eliminating all evidence surrounding the Ross 128 aliens.

Her shoulder ached more than it had in a long time, a stark reminder of her need to quit field operations. She pulled out the flask and held it in both hands, rubbed her thumb over the simple design in the silver, then put it back in her pocket.

I do not understand.

Patience.

This last mission—to save Mary and keep her from harm—was a disaster. She had a dead surgeon who could have helped Mary to account for, a backwoods pilot in custody, and the head of Prussian espionage making a personal visit. If Jim's story about the rescue and escape in space was true, Winter wouldn't be the only one out to scrape Mary's mind.

Heavy rain hammered the road as the hovercar screamed through the countryside. On both sides of the vehicle, evidence of the horrific American conflict remained: deep craters, a handful of broken earth-crawlers, and rubbled buildings dotted the landscape. Human activity out here did not exist.

THE FARMHOUSE AT THE END OF PETERSON ROAD listed to the east. As the hovercar purred to a stop behind the dilapidated building and rested on its parking skids under a smear of pines, Janet quickly surveyed the area. Convinced the grounds were clean, she told the others to stay put until she'd cleared the house itself.

A couple minutes later, she motioned for them to join her under the shelter of the veranda. Mary held on to her dad. She looked even worse now and for a moment, an ancient memory tugged at her, pulling her to comfort and hold Mary the way only a mother could. Instead, she folded her arms across her chest and turned to Jim.

"It's a mess inside, but there's a fireplace and dry wood we can use. Watch your step . . . some of the floorboards are soft."

She led them across the threshold into the gloomy main room comprising a kitchenette with yellowed linoleum and stained cupboards, a sofa and chairs by the fireplace, and broken glass everywhere. Janet pulled the doctor's mem stick from her pocket and plugged it into her indie-comm.

"Jim, can you build a fire?" She threw him a lighter.

Atteberry checked the flue mechanism, found some old paper and within a few minutes, the red glow and rush of warmth from the fireplace chased the gloom of the old house away. Mary pulled a soft chair in front of it and held her hand to her face. He sat beside Janet at the kitchen table.

"How long are we staying?"

She focused on her indie-comm as she answered, "Depends. Maybe a few hours. I need to hack into this guy's files and see what he was up to before we bug out."

"I didn't realize you were a hacker, too."

Janet stared into his eyes. Fatigue and worry scarred his face, yet there remained that light, that spark of curiosity that first attracted

her years ago when they were kids. "There's lots of things you don't . .
." She paused, clenching her jaw. "Kate Braddock isn't the only one
who can hack into files." She smiled thinly and continued her analysis.

"What do you hope to find?"

"Anything that uncovers a solution to Mary's brain. These
researchers rarely work in isolation. Hell, you saw the team around
Elliot at the medical center. Look how fast he pulled a goddamn
surgical unit together. No, he may be the lead, but he's not the only
one involved. I want to understand who else is, so we can find them
and get Mary the help she needs. If nothing else, perhaps others can
use their findings."

Atteberry glanced out the window at the driving rain. "Is there
anything I can do?"

She reached across the table and squeezed his hand. "Spend as
much time with our daughter as possible. Keep her company."

They peered toward her slouching in the recliner, bathed in the
warm flicker of burning logs. Atteberry heaved himself up and
dragged his chair beside her in front of the fireplace. Mary looked
sleepily into his face, as if she couldn't recognize him.

Mary

I UNDERSTAND NOW.

*Mm . . . you see why I chose you and not Kate. Good. But you and I
together cannot continue much longer. Your body is not sound enough.
I feel . . . shame.*

I'm ready to see more.

There is no more see. There is only feel.

Show me, Keechik.

*I cannot. Too much, little one. Too much, and time floats away. You
already understand all there is about my world. The historical
information. The knowledge I bring you of my home, my people.*

You alone remain.

Yes.

And there are no others.

There are no others. All have perished.

Keechik, I don't want to die.

We will soon no longer exist here or anywhere else together. I brought you into my mind, believing that my people would live on through you. A miscalculation. It is too much for you. Can you feel my . . . mmm . . . the word is . . . sadness. Only larger. I should have remained alone.

Please don't let me die like this.

Titanius Resources Corporation Headquarters
New York City,
Northern Democratic Union

Carter

HEAVY WIND HOWLED AND SWIRLED outside Carter's tinted windows as he pored over the draft report on the *Echo*'s rescue mission to Luna and subsequent conflict with the Prussian Consortium. Even though the sky rumbled grey and ominous with thickening clouds tumbling in from the east, creating an ethereal mosaic of dreariness in the office, he refused to turn on the lights. In a deeply seated reflection of his childhood growing up in the projects, the absence of artificial light comforted him, and made the room closer, familiar.

At first, he ignored the rapping on the door but when it persisted, he grumbled, "Come in."

Marla Sullivan poked her head in the doorway. "Ed Mitchell is here, Mr. Carter. Would you like me to send him in?"

"Yes, thank you, Marla."

She bowed out. In a moment, Ed appeared in his rumpled brown suit, old-school glasses and ubiquitous grin. Carter leaned back in his chair.

"How's the report coming along, Clayton?"

"Just fine, old friend. Compliments to the holder of the pen."

Mitchell nodded once. "It's difficult to bullshit convincingly, but I have a God-given talent in that area, it seems."

"Indeed you do." He motioned for him to sit, and took the chair across the desk. "But there is something nagging me, Ed, and I wonder if you can help me understand."

"What is it?"

Carter leaned back, flipping a couple of pages in the report. "This part here about the *unknown object* on the eastern limb. We both recognize this was the Rossian ship from years ago that, for whatever reason, camouflaged itself on the Moon." He narrowed his gaze. "Does the NDU or anyone else need to learn about this finding?"

Mitchell's smile disappeared. "I'm not sure I follow. Is this not accurate?"

"Oh, it certainly is. But I prefer not to advertise what we saw up there. My god, man, everyone and his mule will be on the trail of the aliens. We don't want that. *I* don't want that."

The two men eyed each other. Carter continued. "The point I'm making, Ed, is practical. Let's consider the facts that we cannot dispute. First, something destroyed our lab."

"Yes."

"Second, we rescued the kid, but Kate Braddock disappeared with the aliens."

"Agreed."

"Lastly, the alien ship, thanks to faster-than-light technology, is nowhere to be found. Now, how many others actually know about that ship and its capability?"

Mitchell scanned the office ceiling as if the answers were all written there in the tiles. He placed his data tablet on Carter's desk and asked, "What are you getting at with these questions?"

Carter understood well that Mitchell always thought several moves ahead, like a chess player. "If most people are ignorant about the alien ship, why mention it?" Then he added, "As far as I can tell, the only ones aware of the Rossian vessel are you, me and the crew of the *Echo*, Jim Atteberry, his daughter, and Esther Tyrone. Now be honest, is that right?"

Bits of wind-blown dust and paper scratched at the window as Mitchell contemplated his next words. He blinked and said, "Yes and no."

Carter opened his mouth to protest but Mitchell cut him off. "Look, Clayton, you're correct. The number of people who saw the Rossian vessel is few. But that said, the rumours are already circulating about bug-eyed aliens on the Moon. True or not, it's almost impossible to change the channel on that kind of discussion." He shook his head. "But you know that, so what's really on your mind?"

Carter stood and ambled to the massive window, holding his hands behind his back. "Just this. The others who may have an inkling about the alien ship are the crew of the *Sara Waltz*. Remember, they're the ones who shot at us and chased our butts around Luna. I have no doubt they also saw the other vessel on the Moon's surface, but might not have understood the significance of it." He turned to face Mitchell. "Ed, I have to assume they recognized where that alien ship came from and our interest in it."

"That may be a stretch, Clayton, but let's suppose they do."

"Well that brings me back to the report. Here, you go into great detail about that vessel, Braddock, the girl we rescued, and on and on." He raised his voice. "I won't have it, Ed. Why give this information to the clueless idiots in the world? I don't understand. Why would you do that?"

Mitchell shifted in his seat and adjusted his collar. "The issue has moved beyond this room, way beyond Titanius. That's why. We had our chance to secure that alien tech, but we didn't. Pretending we overlooked the Rossian vessel up there would be disingenuous and to invite ridicule and mistrust." He clasped his hands together in front of him.

Carter scowled, working his jaw. "Perhaps, but sharing that information with international governments is inviting meddling the likes of which we've never seen before in the space resources sector." He paused, then a sly grin unfurled on his lips. "There is another angle."

"Which is?"

"Mary Atteberry. Something happened to her, Ed. When my team questioned the specialist at Gotham Hospital, he told us all about this brain problem she has. Apparently, the alien changed her, and she now possesses knowledge and abilities unheard of in a human being."

Mitchell's mouth tightened. "But she's just a kid. We can't—"

"Can't what? Ask her questions about what she knows? Learn from her about creating our own faster-than-light tech? Provide her with the best medical care in the world?" He paced around the room. "Remember your history, Ed, about how science developed throughout time. Years of boring, routine info gap-plugging interspersed with brief yet powerful flashes of insight. And those times of breakthrough elevated all humankind to greater heights in an instant. Like that." He snapped his fingers. "Mary Atteberry is the key. We must find her and speak with her."

Rain now slashed across the window, distorting the view. Mitchell sighed. "Where is she now?"

"Back in San Francisco."

"How do propose we catch up to her?"

Carter grinned. "I've asked Esther Tyrone to help. She's in tight with the father and wants the same things I do: space exploration dominance."

"Is this part of the partnership negotiations?"

"In a sense, yes. I, er, demonstrated the benefits that helping us would have on her career." He smiled coyly.

"That being the case," Mitchell said, "we need to expunge Mary Atteberry from that report. Everything except for the common fact that the *Echo* rescued her. All the other material, her illness, the description of the alien she provided, and that strange thing she did to hide the ship from the Prussians . . . all that needs to be deleted. Let the others chase rumors of the alien vessel. Our focus is now on the girl."

Carter stroked his chin. "I expect you'll take care of that?"

Mitchell gathered the draft report from Carter's desk, stood up and said, "Consider it done." He bowed with a sour grin on his face, then scurried out the door.

FIFTEEN

Atteberry

AN INDIE-COMM PINGED, INVADING THE DROWSINESS of his woolen mind like a predator. He checked his device. He'd been asleep several hours, and it was early afternoon.

"Yes?" Janet's voice. "I see." She tossed the device in her pocket. "Gotta run." She disconnected the data stick, then doused the fire. Atteberry, confused but now alert, gathered Mary up and waited at the front door. The sweet smell of booze permeated the still air.

"What's happening, Janet?"

"The pilot, Castillo. The confeds are planning to turn him over to the Prussians any minute. We gotta find him and pray he's still in one piece."

The hovercar pulled up from the trees and they tumbled in. Janet plotted a route to the airport through back roads, then settled in as the vehicle flew off. The rain intensified and slashed at them in waves. Mary, in a drowsy state, mumbled gibberish.

An hour later, they glided over an old weed-infested service road at the south end of the tarmac and purred to a stop behind a cluster of storage buildings and small hangars. Across the tarmac, about half a kilometer away, Castillo's heli-jet stood idle, chocked and guarded by a pair of confederate soldiers.

"See that low-rise office?" Janet pointed out an ugly white building with generous windows in the distance. A handful of hovercars sat at recharging stations beside it. "That's where the pilot is according to the intel. We've gotta find him, remove those guards and take off." She slammed a clip into her gun. "Won't be easy, so if we're separated, make sure you and Mary get to the heli-jet once Castillo fires up the engines."

Fear surged through his body and that same feeling of helplessness he experienced on the *Echo* returned. "Janet?"

She buckled a hand taser to her belt and looked up.

"I don't think I can do this."

"For crissakes Jim, don't go down that road."

"But this is so messed up. This isn't the world I understand."

She narrowed her gaze and clenched her jaw. "Yeah, you think your little life of books and green-pastured campuses and sunny days is the truth, hm? But under the surface of that cheery facade is the real world, *this* world. And guess what? It's dirty and ugly and people get hurt so others like you can sleep at night. Listen: all you have to do is stick close to me and protect Mary. I'll do the rest."

He swallowed hard and rubbed his thighs.

"Let's go. Move fast, we're being watched." She pointed to a security camera on top of a comms tower.

A series of outbuildings separated them from the hold where Janet believed the confederates detained the pilot. She took off through the rain, ducking between the sheds and hangars, burning across open spaces toward the office. Atteberry and Mary followed, but clumsily. Her lack of balance caused her to stumble every few

125

steps, and she grabbed on to his waist. Within moments, Janet was a hundred meters ahead of them.

Mary stopped under the eaves of a sheet metal structure, her drenched hair clinging to her head, and looked into Atteberry's face. "Dad," she said, "We need to rest."

He gazed around. No soldiers approached them yet.

"Okay, let's stop for a minute."

She leaned against the corrugated wall and swallowed deep breaths. "Janet's something else."

He stroked her cheek. "She's determined and persistent, like you, Mares."

"Do you miss her, Dad?"

Atteberry chewed his lip, scanning from Mary's face to the tarmac, catching glimpses of Janet's dark form dashing around buildings like a cat. "Honestly, I don't know her anymore." A security vehicle rolled up where they'd abandoned the hovercar on the service road. Two soldiers in olive ponchos, weapons shouldered, poked and sniffed at it.

"You ready to go?"

Mary dragged herself into action, and they ducked around the corner and hobbled toward the next building. Janet knelt close to the ground in the distance, motioning them forward.

A diesel-powered truck screamed a couple hundred meters ahead, road spray fanning out of it like smoke, then half a dozen heavily armed soldiers jumped off and assumed positions around the office.

Atteberry knelt beside Janet and gasped, "What'll we do now?" She ignored him and instead, stared directly at Mary and said, "You know what I have to do if it comes to that, don't you?"

Mary's bottom lip trembled.

"What are you talking about?" he whispered, but he didn't expect an answer. He already knew the most unconscionable thing on her mind.

A sleek hovercar then arrived at the building and a short, thick-haired man emerged wearing a stylish leather coat, hands in pockets. Janet studied the figure as he marched head down into the office.

When he glanced back, she noticed his full eyebrows and hard facial features.

"Winter."

"Who?"

She slammed a tiny scope on her weapon. "Benedikt Winter. He leads space intelligence in the Prussian Consortium." She turned to Atteberry. "This is worse than I thought. He doesn't get directly involved in field operations. Prefers the Berlin lifestyle. But if he's out here personally. . ." She looked at Mary. "Sorry, he's come for you."

Rage boiled in Atteberry's chest. *Screw him, and Janet too!* He gripped Mary's hand.

"We need a diversion," Janet said matter-of-factly. She peered through the scope on her weapon, aiming it toward the heli-jet. She squeezed off two rounds in quick succession, dropping the guards in front of the aircraft. Shouts rose from the office and four soldiers raced over to the fallen men, taking turns moving and covering.

Janet pulled a sling from her pocket and launched two walnut-sized devices across the tarmac one after the other. Within seconds massive explosions rumbled over the open space. The shock wave rose through Atteberry's legs.

"Let's move!"

They tore toward a deep run off ditch and jumped in. Janet moved with the grace of a predatory animal through the muck and weeds of the gully. Then, in a flash, she picked off two more soldiers guarding the office. Other men fired indiscriminately at them. Atteberry, drenched in rain and dirt, covered Mary's head with his arms.

Janet crept back. "When I yell, move your asses to the heli-jet. Don't stop to look around, just run like hell. I'll meet you there. Understand?"

"Y-Yes."

She disappeared again into the rain.

A moment later, a flurry of shots rang out. He lifted his head and peered across the tarmac toward the aircraft. More bodies littered the asphalt in front of the vehicle. Then, a flash and rumble of another slinged explosive cracked the air. More shouts ensued, and someone near the office building shrieked in pain.

Janet?

He gulped.

Mary grabbed his arm. "Don't let them take us, Dad."

"I won't."

She brushed her bangs from her face.

"Now, Jim!" Janet's voice carried across the open space. "Go!"

At first, he hesitated, then gathered his courage and slipped in the mud as he and Mary scrabbled up the side of the ditch. Smoke rose from different pockets on the tarmac and from the office itself, and the exotic smell of sulphur, cordite and chemicals filled his nostrils. No sign of Janet anywhere.

"Come on."

He pulled her close and raced toward the heli-jet. A fresh wave of bullets sailed overhead. Atteberry instinctively ducked, protecting Mary. Within a few meters of the jet, a bullet ripped into his leg, pain searing through his bones. He tumbled to the ground, inadvertently pulling Mary down. She screamed and dropped, and more bullets flew over their heads.

"Get to the other side of the jet, Mares," he groaned, his voice sounding distant and foreign.

They crawled the remaining few meters to the craft. Atteberry couldn't feel his leg but knew he'd have to staunch the gush of blood. He pulled himself over the body of a dead soldier and found refuge behind the fuselage. The last thing he remembered before darkness cloaked his vision was Mary rocking him in her arms.

Esther

AFTER RECEIVING THE NEWS FROM KAPOOR that he'd taken away part of her job function and given it to that traitor Mark Jefferson the previous afternoon, Esther left the Terran Science Academy without speaking to anyone. Once back in her apartment, she showered, changed into comfortable clothes, ordered up some Wagner on the audio deck, and poured herself three fingers of rye that she gulped down before filling her glass again. Within half an hour, she'd fallen asleep on her sofa and found the dreamless world she'd pined for earlier.

The following morning, she awoke under a brilliant sunrise burning off the vestiges of fog, refreshed and with a brand-new plan. As she finished dressing in front of the bathroom mirror, she walked through the steps unfolding in her mind and smiled smugly at the beautiful, subtle perfection of logic, the conviction of an alternative way of seeing the world evolving. She should have done this years ago. Taking the time—even a few minutes—to consider what she truly wanted proved to be well spent. Rather than scuttling through life *hoping* for certain things to happen, wondering *if only* this or that would appear, she now understood the power that true self-honesty and fundamental desire revealed.

Jim said that even though in the end we're always abandoned, the finality of life shouldn't deprive us of wonderful connections in the interim. But that rang hollow, and now she leaned closer to Carter's way of seeing the world: it's all there for the taking, and by satisfying our own self-interest first, we can help others achieve their goals too. Nothing more complicated than that. Nevertheless, that philosophy was insufficient. No just God existed to mete out rewards and punishment that she could see, no heaven, no hell to keep us all in line. Carter summed it up succinctly when he said morality in a godless world was nothing more than a bowl of soup. Only this, the present, was real. And if this realm was it, with no judge or jury to fear, why not take what you can?

Is this what you've become?

Why not?

MARK JEFFERSON, LATE TWENTIES, lanky and good-looking, met her in his basement office of the TSA where the Space Operations lab was located. He appeared nervous as he invited her to sit down across from him at his cluttered desk.

"I wasn't gunning for your job, Esther. I hope you understand that." His fingers skated over various documents and graphs in front of him.

She scrutinized the young man. "It is what it is. I have no beef with you, in fact, I'm here to offer you some assurance."

"Oh?"

"Yes." She shifted on her chair. "The truth is, Mark, I've been wanting to reduce my workload for some time and my adventure on the *Echo* reinforced how important my first love is to me. Operations can be a thrill, but my overriding interest is the search for extra-terrestrial life." She studied him. "Keiran took Ops away from me which turned out to be a blessing."

The corners of his mouth twitched. "Then . . . you don't mind that Dr. Kapoor gave Ops to me?"

"Do I look like I mind?" She noted the early worry lines on his face, and quelled the rising outrage bubbling up in her chest. "I'm happy for you. Not many scientists your age are given the opportunity to lead a whole directorate."

Mark exhaled and relaxed. "I'm so glad to hear you say that. When Dr. Kapoor approached me and gave me the position, I feared you'd be upset."

"Well," she said, "the timing wasn't great, but I suppose there is no best moment for these matters. Anyway, I will do whatever I can to ensure the transition from my office to yours is smooth. I'll have my assistant contact yours later this afternoon to work out the details, but you're already on top of the workload so there shouldn't be any surprises." She folded her hands in her lap. "Of course, the politics at this level are nastier, and will eat up your time. I can't count how many sleepless nights I've had worrying about situations like the Ross 128 fallout, for example."

His face blushed. "I was afraid of that. It's challenging enough right now getting everything done and finding time to see my kid. Will I have to give up the hands-on work?"

"Oh, no doubt." She controlled her breathing as her pulse raced. "But you're bright, and you'll figure out how to manage. If there's any advice to tell you, it would be to keep your priorities straight and delegate as much as possible."

"Thank you, I appreciate that. I've always considered you as a mentor to me, and I hope we can maintain that relationship as colleagues."

She brushed some lint off her jacket sleeve. "I'd love that," she lied. Then, tilting her head, she added, "The major issue that you may not know is what happened on Luna and, specifically, during the return flight."

"Only bits and pieces."

"Well, you must have heard about Mary Atteberry's encounter with the alien, right?"

He paused, his cheeks flushing. "Yes."

"It's generating a lot of interest which is one reason I'm glad you're taking over Operations. It frees me up to focus on negotiating a fleet of exploration vessels with Titanius."

"Of course."

Her indie-comm pinged and she glanced at the screen. "Alas, duty calls." She stood, and Mark followed her to the door. "Congratulations again. I'm so happy for you and I'm looking forward to working with someone I trust."

"Thanks, me too."

She marched toward the elevator bank, head high, back straight.

Yes, it is what I've become. He won't know what hits him.

Janet

MARY'S SCREAMS CUT THROUGH THE RAIN and howling wind, stinging Janet's ears as she crept closer to the building where the confeds held Castillo. One soldier she'd hit groaned. He lay in a heap a couple meters from her at the entrance. Nothing else moved.

It's too quiet.

She skulked up to the wall and caught the dying soldier's pleading eyes, wide and tearing. Half his stomach and intestines sloshed around on the gravel beside him, oozing between his hands. Some kid not much older than Mary. She crawled to him and placed her fingers on his trembling lips.

"Hush, now, you'll be okay."

She gazed at the windows and entrance, finger itching on her weapon's trigger, then knelt hard on the boy's windpipe, crushing it, until his body relaxed.

The door listed on its hinges, straining to open. She glimpsed a shadow of movement inside.

Castillo?

Janet tossed a smoke bolt through the crack. It hissed and grey plumes billowed out. Someone coughed. Like a flash of lightning, she kicked the door free and rolled in. "Castillo!"

A man groaned from the other side of the room and Janet ducked behind a bullet-riddled desk. Then, as the fog lifted, she saw the pilot. He slumped forward on a chair, hands cuffed and, standing beside him with a gun pointing at his head, calm and expectant, was Benedikt Winter.

"I salute you, Frau Chamberlain, but suggest you drop your weapon and join the party." He scraped his shoe across the floor. "It's just the three of us now. You took care of the others, and additional Confederate soldiers remain several minutes away." He waved the remaining smoke with his free hand. "Your pilot is alive, by the way; however, the guards roughed him up a bit before I arrived."

Janet swallowed hard and rose, aiming her weapon at Winter's forehead.

"Ah, there you are. So we finally meet." He grabbed a nearby chair and sat down, keeping his weapon on Castillo. "I did not expect to find you here. Please join me, we have much to discuss."

The desire to put a bullet through his skull overwhelmed her, but something held her back. *What does he want? What does he know?* With her free hand she pulled out her indie-comm and scanned him for additional weapons. Other than the luger he held, he was clean.

"I'll stand, Winter."

He shrugged. "As you wish. So a stalemate, yes? You shoot me, I shoot the pilot, the confederates shoot you and grab the girl. All very messy, wouldn't you agree?"

Castillo peered up from under his dishevelled hair. His mouth had been taped and dried blood caked his face.

"You've piqued my curiosity," she growled. "Word is you prefer staying home in Berlin, so what brings you to republican territory?"

He cocked his head and croaked. "To be frank, your child does."

"What do you want with Mary?"

"The same thing you do. To protect her, help her recover from her experience on Luna. It's unfortunate your surgeon got himself killed in the crossfire at the hospital this morning. We could have prevented all this. Now please, drop your weapon and let's talk like civilized people."

She flexed her grip on the gun and remained silent, but did not lower it.

"The child acquired some unique powers from the aliens. I wish to know precisely what those are."

"I'll bet."

"Oh, you misunderstand, Frau Chamberlain. My intentions are not to keep whatever she knows from others. On the contrary, I believe if we work together, all people can benefit. My goal is peace, and as long as military parity exists in space, we shall have it. My consortium is not served one iota by gaining such a powerful weapon as the child if all it does is cause war. You see?"

"Weapon?"

"Ah, a poor choice of words. My English is . . . incomplete."

She glanced at Castillo and through a window opening up on the tarmac. "If you wanted, you could've killed us both by now. So what are you proposing?"

"Quite simple. You need to quit this territory before the entire assassin community finds you, never mind the Confederates. My consortium has some of the best doctors in the profession, and the facilities in Munich are second to none. I propose we all leave together, assuming Herr Castillo is able to fly. I help your girl, and in exchange, you turn yourself in to me. But we must hurry before the Confederates arrive in force, otherwise, there is no further discussion."

Janet wasn't in the habit of negotiating. If it had been anyone else other than Mary, she wouldn't hesitate putting a bullet in his head.

Don't be so indecisive. Shoot him, then we can relax.

"Well, what do you say, Frau Chamberlain? Will you come with me?"

She spoke through clenched teeth. "Release the pilot."

"Of course. A sign of my goodwill." Winter stood and unlatched the mag-cuffs holding Castillo's arms behind him. He groaned and fumbled with the tape across his mouth until it came loose.

"Are you able to fly, Sam"? She shouted.

He coughed and spat blood on the floor. "Yeah, I can manage."

Janet's mind whirled and her intuition screamed, but she shoved that noise down. This was an opportunity to correct past mistakes, to stop the spider too. To end it.

"I suppose I have little choice at this point."

"Drop the gun and let Mary live, or shoot me and then you die in a few minutes, and the confeds have their way with the fraulein." A gust of wind rattled the windows. "My life means nothing compared to the importance of the Consortium. You kill me, a replacement comes along. So you see, if you want all this to stop now, you will give yourself over to me and we'll disappear."

Janet's mind spun, but she couldn't shake the over-riding need to protect her daughter, even if she was a stranger, even if Mary and Jim both held her responsible for the mess they were in. She lowered her gun, placed it on the floor in front of her, and kicked it away.

"All right, even in the absence of trust, we prefer not to kill each other. Fine. An excellent choice. Now, we must move and you're coming with me, so let's go." He pointed to a door leading to the tarmac. "Castillo goes first, then you, Frau Chamberlain. And if I think you're playing a trick, I won't hesitate to put a bullet through your skull."

Castillo struggled, but picked up his pace in the rain as they marched to the heli-jet. Janet kept her hands at her side, away from her body, careful not to spook Winter into doing something rash. Mary peeked from behind the aircraft, her face a ghostly apparition.

"We're all getting out of here, Mary," Janet hollered over the wind.

"Dad's hurt bad."

When they reached the machine, Castillo kicked away the chocks and unlocked the cabin with his thumb print. Janet helped push him into the cockpit. Within moments, the engines hummed to life. Winter kept her close to him as she examined Jim's shattered leg. Mary had tied a piece of webbing from one of the soldiers around the wound to prevent bleeding, but he was in awful shape, his skin ashen.

"Get him inside," Winter mused.

Mary couldn't do much, but together they shoved his dead weight into a flight seat and elevated his leg across an arm rest. Then she wriggled into the small cargo area where she unfolded a portable seat from the bulkhead.

"You next, Frau, and go slow."

Janet moved with care into the seat beside Jim, keeping her hands high and away from her body. Then Winter climbed in.

Looking out the window, she glimpsed additional Confederate troops pulling up to the airport in two old-school, diesel-fuelled troop carriers. Castillo must have seen them as well because the engines revved. Winter hauled himself into the cabin and took the seat beside Janet. He jammed the business end of his luger in her ribs.

"Mary, you have your harness on?" she asked.

"Yes."

"Take off, Sam," she yelled over the noise of the rotors.

The craft groaned and inched off the tarmac. When they were about fifteen feet off the ground, just before Castillo pushed the throttle forward, Janet reached across Winter's chest in a flash of movement that even surprised her. She snapped his wrist and the weapon fell to the floor. In a millisecond, she opened the cabin door.

"What are you—"

Before he finished his sentence, she kneed him in the head, pulled the harness off, and sent the Prussian halfway out the open door. He scrambled to find purchase, grabbing onto the frame. Mary screamed from the cargo hold, but the noise and confusion smothered her words. Winter turned to face Janet, his calm confidence replaced by stark panic. She struck again, pounding him with a swift kick in the small of his back and this time, he lost his grip and tumbled out of the craft toward the tarmac. The heli-jet bobbed with the sudden loss of 175 pounds. Janet slammed the door closed and yelled, "Go! Go!"

The heli-jet whined forward and gained altitude before screaming into the wind. On the asphalt, Winter lay on his side, reaching out to one of his legs. Flashes of light erupted behind them as the confederates, now positioning themselves on the runway, opened fire. Seconds passed like hours until the craft put sufficient distance between them and the airport.

Then she remembered to breathe.

SIXTEEN

Winter

BENEDIKT WINTER MUSED ABOUT THE ODDEST THINGS in the strangest of times. For instance, as he struggled to sit upright on the rain-soaked tarmac, clutching a shattered ankle, he remembered some old chestnut he'd heard at a conference on the physics of space flight years ago in Mumbai: it's not the fall that kills you; it's the landing. But death would not come to him this day, and he sensed that if Frau Chamberlain had really wanted him dead, she would have finished the job. *She grows soft in her old age.* Still, the shock of his injury and humiliation at her hands shot through his entire body. His vision darkened, and he fought to stave off unconsciousness from the pain. He needed to contact the *Sara Waltz* in space dock above New Houston for repairs. Fast.

A squad of Confederate troops, weapons drawn, raced toward him from the other side of the tarmac. After demanding to know who he was and what he was doing, amid shouting and carrying on like children, they relaxed when they realized he was unarmed and in no shape to flee.

"*Bitte,*" he hissed through gritting teeth, "where's your medic?"

The squad leader radioed for medical assistance and within moments, one of the troop carriers squealed to a halt beside them and a slight, fit woman hopped out carrying a camouflaged bag and a bio-scanner. She deftly examined Winter's ankle and administered a painkiller. After grabbing a pressure pad from her kit, she paused and studied his face.

"I'm Collins. It's not my business, but how the hell did y'all fall out of that heli-jet?" She wrapped the pad around his leg. "Hm?"

"Doctor, thank you for your attention to my medical needs, but I am in no mood to chat."

"Ah, you're German."

"I prefer Prussian, but as you wish. Now if you'll forgive me, I must be on my way. I have an important call to make."

The squad leader, hovering two steps from them, growled. "You're not going anywhere or calling anyone until you tell us what this is all about."

Winter sized him up and noted the stripes on his uniform. "Captain, please. I'll brief you on everything you want to know in the fullness of time, but I must insist you let me at least contact my ship."

Dr. Collins scanned his bio-signs again and appeared satisfied. Then, turning to the captain, she said, "He won't get too far on his own with that ankle and all, but he's clear to travel."

"Roger." He motioned to a pair of soldiers and they hauled a stretcher from the back of the carrier. Winter resigned himself to being treated as a patient for now but had to contact the *Sara Waltz* somehow. He shifted his weight on to the stretcher and lay down.

"Where are you taking me?"

"Military hospital north of here."

Winter grunted. The painkiller had kicked in and his muscles were heavy and languid. As the soldiers loaded him on the back of the truck, he reached into his pocket and, by feel alone, coded a message to the *Sara Waltz* on his indie-comm.

Targets moving north-west. CCR? Helijet. Trans freq 147m800. Must intercept.

Then, with the combination of the injury, painkillers and dissipating adrenaline, Winter allowed his vision to darken and he resigned himself to unconsciousness, the last thing he remembered was the truck rumbling underneath and the smell of diesel.

DISTANT VOICES AND METALLIC SCRAPING NOISES awakened him. Winter peered through the room and recalled the soldiers taking him to a hospital. The only clothes he wore were his shorts, and his broken ankle had a thin flexi-cast wrapped around it. His lower leg throbbed but he'd been in worse shape before and could manage that, but first, he had to speak with Captain Krause of the *Sara Waltz* and get out of this place.

A junior nurse with soft features and mysterious black hair entered the room. "Oh, you're awake. How are you feeling, Mr. Winter?"

He feigned fatigue and kindness. "Woozy from the medicine, but the ankle has improved . . . *danke.*"

She checked his bio-signs on the reader above his head. "I'll be back in a few minutes once I've found the doctor."

The moment she left, he sprang to his feet and almost collapsed from the pain shooting through his leg. But he grabbed his clothes sitting on a nearby chair—his indie-comm was still there—dressed and, peeking around the room's entrance until the hall was clear, he scuttled down a stairwell.

The concrete steps were challenging to navigate with his limited mobility and muddled head, but he'd been on the third floor and didn't have far to go. Once on the ground, he burst through an exit and hobbled into a stand of nearby pines. The place, being a military hospital, was secure with wire fencing and barricades. Escape would not be easy. After he'd put some distance between himself and the clinic, he opened an encrypted channel on his indie-comm.

"*Sara Waltz*, this is Winter. Do you read?"

Within a moment, one of the ship's comms officers responded. "*Sara Waltz* here. Go ahead, sir."

He shot a nervous glance through his surroundings. "I have little time. I'm at a military hospital north of the small airport in New Houston. Lock onto my device's coordinates. Have you dispatched interceptors yet?"

"Benedikt, it's Captain Krause here. We have three ships en route from low orbit." He paused, then added, "And we've picked up the target aircraft. We should engage them within a few minutes."

"Perfect. Please remind your crew that the occupants must not be harmed, especially the child."

"Understood. Now what about you? Do you require an evac?"

"Yes." He peered through the trees and shrubs. "There's a wire fence around the perimeter but if one of your smaller craft were to float in undetected, I could rendezvous in a small clearing about 50 meters from my current position."

"There is no need for subterfuge, Herr Winter. We have an excellent relationship with the Confederate Union, and—"

"Don't argue, Captain."

"Very well. I'll send a stealth jumper down to get you now."

Winter signed off and caught his breath. His ankle barked and he focused his mind to release the pain. Several minutes passed and the mental control method worked, allowing him to navigate through the woods to that small clearing he spied on his device.

He leaned against a massive live oak at the edge of the rendezvous point and paused. His emotions, still conflicted and chaotic, tainted by a mix of pain and humiliation, spilled across his mind. *She is a formidable adversary . . . smart, ruthless, cunning. Extracting her heart slowly from her breathing body in the ancient Aztec tradition will be a pleasure.*

Janet

"HEY CASTILLO," JANET SHOUTED OVER THE DIN of the heli-jet, "where's your first aid kit?"

The pilot glanced at her over his shoulder with vacant stare. He was in no shape to fly, but Jim needed attention. "In the cargo hold on a side storage compartment. It's labeled."

"Mary, can you find it?"

"Say, if there's any extra painkillers, would you toss one my way?"

Rain pelted the heli-jet and thermal-fuelled gusts of wind buffeted the aircraft like a cork in the ocean. Atteberry groaned, passing in and out of consciousness. His lower leg had a chunk of flesh blown out of it, reminding Janet of the shark attacks she witnessed in the South Pacific during one of her first missions as a grad student.

Mary handed her a box. "This is it, right?"

"Yeah, thanks." Mary's own condition had worsened during the fray. The deep circles under her eyes and sweat across her face showed the extent of her own frail health. She pulled a package of painkillers from the kit and shoved a tablet in Mary's hand.

"Chew this, Mares. It'll take the edge off."

She examined it, then popped it in her mouth and crawled back to her seat. Then Janet reached forward, tapped Castillo on the shoulder, and handed him a couple of tablets too. Turning her attention to Atteberry, she placed a mask with a pseudophine inhalant to his nose and mouth and pumped it twice. Within seconds, he lost consciousness and his body relaxed.

The injury to his leg was more severe than she realized. After applying a proper tourniquet above the wound, she unwrapped the blood-drenched webbing and the sight of shattered bone slivers and shredded muscle almost caused her to retch. She grabbed a bottled water from the kit and flushed out the area, then found a packet of syntheti-skin and a pair of tweezers. She poured disinfectant over the gash, and carefully picked out the visible splinters. With her indie-comm, she scanned the wound, discovered another shard under a muscle, felt around it with her fingers, and yanked it out. Then, after cleaning the mess again, she stretched the skin across the gaping wound, wrapping it tightly around. Within moments, the skin awakened from its dormant state and melded with Atteberry's own.

He still needed medical care to repair the bone, but at least the syntheti-skin would stop the bleeding, prevent infection, and allow the marrow to start healing.

"How're you doing, Castillo?"

"Better now that we're out of that hell-hole, but I'm gonna charge you extra for all this shit."

She nodded. *No kidding.* "Anything broken?"

He raised his hand to his chest. "Don't think so. They did a number on my ribs . . . they're sore but nothing a bit of time and John Barleycorn can't fix."

Oh, we like him, Jan.

She passed him a disinfectant wipe from the kit and he cleaned up his face. Then she pulled the flask from her jacket pocket and handed it to him. "Finish it."

As she settled back into her seat and exhaled, replaying the morning's events, a series of alerts suddenly screamed from the cockpit.

"We've got company, ma'am."

Janet hauled ass into the co-pilot's chair and scanned the horizon. The radar showed three aircraft approaching from high altitude.

"I ain't never seen that before," Castillo shouted, staring at the radar screen.

"They've gotta be coming from an orbiter. That asshole I gave a flying lesson to wasn't hurt enough and must've contacted a ship. Either that, or the Confederates are way more aggressive than usual."

"No matter, those ships are runnin' hard. Don't get me wrong: I love my old bird. The *Relic*'s pulled me out of jams all her life, but she'll never outrun those."

He was right. Within minutes the interceptors would be all over them. "How far to the border?"

"Another 15 minutes." Castillo's voice rose as renewed panic set in. He gazed at her, clenching his jaw muscles. "But do you think that'll stop them? The entire world's on edge these days. I outghta land her and call it square and live to fly another day."

The attack ships continued toward them on an intercept vector at extreme velocity. Janet monitored the radar, unwilling to give up but recognizing Castillo, as the pilot, called the shots. "Okay, let's land and face the music. You've got to know when you're beat. Dammit!"

"Roger that."

Castillo eased up on the throttle and scanned the geography for a suitable place to land. Janet studied the rain-drenched sky, searching for the attack ships but the clouds were too thick, so she returned to the radar. She noticed the blips on the screen break formation and adopt an hostile pattern.

"Shit, I wish I could see." The pilot decreased altitude, but the storm continued affecting visibility.

A new alert sounded in the cockpit. One ship launched a salvo of missiles toward them, tracking their flight path.

Janet instinctively pushed herself hard into the seat, as if trying to disappear. Out-maneuvering the attack ships now that they'd achieved firing range was out of the question. Their best hope was to land and abandon the heli-jet before the bombs destroyed it, but they'd never have the time to do that.

She stared at Castillo and watched him struggle to negotiate the winds and find a clearing. The tracker on the dash displaying the incoming missiles shrieked as the distance between the shots and the aircraft rapidly diminished.

"We ain't gonna make it!"

Mary crawled up from the cargo space. "I can help," she croaked into Janet's ear.

She lifted her gaze from the radar. "What do you mean?"

"I can help us get away." She positioned herself between Castillo and Janet, and took several deep breaths. Then, reaching out toward the power dispersion hub, she fingered it and her body shuddered. A curious blue glow emanated from her finger tips and sweat broke out over her face.

"Jesus the hell are you doing?"

She didn't answer, absorbed in whatever operation she performed on the heli-jet. Castillo glanced at her between scanning the ground.

"I gotta put her down, ma'am," he shouted.

Mary's eyes flickered open. "No," she said, "go higher, as high as you can."

The pilot peered nervously at Janet, but she shrugged her shoulders. Then Jim groaned from behind them, waving his hand.

"What is it?"

He gulped hard and groaned in a barely audible whisper, "Trust her. She's done this . . . before."

Janet studied her daughter. The blue light glowed richer, reflecting off her sweat-streaked face.

"Screw it," Castillo shouted, "If we're gonna go, let's go!" He yanked on the throttle and the *Relic* rocketed into the gloomy sky.

The missiles screamed closer. Janet caught glimpses of them firing through breaks in the clouds. It'll be over in a second. She squeezed her eyes shut and gripped the arm rests.

A blinding light flashed through the heli-jet, followed by a series of massive explosions on the Earth's surface that rumbled through the atmosphere. The aircraft bounced around in the acoustic aftershock, but continued climbing.

Moments later, the attack ships appeared, regaining formation and slowing, as if searching for wreckage. Castillo pushed the heli-jet forward, recalculating their course to the Mexican border and assuming an alternative flight path.

Mary opened her eyes. Terror filled them as if she'd seen a ghost.

"You okay, child?" Janet asked.

Whatever she did had exhausted her.

She asked Jim, "Is this what happened on the *Echo*?"

"Yes . . . exactly the same."

"How long can she hide us?"

"Don't know."

CCR territory remained another couple hours' flying time away, but Mary's health deteriorated. Maintaining this effort would kill her.

Mary inhaled again and repositioned her fingers on the hub. "I'll keep us safe for as long as possible." Then, her voice cracking and her lip trembling she added, "We want to live."

Atteberry

ATTEBERRY PULLED HIMSELF UPRIGHT AND GAZED out the heli-jet's window at the grey, mountainous landscape below. Mary continued manipulating space-time but struggled to maintain her position, struggling under her labored breath. Janet monitored her indie-comm in the co-pilot's seat, and Castillo had returned the bird to a more comfortable altitude.

"Where are we?"

Castillo tilted his head back. "West of Yosemite National Park. I'm bringing us in over the mountains en route to my base in Oakland. Not far now."

"I'm worried . . . about Mary. Is it safe to return to space-time prime?"

The pilot glanced quizzically at Janet. Atteberry added, "Normal space-time, so everyone can see us."

Janet peered out the side window and checked the radar. "Yes, we should be okay now. Castillo, keep us hidden as best you can." Then to Mary, "That all right with you, Mares?"

She agreed and released her fingers from the power dispersion hub one at a time until she freed her touch completely. She slumped back into her seat. Atteberry reached over and stroked her moist hair.

"Jan, we can't carry on like this."

She turned herself around to face him, leaning on the seat's arm rest, and grimaced at Mary's strained look. "You two both need a doctor, but I can't see getting one without giving ourselves away." In a softer voice, she said, "How are you doing?"

"The pseudophine's working. I don't feel anything in my leg now, but that's as much the loss of nerve endings as anything else, I imagine."

She inspected his leg. "Looks like the new skin's taking."

"It's Mary I'm worried about."

"I know," she said, and pointed to her device. "I've been tackling this data stick from that surgeon's house. Punched through the encryption on some of his files, but not his research. Understandably, he took more precautions with that. But what's interesting is this . . ." Janet swiped the screen until she found what she wanted. "In his normal correspondence, he chats a lot with two other researchers: a surgeon in London he refers to as Abigail—no last name—and this other fellow called Lewis. If I'm not mistaken," she said, "He was that other doctor who protected Mary when all hell broke loose, remember? Lewis Palmer."

Atteberry nodded but his memory was fuzzy.

"Regardless," Janet continued, "if he's the same guy, then we may be in luck."

"How so?"

"Dr. Lewis Palmer is not a UCSA citizen. He's Californian, and his home is in the CCR."

Atteberry bolted upright, shaking the cobwebs from his head, grimacing with the effort. "If that's true, he might know enough to continue Mary's operation in familiar territory, safe from the Confederates and whoever else wants a piece of her brain. He might even get CCR forces to provide security. Esther must have contacts."

"Before you get too excited, Jim, he may not have a practice in the California Congress. From what I'm reading in Elliot's correspondence, they spent a lot of time at that medical center in New Houston. Still," she said, adopting an optimistic tone, "it's something to go on. If I crack the remaining files, I might find additional info on the man."

The heli-jet dove and Atteberry jolted forward, grabbing the arm rest. He and Janet peered out the windows.

Castillo said, "It'll be like a roller coaster as I follow this waterway through the hills. There's barf bags somewhere if you need 'em."

Atteberry poked around by the side of the seat just in case, as the pseudophine messed with his stomach. He didn't find any bags, but uncovered a ratty, oil-stained blanket, a little on the thin side, and wrapped it across Mary's resting body. Guilt rose within and he fought to keep it abated.

What did she mean when she said we *don't want to die?*

"Can I ask you something, Jan?"

"Sure."

"Why are you here? I understand Mary's your daughter too and all, but you never once contacted us since that night at Mount Sutro when your team destroyed the tower. And now, all of a sudden, you're here in the thick of it again."

Her face blanked, and she turned away. "Long story, I'm afraid. Not even sure myself. Maybe we can discuss it when this business is over."

"You planning on sticking around?"

She didn't answer, but Atteberry studied her profile and remembered that same detached look from long ago. She never discussed her feelings much, hell, if at all. Nothing more than mundane day-to-day things. Certainly nothing at the core of her soul, and after a while, they settled into their personalities and didn't deviate from their norms. But these odd, far-away looks crossed her face once in a while when she didn't realize he was watching, as if the facade of "policy wonk", of "wife and mother" loosened, and glimpses of the real Janet—Janet the agent provocateur—emerged.

But who was she?

Earlier, when Mary asked if he still missed her, Atteberry had answered her honestly: he didn't know this woman any more, this soldier or terrorist or agent or operative or whatever she called herself. But now, the truth settled over him with the heaviness of a suffocating dream: he hadn't truly known her back then either. He'd fallen in love with, and married, an imposter. And, she'd appeared in his life again.

Several minutes of silence passed as Castillo maneuvered the craft through the hills. No additional alerts sounded, but that didn't stop him from checking the radar and flicking between different data screens. Atteberry resumed gazing out the window, his hand resting on Mary's.

"They drafted me in high school."

"Hm?"

"The agency I work for recruited me when I was fifteen."

Atteberry's shock caused his mouth to open. "Jesus, why didn't you tell me that years ago? What was so goddamn important you couldn't have told me even that before we married? It wouldn't have made a difference."

The abyss expanded between them. "They swore me to secrecy." Angling toward him, she added, "I wanted to, Jim. I even told them I'd quit before we were engaged. They hinted that if I said a word about any of my actual work to anyone, they'd kill you." She sighed. "Look, I know what they did to others. Hell, I'd killed dozens of targets myself by the time we met at college. I couldn't let them do that to you . . . not to you."

A flicker of familiar emotion crept over him, that same unbearably light sentiment that crushed him the moment they'd met at a campus rally and the world finally made sense to him. The damn, rapturous state of insanity reminded him he once loved her deeply— or at least, the image she projected. Now the words, the feelings, the history tumbled over each other into a muddle of desperate memories.

"I don't know what to say," he whispered.

"Well, perhaps we can clear the air someday." She squeezed his hand and fixed his eyes. "No more secrets. I promise."

She held his gaze a moment, then turned away, frowning.

SEVENTEEN

Carter

MARLA SULLIVAN INTERRUPTED CARTER IN HIS OFFICE with a communique from Captain Russo on the *Malevolent*, somewhere in the void between Earth and Luna. He tore the paper from her hand. She stood in silence as he read:

NDU supply ships abandoning Titanius. Agreements meaningless. Claim we're in breach. Flying solo. Capt. LR, Malevolent.

Carter slammed the note on his desk and growled at his assistant.

"The NDU blames *us* for this mess in space? Do they not understand that our mission to rescue the Atteberry girl was a success? And now they're pulling their supply ships. Dammit, Marla, what's the matter with those pencil-necked bureaucrats!"

She flicked a brown curl from her face and pursed her lips, holding a data slate against her slender hip. "It does baffle the mind, sir."

He grinned sardonically. "Baffle, yes." Carter sighed and worked his jaw muscles as frustration roiled in his gut. He fingered the note on his desk, considering his next moves.

"We must go it alone, then. If that's the way the bureaucrats want it, fuck 'em all." Turning to her, he said, "Sorry, Marla. Get me Captain Powell on the line and put him through to my boardroom."

Marla nodded and disappeared. A moment later, the comms panel in Carter's boardroom chimed, and he marched in from his desk and accepted the call.

Powell appeared on the massive wall screen wearing an olive-green work shirt, sleeves rolled up. Grease stains scuffed his forehead. The *Echo* rested at some distance from him in the background, with workers in light blue coveralls crawling over her like ants on a honeycomb. He wiped his hands on a cloth.

"Good afternoon, Clayton, what can I do for you?"

Carter grinned curtly and rapped the top of his boardroom table with his knuckles. "Hello John, I didn't expect to be calling you so soon after our return, but the diplomatic situation here is fluid and disintegrating as we speak and I need your help. But first, how go the repairs?"

The captain glanced over his shoulders and dabbed his face with the cloth. "Well, as you can see, I've got a full crew on her now, another coming in overnight. There's no shortage of items on the repair list, but we're making progress. Listen, I've been following the global fallout from our skirmish and rescue mission, and in fact I expected your call."

"Excellent, John. When do you think she'll be ready to fly?"

"Fly? Oh, we're nowhere near flight capability. I've gotta install new antigrav coils and they won't arrive for another couple weeks, so—"

"We can't wait that long, I'm afraid."

Powell caught his breath and faced the camera. "What's going on?"

"All hell's breaking loose across the world. The NDU just pulled their support from our fleet, and we're still playing cat and mouse with the Prussians in the Earth-Moon system. God knows what else is happening in the sector . . . but never mind all that. I want to return to Luna as soon as possible."

"Okay. We've got other ships available. Why not take one of those?"

Carter inhaled. "No. It's clear to me after being in space that the *Echo*'s speed and maneuverability are critical to this next mission."

"And what is this *mission?*"

"A trip to the *Mare Marginis* so we can search for any residual clues about that Rossian vessel's disappearance."

A tech excused himself and interrupted Powell by shoving a data slate in front of him. "Give me a moment, Clayton." He swiped through the tablet, studied a page here and there, then mumbled instructions to the worker before returning his attention to the screen. "What's the timeframe?"

"I'd like to leave tomorrow, day after at the latest."

Powell frowned. "My crew hasn't recovered yet. Jenson's still shaken up over that firefight with the *Sara Waltz*, and Dub's MIA in Montreal."

Carter's shoulders slumped, and he dropped into a chair. "Please, John, the political situation here is tenuous. We need to at least establish a powerful presence in space before it all turns into the wild west up there."

He paused, looking around. "Well," he offered, "I could double the work crews and put my own on standby. Cut the repairs to flight essentials only. One of the engineers could try to refurbish the antigrav coils I've got . . . I suppose the worst thing that might happen is we don't get all the bells and whistles installed."

"That's better. Let's do that, but it's clear the fitting of our medical bay needs finishing. I'll put the word out for a medic and see who crawls in."

"Agreed. We should also shore up defensive systems." He paused and surveyed the hangar. "Listen Clayton, I've gotta get back to work and call in that extra shift, so if there's nothing more, I'll keep you apprised of our progress." Powell reached out to end the call when Carter stopped him.

"I have one more question for you, John."

"Sure."

"You understand what that alien ship did. The damn thing disappeared in a flicker of light. Any thoughts about how they developed FTL tech?"

Powell kicked the floor. "It's too early to speculate on that. I saw the same as you." He looked straight into the camera. "But what's even more intriguing is what the young lady did on the way home, you know, with the space-time dimensional shift. I didn't buy Tyrone's explanation and the logs back me up. Any chance the girl might join us on this next Moon run?"

"That's highly improbable. She's struggling with after-effects from the alien encounter." He grinned. "But I hope to have her knowledge extracted once I track her down. If it's only the *Echo* against the Prussians, Chinese, and everyone else, we'll need all the help we can find." He added, "Thanks again, John. We'll talk soon."

Janet

Rain bowed away to sporadic showers and a sluggish, early afternoon sun broke through a bank of low-lying clouds to the west as Castillo's heli-jet touched down on his property north of Oakland. No additional interceptors or CCR forces had appeared as they meandered through the California hills, and Janet exhaled when the machine's rotors eased to a stop, releasing her anxiety over the attack. All she ached for was to hide and drink for a few days, alone with the spider.

She shook Castillo's hand and thanked him, then punched her indie-comm. "I've transferred double our agreement."

He raised his eyebrows, but didn't protest.

"Go see a doctor, okay?"

"Count on it. And you three stay safe."

A black hovercar appeared in the dirt laneway. "There's our ride, Jim."

Atteberry and Mary leaned on each other as Janet led them to the vehicle and shepherded them inside. She punched coordinates in through her indie-comm, nodded at Castillo in the surrounding gloom, and pushed back into her seat.

"How's your leg?"

Jim's head lolled forward. "Still numb. From time to time, I get these sharp daggers of pain shooting through it right to my hip, but the wound itself seems to be healing." He looked out the window at the passing green-grey of the hills and held Mary close. "Where are we headed?"

"There's a safehouse in the woods near here."

"Shouldn't we get to a hospital? See if there's anything we can do for Mares?"

Janet faced him. She'd lost the spark that filled her during the escape and attack, as if to say now that the immediate danger had passed, life had become dull again. She felt emotionally isolated, unable to process what happened, and unwilling to take any more chances. *I should have killed Winter.*

"We can't show our faces here, especially not me. The safehouse offers protection and I need time to hack into Elliot's other files." She glanced at Mary and the tension in her face dissipated. "You know, even now, she's beautiful. You've done a brilliant job raising her, Jim."

He immediately brushed off the comment.

"Let's find this other surgeon and get her well."

THE NONDESCRIPT CABIN GREW OUT OF THE CALIFORNIA HILLS like a natural extension of the earth and rock surrounding it, not exactly camouflaged, but enough to miss if you didn't pay attention. As the hovercar approached with lights out, stealth mode, Janet studied her indie-comm and the car's own sensor screen for heat signatures or other signs of life. All was quiet.

She turned on a thin light as they entered. The house reminded her of an old fishing cabin her grandfather used to take her to when she was a kid, dusty with stale air and the smell of smoke embedded in the upholstery. Sparsely furnished, roughly hewn floorboards, a minimalist design. Off to the right was an oversized bedroom where everyone could sleep, and a corner of the great room spilled into a kitchen. Two practical sofas, a couple of chairs and a small work table completed the functional look.

Mary lay down on one of the sofas and Janet drew a medical kit from a cupboard beside the stove. She injected her with more painkiller, and brushed her forehead. Jim pulled a quilt he found in the bedroom over her.

"Get that leg elevated, mister."

He flopped into a recliner near the fireplace and raised his leg up to rest it on the hearth. Janet stooped over him and took out a small flashlight from her pocket and studied his injury.

"The skin graft is holding. Lots of bruising, but no sign of infection yet." She peered up at him. "Do you need any more painkiller?"

"No, I'm good. Just tired as hell and having trouble concentrating."

"Try to rest."

She grabbed some kindling and logs from the wood box and built a fire. When the flames took, a warm glow filled the room and cut the chill from the late afternoon air. Janet searched the kitchen cupboards and returned with a bottle of bourbon and a couple of glasses. She set them on the hearth and pulled a chair beside him and poured out drinks. The spider came to life.

It's about time. Now we can put the world straight.

She slugged back three fingers, splashed herself another, and downed that as well. Then she set her mind on hacking the rest of Elliot's files.

Jim looked lost, bathing in the fire's warmth. He whispered to no one, "She's not going to make it."

Janet put her device down and sighed. "Time is our enemy now. What she did on the heli-jet, the dimensional phase shift or whatever it was, wiped her out. She's not eating and is barely lucid."

"A cruel joke."

"What do you mean?"

He pulled himself up in the chair and shifted his leg. "When we all returned from space, Esther and I took her to a hospital in New York

City to get her checked out. We had this discussion about the inevitability of death, and no matter what happens, what we do, whether we find someone to love, we all die alone, abandoned."

"That's a little dark for you, isn't it, Mr. Optimism?"

"Perhaps the blinders of youth have disappeared. Anyway, life seems so random and unjust. We get shunted around from one tragic struggle to another, win a few, lose a few, and then we're done. We rescue Mary from Luna, but Kate disappears. We bring her home only to discover that her strength—her photographic memory—can't handle whatever the alien dumped on her and, in fact, is literally torturing her to death.

"And also saved us," Janet interjected.

He ignored her and continued. "So we find a guy in New Houston who might help, and he's killed by a stray bullet from some assassin out for your hide." He turned to her. Reflections of the firelight danced in his tired eyes. He looked handsome in the warm glow. "And we save her, so she can die again a few days later. That's the cruel joke."

Janet returned to her indie-comm. "Exactly what I'm feeling too, Jim. If there's a point to any of this, I don't see it."

"At least you have your philosophical beliefs driving what you do. That's something to hold on to."

She grimaced.

For the next several minutes, the only sounds in the room were the crackling of the fire, Janet tapping on her device, and Mary's rhythmic, labored breathing from the sofa. Jim closed his eyes and his head lolled to the side.

Then Janet bolted upright. "Got in."

Startled, he rubbed his beard while her fingers flew across the indie-comm's screen, swiping through mail and messages and other documents, speed-reading like the researcher she was a long time ago.

"Anything there, Jan?"

"Hang on." She continued tinkering with the device, nodding occasionally, then looked up. "Dr. Lewis Palmer is our man. He and Elliot collaborated on several projects, all related to the safe application of mindscraping techniques to address various brain disorders. That's consistent with what Elliot told us about his research, so at least it doesn't appear like he's working for any nasty agency. I also have his personal cell number." She punched it in and put the indie-comm on speaker phone. After a couple rings, a man answered.

"This is Palmer."

"Doctor, it's Janet Chamberlain. My daughter, Mary Atteberry, was scheduled for surgery with you this morning and—"

"How did you get my number?"

"Believe me, it wasn't easy, but never mind that. What we need to know is—"

"You shouldn't be calling. It's not safe."

"The channel's encrypted, Doctor. We're good"

A silent pause.

"Dr. Palmer, are you still there?"

"Yes. What, er, can I do for you, Ms. Chamberlain?"

"Mary's father Jim and I were hoping the surgery could proceed. Perhaps there's another hospital?"

"How is the patient?"

Jim chimed in. "She's dying, doc. She needs help right away."

Another pause.

"I'm afraid there's nothing I can do now, folks. Dr. Elliot was the physician with the knowledge and skills for this sort of thing. My forte's more on the support and design side." The doctor sighed, then added, "I'm sorry I can't be of more help. We lost a superb man today."

Janet glimpsed at Atteberry and leaned forward with the indie-comm in front of her. "Please, this is a tough time for all of us."

"I can only imagine, ma'am, and I truly wish there was more I could do. Perhaps a hospital at your location can give her something for the pain. I assure you, it will get a lot worse before she . . . before it's over."

Jim spoke, keeping his voice low so as not to disturb Mary. "Could you at least try? I can't watch my daughter fade away like this. Please, doc. She's not eating, and her energy's gone. Just try."

Encryption tones beeped over the channel, accompanying the doctor's calm breathing. They uttered no words for what seemed like minutes. Janet shifted on her chair again and again. She broke the silence. "Doctor, are you there?"

"I'm thinking . . ."

The fire logs popped and Mary whimpered from the sofa.

"Mr. Atteberry . . . Ms. Chamberlain, there may be a solution, but listen carefully. I can't guarantee that what I propose will have any effect on your daughter's condition. As I said, Dr. Elliot—"

"Yes, Doctor," Jim interrupted, "we understand."

"Very well. I'll need access to the quantum computer at the Terran Science Academy labs. Do you know the research institution in San Francisco?"

"I know the TSA intimately," Jim said, his eyes widening.

"Good. If we have a connection to that device, I could undertake what Bob proposed for the operation. I'd need to rig a temporary operating theatre at the Academy where that computer's located."

"I know a director, and—"

Janet reached over and touched his arm, adding, "Once we secure access, what else do you want us to do, Doctor Palmer?"

The physician ran through a list of actions required to prepare Mary for the surgery and be ready to go as soon as the next morning. He suggested they stand by until the quantum computer—the "Q", he called it—and the operating team could be secured.

As they said their goodbyes, Palmer added one more thing. "I've already booked a flight home that leaves in a few hours. That should give me enough time to prepare my material here and arrange for a medical team in San Fran to assist."

"Thank you so much, Doc," Atteberry said, his voice cracking.

"We'll try our best to save her," the doctor said, "but it's a long shot. Let's pray it comes together without any more incidents."

EIGHTEEN

Esther

DESPITE MANY ATTEMPTS, ESTHER COULDN'T REACH Jim Atteberry on her indie-comm. She'd lost track of him after they'd returned from the east coast, and she blamed herself for not staying close, regardless of Janet's ethereal presence. Odd, this aftertaste of jealousy rising in her.

Esther sighed and leaned back in the office sofa. The building took on a magical, spectral feeling at this late hour and for the second night in a row, she remained the only person on the floor. Fog had rolled in across the city, so stargazing was out of the question, but she didn't want to return to her apartment. Not yet.

Where are you, Jim?

She had to find Mary and acquire her knowledge of the alien technology before sickness overtook the girl. Gleaning that information would propel her and the TSA into a brand new world, not to mention the future of humankind, but that wasn't her motivation. Fixing the relationship with Dr. Kapoor, for some deep-seated people-pleasing reason, became the priority. Reacquiring the Space Ops lab and squishing Mark Jefferson underfoot, too. But manipulating Jim to scrape Mary's mind—even if the present was all that existed—didn't sit well now that she'd had time to live it. How does Clayton do it, she wondered? *Perhaps he is soul-less after all.*

Sleep grew heavy and the moment she drifted off, her indie-comm pinged. Esther shook herself upright and grabbed the device. An encrypted call.

"Esther, it's me."

"Jim, where the hell are you? I've been trying to reach—"

The connection crackled and encryption codes beeped. "It'll take too long to explain, but I need a huge favor from you."

"What is it?"

"Mary's not well and a surgeon's flying in to operate on her brain tomorrow, but he needs access to your quantum computer."

Esther stood and gazed out her office window into the dark. "The Q-comp? What for?"

"You know the guy in New York who scanned her and said she didn't have enough physical capacity for all the knowledge the alien dumped in her? Well, this other surgeon believes he can transfer that into a secondary computer and the only one he knows that's capable of the speeds and memory required is yours." He paused. "He specifically mentioned it by name."

Esther pinched the bridge of her nose. "Jim, you know I'd do anything to help Mary, and you," she let slip, "but you've got to understand something." She swallowed hard. "I'm no longer in charge of Space Ops."

"What?"

"Kapoor took it away from me and gave it to Mark Jefferson, so I'd have to get his permission."

Static discharged on the line and the encryption codes beeped again.

"How big a problem is that?"

"First, the Q-comp's hours are all booked in advance, and currently, there's a joint deep space exploration project going on with the Japanese. It's running twenty-four seven through the next week. If we shut it down now, all that data and hundreds of millions of dollars will be lost, and I can't see him allowing that."

Esther paced around the office. The last thing she wanted was for Mary to suffer, so from that perspective alone, she could justify terminating the deep space project. But that would mean telling Mark and Kapoor about Mary's condition, and what her knowledge could bring to the world, and that raised even more problems since neither had any clue what power she held in her brain.

"Jim, where are you now? Can we discuss this in person?"

"I can't tell you. Mary and Janet are with me in hiding. Listen, Es, there's people after us and my girl won't last much longer."

"If I go to my boss with this, he'll want to know what's so special about her that I'm asking him to shut down a major project."

Another pause. "What other option do I have? Are there other computers like yours around?"

She remembered the British military had been developing their own, but they remained at least two years from bringing it online. "No, ours is the sole operational one in the world."

"Maybe if I talked with your boss and explained . . ."

She lowered her voice, an automatic response to sharing secrets. "Listen Jim, we can't do that. Your lives are already in danger, and telling more people about what Mary did and, worse, that she has this knowledge and power within to manipulate space-time, well, that's inviting more trouble than anyone could handle."

Jim protested, but Janet's voice rose in the background and he settled down again.

"Please, Esther."

She hesitated, then shook her head in resignation. "I'll ask Mark about the status of the deep space project and get a firm understanding of the timeframe. Perhaps I could persuade him to squeeze in this operation once it's finished in a week."

"Mary will be dead by then."

Dammit. "Okay, well, I'll speak with him, anyway. He might have a solution I haven't considered."

Jim sighed, relief in his voice. "Thanks, Es."

"Don't thank me yet. It's a hell of a longshot, and right now Mark isn't my favourite person in the land."

"We're meeting with the surgeon in the morning. Can you call me as soon as you can?"

"Yes. I'll talk to Mark tonight and see what he says."

She ended the call and tossed the indie-comm on her desk, then stared out the window into the foggy gloom. *He'll want to know why, and all the details, and then remind me of the cost of the deep space project and the fallout from stopping it even for a few hours.*

From her computer, Esther prepared an urgent note.

Mark, any chance I can use the q-comp tomorrow. It's a life/death thing.

She paused, wondering if she needed to say any more. After reflecting a moment, she signed her name and sent the missive. A few moments later, her device pinged with an incoming message.

Sorry, Esther, the Q's running Deep Space for the next 6 days. I could let you use it then, if that helps.

She tried again.

Please, Mark. I can't explain, but it's Ross 128 related. Half a day?

Fatigue swept around her like a storm as she picked at her scattered work, preparing to go home, knowing his answer even before the inevitable message appeared on her screen.

Sorry.

Wrong answer. She grabbed her indie-comm and marched from her office to the escalator, then descended to the lobby. She had to figure out a plan to hijack the Q without jeopardizing the deep space project and without letting Jefferson or Kapoor in on the reasons. Either way, she would secure the Q for Mary no matter the fallout.

The commissionaire wished her a good night and Esther replied with the same, glimpsing herself in a wall mirror near his desk. She flinched at what she saw behind her image.

What have you become?

Atteberry

"WE'LL NEED A BETTER BACKUP PLAN." Atteberry's voice bordered on a whisper as he pulled himself straight and repositioned his injured leg.

Janet glanced up from the small table in the firelight. She'd been cleaning her weapons. "Why do you say that?"

"If Esther can't secure the quantum computer, we have no alternative."

She grimaced. "That's why I'm following up on Elliot's research. I've learned there are always other options if we dig deep enough." The light bathed her face in a warm glow, and for a moment, her eyes lingered on him. Atteberry's distant feelings ached to resurface, and he fought to quench the untimely longing appearing in his chest.

"I hope you're right." He paused. "Do you hear Mary breathing in there?"

Janet turned her head toward the bedroom where Mary lay. Her labored breath rattled in her lungs and had long since lost the rhythmic pattern of a sound sleep.

"Dad, you there?" Mary's frail voice cracked the still air in the cabin like death.

"Yes, honey, you okay?" The bed and floorboards creaked, then Mary appeared in the doorway, hidden in the shadows.

"I—We're running out of . . . time."

"Come here, Mares. Sit with me."

Janet stood and placed her arm around her waist, guiding her to her chair and easing her into it.

Tears streaked across her cheeks. Thick dark veins showed on her forehead and around her eyes as she struggled to keep her head upright. Janet remained behind her, cradling her shoulders, and Atteberry strained to be strong for her, keeping his own fear in check, and failing. He reached out and took her hand. It was cold as a snow.

"We're working on it, Mares. The procedure could begin as early as tomorrow and then you'll be up and at it like old times." The room shifted around him and he cleared his throat.

"You were never any good at . . . at lying, Dad."

He turned away and stared into the wooded gloom outside the window.

Janet said, "Is the alien still with you?"

"Yes. The Keechik mind and . . . we are . . . mm . . . together now. He's struggling to keep things from me but its . . . not working. We'll both die soon."

"How much time, Mary?"

The girl gasped, then said, "Organs are shutting down."

Janet stroked her hair. "Can you hold out another couple of days?"

"Don't know. I—We will fall into a coma at some point. Eighteen hours, perhaps."

Atteberry scratched his beard, desperately holding on to his own consciousness. The fire glow traced an outline of grotesque shadows out the window, and a glint of a reflection twinkled in the dark outside. This was too much. He caught the detached worry on Janet's face.

"Jim," she whispered, "are you prepared for the worst?"

"Jesus, how can you ask such a thing?"

"Dad, you must be ready. We're okay with the end . . . whenever it comes."

He choked back the rising tears, wishing he could find the courage to stay positive, desperate to trade his life for hers.

The fire whined and crackled, then a couple of sparks flared up.

"I'll give you some more pseudophine for the pain," Janet said. "That'll help you sleep. You must rest before the procedure." She crossed the room and rummaged around in the kitchen, then returned with an inhaler.

"Here . . . breathe deeply into this." She placed the pump into Mary's mouth and fired the painkiller into her. Mary coughed, but kept inhaling for several seconds. Janet shot another blast, and her head drooped as the drug kicked in.

Janet lifted her out of the chair and half-dragged her toward the bedroom. "I'll stay with her a while if you want to grab some sleep, too." Then they disappeared into the shadows. Atteberry heard the bed groan as Janet lay her down, then silence enveloped the cabin like a dream.

He exhaled and wiped his face. Outside the window, something caused another reflection in the faint fire glow. He squinted, examining the darkness, but whatever he thought he saw had vanished and he didn't think about it again.

Winter

THE CHIME FROM HIS INDIE-COMM PERMEATED Winter's sleep as he dozed uncomfortably in his weary hotel room. Despite the painkillers and persistent dullness fogging his mind, he rose with a start, stretched, then glanced at the device. An incoming message from Berlin Operations. Early morning there.

He punched the return call function and his second-in-command Cornelia Wagner appeared in the viewer. "What do you have for me?"

She got straight to the point. "Satellite imagery picked up the location of the heli-jet, Herr Winter. She's partially hidden close to your position west of Oakland. No sign of anyone there now, however."

"How recent are the images?"

"Real time, sir."

"Excellent." He grunted as the throbbing in his legs gained traction. "Have you analyzed that area over the last 12 hours?"

A hint of a smile curled her lips. "Indeed, we have. I'm bringing up some photos. Stand by."

Winter hobbled over to the small worktable, fell into the desk chair, and transferred the call to his tablet. In a moment, grainy images of the heli-jet appeared in various degrees of descent.

"Are you receiving—"

"Yes, Cornelia. Keep them coming. I'll tell you when to stop."

The images flickered across his screen, a fresh one appearing every three seconds. After seeing the pilot and his targets gather in front of the craft and turn, he narrowed his eyes and hissed, "There."

The scrolling stopped and Winter zoomed in on the four persons of interest, to the extent possible with the satellite's resolution. The girl was still alive, but possibly wounded. Her father's leg appeared bandaged now, but the pilot and Janet Chamberlain remained *intact.* He stared at the fraulein, fueling the revenge brewing deep in his chest and solidifying his resolve to stop at nothing until he had her.

"How long ago was this taken?"

"That image was recorded at 21:07 your time, Herr Winter."

It was now just past midnight.

"Where did they go from here?"

Cornelia's face returned in the screen's corner and she looked off camera and adjusted something. "The pilot entered that principal building, but the other three drove farther east into the backcountry. Their location proved challenging because of heavy atmospheric interference, but I ordered an agent to the coordinates of an isolated cabin in the area." Before Winter spoke, she added, "He has yet to report, but the next scheduled check in is . . .19 minutes from now."

Winter grimaced. "Cornelia, be frank with me. How confident are you that your man is on the right path?"

She scrutinized him and said, "Extremely."

"You know who is with the girl, yes?"

"I know Janet Chamberlain is one of the three, yes, and that she's been a desired target for several years, but Herr Winter, I would not lie or mislead you. The team has surveyed that area extensively throughout the night. We have considered every contingency, every viable route in and out of that sector and we narrowed their location down to this cabin." She flashed a new, real-time image on the screen showing a tiny building and what appeared to be the outline of a hovercar in the bushes. "Do you see the heat signature from the structure?"

A wispy plume rose from the chimney. "Yes."

"It's the only signature we've picked up in that spot. I bet my life the targets are in that cabin, and I expect to confirm that as soon as the agent checks in."

Winter studied the infrared image unfolding on his screen. He squinted at an anomalous figure in the woods. The agent? Perhaps, or it could easily be the trunk of some tree or a rock—it was impossible to tell from the image—but he understood why Cornelia's confidence exploded.

"Most excellent work, Cornelia. Keep me apprised the moment you hear from your man in the field."

"Naturally, Herr Winter."

He ended the connection and leaned back in his chair. The pain from landing hard on the tarmac after Chamberlain kicked him out of the heli-jet had not ceased. A cold sweat broke out on his forehead and shivers rattled his spine. He glimpsed the bottle of painkillers on the coffee table in front of the sofa where he'd dozed. Half the bottle was already gone, and he wondered how much longer he'd last before dipping into the pills again.

He needed a distraction.

There was nothing but American trash on the television. Most channels showed ugly people eating from extreme close up viewpoints. Tongues and teeth and saliva swirling around disgusting bites of half-consumed fruit, red meat and thick creams, interspersed with random shots of genitalia. *This land is a sewer.* He landed on a quiet channel showing images of weather patterns set to classical guitar music. Following the fingering in his mind, the chord progressions, the nuanced key changes occupied his thoughts until, after a passage of time, his indie-comm pinged again.

"Herr Winter," Cornelia said, her voice no more emotional than before. "The agent has confirmed the target family in that cabin I showed you."

"Wonderful. What more can you tell me?"

"Ms. Chamberlain is with the girl in a bedroom. The father appears to be sleeping in front of the fireplace. There has been no movement for a couple of hours."

"Perfect. Do you have a team to send in?"

"Negative. Just the one agent."

He frowned. This was not sympathetic Prussian Consortium territory, and he dared not ask about co-opting confederate agents in California. Far too many eyes, too many hands, too many whisperers.

Cornelia added, "I can assign independents to a team, Herr Winter, and have them on site at the cabin within a few hours. Shall I order them?"

The dull throb had moved from his legs and spine into his mind. Clarity of thought and action was difficult, but he pushed through the encroaching darkness in his thinking and determined the path to take. Relying on Cornelia's judgment was a non-issue. The two of them had been on many missions together in the past and, as his 2IC, she'd proved her worth over and over. No, Cornelia was not the issue. But relying on independent mercenaries, well, that was the problem.

"You know I don't like to use independents for anything but routine work, yes?"

"I do, but—"

"No buts, Cornelia. This is far too important to leave to agents who trade their skills solely for filthy lucre. I need a team of our agents. Men and women who are prepared to die for a principle. Agents like you."

"Or you, Ben. I mean, *Herr Winter*."

Her slip amused him.

"The *Sara Waltz* is in space dock at the New Houston elevator, is it not?" she asked.

"Yes, why?"

"Perhaps they can deploy a security squad to the cabin coordinates?"

Winter considered the option. He pushed through the thick fog covering his thoughts, assessing possible outcomes, contingencies, risks, and the ultimate reward: securing the girl and destroying Janet Chamberlain.

"I like that, Cornelia . . . a lot."

"Shall I contact Captain Krause?"

"Yes, please do. I remain in considerable pain from the earlier accident and require a couple hours of sleep."

"I'll take care of this post-haste, Herr Winter. Once the targets are apprehended, I'll contact you again."

He shook his head. "Call me before they move in. I want to be there when it happens. I shall enjoy seeing the fear in that creature's face when she encounters her day of reckoning."

NINETEEN

The Mergeling

THE DEEP VIOLET DREAMSCAPE FILLED the Mergeling's mind as experiences and knowledge swirled like a cosmic maelstrom. What remained of Mary lay dormant in a pocket of chemical reactions somewhere in the murky surroundings, somewhere *under*. They thought together, saw together, as one. In the grasp of these changes, the Mergeling understood the notion of hope that something outside of it may help it exist beyond the present physical circumstances.

We must find a way.
There is always a solution.
How can we be certain?
We cannot.
We speak in riddles.

A flicker of light emerged in the distance, cutting through the infinite indigo hue, imposing a fresh depth of perception to the being. The erstwhile Mary Atteberry, the remnant in the synaptic puddle, gazed awe-struck at the beauty of the thick, brilliant blue. Somewhere in the merged memory, her old self recalled that same color on Luna when she and Kate scratched out their survival in the grey dust. She recognized it again as the alien Keechik.

We know how to conduct this operation they speak of. We know.

Yes . . .mm.

We must tell them how.

They would not understand. It would be like explaining the fundamentals of physical manipulation to an earthworm. They are too small.

Still, we must try.

The cold flicker grew more intense. The Mergeling patched new thoughts into a mental mosaic these beings could never grasp, but it did so regardless.

Let us try anyway. Perhaps the physical remnant can assist?

Janet

THE MORNING SKY BROKE FROM THE INCESSANT CLOUDS and rain, momentarily blossoming into deep purple and blue striations, interrupted by a smattering of alto-cirrus clouds, reminding her of the simple, complex beauty of the natural world. Janet stared out the living room window of the quiet cabin into the surrounding woods, still shrouded in darkness, the shapes of dormant trees emerging like statues from a ground-hugging fog.

Everything slept outside.

Jim sighed and shifted his weight on the sofa where he'd been sleeping.

He doesn't know I'm awake.

The rattle from Mary's fractured breathing punctuated the remaining silence of the room. Janet stretched her back, peered out the window one more time, and rose.

"You awake, Jim?"

"Hm? Yeah, I suppose."

"I'll check on Mary."

She crept into the bedroom where Mary lay on her side, shivering under a mountain of blankets. She was awake but didn't register Janet's presence at first. The bed creaked under her weight as she sat on it and brushed Mary's matted hair with her fingertips.

"Morning. Are you okay to travel?"

Mary reached out and took Janet's hand. "So . . . exhausted, Mom."

Janet gulped.

That word.

She hadn't been called *that* word for years. Even after she reappeared in their lives in 2085 to protect her during the initial alien panic, her daughter hadn't called her by *that* word. And something familiar struggled deep within, an ancient calling, like a childhood tune on the tip of her tongue she couldn't quite remember, lingering there, taunting her. Then, unable to quell the rising desolation that had remained buried for as long as she could remember, Janet wept. In the still darkness of the small bedroom, tears pooled.

She brushed them aside. "Come on, kiddo, let's get going. We'll get you to the doctor and extract the alien mind from yours. You'll be back to normal in no time." She pulled Mary up from the bed and helped her stand and get to the bathroom—a positive sign. Some organs still functioned.

Jim boiled a kettle in the kitchen and, after rummaging about in the cupboard, pulled out a box of tea. In the living room, Janet studied his movements, the obvious discomfort in his leg, the quiet eyes, the beard she loved on him, the broad shoulders. Maybe it was *that* word, or something as simple as spending time together as a makeshift family again, but Janet's mind slipped and softened from the disciplined focus she needed more than ever before.

I'm becoming a danger to myself and the others.

Jim handed her a steaming cup of tea and gave Mary a glass of water. "Sorry, Mares, no grape juice in these parts."

She frowned at him and took a few sips before setting the cup down on the coffee table. Then, he looked at Janet and his face darkened. "You okay?"

"Yeah, just indulging myself for a moment." Janet wiped her eyes. "I'll be fine."

They sat in silence, nourishing their drinks, gradually waking up. The sun had risen and the tree tops glistened in warm yellows and oranges. Mist continued meandering through the woods, and Janet studied their surroundings through the window, keeping a sharp lookout for anything that appeared *other*, out of place. So far, so good.

Soon, she announced, "It's time to go." She packed some medication into a small shoulder bag and opened the door. Cool, damp air greeted her, and she inhaled deeply, her gaze darting from side to side. She punched a code in her indie-comm and the hovercar purred toward the cabin from its overnight resting place in a tiny hollow. Janet helped Mary and Jim get in, then she took a final look back at the cabin and joined them.

Mary searched the scenery as the hovercar rose and floated toward the county road. "Where are we going again?"

"There's a commuter train station near here. We'll take the Maglev to San Francisco, then cab it to the TSA. I've already sent a message to Esther Tyrone and she'll be ready for us as soon as we've met the surgeon," Janet said. Jim held Mary close in a protective hug.

She commanded the car's AI to monitor traffic patterns in the immediate vicinity, searching for anything out of the ordinary. On the car's view screen, various icons representing other vehicles appeared, and after scrutinizing the data for a minute, Janet turned away, satisfied no one followed them.

They whirred into the Maglev station in San Ramon at 6:30. Various hovercars, scooters and bicycles already filled half the lot with workers on their way to Oakland and beyond. Well-dressed men and women carrying tablets and shoulder bags pushed their way to the train platform, and city staff helped manage the flow.

Janet peered sharply around the station, watching the travelers, searching for anything that looked *other*, especially couples and loiterers. *Something doesn't feel right.* She and Jim held Mary upright and kept her moving onto the platform where they sat her on a bench. A few commuters stared at them, especially Mary.

And no wonder. Her dishevelled hair and stained clothing gave her the appearance of someone who'd run away from home and had been living on the streets for the past couple weeks. Mary's glazed eyes were ringed with black circles, and she struggled to focus, while Jim didn't look much better. His skin was a grim shade of pale grey, and his injured leg was an obvious point of interest to those standing around the platform with nothing else better to do.

Janet studied every one of them: the man wearing sunglasses, sleeves rolled up, and carrying no tech. The fit woman in shorts and sneakers, speaking into her indie-comm while frequently glancing at her. Two other young, attractive men sitting a dozen meters from them, glancing around, their gaze resting on Mary and whispering to each other.

Hard to tell, dammit.

The Maglev hadn't arrived yet from its point of origin. Travelers worked on their indie-comms or chatted with each other, some of them peering down the corridor for the train. Janet's anxiety boiled. She worked her jaw muscles and fingered the weapon under her light jacket.

When the Maglev flew in silently and eased to a stop, passengers lined up, awaiting their turn to board. Jim stood and lifted Mary. "This is it, Mares. You'll soon be good as new."

They fell in line with the others and slow-marched toward the humming train. Janet searched the platform, all her senses alert, prepared for any movement, watching those with their hands in pockets cautiously. Despite the lack of overt activity—or perhaps because of it—she remained vigilant.

It still doesn't feel right.

They were close to boarding and Janet grew increasingly nervous. She didn't want to be trapped on a high-speed Maglev and encounter other agents, and she had no rational reason to suspect that would happen, but she couldn't shake this feeling that one of these passengers, perhaps more, had been watching them.

A passenger in front of them fussed at the doorway leading onto the train. She blocked the entrance, searching her bag for something and grumbling aloud. Another man shouted, "Any time there, lady."

"Someone needs another coffee," Jim mused.

But Janet gripped the gun handle inside her jacket, her head on a swivel as she instinctively moved closer to Mary. The lady ahead found whatever she'd been searching for and continued boarding, chiming, "Sorry, I'm sorry."

The other man who'd urged her to hurry turned and greeted Jim like any other friendly commuter might. Although his face was pleasant and good-natured, an underlying, calculating evil in his eyes chilled Janet to her core. Before she could process her intuition, it happened.

"Good luck," he whispered with a slight pull on *good*, nodding at Jim, glancing at Mary.

"Thanks."

And Janet *knew*.

TWENTY

Carter

"THIS IS MADNESS, LAURA, AND I WON'T STAND FOR IT!"

Clayton Carter fumed in his private boardroom, set down his morning coffee, jaw clenched, staring at Captain Russo aboard the *Malevolent*, shocked at what she'd told him.

"I agree, Clayton, but what other choice do we have? We're still in a standoff with the *Volmar*, and we'll soon be facing this rag-tag collection of Prussian, Chinese, Russian, Brazilian—"

"I get the picture."

"I'm not sure you do." She glanced off-screen and nodded. "Weapons is tracking 18 vessels en route to our location. Granted, some of them are cargo scows and science ships, but most are equipped with some serious weaponry. There's a snowball's chance in hell that we could ever survive a full out attack."

Carter inhaled deeply and rolled his eyes. "Are you suggesting we cut and run? What kind of message does that send, hm?"

"It says we wish to live and fight another day. Clayton, you understand first-hand what these ships can do. The *Echo* barely escaped the barrage from one heavy cruiser. There are a dozen similar boats on their way. We'd be fools to stay here and provoke them."

Ed Mitchell rapped on the boardroom door and entered, concern stamped on his face. He handed Carter a bottled water and faced the screen. "Are you discussing the convoy?"

Carter motioned for him to sit. He remained standing.

"Laura, what's the status of your own weaponry?"

"We're at full capacity and believe me, some of my crew are itching for a showdown, but this is too much."

"How long before the Prussian cruisers are in range?"

Captain Russo checked her console. "At their current velocity, we have a few hours tops."

The room grew deathly silent except for random bursts of static and background chatter from the connection with the *Malevolent*. The strain in Russo's face showed, and her constant shifting and fidgeting telegraphed an anxiety that Carter had not previously witnessed. One trait he admired about her was the ability to remain calm and professional no matter the danger—the same way Powell handled the crisis on the *Echo*. *She wouldn't be calling in unless this was damn serious.*

"So if you hold your position, it's all-out war."

"Affirmative."

Ed touched Carter's arm to get his attention. "This won't end well for the *Malevolent* or for our other interests, Clayton. The rest of the Titanius fleet is days away, except for the *Echo* and she's still in the shop."

"We must be able to do something other than bail."

"It's the only reasonable course of action to take."

"But the *message*, Ed. Come on, if we blink now, we'll never hear the end of it. Aren't you the man who told me our strength lies in what other nations, other corporations believe we *could* do to them? If we run, they'll assume we've got nothing of value, but I want them to think we found something on Luna that will change the course of humanity forever. A weapon more powerful than any nuclear torpedo they dare launch our way. Do you see?" He grinned.

Ed rocked on his heels. "You want to bluff them?"

"Poker was never my game, but yes, if only to buy us time to get our own fleet back, and fly the *Echo* again."

Russo broke in. "What've you got in mind?"

Carter clapped his enormous hands together. "Yes, that's it! We shall use subterfuge to gain the advantage." Turning to the captain on the massive screen, he said, "Laura, I need to think this through with Ed and don't want to keep you from your duties. But before I let you go, what's the latest you can remain in your current position before the ship is in danger?"

"Two and a half hours," she said. "If I don't hear from you then, I'm pulling out and we'll regroup with the rest of the fleet on the far side of Luna."

"Understood." Then, in a softer tone, he added, "Thank you, Laura. I'll buy you a drink at the Chez Martin when this is all over."

"You'll have to do more than that," she said with a mischievous, deadly smile. "*Malevolent* out."

Carter invited Ed to sit again at the board table.

"What's on your mind?"

"Simple. We don't have any superweapon, but the Prussians know how deftly we escaped sure destruction on the return from Luna."

"Yes, when Mary Atteberry manipulated space-time and took the *Echo* out of prime."

"Right, but the girl is still missing on the west coast somewhere, and it may take a while to get her back with us." He grinned, pausing, but Ed didn't follow. "Okay, if the *Volmar* thinks we have the power to walk through a firefight unscathed, would they remain so eager to attack?"

Mitchell considered his response. "Uncertain."

"Which is the reason the Prussians haven't engaged the *Malevolent* yet. They have no idea what we have. For all they know, we may have equipped our entire fleet with this tech."

"But if that was the case, it wasn't clear earlier when Captain Russo fired volleys back and forth with the Prussians. They must realize she doesn't have the same capability as the *Echo*."

"Unless we leak a message to the effect that she does, and to use it however she sees fit to wipe out any hostile attack."

Ed drew tiny circles on the polished mahogany table with his index finger. "I see now . . . yes . . . that may be enough. The threat of a weapon so powerful they won't even consider calling us on it." He shrugged. "This plan might work."

"Right, but in the meantime, I must locate that Atteberry girl and get her back aboard the *Echo*. As soon as Captain Powell gives the green light on the repairs, I want the ship *flying* and I need her on it."

"What's the latest news?"

"Nothing this morning. I've left a thousand messages with Esther Tyrone, but it's still early in California and she may not even be up yet. However, she's agreed to help us find and hold the girl until we bring her here."

"I'm sorry," Ed continued, "but under what pretense would her father ever agree to come back here? A few days ago, Dub tried and failed to detain her, inviting his wrath. If I were the parent, this is the last place I'd come."

Carter's jubilant mood quickly soured, and he pursed his lips. "Yes, yes, I know all about the screw up at Gotham Medical. But one thing I've never accepted my entire life, Ed, is quitting. There is a way to convince them it's in her best interest to join us. I simply haven't uncovered it yet."

"Well, we've been through a lot of adventures over the years, and if anyone can solve a puzzle like this, you can." Ed stood and pushed in his chair. "I've got to get on this fake message and apprise Laura of the plan so she can prepare, but I will tell her to bail if there's any sign of imminent warfare, Clayton. We can't afford to lose her or that ship."

"I understand completely." He rose and tugged on his jacket. "In the meantime, I'll put eyes on the TSA and find out what's happening with the girl."

The two men exited the boardroom, but before Ed left the office, Carter stopped him, leaned in close and said *sotto voce*. "When the *Echo* flies, Ed, mark my words: that girl will be on board."

Atteberry

IN A SPLIT-SECOND, JANET GRABBED THE MAN'S ARM, spun around and snapped it at the elbow, dropping him to the concrete platform. Passengers scattered, and someone screamed.

"Run, Jim!"

Atteberry snatched Mary around the waist and hobbled as quickly as possible toward the station. He glanced over his shoulder. Janet crouched over the twisted body of the fallen agent, her weapon drawn back to the train.

"Come on, Mares, inside!"

She struggled to remain upright and Atteberry shoved her through a sliding door. There, in the morning light of the station lobby, three agents encircled him. One of them, a six-foot-tall woman with a buzz cut, ripped Mary from his arms while the other two men held him back, their hands like vises on his wrists.

"No! Let her go!"

They pulled her aside and clutched her, holding her arms behind, but Mary was in no shape to resist. He looked around for help. Other passengers in the building stampeded for the opposite doors and disappeared, leaving the muscle, him and Mary, and a wide-eyed paralyzed clerk behind the information counter. More shouts and the noise of a struggle on the platform trickled in. When Janet screamed, he fought against the men holding him. It was a fruitless struggle.

Mary vomited across her captive's shoes and pant legs, and the woman swore, smacking her across the back of her head. She slumped down, unconscious, spittle dripping from her open mouth.

Atteberry yelled, but his words caught in his throat. One of the men leaned in on his injured leg. Intense pain shot up his limb and through his spine as his vision darkened. He gaped at Mary, fighting to maintain consciousness.

Two other agents entered, dragging Janet into the station by her arms and dumping her in front of him. Blood oozed from her nose and someone had ripped out a chunk of her hair. Her face was swollen and badly beaten. She coughed and groaned, but otherwise remained motionless in a heap.

The smaller of the agents who brought her in grumbled something into his indie-comm that Atteberry didn't understand, but he recognized the language: German.

An old school three-quarter ton diesel truck rattled up by the door leading to the platform and squealed to a stop. They pushed Atteberry out first. A door on the rear of the truck swung open and more hands grabbed him and hauled him up inside. Someone slammed him onto a metal bench and secured him to it with mag-cuffs.

Next, they tossed in Janet. She must have been semi-conscious because she tried getting up but fell hard on the metal floor. Then they threw her on the bench and cuffed her.

"Mary?" Atteberry shook his head, chasing the veil of encroaching darkness away.

A man deep in the shadows of the cargo hold growled in English, "Careful with the girl, *dummkopf*. You must not harm her." They lifted her into the truck and lay her down on a cot opposite him. The buzz cut woman placed monitoring pads on her head and chest, and a bio-screen blinked to life. The vital signs, Atteberry recognized, showed mostly red and a swirl of panic coursed through him. Then the others piled in and one of them slammed the rear door shut. They took up various positions on the benches around the gloomy interior and the truck pulled away.

"Who are you? What are you doing?"

The voice in the dark corner rose calmly above the din. "Hush, Herr Professor. We shall help your daughter get better."

"Wh—Who are you?"

The man behind the voice emerged from the shadows. Although Atteberry's vision blurred and danced with lights, he remembered that set jaw, the pinch-thin lips, those cold eyes.

"You!"

"Yes. We meet again."

Winter struggled to walk: his legs had been badly damaged from the heli-jet fall, and he grunted as he sat beside him, leaning back.

"I'll be brief. It is only because I like your spirit that you're still breathing. And I have some sympathy for your daughter." He gazed over at Janet's hump. "And she is alive for my personal pleasure later on. But first, some delightful news. We shall take a brief respite near here, where Helga can stabilize the girl. Then we fly to Munich to heal her."

"You—You know about her brain?"

"We suspected something happened when your *Echo* phased out of space prime, but I understood the truth only when her medical reports appeared and we did our homework in New Houston."

Atteberry's rage boiled over. "Damn you, Winter, we were trying to save her life!" He struggled against the cuffs.

"Oh, hush now. As I said, she will be saved. But on my terms." He pulled a piece of chewing out of his pocket and popped it in his mouth. "You see, the fraulein is too important to global security to have her poked and prodded by the NDU or anyone else. In the old days, people learned through books and databases. But today, I wager the alien mind working its way through her brain contains far more knowledge than we could ever learn in our brief lives. And I intend to extract it."

Atteberry groaned.

"Oh yes, your only interest as a father is saving her, restoring her health. Any parent would feel that. But her value, begging your pardon, is more than sentiment. So much more."

Janet stirred beside him and awkwardly pulled herself up with her cuffed hands to a sitting position.

"So nice of you to join us, Frau Chamberlain."

She mouthed something inaudible.

"Quiet, *bitte*. You and I will have our little conversation soon. Alone."

"Listen to me, Winter," Atteberry demanded, "We were on our way to a surgeon right here in San Francisco . . . one of the surgical team from New Houston. He said he could help her. There's no need to—"

"Ah," he grinned. "Dr. Palmer. I know all about him. But from what I understand, he's hardly equipped to conduct a delicate procedure like this. No, we have our own surgeons, our own method for extracting knowledge."

"Mind scraping, you mean."

Winter snapped his gum. "You make it sound barbaric. No, there are ways to dive deeply into someone's mind these days without turning their brains to cabbage. In Munich, we'll carry out the procedure and hopefully your beautiful daughter will be . . . what is the expression I heard once?" He searched for the words. "Ah yes, she'll be right as rain."

"'Hopefully'?"

"Well, there are no guarantees. We have the finest surgeons in the world, but until they get in there, one can never be sure of what one may find. You understand."

Atteberry's mind raced with both terror and a faint hope that perhaps Mary could still be saved, but at what cost to the world? He didn't care. Mary needed the operation now. "Do the surgery here with Dr. Palmer. Mary's not well and can't survive a flight to Europe." He looked into Winter's black eyes. "She's dying."

The man peered over at the bio-signs monitor attached to Mary. "You have a point. She does not appear as vigorous as I had wished. Nevertheless, Munich it is." He rose, motioned to one of the goons by the rear door who barked an order into his radio.

"Look at her, Winter. She's barely hanging on. Please. I'm—I'm begging you to help her here in San Francisco."

The man stepped toward the dim front of the cargo area but stopped short and turned. "I'm sorry. You see, Herr Professor, Dr. Palmer cannot perform the procedure."

"What are you talking about? We confirmed with him again this morning. Everything's in place, and all we need is access to the quantum comp—"

"No, you misunderstand. He won't perform the operation because, well, he's dead."

Atteberry's jaw dropped. Paralysis enveloped him. "You're lying," he sputtered. "Please tell me you're lying."

Winter spat out his gum. "Here," he said, pulling an image from his shirt pocket and handing it to him. "You tell me if he's up for the task."

Atteberry reached over and grabbed the paper image in his shaking, cuffed hands. Janet leaned in to look, then turned away. What remained of Dr. Lewis Palmer was slumped in a straight-backed chair, arms tied behind him, his head pulled back as if in prayer. A gloved hand held it in place. Remnants of flesh and bone clung to his mouth and chin by tendrils in his swollen nose, loosely decorating his sunken chest.

TWENTY-ONE

Atteberry

BILE OOZED UP HIS THROAT AND ATTEBERRY swallowed hard to choke it down. The truck's hot, diesel fumes swirled around and he saw multiple images of Winter fading away into the shadows of his vision.

This can't be happening . . .

"Jim?"

Janet's voice, in contrast to the rumbling truck, pierced his isolation.

"Jim, look at me," she whispered.

Atteberry held his breath and the spinning mercifully stopped, but the unresolved ache in his gut refused to abandon him. Someone touched his arm. He caught Janet's face, her cuffed hands on his wrist.

"It's hopeless, isn't it?" he said.

She remained stoic, but her eyes told him the truth. Their last hope of saving Mary by extracting the alien's mind had vanished, and she would die despite Winter's goal of flying her overseas for surgery. He glanced at the monitor above the cot. Vital signs continued bleeding red with flashing alerts.

"What does it all matter, Jan? I wish I'd never heard that damn Ross 128 signal. See what it's brought us?"

She squeezed his wrist and sighed. "It's not over yet."

His mind snapped at her words. *How dare you spew some ridiculous feel-good gibberish!* He gulped like a drowning man gasping for breath and said, "Look . . . around you. This *is* the end. There's nothing . . . more we can do. Winter will kill us, and Mary, and we're . . . sitting here, useless. How are you not . . . getting that, Janet?" He squinted and added, "What have you become?"

She released his wrist.

In the truck's gloom, Atteberry saw the glisten in her eyes, and shame overwhelmed him. The lump in his own throat grew. "I'm sorry, Jan, that wasn't fair."

She fell back against the side panel.

Time played tricks on his mind and he recalled how they first met on campus as freshmen, how intoxicating she'd been with her natural beauty and energy, protesting whatever the hell it was and, from all the other suitors encircling her, she chose him. Atteberry snorted at the image of his younger self, lost in books, tinkering with archaic twentieth century radios, adrift in soft summer nights gazing at the stars and planets and contemplating creation. Those halcyon days seemed ridiculous to him now, even wasted. He'd loved her like none other, so much that sometimes after they'd made love, he cried because he ached from the depth of subconscious emotion pulsating through his veins.

But it was all a ruse.

Some agency had already recruited her by then, and she worked for the NDU government as a . . . what? He didn't know. And he did not understand what or who she truly was until that mysterious signal appeared six years ago.

The truck hit a bump in the road and jostled them against each other. Janet leaned into him. That's when he heard the faint rise of her muted crying, her breath escaping from her open, swollen mouth.

His pain subsided like morning fog in the June sun, and from deep in his jumbled thoughts, a new voice pushed its way through to his consciousness, one he'd never been aware of before, yet now it appeared as an old friend, with wisdom and authority.

Fight back, Jim.

He peered around in his confusion, wondering if Janet or perhaps Mary had spoken to him, but all he saw was the massive woman called Helga hovering over Mares, the other goons watching him from the rear door, weapons lowered, and the outline of Winter perched in the stygian gloom.

Fight back.

He reflected on how Captain Powell handled the danger on the *Echo* with calm confidence. The man barely broke a sweat and seldom raised his voice yet commanded the respect of the entire crew, even that asshole Carter. He never gave up, but continued taking one step forward at a time, as if in some bizarre prophetic way, he either realized he'd save the ship or didn't care. Well, he couldn't have known about Mary's ability to shift space prime, yet Atteberry realized Powell was totally devoted to his work. No, it must have been something else.

Fight back.

Perhaps this drive, this courage in pursuing various options without dwelling on the outcome was the same trait Janet had: a singular focus on the *now*, taking action and leaving the unpredictable result to destiny or providence. Yes, maybe that's what she meant.

His breathing returned to normal, and the pounding in his head eased. He asked himself, *what can I do?* And waited, straining to uncover whatever might present itself in his mind.

A moment passed.

And another.

Fight back, Jim.

He clenched his teeth and stared across the gloomy space at Mary, his only child, and remembered she'd already faced death on Luna, again on the *Echo*, and the *Relic*. Yet, despite her wish to live, she expressed no fear of dying—that same courage, same ability to work the problem that Janet possessed. Perhaps he had the spirit too and didn't realize it.

Fight back, whatever the outcome.

And in that moment, with his confusion abating, replaced with a convicting power he'd never experienced before, he approached his dilemma with fresh insight, renewed strength.

I'll do what I can to save you, Mares, or die trying.

Gathering data, he considered their options and released all holds on any result he desired as the truck rumbled along, zigzagging, and dropping its speed.

If this life was all there was, which he only now doubted, then he vowed to fight to the bitter end awaiting him.

Winter spoke from the dark. "How is the girl?"

Helga shook her head and remained silent. The truck's brakes squealed, and the vehicle rolled to a stop. The goons by the door prepared to disembark.

Janet stirred and brushed her bloated face with her palms, straightening up. Before he realized what he did, Atteberry whispered, "I love you, Jan."

The unfolding silence of the moment between them expanded to blanket eternity. She gazed over at him, stroked his cheek with a bloody finger and said, "I love you, too."

Esther

THE COMMUTE TO THE TSA WAS UNEVENTFUL save for the deep churn in her gut over what she prepared to do next. Shutting down Mark's experiment on the Q comp without authority would not only end her career; it could also get her arrested for sabotage. The decision rolling around her head was clear: tell Mark and come clean about Mary and the events on the *Echo*, or, allow Mary to die when the technology existed to at least give her a fighting chance.

For a moment last night, she considered telling Jim the computer was not available, but she sensed what he'd do: he'd show up for it anyway, and that whacko ex of his would no doubt kill anyone who stood in their way. No, what she planned to do was something she'd never expected before in her entire life: terminate the Deep Space experiment first. With the computer free, she and the others could use it for Mary's operation.

It was too easy. After she messaged Jim the night before, she walked with a singular focus to the Q comp, ignoring the two grad students beavering away in the corner, accessed the project because Mark had stupidly left the security codes unchanged when he took over, and programmed the machine to shut down at 0600. The time on her indie-comm displayed a few minutes after seven o'clock as the hovercar glided to a halt and grounded itself in front of the TSA's primary entrance.

She messaged Jim telling him she'd arrived at the TSA, but no response came back.

Odd.

Once inside her office, she sent another message to him.

More silence.

She pulled a tote from the supply cabinet and grabbed her personal effects from the desk, and stared at her wall of books and telescope tilted upward by the picture window overlooking the ocean. She'd have to get all that delivered to her wherever she ended up and assuming Kapoor showed a measure of mercy.

The ping from the indie-comm startled her. It was a message from Mark Jefferson: *join me in space ops.*

So he now understood. The system would have alerted him to the breakdown of the experiment, and after asking some questions and checking the machine, he'd realized she was behind it. Time to face the music. Before she responded, Esther gazed out the window at the lifting fog and muted blues of the morning sky.

Was this the right thing to do?

Too late to reconsider: the deed had been done, and now she plumbed a well of courage to push back at Mark and Kapoor. All she'd ever intended was to protect the Academy, engage in science, and help the Atteberrys. She exhaled, checked her hair in the window's reflection, and began the lengthy walk down the hall, down the escalator, and down the elevator to Space Ops.

As she entered the lab, the small group of scientists and technicians hovering over the quantum computer stopped talking and stared at her, like Rembrandt's *Syndics of the Drapers' Guild*, she thought. Mark wasn't with them, so she searched around the cavernous room and found him speaking with Dr. Kapoor outside her old office.

As she marched toward them, she recognized she'd made the right decision. Mary's life hinged on the use of the Q comp. Saving her also implied extracting Keechik's memories and storing them on the Q's massive network. If the rest of that knowledge was anything like the manipulation of space-time and FTL technology, Kapoor should thank her profusely, but to tell him meant putting future exploration in the hands of the politicians, the UN, and the other weasels in Kapoor's circle. She couldn't let them find out. If the decision about who should have the alien's power was hers, she'd rather see Clayton Carter get it than any government.

Funny how he keeps popping into my head.

The two men looked up stone-faced as she approached. Mark showed concern more than anything else. Kapoor was full of muted rage.

"Dr. Tyrone," he said, "What the hell have you done?"

She stared him down with a defiance she hadn't known. "What do you mean?"

"You know exactly what I mean. You shut down the Q and sabotaged the Deep Space project. Do you have any idea what this will cost us?"

She narrowed her gaze and bristled. "Of course I do."

He waited for her to say more, but she offered him nothing. Instead, she glanced at Mark, who pursed his lips and ran his fingers through his thick hair. "Well? What could possibly compel you to terminate one of the most important, most expensive projects we've ever undertaken?" He hesitated. "I sure as hell hope this isn't your idea of revenge for being re-assigned."

189

Esther snorted. "Not a chance."

"So tell me!"

The other technicians had wandered over within hearing range and struck various scowling poses—some with their arms crossed, others with their hands shoved deep into their lab coat pockets. Esther acknowledged them with a nod.

"I'm sorry, Kieran. I understand how this appears, but you gave me no choice," she said.

"What are you talking about?"

"If I may back up for a moment . . . what happened at Mount Sutro six years ago was only the beginning. I didn't apprise you of the full gravity of that situation because I needed to protect the TSA's reputation. What do the politicos call it? Ah yes, 'plausible deniability'."

He chuckled. "You mean to say that you were protecting me? What the hell from?"

"From everything going on. Mark understood that, right?"

Jefferson's gaze fell to the floor, and he stammered an inaudible response.

"Hey," she continued, "you really don't understand what's happening, and I won't tell you all the details down here. I'm sure you'll find out soon enough, but the bottom line is that a whole lot more happened on Luna and in the *Echo* than you're aware of, and what takes place here in the next few hours will affect humanity forever."

Kapoor's countenance shifted from hostility to confusion.

Esther pressed on. "In a little while, Mary Atteberry—the summer student—will arrive with a team of physicians who will perform surgery right here in this lab. The Q is a critical piece of equipment needed for this operation to be successful. By refusing to shut down the Deep Space experiment which, I might add, could be started up again soon, Mark sentenced Mary to die. I told him last night it was a matter of life and death although, in his defence, I didn't say whose life, not that that's important."

"You didn't tell me it was *her*, Esther!" he protested, but now everyone stared at him. "You said nothing about that student!"

190

Kapoor stepped away from him and asked, "Is this true, Dr. Jefferson? Did she ask about the computer?"

"Y—Yes, she did."

"And did Dr. Tyrone say it was of life-threatening importance?"

He glared at her, then returned Kapoor's gaze and whispered, "Yes."

"And you," he said, motioning to Esther, "you cannot tell me what this is all about?"

"Correct, sir. Not yet, at any rate. Perhaps when the surgery is over and we save the girl, we'll be able to sit down for full disclosure."

"Dammit." Kapoor pulled on his chin and struck a new pose with hands on hips, gazing around the lab and stopping on the quantum computer. "I remain shocked by all this, Esther," he said in a soft voice, "but there's nothing we can do now for Deep Space or the lost data. When is the patient arriving?"

"Any time. She's meeting with the surgeon this morning and they plan to operate. That's all I know."

His tongue darted out between his lips. "All right. Esther, keep me apprised of everything that happens here."

"Understood."

"And you, Dr. Jefferson, walk with me."

Kapoor pushed his way past her and the gaggle of technicians, marching toward the lab entrance. Mark following him cautiously.

Esther scrutinized the techs who remained transfixed, making eye contact with them all, until, one by one, they returned to their workstations. She'd won this round but wouldn't allow any satisfaction to creep into her thoughts. To protect Mary, she needed backup. After searching her indie-comm, she uncovered the name of a CCR agent who helped them escape from Mount Sutro: Franklin Meadows. He'd told her to call anytime if she ever wanted help. *Let's see if he meant it.*

As she prepared to punch his number, the indie-comm pinged. A new, urgent message from Clayton appeared on the screen: *Have you found the girl?*

Atteberry

ATTEBERRY STEPPED FROM THE REAR OF THE TRUCK into a deserted alley surrounded by decrepit factory warehouses in various stages of decay. His injured leg, although healing, continued firing needles through his nerve endings as he followed Janet and the guards through a solid metal door into a cavernous, dimly lit storage area. Their hands remained cuffed in front of them. Helga and Winter came next with Mary, maneuvering her antigrav cot across the concrete and into the building.

The sight of those bastards hauling her around like cheap luggage infuriated him. Atteberry wasn't familiar with violent emotions, but he vowed under his breath the moment he got the chance, he would crush their skulls under his boot.

The warehouse smelled of grease and rubber. Some pigeons roosting in the high ceiling flapped and cooed at being interrupted and flew through the dust motes and streaks of daylight from broken windows, coming to rest on an iron beam on the far wall. The stench of their shit was palpable. Overturned chairs speckled the floor, along with scraps of paper and a desk—probably where a foreman sat once upon a time—and various doors on the left-hand side led to a handful of small, individual offices, some with windows, some without.

Winter, in a gentle voice, said, "Bind the woman to the water pipe in that corner. Don't take your eyes off her." He motioned to Helga to take Mary there as well and stay with her. "Make sure the girl is secure, too. It's unclear what she's capable of doing. The moment she regains consciousness, I want to speak with her."

"What the hell's going on?" Atteberry said, panic rising in his voice. "I thought you wanted to get to the airport."

"Winter gazed absently at the ceiling. "All in due time, Herr Professor. "First, we must talk."

"What do you mean 'talk'?"

"Come with me. Let's see if we can reach a . . . mutual understanding."

"I'm not leaving M—"

A goon slammed the butt end of his weapon into Atteberry's kidneys and he buckled over.

"Let's not make this difficult, Herr Professor. Georg is not your friend, and he hasn't eaten in a while."

The guard grabbed Atteberry's cuffed hands and twisted them before pushing him to the first enclosed office. Winter turned on the light and pointed to the one chair. "Sit."

"Not until you—"

Georg slammed him down on the chair and slugged him across the cheek.

"You are making this so difficult, and it needn't be."

Atteberry grunted and stared daggers at Winter, hate building like an overloaded circuit ready to explode.

"Tell me about the *Echo*. How does she fly so damn fast?"

"I know . . . nothing about that ship. I'm not an engineer." He spat some blood on the floor.

Winter raised his eyebrows and Georg, not missing a beat, grabbed Atteberry's right thumb and folded it back against the joint. He shrieked in pain until he shouted, "Okay! Okay, I'll tell you what I did, what I saw." Georg released his grip and flashed a mouthful of chipped teeth.

For the next ten minutes, Atteberry sputtered out what he remembered from the rescue mission to Luna. Winter interrupted him only once, when he recalled how Mary left the alien ship and Kate had remained aboard. He leaned against the office wall, expressionless.

After several moments of silence, he asked, "What about the voyage home from Luna? How did the *Echo* evade the firepower of the *Sara Waltz*?"

Atteberry hesitated until Georg stepped toward him. "I don't understand how it happened," he said, his voice rising. "All I saw. . . Mary did something and apparently that made us invisible to your ship. Someone said we'd shifted out of space prime but I can't remember."

"And where did Mary get this power? Is it from the alien?"

"Yes, I'm telling you that's why she needs this operation we're supposed to do this morning."

"Where is the alien now?"

"I have no idea."

"Don't lie."

"I—I'm not! Clayton Carter and the others kept talking about faster than light technology, but I know nothing about that."

Winter curled his lip. "But you understand subspace communications. And the girl does too, yes?"

Atteberry remained silent.

"I'd like to discover what else she knows, and that's why I'm taking her to Munich for a . . . cleansing."

"What's that?"

"You may recognize it as mind-scraping. It's a tricky procedure, but we extract the knowledge we require from her brain, while leaving her substantial memories intact."

Fear crossed Atteberry's face.

"Yes, now you understand, Herr Professor. We both want the same thing. Dr. Palmer was preparing a similar procedure until he chose not to cooperate. You see, there's no need for us to fight. We should solve this problem together."

"I don't . . ." He shook his head in disbelief. Was Winter offering him a fresh chance to save Mary's life? He understood mind-scraping and the damage it inflicted on people's brains, but if a chance existed to siphon off the alien mind and restore Mary's health, he couldn't object. Perhaps the Prussians had found a less invasive way.

"Regardless," Winter continued. "I'm done with you." Then to Georg, "Return him to the others, secure him there, and go eat."

Georg grunted and lifted Atteberry out of the chair, pushing him through the office door. Janet lay on the concrete floor, her cuffed arms above her attached to a thick pipe. She looked up as Atteberry approached. Mary remained unconscious on the cot, covered in a thin blanket. Helga rested on a stool by the window. The guard slung some chain around his cuffs and secured him to the pipe beside Janet. He gave them a yank, and marched out the warehouse, nodding at Helga.

"What'd he do, Jim?"

Atteberry sighed. "He wanted to learn about the *Echo*, but I don't know how the thing flies. And he focused on Mary and how she made the ship disappear. He plans to scrape her mind and extract that information without damaging her own memories. That'll help her get better, won't it?" He watched her shift around. Janet's face looked ragged and worn now. Deep bruises blossomed on her cheeks. Not quite the way he remembered her, but he didn't care.

"Mary still sleeping?"

"Yeah," Janet said in a lowered voice, she added, "We can't let him take her to Munich."

"Why not?"

She struggled to find the words. "Because mind-scraping is torture, Jim. There is no clean method. One reason Palmer needed the TSA's quantum computer was to capture the alien memories while preserving Mary's brain. That doesn't happen in scraping. The process destroys fundamental brain activity."

"I don't understand."

"If he goes through with this, and Mary somehow survives the flight to Europe, he plans to extract what he wants and leave her in a vegetative state." She paused. "I've seen how it's done, Jim. There's nothing left of the . . . patient."

"That's why he's never mentioned the need for the quantum memory." He hung his head and inhaled. "We have to stop him." He tugged at the chain holding his cuffed hands to the pipe.

"We must do more than that."

"What do you mean?"

"Winter isn't the only motherfucker after her. No one can scrape her mind, Jim. And there's only one way to prevent that."

"Right, get out of this place, find another doctor and save her."

"No."

"Then what?" Dread again bubbled in his gut.

Janet paused and set her mouth. "Mary herself must die."

Before he could process the words, his daughter stirred from her cot. "Dad?"

"I'm here, Mares."

"I—We overheard your conversation."

His shoulders slumped, and he threw Janet a horrified look. "I'm so sorry you had to hear that. I won't let them kill you, Mares."

"Please, Dad, listen." Mary struggled to raise her head and face him. "Janet's right. *Mom's* right."

"Hm?"

"You must kill us . . . before it's too late."

TWENTY-TWO

Winter

WINTER EMERGED FROM THE INTERROGATION ROOM with a wry smile on his face. He waved Helga over to join him outside the office door. The woman towered over him, keeping a sharp eye on Mary and the others. He liked that.

"How is the fraulein?"

Helga screwed her face up and said, "The girl is a resilient creature, Herr Winter. Drops in and out of consciousness. I've pumped her with painkillers and medicine, and vital signs are stabilizing."

"Can she travel?"

"No, she is far too weak. Her bio-signs are not sufficiently strong."

"But stable, yes?"

"Yes, Herr Winter, however, not improving. We must wait another few hours."

He spat and wiped his mouth with a handkerchief. That wouldn't do. "I would prefer to interview her now."

Helga bristled. "I cannot recommend that. She is incapable of being questioned."

"Then get her in shape with more stimulant. I should like to speak with her now."

"But—"

He stared into her deep green eyes. "No 'buts'", he asserted calmly. "Pump her up and bring her to me."

"Yes, Herr Winter, right away."

She marched back to the corner and opened a med kit, poked around, and retrieved a hypospray. The father protested, asking questions, but Frau Chamberlain remained silent. The once powerful mercenary that caused so much torment over the years slumped on the floor, beaten.

Winter returned to the office and drew his indie-comm from a pocket. After scrolling through the messages, he stopped and opened one from Cornelia: *Med team in place. Too dangerous to use Sara W. shuttle. Must take a charter. Arranging now. Will keep you apprised.*

He pursed his lips and considered the timing. He trusted Cornelia and made a mental note to see her again socially upon his return. Perhaps they could still repair their fractured relationship despite the difference in corporate status. Perhaps he had broken it off prematurely. His mind drifted to their weekend in Paris a couple years ago.

Helga rapped softly on the doorjamb. She held Mary by the waist and guided her onto the chair, then prepared to leave.

Winter intervened. "Please, Helga, remain here with the girl."

"Thank you, Herr Winter," she said, her face softening. She grabbed another chair from outside the room and placed it beside the fraulein.

Mary lifted her head, gazed at Helga with confusion, and turned to him. "I'm not . . . where are we?" She surveyed the room, mumbling.

"Hit her again with the stimulant, please."

Helga hesitated.

"I won't ask a second time."

She pulled the hypospray from her shirt pocket, placed it on the girl's neck and pressed the plunger. Mary blinked rapidly and, in a moment, shook her head as if fighting off a shiver, then fixed her gaze on Winter. Helga scanned her vitals on a portable data slate.

"Welcome back."

"Where are we?"

"Fear not, Fraulein Mary. You're among friends here." He rolled his tongue over his teeth. "I will ask a few questions, and you shall answer them."

She glared at him, then attempted to get out of the chair, but her legs wouldn't hold her weight, and she collapsed back down. Helga placed her hand over hers.

"But—we need to leave for the surgery. Dad . . . there's a surgeon from New Houston coming. We have to hurry."

"Yes, and the medical team is standing by. But before that, I must learn certain things. As a precaution, you understand."

"Where's Dad?"

"Please, Fraulein, I shall ask the questions. Time is of the essence and if we're to save you, I require complete cooperation."

She lowered her eyes. "Okay."

Winter circled around in front of her, tenting his fingers. "Danke, now I should like to learn what happened on the alien vessel when you and Braddock were abducted."

Mary's mouth fell open. "No . . ."

"Please, Mary, it's for your own good. The surgeons must hear everything."

"We can't."

Winter considered his next words. "Let me clarify the situation then. If you don't explain what happened, I shall relieve my frustration on your father. Do you understand *that?*"

Mary's face remained unchanged but her eyes softened.

"So tell me exactly what happened when the creature seized you."

She gulped. "We weren't taken against our will. The alien, Keechik, saved us."

"How so?"

"Kate and I were running out of oxygen, trying to find an entrance into that ship . . . a portal or hatch . . . anything. I passed out and when I woke up, I was inside the vessel."

"And the Braddock woman?"

"Yes. We were separated at first because—"

Her head dropped. Helga stroked her hand and said, "It's all right, Mary, you're doing fine."

Tears filled her eyes. "He attached me to a neural device, and I interfaced with . . . a strange network. Keechik's entire record, all his memories, all his knowledge transferred into me."

"Curious. Why?"

"He's the last of his kind. All he wished to—" she swallowed hard and cleared her throat. "He wanted to preserve his civilization's history."

"Why you and not Braddock?"

"I'm eidetic. I can't forget something once I've seen it. His memories are as fresh to me now as my own, as if I've lived . . . we've lived multiple lives."

Winter continued pacing, hands behind his back. "So you have absorbed everything the alien knows, yes?"

"Yes. I mean, I'm trying to understand everything, but my brain . . . I can't process it. Our memories are merging, but it's all jumbled. I'm struggling to figure out what's me and what's him."

"Fascinating!"

"Please, we must get the surgery done or both of us will die."

"Where is the alien ship now?"

Mary blinked a few times, then said, "We cannot say. The real Keechik is still on it, I believe."

"But where?"

Mary's voice raised. "I don't know!" She slumped over.

Winter glanced at Helga.

"More stimulant, please."

She implored him to stop, but he focused on getting the answers he needed. She sighed and pumped the hypospray into Mary's neck again. The girl twitched and shook.

"Now then," he continued, "if this alien's mind is part of you, is that how you shifted space-time?"

"How do. . .?"

"Ah, I know more than you realize."

She bit her lip.

"And you can still do this? Don't lie, Fraulein."

"Yes," she whispered.

Winter stopped pacing and bent down in front of her, glaring. He grabbed her chin. It felt cold and clammy. "Tell me, do you understand how the alien ship travels faster than the speed of light?"

She nodded, tears pooling, her face turning white.

Winter hadn't counted on this, but in his hand was all the knowledge required to establish the Consortium as man's future. All he needed to do was extract it before her body decayed.

"But I can't—we can't survive without the operation."

"Of course, Fraulein, I understand." Winter's indie-comm pinged, and he punched open the message from Cornelia: *Charter standing by. SF Int'l. Hangar 13.* He motioned to the bio-signs device. Helga glanced at it and pursed her lips.

"Can she travel now?"

"I—I wouldn't risk it yet, Herr Winter."

He straightened his back, and stroked Mary's sweat-laden hair. In a gentle voice, slow and deliberate, he said, "More stimulant. Then we shall go."

Janet

ATTEBERRY LOOKED TO HER WITH HATE-FILLED EYES. "What do you think he's doing?"

He spoke in a low voice, even though Helga remained in Winter's office and Georg hadn't returned from lunch. As if it mattered. Despite several attempts to find a weak spot in their chains and mag-cuffs, he and Janet weren't going anywhere.

"She's too important an asset to harm, so he's likely asking lots of questions, trying to figure out what she knows, what else she can do." Janet shifted on the floor and grimaced. "The way she's half out of it, though, I doubt he's learning much."

She explored the inside of her broken mouth with her tongue, imagining her face had swollen into a grotesque caricature. She threw a brief, apologetic smile, then continued testing the cuffs. He was determined to save Mary, that was clear. But Janet understood the larger stakes. Her assessment—and Mary's agreement—that she must die rather than go through whatever experimentation Winter had planned was the only goal now. Palmer was the surgeon capable of understanding the procedure that might save her life, so Winter likely had something more planned for her in Munich. Mind-scraping, to be sure, but what else?

She shrugged. Wouldn't matter. Once the fucker got what he wanted, he'd discard whatever remained of Mary's body and brain like dinner scraps. No way could she let that happen. Yet, if they somehow escaped this mess, assuming the worst, she'd turn around and put a bullet in Mary's head and not think twice. Mary's life, and the knowledge she held, would be sacrificed for the good of the planet and human race. Madness, certainly, but the Prussians could not be allowed to dictate scientific evolution.

She had to die.

We need to drink.

No. If she's going to escape, she'd have to do it by herself and keep Jim out of it. Despite the messed-up feelings, she didn't trust him for this.

"What're you thinking about, Jim?"

In the old days, he struggled with telling the truth, but perhaps he'd changed. Their shared history and current predicament interfered with her ability to process his actions. He wanted to protect Mary, but if anyone had the know-how to escape successfully, it was Janet.

"I want to save Mary, even if it means she dies naturally in my arms with me."

She squirmed and said, "Believe it or not, this is difficult for me, too. After all, she's still my daughter."

He opened his mouth to protest, but she cut him off. "Sure, I get it. We don't have any sort of relationship, and I'd never claim to be a parent to her, but please understand how I've struggled with my choices, too. Putting my values and principles before her welfare. Before you."

"What is this, some kind of last-minute expression of remorse? Guilt?"

"I had no choice, Jim."

He fumed. "Bullshit. You could have said 'no' to whoever you worked for. You could've dropped out of that sordid business, or at least have been honest with us. But no, you simply disappeared in the night without a word like a goddamn shadow."

Silence enveloped their corner of the warehouse. Helga's voice rose from the office, but her words were indistinguishable, spoken in a foreign language. Then the metal door to the street swung open and Georg entered. He sauntered toward them, grabbed Helga's stool and sat, watching them, picking his teeth.

Janet continued working the cuffs even though Atteberry no longer tried. Despite the circumstances, she would never give up. "This may seem ridiculous, but if we're finally having an honest conversation, I'm telling you, I had no choice but to leave."

"Janet, for the love of god, what were we supposed to think?" He lowered his voice, but Georg remained obtuse, unconcerned. "Why didn't you tell me, or leave a note, or call? Those days were so dark. I went crazy with worry. Mary pulled out a mitt full of hair follicles one by one in some bizarre response to being abandoned. Took months for her to adjust. All you needed to do was tell us you were okay." He shifted his leg, flinched, and continued. "Anyway, I suppose it doesn't matter. That was all in the past and we've moved on. But don't you dare say you had no choice."

Janet frowned, debating whether to respond. The spider scratched and picked at her mind, reminding her of its omniscience. She shook it off. Then, glancing away, she whispered in a ghostly, unrecognizable voice, "They threatened to kill her in front of me, Jim."

"What?"

"I didn't want to leave you. I tried negotiating with them, find a desk job or do something peripheral, but they wouldn't listen. Said they needed me for the field ... what I'd signed on for in the first place, and what I *was* good at."

"Wait, they did what?"

"The squad leader was in on it. I'd find little clues that they'd been in the house, in Mary's room. At her school. I suspected one of her teachers was watching me. Anyway, as you say, all in the past but understand, they swore me to secrecy, and to never contact you or Mary again. Even years later, I still found gruesome reminders of the deal. Photos in my kit. Video of Mary playing in the yard ... things like that."

He lowered his head, processing her words.

Janet peered at him sheepishly. "They relaxed the protocol at one point before Mount Sutro, but that's the way it was back then. None of us had any real, practical choice, Jim. I saw what they did to a colleague who broke. They stripped the muscle off her mother's bones in front of her. Recorded the damn thing and forced the rest of us to watch, over and over and over. Did it for sport."

"But ... but I thought you were the good guys ... the morally incorruptible?"

"There are no good guys in this business, Jim. No bad guys, either. Just us and them."

Jim shook his head.

"I did what was necessary to protect my ... family."

He stared deeply into her eyes. "God damn you."

Janet slammed her cuffed wrists against the pipe anchoring them to the wall. Georg peered up from his chair and grinned. "Wallowing in the past won't help now, and I can't figure a way out of these yet."

"Perhaps there's another solution."

She snorted through her swollen face. "Well, are you still built like that? An optimist, I mean?"

Jim swung his head toward the room where Mary's inquisition continued. He'd always been an idealist for as long as she'd known him. His desire to share the Ross 128 signal with the world in '85 was born of it, but she had a better understanding of how evil truly operated.

"Kate used to remind me that the world wasn't as kind as I'd hoped. She'd rein me in constantly. But I've lost that innocent belief in humanity, that fundamentally, we are marvellous creatures all wanting simple things: a chance to work, a safe place to raise our loved ones." He looked around. "If Winter's fancy mind-scraping surgeons can save her, perhaps it's best to go along with them so I can get Mary back."

She wasn't prepared to play those odds.

Then, as silence blanketed their conversation, the office door clicked and swung open.

TWENTY-THREE

The Mergeling

WHY DID YOU DO THIS TO US?

Mm ... if we return in time and choose another way, we would. We regret this now.

How do we talk like this?

We, the Keechik, is not real. We are a ... simulacra. We combine all thoughts and construct speech from that.

A pause. Motion.

We move again.

Yes.

We must destroy them all.

Yes.

Janet

HELGA LED MARY BACK TO HER COT. Her ashen face hadn't changed, but her eyes seemed sharper, taking in her surroundings, and she appeared steadier on her feet. Her fingers twitched, a known side effect of neural stimulant she'd seen many times in the field. After helping Mary lie down, she covered her with the blanket and checked vitals on her data slate.

Mary acknowledged Janet, then focused on Jim. He yanked on his mag cuffs and asked, "Are you okay, Mares?"

"Yes . . . just tired," she said, lifting her head, sounding like her old self.

"What did they do—"

"Please, Herr Professor," Helga interrupted, "the girl must lie down. She is full of stimulant but it will wear off soon and she needs rest for the flight."

Winter emerged from the office. "Ah, Georg, you are well-fed now?"

"*Ja.*"

"Good. I should like to have a conversation with Frau Chamberlain. Bring her to me in ten minutes. I need to arrange a few things first."

"Yes, Herr Winter."

The Prussian pulled a pair of black leather gloves from his back pocket and a long, thin knife — a Gerber Mark IV — from a sheath at his side, stared at Janet and grinned sadistically. But she met his stare, defying him, daring him, and smirked. He turned and closed the door.

She lowered her head, cursing for not being better prepared. The previous night in the cabin had been too easy. She wondered if her drinking had affected her judgment beyond her comfort zone. Winter wasn't the type of man to back off. Although she hadn't encountered him personally until New Houston, his reputation as a ruthless strategist and indefatigable, persistent killer was well known throughout the NDU operative community. And she'd become soft, lazy, less attentive. And old.

No wonder they're pushing me out. I'm a threat to my team now.

She shifted again and peered at Jim. He remained fixated on Mary, a helpless yet determined look on his face. And in that moment, with Mary dying on some prehistoric, antigrav cot, attended to by a nurse with massive forearms, and her ex-husband sprawled on the floor, an overwhelming peace embraced her. From what? Surely, Winter planned to torture, then kill her. On its own, she could handle that: she'd prepared for this scenario since she was 15. The peace did not derive from some arbitrary training or acceptance of the inevitable. No, this was something more.

Perhaps because the end of her life was near, she relieved the burden that had nagged her ever since she first met Jim and escalated when they married and brought Mary into the world. The secrets, the lies, the subterfuge . . . all added to her internal misery like the seed of a childhood regret growing over time, a black pearl of remorse, the feeling of being trapped by her own history that she could never forsake. But, having shared the truth with Jim, after confiding in the man she once loved with all her heart, the burden dissipated. She felt lighter, despite what lay around the corner. Coming clean held more value than she ever believed possible, as if some providential plan unfolded.

"Helga," she asked in a gentle voice, "will she make it?"

The woman's face showed concern, and she shrugged her shoulders.

So she's a caregiver first, not a merc.

Mary fidgeted on the cot to get comfortable. Janet had seen this reaction many times, not only in others but in herself too. There were missions where her entire squad had juiced up on adrenaline and other mind-altering stimulants to undertake the dirty work needed to preserve order in the world. One particular time when Mary was about four, in England, her leaders ordered her to destroy an elementary school harboring a Russian strategic comms unit in the basement. The only way to take it out was during the day when the children were in class. She protested, seeing Mary in every kid running in the schoolyard, but her orders were clear. The team needed more than juice for this: they loaded up on meth and slaughtered every kid and teacher in the way before torching the basement. She shuddered at the memory, as vivid as if it happened yesterday.

"What did you give her?"

Without looking up from her data slate, Helga answered, "60 CCs of standard polyamphetamine."

"That much? Jesus . . ."

She sighed, resignation crossing her face.

"I don't understand," Jim said.

Janet stated, "A normal daily max for an injured person is 20 CCs."

He yanked hard on his cuffs, catching Georg's attention. "Is it . . . safe?"

"The next half hour is critical," Helga offered. "Please, no more questions. The fraulein must rest."

Several minutes passed in silence save for the cooing and wing-flapping of the pigeons in the rafters. Mary was in no shape to travel, and it seemed Helga realized that. Perhaps that's what she and Winter had discussed when they heard her voice in the office a while ago. Freedom was her only goal now, and Jim, not thinking straight, injured leg, would only slow her down. She clenched her teeth, grimaced at the pain shooting through her jaw, and came to the only logical decision available: she would have to escape alone, retrieve her indie-comm (wherever that was) and contact any available NDU agents in the area. Then, with their help, take out Winter and save Mary and Jim. And, if necessary, murder her daughter.

Unfortunately, the mag-cuffs were solid and the chain holding her bound wrists to the factory pipe showed no sign of yielding at any pressure points. Even if she broke free, the separation between her, Georg, Winter and, yes, Helga was impossible to overcome. She may kill one by the element of surprise, but not all three. An escape would require a statistically enormous amount of luck, an element of dubious reliability in any operation, and one she preferred to be absent.

She would have to release her dependence on the desired outcome and place her fate in the hands of random chance. To do nothing was not an option she could abide.

"What are you thinking about, Jan?"

Jim's voice startled her. "Hm? Oh, ghosts of missions past." She smiled at him. "You holding up okay?"

He returned her smile, and in that minor act, more of those dormant memories erupted in her and masked the fear and pain coursing through her body. Although forever a mystery to her, she could not doubt what this moment, heightened by the near-death reality they faced, meant. Clarity replaced fear. Awareness overcame uncertainty.

She loved him and knew she always had.

Without speaking, Janet caught his attention. The lump forming in her throat was the sweetest pain she'd known in years, killing the words that struggled to emerge. Across the three meters dividing them, they connected and all time and space dissipated in a flurry of raw emotions.

He returned her gaze with a tenderness she hadn't experienced for years, and nodded before pulling away, shoulders slumping.

TWENTY-FOUR

Carter

THE SLEEK, DUAL-ENGINE TITANIUS HELI-JET cruised at 3500 meters above the Eastern Seaboard in a northerly direction toward Nova Scotia and CFB Shearwater, where the *Echo*, undergoing repairs in her underground hangar, awaited Clayton Carter's inspection.

Gusts of wind buffeted the aircraft, jostling him out of his reverie. He pressed his mic. "How much longer, Samantha?"

The young pilot turned and spoke into her mouthpiece. "Another ten minutes, sir. We're fighting headwinds and that's delaying us slightly."

"Very good."

Carter opened up his indie-comm and punched a secure channel to the *Malevolent* in space above him. Wallace, the comms officer—someone he hadn't met officially but knew Laura trusted—answered his hail and summoned Captain Russo. When she appeared on screen, he noted the concern etched across her face. He didn't waste any time. "Laura, what's the current situation?"

Russo stood on the bridge facing him. Behind her, various officers and personnel worked their stations in what Carter could only describe as controlled chaos. "No change, Clayton. We've spoken with Ed Mitchell and a few of his Ops team about the plan and, frankly, I'm not as optimistic about it as I'd like to be."

"Oh? Any particular reason?"

"Well, yes." She sounded annoyed, but the quick grin on her face assuaged his rising defensiveness. "Yes," she said in a softer, firmer tone. "The challenge with high stakes poker is some idiot will call your bluff. What I mean to say is that I can feign having a . . . a suicidal corbomite-type device on board, for example, but guaranteed there's a jumped up maverick out there wanting to make a name for himself and will challenge me."

"That is the nature of the game, Laura, and it's up to us to play our part authentically."

She paced around her command chair. "Naturally, and believe me, I'm well-versed at role-playing. But if some wing-nut fires on us—and no one has yet—then what? We might take a few of those smaller craft down before the Prussian cruisers eat our lunch." Something grabbed her attention. "It's not exactly the way I prefer to leave this life."

Carter gazed out the window. Clouds billowed on the eastern horizon, borne on the high winds. Something nasty tumbled toward them. "I hear you, Laura, but we should cross that bridge when we get there." She protested, but he raised his deep voice and cut her off. "In the meantime, where's the enemy fleet?"

Russo scowled. "The convoy's en route, approaching our coordinates at the same velocity as before. We count 18 and three of those are heavies. We're standing our ground, Clayton." She glanced around. "For now."

"Where's the rest of our own ships?"

"The two closest martian security cruisers are a day out. Five more heavies from the Saturn loop are hoofing it, but even at top velocity, they won't turn up for several days. If we can hold off the convoy until the martian ships arrive, we might have a fighting chance."

Carter's mood soured. He didn't want another close encounter with the Prussians, not when he needed time to investigate the alien ship site on Luna, but Laura was right: some of those ambitious, hotdog captains wouldn't hesitate launching an old school nuclear torpedo at the *Malevolent* for kicks. He had to introduce the *Echo* into the game and create a distraction.

"The good news," Russo added, "is that the *Sara Waltz* is mired in space dock at the New Houston elevator. Their damage must be more substantial than we assessed. The *Volmar* is nevertheless in front of us, matching our course corrections perfectly."

"A bit of a respite. Excellent. Has there been any contact with either vessel?"

"Negative. We've picked up routine chatter from various ships, but nothing unusual." She looked off screen. "Stand by, Clayton."

Russo's Comms officer approached her with a data slate. They studied it for a moment, Russo nodding, then he left and she returned to the viewer. "I may have spoken prematurely."

"Tell me more."

"Ensign Wallace received some low level, encoded messaging between the *Volmar* and several of the convoy ships . . . in particular, the lead science vessel flying under the Indian banner. Seems the fish has taken the bait."

"Mitchell's bluff?"

"Yes. There's growing concern about engaging the *Malevolent* . . . they're worried that we've incorporated alien tech into our systems, specifically, in weapons." The relief on her face and throughout her body was palpable.

Carter relaxed and leaned back into his flight seat. "Ed Mitchell is clever. They must have intercepted his decoy messages."

"There's more, Clayton." Russo, hands on hips, barked at an unseen bridge crew member, and continued. "The convoy is reducing speed. Apparently, the science vessels want to investigate us further. We're being scanned. Nothing critical. They can't penetrate our hardshields, but I'll let them peek at a few ghost systems full of mazes. That'll give them something to worry about when they discover all the encrypted networks throughout the ship."

"Explain."

Russo focused on the screen, full of confidence now. "We took Mitchell's bluff a step further and established false systems on the ship. These are coded networks with random file generators, mockups of schematics . . . actually, all kinds of insignificant things. We'll make those science vessels work for their access, but once they scan the ghosts, they'll have no clue what any of them mean. They're a rabbit warren of mis-information."

"Brilliant!"

"I must caution you, however. They may see through the ruse in short order. The professional crew of the *Volmar* won't chase shadows for too long, but if we can keep them running scared until the martian cruisers arrive, then we're in a far better tactical position."

"Understood, Laura." He needed the ship's data for the *Echo*, and said, "Send me your telemetry post-haste. I'd like to share it with Captain Powell."

"Stand by a minute for transmission."

The heli-jet pilot broke in on the flight channel to announce they'd be landing in a few minutes and to prepare for rapid descent. "And as a heads up, sir, the cross-winds are brutal near the surface. Be sure to remain buckled in."

The aircraft veered west and adopted its landing pattern, dropping out of the sky over the city of Halifax. The aircraft shuddered in the heavy gusts as it descended vertically over CFB Shearwater, and for a moment, Carter wondered if they'd be slammed into the ground like a meteorite. But the pilot showed her skills in maneuvering the craft gently over the final hundred meters and, despite the knee-knocking turbulence, brought the heli-jet to rest on its designated pad.

The *Malevolent* telemetry file transfer ended and before signing off, Carter said one more thing to Captain Russo. "All we need is a few hours and the *Echo* will be in flight. I'm certain she'll get the attention of that convoy and between the two of us, we'll give 'em a damn fine show."

"Acknowledged. Let's hope time is on our side. Godspeed, Clayton. *Malevolent* out."

Esther

THE SPACE OPERATIONS LAB IN THE BOWELS of the TSA remained quieter than usual with Esther in the room and the public dressing down that Mark Jefferson experienced from Dr. Kapoor. *He'll get over it . . . eventually, but now I've got to get the quantum computer prepped for Mary's operation.* She grimaced as she removed her jacket and pulled a stool up to the Q's control panel. *Strange that Jim hasn't checked in.* A flash of panic crept into her bones and she shook it away, refusing to give in to the possibility that something had gone horribly wrong. *And then there's Clayton . . . I can't ignore him much longer.*

From the time she'd left a v-mail with Sergeant Meadows to now, Clayton had messaged her twice inquiring about Mary, but until she knew her whereabouts—and condition—she avoided discussing the matter with him. Not because she was being coy or engaged in a power play; rather, she doubted her desire to continue working with him, to bring Mary to his side. True, she hated being kicked around and played by anyone, but after she dabbled in looking out for herself first, she didn't like what she was becoming, and the episode with Kapoor and Mark underlined her ability to be strong without being cut-throat. And, piercing through the noise of the entire affair—the Ross 128 signal, the rescue mission on Luna, the alien mind that inhabited Mary's brain—she still liked Jim and preferred helping him to save Mary before anything else.

The Q's operating system was a technological disaster since she torpedoed the Deep Space experiment. Back-up systems continued functioning, but the key relational networks were either offline or completely out of sync. It would take a couple of hours to prepare it for new mountains of data.

As she initiated the overall reboot, her indie-comm pinged. Esther glanced at the screen, and quickly answered the device.

"Dr. Tyrone, it's Sergeant Meadows returning your call. How's business at the TSA?"

She peered around the lab. No one within earshot. "Oh, you know how it is, always something fascinating taking place. Listen, Agent, time is brief so I'll get right to the reason I called. Remember the Mount Sutro event and the alien signal?"

"I do. Has there been recent contact?"

She hesitated, then stated, "Yes. And it's complicated as hell." Esther explained all the events that had taken place since Mary Atteberry began working on Luna with Kate Braddock, including how the alien had transferred its knowledge and memories to her, and how the *Echo* avoided a disaster with the Prussians on the way home. "Now," she continued, "Mary's operation is supposed to take place this morning, here at the TSA. Apparently, they need the power of the Quantum computer, but admittedly, Agent, I'm worried. There's a lot of interest in her and what she knows, and someone may come after her or sabotage the network."

"That's understandable, Doctor. What do you have in mind for me and the CCR forces?"

She swallowed hard, knowing full-well she was overstepping her authority again, but determined to act on her instincts. "I wonder if you could send a few of your soldiers over to keep a watch on things and make sure no harm comes our way." She lowered her voice. "We have spies in here, of that I'm convinced, and your presence could be an important deterrent to any ideas they may have."

Meadows clucked his tongue. "We've heard the rumors too, ma'am, so thanks for calling. I can deploy a few agents to cover the entrances to the lab. I'll despatch them as soon as we're done."

"Wonderful, thank you."

"One more thing, Doctor."

"Yes?"

"I'm coming with them. I'll lead the team and pay close attention to any activity that even remotely looks suspicious."

Esther paused. She hadn't expected that. This man surely had more important things to do personally given the fragile political environment, and yet he planned on leading the security team? Something didn't feel right, but she couldn't place that fear and brushed it aside. "Sounds good, Agent. I look forward to seeing you again."

She ended the call as Mark Jefferson returned through the lab's main doors from his private meeting with Dr. Kapoor. He spotted her and marched over. His tie had come loose, and his face was flushed.

"I'm sorry, Mark. I had to do it."

He ignored her and checked the Q's operating screens. "I suppose we lost all the Deep Space data?"

"Not all. There's a remnant from the last couple hours of operation, before I shut it down."

He shook his head, clenching his teeth. Then, turning to her, he said, "You could have told me, Esther. You could have mentioned this was about the Atteberry kid and all that alien crap from Luna. I would've—"

Defiant rage blistered in her gut. "Would've done *what*, exactly?" She stood up and faced him squarely. "You had a chance to trust me, to open your eyes to what's unfolding here. Instead, you followed your rules, didn't want to upset a client or see one of your experiments get derailed even though I told you, *I told you* this was a life or death situation." She inhaled deeply and tempered her anger. Lowering her voice, she added through her teeth, "Don't you dare come back now and try pinning this on me."

The two scientists stared at each other. Esther's heart hammered at her ribs and her own face heated up. Finally, Mark lowered his gaze.

"Well, for what it's worth, Kapoor said the same thing. I suppose I have a lot to learn."

She relaxed. "We can still make this work, Mark. Help me prepare the Q for Mary's operation. You always were more skilled at manipulating this beast than me."

He unbuttoned his collar, yanking his tie away even more. "You've rebooted it?"

"Yes, I sat down right before you came in."

"How much memory does this, er, operation need?"

"I honestly have no idea, but it's not only that. I think they require the relational abilities of the network. From the mess I saw of Mary's brain at the hospital, time and quantity of data are the two primary concerns. They'll have to transfer a lot of material through multiple venues and into numerous repositories."

He adjusted the synchro pot on the console and watched as the Q's systems, one by one, returned online. "Do you think this'll work? I mean, when I consider the risks of interfacing the Q with a human being, I can't fathom how anyone would survive."

"I've no idea. No one does. Jim, her father, told me it was a long shot even with the proper facilities and top surgeons, but they're gone now and her only other alternative is sure death." She placed her hand on his forearm. "Mark, before this is over today, we may have a dead kid down here, a room full of soldiers protecting us from foreign and domestic enemies, and God knows who else all wanting a piece of her brain. But we must try. Her life is more valuable than . . . than the Deep Space experiment or which one of us leads this division. Can you see that?" She glanced around the cavernous lab and shrugged. "None of *this* truly matters. None of it."

The Mergeling

WE ARE ALMOST COMPLETELY ENTWINED NOW.

Yes. But there is more experience, more memory, with no physical place to go.

Why can we not save ourselves? We could eradicate those that would harm us.

Mm . . .you do not truly wish to destroy.

Keechik, if we are to preserve our history and make it available to other life forms in the universe, then we must survive. We must neutralize the human threats.

And where would it stop, the friend Mary?

We don't understand.

Suppose we eliminate the threat as we suggest. When do we perceive the absence of malice?

We . . . we do not.

Mm . . .

Unless . . .

Yes. They all must perish, for none of them is incapable of . . . mm . . . scraping our mind. Not one is above that. Not one.

Not even Jim.

No, not even Jim.

We do not wish to die. We yearn to return to the friend Mary.

TWENTY-FIVE

Winter

"THIS IS FAR MORE COMPLICATED THAN I HAD EXPECTED, Cornelia," Winter mused. "The girl is in no shape to travel . . . not yet, at any rate."

"Understood, Herr Winter. The surgical team is standing by in Munich, informing themselves about the operation."

He detected worry in her voice. "What's on your mind, *Schatz*."

"Herr Winter, I—"

"Please go on. I can always tell when you disagree with me." He listened to Cornelia's soft breathing.

"Mind-scraping is invasive, and the delicate nature of this procedure—one that has never been performed—has given the lead surgeon, shall I say, pause. They're arguing about additional computing power. Insisting on quantum efficiency." The encrypted connection between them crackled. "Without the machine at the Terran Science Academy, it may not be possible to preserve the data and the girl's life."

Winter hobbled around the small office, chewing his lip and scowling. Cornelia had arrived at the same conclusion that transporting the girl overseas would likely kill her before the operation could even take place. And, despite the proven methods for extracting information from recently deceased patients, the risk of losing what she carried in her brain increased with every passing minute. The glory of the Prussian Consortium beckoned him, drove him to continue scraping the girl's mind. If travel was out of the question, he needed to consider alternatives.

"Cornelia, how long would it take the team to come to California? I share your concerns, and this operation is far too important to leave to chance."

"Logistically, it is straightforward. However, we will then face the challenge of finding an appropriate hospital or medical center. You only have a handful of operatives with you, and the CCR forces are many and powerful."

"Yes, that remains an issue." He sneered, craving a cup of dandelion tea. "Well, leave it with me for now. Let's continue assuming Helga can prepare the girl for the flight and I'll make a call when the time to quit is upon us." He prepared to cut the link when she interrupted him.

"I suppose it is possible," Cornelia added, "for you to scrape her mind completely with the instruments Helga already possesses. The girl would not survive, of course, or if she did . . ."

The silence over the connection grew. Winter did not want to put Mary through the torture of full-on memory extraction, but Cornelia was right: it was a viable alternative.

"I'll give it consideration." Then, changing the subject, he asked, "What is the status of the *Sara Waltz*?"

"Yes, well, repairs are almost complete. She'll be fully capable of normal space flight within hours."

"Excellent. Finally, some good news. And the stand-off between the *Volmar* and the *Malevolent*?"

"The latest intel shows nothing has happened. We continue to stare them down. The convoy of Consortium-friendly ships is en route to their position and will arrive shortly."

"Excellent."

"However," she interrupted, "you should know the girl has apparently altered the *Malevolent*."

Winter stopped pacing. "How so?"

"Uncertain. We're trying to confirm what we've learned through intercepted messages, that the enemy has incorporated new alien technology in many of its systems, including weapons."

Winter resumed his path in the office. "Why am I only finding out about this now?"

"With respect, this is a recent event and before alerting you, the leadership here and on the *Volmar* preferred to confirm such rumors before taking action."

He clenched his jaw and narrowed his gaze. "All right. We must trust the captain on this one, but Cornelia, I want to learn everything about this . . . which systems, what messages, all of it. Do you understand me?"

She hesitated. "Yes, sir."

"Is there anything else?"

"The *Echo*."

"What about her?"

"Our agent in the tech crew in Shearwater informs me that she'll be ready to fly in an hour, two at the most."

"No doubt Herr Carter wants to protect the *Malevolent* at the stand-off. The *Echo*'s weapons are no match for our firepower or our numbers. He'd be wise to remain grounded."

"Perhaps," Cornelia added, "but our agent says they have secured additional weaponry on the ship, and Herr Carter himself plans to board her again. If he was strictly interested in a military intervention, it seems to me he should wish to stay in New York."

"Indeed. What could he be up to?"

"At this point, we don't know. But we can only assume he wants to return to Luna. Perhaps they have abandoned important data tubes or equipment at their destroyed lab site?"

"Or maybe he knows something about the alien vessel's whereabouts." He paused. "Nevertheless, we cannot worry about that now. The fraulein's knowledge is our priority."

"Yes, Herr Winter."

Then, flexing his fingers, he said, "If there's nothing else, Cornelia, I should like to have a conversation with Frau Chamberlain."

"Understood. I'll keep you apprised."

"*Danke.*"

Winter ended the call and considered contacting Captain Krause on the *Sara Waltz*. That cruiser in space dock must have a well-equipped medical bay and be better positioned to manage the girl's operation. Less travel, more protection. Before he hailed the ship, a knock interrupted him.

"Enter."

Georg swung the door wide and whispered, "Herr Winter, it has been ten minutes. Shall I bring the woman?"

"Yes, soldier." Adrenaline surged through his body at the prospect of crushing that agent who caused the Consortium immeasurable grief over the years. "I should like to have a pleasant chat with her."

He backed away, right into Helga, who had appeared behind him.

"Helga? Is something wrong with the girl?"

"If you please, Herr Winter, may I close this for privacy?"

He sighed and rubbed his forehead. "If you must."

Helga elbowed her way past Georg, entered, and clicked the door shut. "Sir, I insist we not move Mary. She is not well and—"

"Has her condition changed in the last few minutes?" he asked, with ice in his breath.

"Sir, it's the stimulant. She's absorbed so much and, although it allows her some limited functioning, it is killing her."

Winter stared at the nurse-agent, scrutinizing her face. "And you are certain of this because?"

"Please, Herr Winter, examine her bio-signs." She pulled the data slate from behind her and handed it to him. He swept through various pages and his frustration mounted.

"I do not understand why her vitals are diminishing like this. The stimulant should not have this effect." He looked at her suspiciously. "Are you sure you administered the correct dosage?"

Helga frowned. "Positive, sir." She sidled up beside him to point out a few markers in the data. "These signs, I expected. Here . . . and here. But her neural activity is in total chaos. I can only imagine this is affected by the alien mind within her brain."

Winter studied the data and noted the vast array of anomalous readings. "Is this alien consuming the host? Is that what we're seeing here?"

"Impossible to tell, sir. We don't know enough about it to hazard a guess, and I have no equipment on hand to confirm either way." Concern crossed her face. "The girl is dying, that's all I can say with certainty. I do not believe she'll live more than a few hours assuming she survives the effects of the stimulant."

Winter's rage grew like a black monster, a vicious animal churning in his gut. He sneered. "Very well. Keep monitoring her condition, Helga. I have some business to attend to with Frau Chamberlain that cannot wait."

"Yes, Herr Winter."

She turned to leave and before opening the door, he added, "Oh, and Helga. I should like to remain undisturbed unless the girl expires."

She motioned imperceptibly, then reached for the handle. He grinned coldly.

"Time to play."

Atteberry

THE SOUND OF GEORG'S CHAIR SCRAPING ACROSS the concrete floor pulled Atteberry from his reverie. The man fumbled for something in his pocket, then produced a handgun from his jacket. Georg's attention shifted between Winter's office, where Helga remained in conference with their keeper, and Janet.

The guard muttered as he approached her cautiously. "It is time, Frau Chamberlain."

"For what?" she whispered in a daze.

"Oh, I think you understand. Herr Winter grows irritated. He should like to speak with you."

Atteberry understood what was about to happen and instinctively tore at his chains with no effect. Mary, meanwhile, had slumped down on the cot.

Janet sighed and shifted to a kneeling position. "Well, let's get this over with."

"Thank you for your cooperation and understanding."

Atteberry panicked and snapped at her. "How could you give up like this, Jan? You understand what he'll do in there, and . . ." That this would likely be the last time he'd see her alive hit him like a sledgehammer. "Janet, I . . ."

"It'll be okay, Jim. Look, we all have this day coming. The only unknown factor is when, but make no mistake, death comes for everyone. Better to face it with dignity than go out mewling like a fucking coward." She glanced at Mary, shivering and twitching on the cot. "Sometimes it arrives when we're young. Sometimes when we're old. But it always comes."

Atteberry tried to rise, but flinched as fresh pain shot up his injured leg. He collapsed again and, knowing this was the end of her, at least he took some comfort from understanding the depth of feelings he still held, and that apparently she held for him too.

Georg approached with caution, as if he expected her to squeeze out of her cuffs any second and come at him, guns blazing. But her stolid face betrayed a look of resignation and fatigue, her swollen skin mottled and wavering between pale and ashen. Perhaps she welcomed the end now?

"Listen Frau Chamberlain, I shall release your cuffs and you will rise slowly. No funny business. Understood?"

She agreed and held her hands away from her chest. Georg drew the release pin from his pocket while holding the gun on her, aimed the device at the cuffs, and pressed the button. They buzzed and dropped from her wrists, dangling precariously on the chain that wrapped around the pipe. She grabbed the wall and pulled herself up, suppressing a groan as she straightened her back.

"Very good. Now if you please, put your hands behind your head and face me."

Janet complied, turning toward her captor, squeezing her shoulders. She glanced at Atteberry and threw him a half-smile. He couldn't bear it. *This is how she says goodbye?* "Please, Georg, don't do this. Let us go. I'm begging you."

The hulking man ignored him, keeping a watch on Janet. "Move slowly to the office."

She took a couple of tentative steps, feeling the weight on her legs and, as she began moving, she stumbled. Georg, reached out to grab her arm. In a rapid movement, faster than anything Atteberry had ever witnessed, she pulled a wire no thicker than fishing line from her sleeve and twisted her body behind Georg. In a flash, she laced the wire around Georg's neck and yanked. Hard. He squeaked, surprise washing across his face. His frightened eyes bulged as the garotte sliced into his larynx, destroying his vocal cords in an ungodly fountain of blood. His weapon fell to the floor and clattered. Janet used the man's own weight to increase the pressure on his neck. Before Atteberry processed what she'd done, Georg's face turned deep lavender. His eyes rolled to the back of his head, and he collapsed silently in a heap.

Janet kneeled on the man's throat, thrusting her body on it for what seemed an eternity. Atteberry cast furtive glances at the office and at the warehouse entrance, expecting any moment for the Prussian guard stationed outside to race in and kill them all. But he didn't. Helga's muffled voice in the room continued piercing the still air around him, and Mary's breathing remained steady, if not labored.

She rifled through his pockets, found the pin for the mag cuffs, and released Atteberry. Then, after retrieving their indie-comms and stuffing them in her pocket, she pulled a knife from its leather sheath, and a couple clips of rounds. Georg's body had fallen on the handgun.

She rolled him over, reached behind his chest, grabbed it and handed it to Jim.

"You know how to fire this?"

Atteberry turned the weapon over in his hand with a sheepish look. "The only gun I ever shot was on a range 20 years ago, but it doesn't appear the technology's changed much." He paused. "Shouldn't you take this?"

"No. I need stealth for what I'm doing," she whispered. "You stay here and protect Mary. If the guard outside comes in, don't hesitate. Kill him."

He protested, but Janet cut him off. "Solve your damn moral issues on your own time after we get out of this mess, but for now, do whatever you must to save her. Got it?"

"Yes."

"Winter's mine." She squeezed his shoulder, wiped the blood and sweat from her forehead, then crept across the warehouse to a stand of metal cargo containers lined up against the wall. Atteberry kissed Mary on top of her head and took up a position in front of her where he kept a watch on both the building entrance and the office door.

The voices fell silent. The click of the door caused Atteberry's heart to pump like a piston. He moved his fingers on the gun and waited.

Helga stepped out, surveyed the area, then jumped back into the room, slamming the door behind her. Janet raced around some containers and crossed the gap to a covered position. Muffled hollow sounds wafted toward Atteberry. When the door opened again, Helga exited with her hands up. "Please, I am unarmed. I only wish to check on the girl."

From the shadows in another part of the warehouse, Janet said, "Where's Winter?"

"He has left."

Cold sweat now covered Atteberry's palms as he watched Helga take a few paces toward him.

"I am a nurse, not a soldier, Herr Professor. I am unarmed. Please."

He didn't know what to do. Despite what Janet said, he couldn't kill an innocent person. He licked his lips and lowered the gun.

Movement in the shadows caught his attention, and Janet positioned herself beside the office door. She threw him a questioning glance, then turned aside.

Helga ambled toward the cot. "I should like to retrieve my slate with her bio-signs, if you please. It is in my pocket." She paused, hands high, waiting for Atteberry's agreement.

"Okay, but do it slowly. My beef isn't with you and I don't want to harm you, but I will to save Mary."

She lowered her right hand and reached into her pocket.

Atteberry, his weapon lowered, fixed his gaze on her hand. She hesitated. He looked at her face and caught a wispy smile. He returned it. Then, just as he relaxed, Helga drew a gun from her pocket. In the eternal moment where she raised it toward him, a dart-like object pierced the air with a *ffft* sound. Helga, her mouth suddenly agape, released the weapon, teetered on her heels, then collapsed on the floor where her head bounced twice on the concrete before coming to rest.

Atteberry gulped.

A thin, black-handled knife protruded from her neck at the spine.

Janet pulled out of her follow-through and tore through Winter's office, but returned moments later. Then cautiously, silently, she raced toward the fallen nurse, checked her pulse, and tugged at the knife until the flesh and bone released it with a slurping *thuck*.

Atteberry's stomach flipped, and before Janet said a word, he dropped to his knees and retched. After wiping his mouth on his sleeve, he uttered, "What . . . what just happened?"

"Winter's gone. Took off through a rear door behind the office. Florence Nightingale here was about to kill you, by the way."

"I don't understand."

"You're far too trusting, Jim Atteberry." She inspected Helga's weapon, then grabbed the data slate. "We've gotta move." She glanced around the warehouse. "The other fucker must know about us now."

"You threw a knife at her."

"Yes."

"Like it was nothing."

Janet stopped moving for a second and looked at him sternly. "That's right. It severed her spine." Then she stood up, grabbed the cot and shook Mary awake. "Mares, sweetie, we've gotta go."

"Hm?"

"Jim, help me. You get Mary up and walking. I'll take care of the guard."

He gathered his courage from a well he hadn't known, and roused his daughter, his mind pulling itself from a daze. The cumulative effect of killings and dangers had taken its toll, and he trembled in response to the shock, but determination also coursed through his body now. *This is what fighting back looks like . . . to fight for a cause you believe in.*

Janet reached the entrance leading outside. She crouched, pointing Helga's gun chest high, then swung the door open hard and pressed against the wall. She searched for a target, expecting a volley of bullets. Instead, no shot was fired. She pulled an indie-comm from her pocket while leaning against the entrance wall and punched it. Returning her gaze to Atteberry, she said, "Let's go," and he dragged Mary across the floor, her legs and feet unable to keep up with him.

Janet exited and moved to the left. When Atteberry saw daylight, his heart jack-hammering in his chest, he found her crouching behind a stand of squat metal containers and rusted garbage bins. Then she motioned for him to come.

Mary could barely hold herself upright. Most of the stimulant had worn off, but not the hallucinogenic effects, for she babbled at him as he threw her arm over his shoulder and grabbed her waist. She spoke gibberish, something about ancient moonscapes and blinding light in the heavens. No matter, when they arrived at Janet's location behind the bins, he released her and eased her to a sitting position on the ground.

"What now?"

"We wait. An agent's on his way to lift us and he's coming in hot."

"What happened to the other guard?"

Janet pursed her lip. "He could still be out there, hiding. But I suspect he left to protect Winter. They'll regroup and come after us soon enough, so we've gotta figure something out, Jim. I need time to think this through and clean myself up."

Atteberry grabbed the shaking fingers on his hand and held them tight.

Several minutes passed before a scratched and dented hovercar screamed down the alleyway to their location. The door popped open and a hand with an assault gun beckoned them.

"You and Mary go first. I'll cover you."

Atteberry picked her up in his arms. Her body was a dead weight now and for an instant, he couldn't detect her breathing, but a deep, forced rattle told him she was still alive. Janet fired shots randomly while he stumbled on his bad leg toward the car and placed Mary inside before scrambling in himself. Janet hopped in a second later and the moment she entered, the hovercar accelerated through the maze of boxes and abandoned machinery scattered throughout the lane.

The olive-skinned operative seemed barely old enough to shave, but he was all business as he secured Mary on a seat and cleared Helga's weapon. He paused briefly only when he saw the mess on Janet's face. As he continued helping Mary, he updated them on the situation. "Winter was last seen with another agent heading west, but we've lost him. Sat-comms is working on it, but so far, nothing."

"That op must be the other guard," she said. "What about our agents here, Mikos? Where are they?"

"They were made and bugged out an hour ago, moving north." He shoved Helga's weapon and ammo in a pocket, then lowered his voice. "CCR agents are crawling all over the place, ma'am."

"They know about us. Congressional intel was always state-of-the art." She peered out the window at the city skyline. "Are we safe for now?"

"Clear, yes ma'am, as long as Winter's in hiding."

"Then we need to get to the TSA. We've gotta secure their quantum computer for the operation and then find a neurosurgeon."

"There's more," Mikos said. "Word's out that you all are in town, ma'am. CCR ops have been chatting up a storm, trying to locate you."

She patted her face with a cleansing cloth from a first aid kit and shrugged. "I'm not important. We must get this procedure done. I don't want to think about the alternative right now."

Atteberry piped up. "But the surgeon was . . ."

Silence filled the car as it veered onto the skyway.

"Wait a minute," Janet said, her voice calm. "There was someone else in Dr. Elliot's inner circle, a physician in London. Her name came up a few times in those encrypted messages I read last night." She grabbed her indie-comm and scrolled through various screens. "There she is. Abigail Lamont. Based in Chelsea."

Mary groaned loudly and her eyes flicked open, shock etched on her face.

"Jim, call this Lamont woman and convince her to do the operation."

Janet handed the indie-comm, and he punched the number he found beside her name on an encrypted channel.

"Make them stop!" Mary screamed. "We can't . . ."

Mikos tossed a hypo of pseudophine to Janet, and she pumped the painkiller into her. Mary's face and body relaxed, and she slumped back in the seat.

"We can't keep feeding her drugs," Janet whispered, "or her liver will explode. We've got to stabilize her."

No one answered Atteberry's hail. Perhaps she was busy, or turned her unit off. Or was in hiding.

"Keep trying," Janet said, "We've gotta contact her."

Mikos uttered a Greek profanity and ran his fingers through his thick hair. He monitored his own device and frowned.

"What is it?"

"Sat-comms has picked up our boy Winter, ma'am."

"Where is he?"

"About a kilometer behind and moving fast."

Janet pulled her weapon up and prepared for an attack. Mikos commanded the hovercar to take an evasive route. The vehicle decelerated and burned off the skyway into a maze of rolling streets.

Atteberry glanced at his indie-comm. An encrypted message appeared: *who is this?*

"Got her!"

He messaged back with his name and explained briefly Mary's condition and the failed surgeries they'd planned with her colleagues to extract the alien's mind from hers. He finished with a desperate question: *Can you help?*

Several moments passed, but no answer appeared.

Atteberry sent another: *please, my daughter's dying.*

More time crawled by.

"Come on, dammit."

Lamont messaged: *Sorry, can't. I'm being watched.*

Please doc, you're our last hope.

Atteberry scanned the busy streets outside, all the normal people oblivious to what was happening. He brushed his hand across Mary's forehead and prayed silently. Still, Lamont didn't respond.

I'm begging you.

After what seemed like an eternity, Lamont finally responded: *I can't. Don't message me again.*

TWENTY-SIX

Janet

"SHE REFUSES TO HELP," ATTEBERRY SAID DESPONDENTLY.

Janet, desperate for a drink, had watched him closely for the past several minutes. His fingers continued trembling but the color in his skin returned and, if experience was any indication, he'd be over the initial shock of watching someone die in front of him soon. She'd forgotten how much of your soul death can rip from you.

But this doctor bowing out cut her. *This is exactly the problem we face in this world. Too many people unwilling to step up.* "Tell her I'm calling her in a minute on another encrypted channel, and she'd better pick up."

Atteberry typed the message into the indie-comm, then when Janet reached out her hand for it, he gave the device to her and refocused on Mary. Meanwhile, Mikos continued scanning the streets, checking the viewer on Winter's whereabouts, and commanding the hovercar to continue with chaotic course patterns. He pulled a small bottle from his pocket and handed it to her.

"Bless you." Janet downed two big gulps, wiped her mouth, and punched the device, waiting for the connection. A minute passed, but she kept the hail going until the familiar encryption beeps of a new contact appeared.

"Yes?"

She straightened her back and leaned forward. "Dr. Lamont, my name is Janet Chamberlain. You already know the details of what happened in New Houston, and now that some asshole murdered Dr. Palmer, you must worry you'd be next if you get involved."

Static crackled across the connection. A faint voice responded, "Yes."

"What you may not understand are the implications of your sitting on the sidelines while my daughter lies in front of me dying." She gulped, overcome by a strange, ancient sensation of protection toward Mary, something that had eluded her until this fiasco began. The booze started kicking in. "She has two minds, doctor. Her own, of course, but also this alien's memories, too. They're overwhelming her synaptic system and in effect, she has nowhere to store them in her brain. Moreover, she's eidetic."

"Oh?"

"Do you understand what that means?"

Lamont paused and stuttered. "I—I know that eidetics canna forget what they've seen. Most of us only keep scraps of our recollections, but she will experience them as if they happened yesterday."

Janet placed her accent as originating from Yorkshire. "Right, and because this alien was the last of its kind, the creature dumped everything it knew into her for that precise reason. Doctor," she continued, looking at Mary slumped and strapped in the hovercar's seat, "whatever memories this thing put in her are slowly torturing her to death. We must remove them."

A pause. "I'm sorry, but I—"

Janet pulled her shoulders back. "Hang on. This alien isn't some bug-eyed creature like you'd see in the movies. It gave Mary the knowledge and experience of a whole new world of physics, of medicine, you name it. I mean, she can heal others with a touch of her hand for crissakes. Manipulates space-time. There's a wealth of technology in her that would revolutionize our understanding of, well, everything."

"I had no idea."

"Listen, no one knows the extent, the breadth of information Mary holds. But I assure you there are evil forces who would love to exploit her for their own gains. And not just to build faster spaceships for mineral resource extraction. We're talking military, political, technological domination." She stared at Jim who now faced her, eyes fixed on the bottle in her hand. "We cannot let her fall into the hands of the Prussian bastards chasing her out there. But if we can save her, then at least she'll be able to protect herself."

A pause permeated the connection, followed by bursts of static. Then Lamont spoke, her voice reflecting more of a detached, scientific mind, a curious mind, one less prone to fear. "Dr. Elliot briefed me on the operation he planned for the wee bairn. I don't rightly know, but he seemed confident. Lewis Palmer had his own reservations, and I have mine. The biggest issue is where to put the alien's data. Robert wanted to syphon it off but we dinna believe that would be effective."

Janet shifted in her seat and stole a glance at the passing streets and alleyways. She touched Mikos' arm, and he shook his head. *Winter's still on us.*

"Doctor, are you saying you're willing to help?"

"No, far from it," Lamont blurted, a slight note of panic in her tone. "Even if I wanted to, if I could do summat, it wouldn't change your daughter's prognosis."

Janet's frustration rose and her entire body tensed. "Dammit, are you saying that Elliot was completely up the pole? That he used my daughter for some weird experimentation? Validation of his theories?"

Atteberry turned toward the window, his head bowed.

"The truth is, this operation was experimental. Nowt's ever been attempted of this complexity before. Look, we're all guessing when it comes to non-invasive mind-scraping practices, Ms. Chamberlain, but make no mistake: the risks of summat going terrible wrong were extremely high."

The uncertainty of Elliot's procedure dawned on her and passed through her like an elusive memory. *Perhaps that republican agent did us a favor by killing that asshole in New Houston.*

The booze caused her mind to drift. A scene of the three of them at home in the kitchen, when Mary was about four, flashed in her thoughts. Sunlight streamed through the windows while they played an old-fashioned board game at the table. Jim kept landing in jail and Mares squealed with delight as he feigned crying, then sulking, with a gleam in his eye. They'd looked at each other and understood how much they ached to make love once she went down for a nap.

"So, even if I could 'elp, if I weren't being watched an' all, I canna save your daughter."

The doctor's voice pulled her back. The image of lying next to Jim in their bedroom vanishing.

"It's hopeless, then?"

Lamont remained silent but stayed on the link.

The protective force surged, and Janet tried a fresh approach. "Doctor, suppose we're all willing to take the risks and the surrounding danger was gone, what would you need to attempt the procedure?"

"Oh, but that's not the case, eh?"

"Humor me and pretend it is."

"Well, assuming a team was in place, the issue for me is an outflow solution."

"What do you mean?"

"Like I was saying, Dr. Elliot suggested that siphoning the excess memories was the best route, but I disagreed. Those remembrances must go somewhere. They don't just disappear into the ether, eh? So

I'd require storage capacity for significant amounts of data in terms of volume, flow rate, integrity, and . . ." She paused a moment. "Perhaps I could knock several powerful networks together if I find enough of 'em. We'd discussed that at one point."

"Your pal, Dr. Palmer, planned to use the quantum computer at the Terran Science Academy. Would something like that work?"

A static crash masked the beginning of Lamont's response. " . . . if you get it to New York City. The Gotham Medical Center is the only hospital equipped to handle this now that New Houston is inaccessible. They have specialists and facilities . . . what they lack is the siphoning solution and, well, someone to take the lead."

"Doctor, you're playing with my feelings here and that's a dangerous game. I've killed two agents in the last half hour, I'm beat up bad, my demons are screaming at me, and I don't have time to screw around." Adrenaline flowed through her veins as she gripped the indie-comm tightly. "I can get you the damn quantum computer. I'll fly the machine to New York, so tell me straight: if I line up protection and put your ass on a flight to Gotham, would you perform this surgery?"

"I—I . . ."

"Don't mess with me, doc. Yes or no?"

Lamont sighed, then with fierce resolve, she said, "Yes. If you do all that, I'll attempt the procedure, but—"

"No 'buts', doctor. My team in London will contact you and arrange transport. I expect to see you in New York in a few hours." She terminated the connection and exhaled, slamming another pull of booze down her throat.

Jim raised his head and peered at her, eyes swollen and red. A haunting, chalk-face smile cracked his lips.

Atteberry

A FEW MINUTES LATER, THE HOVERCAR PULLED into a hidden alley near Carson Road, pivoted to face the street again, and eased down to the asphalt. Bits of cardboard and garbage littered the gutters. Graffiti shocked the tired brick walls that yawned several stories high. Janet had ordered Mikos to find a secure area to stop so she could think through the next steps. She said they needed to procure Esther's computer, transport it to New York, and keep Mary alive. Meanwhile, she contacted the London cell and despatched a security team to pick up Dr. Lamont and fly her across the Atlantic.

And she continued to drink the remaining booze.

As Janet and Mikos discussed operational matters and confirmed that they'd given Winter the shake, Atteberry checked his own indie-comm and noticed the slew of messages from Esther. He punched through them, all asking about where he was and Mary's condition. He hit her number and waited for the link to be established.

"Tyrone."

She sounded upbeat. "It's me, Es."

"Jim!" She lowered her voice. "Where the hell are you?"

"On the run. Listen, I don't have much time. Were you able to secure the quantum computer?"

"Long story short, yes. Mark Jefferson is standing by with a team of technicians to facilitate the operation. When will you arrive?"

Janet mouthed, "Twenty minutes."

"Es, we can be there in twenty. We've gotta be careful. There's some nasty people who want to take Mary to Munich and—"

"Okay, well, you'll be protected once you get here."

"How so?"

Encryption chirps infiltrated the connection. "Look, I had some trouble down here in Space Ops earlier. Kapoor's been all over me like a schoolboy about this operation, but Mark took the brunt of his wrath. I figured we needed help to ensure the operation goes smoothly. I still don't know who to trust anymore, so I called this Sergeant Meadows from the CCR forces. Remember him?"

The name sounded vaguely familiar, but he couldn't place it.

"Doesn't matter, but he was one of the soldiers who helped us escape Marshall Whitt and his cronies at Mount Sutro."

"Okay, yes."

"So I contacted him, explained what was happening—"

"You what?"

"Jim, I briefed him about Mary's condition and the need for the operation and that it would take place here. Anyway, he's sending a few soldiers over."

Inviting additional shadowy types into Mary's world ate away at him like a festering sore, but he rationalized they wouldn't be at the TSA any longer than was needed to load that computer onto a heli-jet and travel to the east coast.

"Sorry, I over-reacted. That sounds good."

Janet motioned to mute the call. When he did, she said, "You've gotta explain we aren't doing the operation there and to prepare that precious computer of hers for transport."

Atteberry didn't move.

"Jim, come on. Get Esther going."

He scratched his beard and unmuted the indie-comm. "Es? Yeah, sorry about that. Listen, can you prepare the quantum computer for travel? Turns out we can't do Mary's procedure there anymore, but there's a team in New York and—"

"At Gotham Medical?"

"Yes, there's a doctor flying in from Europe and they'll do the surgery there."

"What about the guy you lined up here?"

Atteberry exhaled slowly. "He's dead. The Prussians got him."

Silence flooded the connection. When Esther spoke again, a hint of fear tinged her voice. "I see. Well, we're pretty safe with all these soldiers milling about, so it's better if the operation were done here."

"It's gotta be New York. We can't stay here any longer than is absolutely necessary."

"But Jim," Esther said, "the Q isn't portable. You don't just pick it up like a data tablet and carry it under your arms."

"We'll put it in a heli-jet."

"That's not what I'm saying."

"Then what *are* you saying?"

"It's bolted to a concrete block 64 cubic meters big under the floor. Also, the machine rests on a dampening system to eliminate micro-vibrations. And there's the cooling systems, the power supplies too. I'm sorry, Jim, it's not going anywhere."

"Let's ask those soldiers to cut through and lift it out, and maybe—"

"Not a chance. I'm no engineer, but I understand how forces work and I'm telling you, there's no way the Q is moving. Not in a million years." She paused. "What the hell?"

"What is it?"

"There's more than a handful of soldiers showing up. Gotta be at least thirty, all stationed around the campus and guarding the entrances to the lab. Remember how we escaped that night? They've blocked that delivery port entirely."

Atteberry remembered that evening six years ago. He and Kate had been held captive by Whitt's henchmen. Esther found an escape route with the help of the CCR soldiers through a maze of hallways and out via a service entrance in the middle of a firefight.

She continued. "Well, there is really is no safer place around now. Maybe you can bring that team from Gotham Medical here?"

"Wait, why so many?"

"Meadows wouldn't say, only through intel there was more happening and he didn't want to take chances. He likely knows about the moles in the TSA and wants to be careful."

Janet turned away from Mikos and frowned. "They know I'm with you, Jim. They're after me."

Atteberry's jaw dropped. *When will this end?*

"Wait a second, Esther."

He muted the call and scowled. "This is your past coming back again, isn't it?"

"My present and future, too. Look, it's no big deal. We'll take you close to the TSA, then you and Mary grab a hovercab for the rest of the trip. Mikos and I will find a safehouse, go to ground, and pull together a squad of our own agents."

"And suffer more violence? Not a chance, Jan. Besides, you have to be there. You're the only one I . . ." he chewed over the words carefully. "The only person I *trust.*"

She wouldn't be dissuaded. "Thanks, but think about it. I'm a huge distraction now. Those CCR soldiers? I guarantee they don't give a rat's ass about Mary or aliens or anything else. I'm the bitch who blew up that tower and killed their colleagues, remember? They want to hold me to account for my actions." She paused, gazed ahead at the street through the car window. "You've got to go by yourself. Only you and Mary."

Mary stirred on the seat beside him. She raised her head, smiling as she recognized Janet. "We are safe?"

Jan spoke first. "Not quite, honey, but closer. There's a team in New York preparing to assist, and one of Dr. Elliot's colleagues is flying in from London. We'll have to get the quantum computer there."

She shivered and wrapped her thin arms around her chest. "The machine is critical. We must learn how to interface with. . . ensure it's configured correctly."

"And you will. You and your dad are heading to the TSA to check it out."

A look of confusion crossed Mary's face. "What about you?"

"Sorry, I can't go. Too dangerous for me, but I'll catch up later."

Mary shook her head lightly. "You must come."

Atteberry put his arm around her and held her tight. "We can do this, Mares."

"We know, Dad, but we... *I* need you both there. In case . . . " She gulped, locking on him with a desperate, penetrating gaze.

He looked at Janet, his eyes beseeching her to stay with their daughter. She shook her head and turned away.

TWENTY-SEVEN

Canadian Forces Base Shearwater, Nova Scotia

Carter

A MILLION DETAILS RAN THROUGH CARTER'S MIND like a pixilated stampede, crushing everything in their way. As he descended to the *Echo*'s underground hangar—the faint chime signalling he'd reached the desired level—he mulled over what exactly he might do if she came under attack by Prussian ships lying in wait between here and Luna. As much as he despised the idea, he concluded that he'd have to—again—rely on Captain Powell's leadership.

The elevator door snapped open, and he stepped into the main hangar buried 100 meters underground. Bright lights assaulted him, and he stood quietly for a moment, allowing his eyes to adjust. A warm glow bathed the *Echo* as she rested on her own moveable platform. A wide assortment of technicians, some dressed in blue overalls, others in white, ant-crawled over her while several workers oversaw the loading of weapons and additional supplies through her aft cargo port.

He grunted with deep satisfaction. This was his pride and joy, a beautiful ship, the first of many planned vehicles using his innovative engine technology to out-run anything else the world could offer. *But I must have more.* His focus returned to the Rossian vessel, the one those two women encountered on Luna, the one that disappeared faster than the speed of light, taking Braddock with her. He yearned to return to the *Mare Marginis* and scour the area for clues about how that ship did it, how long she may have been watching the Earth, and where she might have gone.

Captain Powell waved from below the bridge section of the spacecraft and jogged lightly over to greet him.

"Welcome, Clayton! Have you been standing there long?"

"No, John. I was admiring all the activity. She looks great!"

Powell followed Carter's gaze toward the *Echo*. "We're still adjusting some secondary navigation systems, but mains are all functioning, the new med bay is amazing, and remember that antigrav coil I needed to replace?"

"I do."

"Well, Aminidab—one of my techs—could refurbish it to spec. It won't hold forever, but it'll do short term so we can get her airborne again."

Carter slapped his captain on the shoulder. "Fantastic, John! I knew I could count on you."

Powell grinned, downplaying the compliment. "There's more clean-up required, but she'll be flight ready shortly and we can get back to Luna."

The two men marched toward the *Echo*, Carter in front. Techs pushing antigrav sleds carrying instruments and heavy laser-welding equipment hurried across their path. At the craft, Carter ran his fingers along the port nacelle, marvelling at how quickly Powell's teams had effected repairs.

"She looks brand new, John."

"Thanks. She's better equipped this time around now that we've fitted her up properly. Getting some of the redundant systems operating will allow her to stay in space longer, and the operational med bay helps. We put in some high-power comms units to bolster transmissions to the Saturn loop. And that's just the start."

Carter fingered the nacelle exterior. The ship was painted an iron ore grey, but now had flecks of red to the rear and around the identification markings. "Fresh paint too, I see."

"Yes." Powell, who had been following Carter along the port side for his inspection, stopped. "Clayton, there's something I'd like to discuss with you before we go too far here."

Carter continued walking, but said, "What is it?"

"I know you'll be on board when we return to Luna in a few hours and do whatever needs to be done to defuse the stand-off on the way."

He paused and faced him. "Yes, what of it?"

"We need to clarify the chain of command."

Carter's eyes narrowed. "I don't understand. You are the captain."

"I am, but you're the owner." Powell struck a commanding pose. Although not as tall as Carter, his countenance and body language made it clear he was in charge. "A couple of times during the rescue mission, you and I disagreed about what actions to take."

"I wouldn't call those disagreements, John," he chuckled, fighting his defense mechanism. "We discussed various approaches, I recall, but conflicts? Hardly."

"Look, Clayton, let's cut the nuancing crap and talk this out man to man." He pulled him away from the ship and the workers so they could speak more privately. "On the ground, right now, you have full authority and no one questions that. My role is to advise and provide guidance, especially regarding fleet readiness and other operational matters."

"Go on."

"But once those port doors close and the platform rises to the surface for her to lift off, I'm in charge. I cannot have my orders questioned in front of the crew. We can discuss issues, of course, but the ultimate decisions are mine." He tilted his head upward in a challenging stance to meet Carter's gaze. "And to be clear, the operation of this ship—any ship—is not a democracy. Space is an unforgiving environment. There is no room for cowboys, understand?"

Carter fumed and tightened his lips. He did not appreciate these fly-boys, these captains, exerting their authority over *him*. He owned the assets, and he paid their wages. Relinquishing the role of *leader* to anyone tasked him, but he also fully understood his limitations. Despite his warming cheeks and clenching fists, he quelled his passions and said, "Thank you, Captain. You'll have no trouble from me regardless of our respective positions."

Powell studied him to where Carter's self-consciousness hammered at his brain.

"Very well, as long as that's clear."

"Crystal."

"Good, then let's continue with the inspection. Let me show you the new aft weapons systems."

Over the following half hour, the two continued checking the ship with Captain Powell pointing out all the extra equipment and briefing Carter on the modified capabilities. When they finished reviewing the bridge and cockpit where the officers' positions were, Powell escorted him back to the hangar floor.

"You've been quiet these last few minutes, Clayton. Does everything meet with your expectations?"

Carter folded his arms across his chest and bowed his head, deep in thought. Finally, he faced the captain and beamed. "She's magnificent. Truly, I am at a loss for words."

Powell laughed and grinned from ear to ear. "I take it that means we're ready."

"And how!" They shook hands and stood together admiring the ship as the technicians—fewer of them now—finished up the remaining preparations and clean up. Then Carter, pulling his indie-comm from his pocket, said, "All we need is the Atteberry girl's alien knowledge and we'll be all set. I'd like to secure that, or at least bring her here, before we leave. She may be helpful on the return to Luna."

He scrolled through his messages. Several updates from Ed Mitchell. Some other political missives that he summarily deleted. Finally, he saw what he'd been hoping to find: a message from Esther Tyrone.

Clayton, sorry for the delay. Mary A. is coming here for the procedure. Lots of danger all around us. CCR soldiers stationed on campus. Need the use of the Quantum comp. New surgeon flying to NYC. Must get M to Gotham Medical, along with the Q. Bad news is, M may not survive the travel, or the operation. Q comp not going anywhere. Negotiating. Will keep you apprised.

Carter shook his head.

"What is it, sir?"

He rubbed his fingers together. *The last episode at Gotham Medical Center hadn't turned out well. And they think they'll operate there? Madness.*

"Sir?"

"Hm? Yes, it's about the girl. She's apparently close to death." It was time to move his plan forward. "John, can we take another tour of the med bay? I want to fully understand its surgical capability."

TWENTY-EIGHT

Braadenton Class Prussian Cruiser *Edelgard*

Captain Adam Beck

"CONTINUE SCANNING LUNA'S SURFACE, BROGAN, and the surrounding void," Captain Beck muttered. "We may be searching for evidence of that alien ship, but let's not get complacent. Weapons and Tactical, keep watch for any other anomalies." He rocked on his heels beside the command chair, scratching the stubble forming on his chin. Tension on the bridge ran high.

"Aye, sir."

Beck had witnessed or taken part in just about every significant event in the Earth-Luna System over the past twenty-five years, so in his current position as captain of the *Edelgard*, he rarely felt his heartbeat rise. Until now. His orders from Prussian Command were to scour Luna for debris or other evidence that an alien ship had landed there, and to ensure no other vessels poked their noses in matters that didn't concern them.

The brandy he nursed an hour ago with his meal rested sweetly in his belly as he studied the data charts and images of the *Mare Marginis*. One side of him—the curious Explorer—wanted nothing more than to prove the existence of the Ross 128 vessel with hard evidence and to learn her faster than light secrets. The other—the warrior—couldn't care less about that. That man preferred fighting and to evaluate his crew in action against another heavy, the cruiser *Malevolent* and her fine captain.

Minutes passed without change, and Beck flopped into the command chair, leaning forward, studying Luna's grey craggy relief. Scuffs and markings on the surface showed where the *Echo* had been, but other than surrounding scars that could not be attributed specifically to any ship, he saw no evidence of a second craft ever being there.

A proximity alert pinged at both the Science station and Navigation.

"Helm, report," he stated casually, thinking that a phantom echo or sounding had passed through the filters and caused the alarm.

"Analyzing, sir," the helmsman replied. Her fingers fluttered over the console as she traced the alert. "Captain," she said, "it's a small body off starboard, bearing 123 degrees-mark-18. Range 90 thousand kilometers."

"What is it, Metzger, a meteor?" Beck approached the Helm and studied the 3D Nav chart.

She shook her head. "Stand by, Captain, more data coming in." She tweaked the resolution of the object as streams of information scrolled vertically down the right hand side of the screen. "It's not a natural phenomenon, sir. The object appears to be a probe or vessel about the size of one of our life pods. Unknown design."

"I confirm the analysis," the science officer shouted.

"Terran?"

"Inconclusive, sir. It bears no markings and presents as dormant."

"Well, pods or probes don't simply appear from nowhere. What's the origin?"

Wendel, the science officer, shrugged. "Impossible to determine, Captain. One moment, nothing but space. The next . . . it showed up."

Beck marched in front of the primary bridge viewer. "Put it on screen, Helmsman."

The sleek body appeared as a smudge against the blackness of space.

"Adjusting resolution," Metzger added while tweaking her console. When the object came into focus, it was lustrous and aerodynamic with a blue energy field glowing around it.

"Science, is this a weapon of some kind?"

"The target has come to life, sir. Reading magnetic and electrical flux fields and . . . oh . . ." He peered up from his viewer and stared at the primary screen.

Beck turned. "What is it?"

"I don't know how to explain it, sir. It simply isn't possible."

"Dammit, Wendel, what's going on?"

"Captain," he began, facing the commander, "we've detected a ripple in space-time prime." The bridge crew stopped and faced the science officer as he approached the captain. "I didn't think it possible."

"Tactical, can you confirm?" The brandy in his belly soured. Beck wrinkled his face.

A slim weapons officer reviewed his console and nodded. "The computer confirms it: we've just witnessed a ripple in the prime."

Metzger shouted from her station. "Captain, the object is in motion on a course to Luna." She looked at the captain. "Shall I lay in a pursuit pattern?"

"Patience, Helm. Hold our position until we know more about this . . . thing."

"Aye, sir."

Beck straightened his leather jacket and raised his voice. "That said, it is prudent to be cautious. All crew, go to Red Alert." The ambient lighted shifted from dull green to crimson. "Wendel, can our scanners penetrate the interior of the object?"

"Negative. But it's hull carries traces of the same environmental parameters we use in our terran life pods. Sir," he exclaimed, "its dimensions suggest insufficient volume for a . . . a *human* to occupy, and it's evidently not terran." He faced Beck. "Nevertheless, I believe this is a life pod, and whatever other-dimensional creature is in it, they're en route to the far side of Luna."

"Comms, are you hailing it?"

"Aye, Captain, on all standard frequencies. No response."

"Understood. All right, listen up." Beck addressed the crew. "We're going in for a closer look and to pick up this . . . vessel. Have Security and Medical stand by in the cargo bay. Weapons, I want you to lock on that pod and track it all the way. If it makes any sort of aggressive move, blast it. Don't wait for my order, understand?"

"Aye, sir."

Helm, Science, Engineering . . . stay sharp. We don't know what we're dealing with here, but if it is the Rossian ship, we must capture it."

"And if it's not, Herr Captain?" Metzger stared at him wide-eyed.

Beck frowned and returned to his command chair. "Let us prepare for anything. Now, plot an intercept course and let's see what this creature is."

"Course plotted, sir."

"Fire it up, Helm, then get me Prussian High Command and patch them through to my office."

The *Edelgard* shot forward, accelerating toward Luna. Beck entered his suite behind the command well, leaving the door open, awaiting contact with his senior commanders. He regretted giving up the battle lines and the Malevolent, but the appearance of the alien object was too much to pass up.

His comms panel chimed and Beck exhaled, long and slow. Before punching the frequency open, he summarized these most recent events in his mind and calculated the critical next steps. *If this is not the Rossian vessel, then what the hell has God wrought?*

TWENTY-NINE

San Francisco, CCR

Janet

PARKED IN A SERVICE LANEWAY ON A HILLTOP off John F. Kennedy Drive in Golden Gate Park, overlooking the Terran Science Academy rising out of the landscape like an extension of an outcrop, the Atteberrys and Agent Mikos observed the activity on campus. They'd apparently shaken Winter (he no longer appeared on the hovercar's monitor), but now they faced an additional problem. Two, actually, Janet realized as she peered through powerful binoculars at a trio of CCR soldiers posted outside the TSA's primary entrance.

First, accessing the lab where this monster of a computer operated. Second, moving the damn thing out, and setting it en route to New York. *So that's three.* And do all this without getting caught. *Four.* And the last swallow of booze already gone. *Five.* A pang of guilt shot through her and, after lowering the glasses, she said, "Jim, I shouldn't go anywhere near that place. If they see me, all hell could break loose again. I'm only putting you in more danger."

This time, Mary responded. "No, you must come."

"I can do more good tracking Winter and making sure he stays away while you secure the computer. The CCR have no issue with you."

Atteberry, resolve set on his face, would have none of it. "No. We're in this together, Jan, win or lose." He smiled, oozing conviction, and that *feeling* hit her again. *What is happening to me? I've gone soft.*

She refocused on the TSA where a handful of other soldiers took up defensive positions on the side of the building.

Atteberry contacted Esther on his indie-comm and put her on speaker. "We're not far now, but you say there are armed forces everywhere. Are they going to help us enter and remove the computer?"

"Hard to tell. Meadows said they're here to provide security and any other support, but how can we be certain? Everyone's tiptoeing on eggshells, especially the scientists in Space Ops. I asked the team to figure out how to move the Q unit and they rejected the idea outright at first, but now they've got the old blueprints on screen and they're looking for release points that won't damage the machine."

"Excellent. So we'll be able to transport the computer?"

"Possibly. Getting it off the floor along with its dampening system is only the beginning. We still must wrench it out of the lab and transport it to the airport."

Atteberry grinned. "One step at a time, Es. I'll contact you again when we're ready." He ended the link and leaned back, grinning.

Janet shifted on the seat and handed the binoculars to Mikos. "I know that look, Jim. Are you thinking of walking up to the front door and knocking?"

"No," Atteberry said calmly, "here's my idea. These soldiers want to arrest you for the Mount Sutro crimes, right?"

"Yes. I can't remember how many people we killed that night under my command, but enough for me to rot in jail the rest of my life."

"Okay, and if you're sure they're here because they want you more than to protect the TSA or Mary or anything else, why not offer a trade?"

Janet frowned. "If I'm following, you're suggesting I turn myself in to the CCR in exchange for access to the quantum computer."

"Not at all. We make them *think* you're turning yourself in, and that you insist the machine be flown to New York with no interference." Then, looking at Mikos, he said, "Are there other agents nearby that could be disguised as Janet?"

Mikos inhaled sharply. "I don't enjoy giving anyone up to the CCR. Who knows what they'd do to one of us, let alone the torture they'd put you through, ma'am. With due respect, Mr. Atteberry, it's Agent Chamberlain they want, not an avatar."

Adrenaline rushed through her system, heightening her senses in anticipation of action. This is what she lived for.

We need more drink.

Mikos added, "And what if they refuse the offer? Surely that's another consideration. They apparently realize you need the Q comp to save your daughter's life, so—"

"Our life," Mary whispered.

"Yes." He cleared his throat. "So rather than give us the computer and a flight out of California, they say hand over Agent Chamberlain, or else Mary dies."

Atteberry set his jaw and fell silent.

Janet spoke. "The problem here is getting the computer to Gotham Medical. Even if we pulled off a ruse with a substitute, we can't blast our way out of that lab. We need their cooperation." Her eyes sparkled as her body responded to the promise of confrontation, and a crazy idea filled her mind. "What if I actually gave myself up?" she mused.

"Impossible," Mikos sputtered. "You must be with your family on that flight."

Janet shook her head. "I'm not planning to get left behind, Agent, but hear me out. We make the offer like Jim says and insist on securing the computer. They'll likely take me off-site for questioning and whatever else they do, but I'll slip away and meet up at the airport. We all leave together and exit their airspace before they can do anything."

Mikos grimaced and folded his arms across his chest.

"Don't look so glum, Agent. Listen, if it helps, call in a field unit to provide cover and clear a path for me. The alternative is throwing a pigeon at them and really pissing them off. We need their cooperation to get the machine, right? This is the logical solution."

"That's risky as hell," Mikos chimed in. "You've been on their wanted list for years, ma'am. You know what that means."

"I'll find a way." She paused. "But I hear you, and understand the risks. The worst case scenario is—" She chose her next words carefully. "I . . . miss the flight. However, at a minimum, you'll get to Gotham and Mary will have the operation." She gazed from person to person, pausing on Mary's strained face. "It's the least I can do."

Despite the pain and fatigue, the danger and risks, Janet relished a shot at taking on the CCR soldiers and mind-twisters after all these years of running. She didn't consider herself much of a negotiator, but if they listened to her side of what happened at Mount Sutro, and Mary's fate, perhaps that would buy enough time for the others to get the hell out of the Bay Area.

Then, having decided, she and the others discussed the finer details of the scheme. Jim would contact Esther and have her set up the exchange. They'd have to rely on the CCR's goodwill, and Esther's presence would solidify that.

Ten minutes later the hovercar levitated a meter off the ground and broke cover from the thicket, heading slowly on a direct course to the TSA's main entrance.

A surge of adrenaline at a daytime operation against serious odds flooded Janet's body. She could almost sense the cortisol and hormones pulsating through her blood, and for the first time in weeks, she truly felt *alive*.

Atteberry

THE MORNING FOG HAD COMPLETELY BURNED OFF, leaving a blue-grey sky marred only by the smears of high cirrus cloud. As the hovercar eased along the campus avenue to the drop off at the TSA primary entrance, soldiers dressed in black and olive fatigues appeared from nowhere and everywhere at once. Atteberry held Mary's hand. She'd been conscious now for some time, murmuring what he referred to as alien talk, and more focused on the surrounding activities.

"I think the stimulant's effects have worn off completely," Janet said, watching her.

A band of soldiers encircled the car as it hummed to a stop and parked on its skids. Their weapons pointed at the vehicle and Atteberry froze.

Janet pressed a button on the door, and the window rolled open. "I'm coming out and I'm unarmed," she shouted, her voice rough and cracked. Before touching the release, she leaned over and kissed Mary on the forehead, then turned to Atteberry.

A veil of awkwardness shrouded him as his head wrestled with his heart. This could be the last time he'd see her, and the ancient dam of unspoken words clogged his throat. She kissed him on the cheek, then stepped out the door and onto the drive. As she did, Esther and Meadows emerged from the primary entrance and strolled toward the car as if they were going to lunch. He held no weapon as he approached. Janet waited a couple of meters away, arms by her side, facing them. Meadows came to a halt in front of her.

"You look familiar, soldier," she said matter-of-factly. "Have we met before?"

He ignored the question and barked in a commanding voice, "Mr. Atteberry, I'd like you and your daughter to exit the vehicle and follow Dr. Tyrone into the building."

He emerged from the same door as Janet, and drifted around the car and helped Mary out, holding her close with an arm wrapped around her waist. As they ambled toward the primary entrance, Meadows stopped them.

"Kenders, check both for weapons."

"We're unarmed," Atteberry said, but his protest went unacknowledged.

One of the nearby soldiers shouldered his weapon and marched up. He patted them down and scanned them. "All clear, sir."

"Very good." Then to Esther, "Go with them and do what you need to do. I've got a truck standing by to take the machine to the airport when you're ready."

Esther, her face withdrawn and tight, led the two toward the main doors. Mary examined the area and put her arm on Atteberry's shoulder. Meadows watched them leave, and before they entered, Atteberry heard him say, "Kenders, clear Agent Chamberlain."

THE FOYER OF THE TSA HAD CHANGED LITTLE since he'd been there last. It remained a cavernous room with high ceilings, an escalator leading up to the management offices, and a bank of elevators to the rear. Where the commissionaire normally resided, two armed soldiers and a man carrying a first aid kit—perhaps a doctor or medic—waited for them. They exchanged nods, and the entire group moved toward the elevators and descended to the Space Operations lab on the final subfloor.

When the doors finished opening, the soldiers led them into the heart of the lab. Half a dozen technicians fussed over the quantum computer while another group stood close by, documenting and checking their data slates. Farther along the back wall, a handful of construction workers waited with various pieces of heavy machinery.

"May we see the schematics?" Mary whispered.

Esther stopped. "Why do you need to see those?" She glanced at Atteberry and the soldiers.

"So we can interface . . . for the operation. We have to understand the input fields and data processing capabilities."

She paused, then said to Atteberry, "This technology is highly confidential and proprietary, Jim, you understand that, and she's, well, I'm not sure . . ." As she mulled over what to do, Mark Jefferson and the director of the TSA emerged from one of the many offices on the floor and advanced toward them. Atteberry remembered him as a graduate student when they first met about the Ross 128 signal in '85. He'd aged and his face had cleared.

"Mr. Atteberry," the older one said, "I don't believe I've had the pleasure. Kieran Kapoor, head of the TSA." They shook hands. "And you must be young Mary." He held out his hand to her.

She stared at him with a confused and distant look. He let his arm drop. "This is something I never expected, but here we are, hm?" A beat. "Esther, how are things going?"

"We just arrived, sir, so I can't say." She called a technician over and he briefed them on their progress. They'd detached the computer and isolated it from the dampening system and were double-checking all the fasteners before calling the construction workers in to extricate the unit from its concrete pad.

Mary interrupted them and said, "We need to see the schematics."

Kapoor and Jefferson stared at her, then regarded Esther.

"She has to understand how to interface with the unit and how the data flow works for the operation, sir."

He wiggled his fingers, looked at a nearby soldier and said, "I suppose I have little choice. Smithson, show Mary whatever she needs to see."

A petite scientist with bulging eyes and a data slate under her arm left the cluster, and helped Mary walk around the unit and swiped through various pages on the slate. Mary murmured again, interspersed with technical questions that Atteberry had no clue about. They disappeared around the far side of the machine.

"Esther," Kapoor said, "I hope you know what you're doing. This is highly irregular."

"I hope so too, sir," she whispered.

Atteberry surveyed the lab, and asked, "How will you get it out? It seems too big to fit through the loading bay."

"It is," Jefferson said. "If we can release the machine from its pins without destroying it, our guys will cut away part of the wall over there to remove it." He pointed to an extensive set of doors with a massive "B" painted on them.

"Like I said," Kapoor complained, "it's highly irregular."

Mary, looking tired and frail, appeared with the scientist Smithson again. This time, Mary held the data slate in the crook of her arm and, leaning against the machine, swiped through it as if brushing crumbs off a table, her eyes flickering and blinking furiously. She continued talking to herself, shaking her head, then caught Atteberry's gaze.

"Will it work?"

She smirked. "The technology is so . . . primitive, Dad." She resumed her swiping, and he recognized how she memorized everything there was to know about the computer.

The technicians froze. Kapoor sputtered something about state-of-the-art, and Jefferson peppered her with questions about what *exactly* the problem was. Esther bowed her head.

Mary returned the data slate to Smithson, and reached for Atteberry and grabbed his arm, steadying herself. In a moment, silence enveloped the group, and he whispered in her ear, "Can you do anything about it? I mean, the two of you?"

She licked her lips and fingered her matted hair. "Maybe, Dad, but I doubt it."

"What's the issue, Mares?"

She glanced back at the unit, as if measuring its dimensions in her head. "It's like using a hammer to swat a fly. It can work, but might destroy more than the fly." She peered into his face. "Does that make sense?"

A hammer to kill a fly. She referred to one of the world's most important, advanced pieces of technology as a heavy, blunt instrument. He took her frigid hands in his and whispered, "You did good, Mares. You did good."

Winter

IN A FIRST FLOOR UNIT OF A THREE-STORY WALK-UP in Kirkham Heights, Winter assembled a new team of operatives. Most of them were freelance mercenaries Cornelia tapped into, except for Fischer, the guard from the failed warehouse interrogation. The group totaled 16.

He lined them up in two ranks in the open living room for inspection and checked their weapons closely. Then, having satisfied himself they could do the job, he popped a pseudophine for the pain in his legs and launched into the details of the operation.

"Some of you have encountered CCR armed forces before, yes?"

A couple of the mercs grunted.

"And others have fought NDU agents, true?"

Several more snorted. It appeared the NDU agents—Janet and her crew—had conducted many missions in the area over the years. *This is good.*

"Ladies and gentlemen, we have little time to prepare. My colleague chose you based on your track records and I cannot emphasize enough the risks associated with this mission." He paced gingerly in front of them, his face drawn, hands behind his back. "Janet Chamberlain, the NDU agent who escaped from me, along with her ex-husband and daughter, negotiated an arrangement. Our mole tells us she surrendered to the CCR authorities in exchange for transporting the TSA's quantum computer."

One of the mercs, a young woman with short-cropped hair and tattoos on her arms, flinched at hearing Janet's name. Winter stopped pacing in front of her. "This concerns you . . .?"

"Tonia, sir."

He looked down his nose at her.

"Only so far as it was that whore who arranged the death of my partner."

"So you would like to kill her, yes?"

"Yes."

He continued pacing. "Perhaps you'll get your chance, but let me clear: she is not our primary target. The girl, Mary, and the computer are what we seek. Secure those two assets, and I shall reward you handsomely."

Glancing at his indie-comm, Winter flashed a live satellite image of the TSA on the bare wall, then outlined the security, the points of access, and other critical intel that Cornelia had forwarded to him. The tall merc on the end, the right marker, interrupted him. "How do you propose we carry this out when the place is crawling with CCR soldiers?"

"Fischer will create a diversion. There's a small personnel door at the rear." He flipped the image showing the back of the TSA where various hovercars sat on skids at a recharging station. "See it? We'll disguise ourselves as CCR soldiers, which will buy us a few minutes of confusion. By that time, we'll be in the building and moving to the lab where the fraulein is."

"But how do we escape?" the tall one asked. "I'm all in for a firefight if necessary, but I'd prefer to live another day."

Winter smirked. "Naturally. Once we secure the fraulein and the computer is safely aboard the transport truck, we use whoever else is there as hostages and human shields." Silence. "We simply walk out, take the truck and drive away. They will not harm us as long as we have the girl."

The revenge-seeking woman, Tonia, asked, "If these assets are so vital to global security as you claim, they may not care if the hostages die."

Winter sighed. "That is a risk we shall have to accept." He picked something out of his teeth. "Nevertheless, I plan to have some serious firepower backing us up . . . if it comes to that. My ship, the *Sara Waltz*, is in space dock at the New Houston elevator, and—"

"You're not thinking of bringing a heavy cruiser in, are you? That seems ridiculous."

Winter clenched his jaw, turned, and faced the man who dared question him. "For what it's worth, no. But there are several well-armed shuttles on the ship standing by should we need them. Do you appreciate how quickly they can move in and out of the Earth's atmosphere, mister?"

The merc gulped and shifted his stance.

"Seconds . . ." With that, he glanced at Fischer and barely raised his eyebrow. The guard marched over, grabbed the surprised assassin by his collar, hauled him out in front of the others, and slit his throat.

"Are there any other interruptions?" He scrutinized the faces of the soldiers, but no one else said a word. "Good. Now there's more of a cut for the rest of you. Let's get on with the mission."

Over the next twenty minutes, the team grouped together around the projections on the wall. They openly discussed the operation, diving into the details, and with Winter's authority established, the mercenaries focused on getting the job done despite the obvious risks. When everyone was clear on their specific roles and tasks, Fischer called up a pair of nondescript hovercars that arrived in moments and awaited them in front of the walk-up. He distributed CCR armed forces patches and affixed them to their shoulders and chests. Finally, he passed them a box of uppers designed to heighten their senses while reducing the innate fears that all in this business grappled with.

"Team," Winter said as they gathered up their kits and weapons, "in a moment, we'll depart. Use the remaining few minutes to review the mission in your minds. There can be no errors today." He retired to a kitchen area in the corner and hailed the *Sara Waltz* on an encrypted channel on his indie-comm.

The *Waltz's* communications officer opened Winter's link, verified the encryption, then put his hail through to Captain Krause, whose face appeared shortly on the indie-comm's micro-screen.

"How are the repairs?"

"Progressing well. The ship will be ready to leave space dock in a few hours."

"Excellent, and I'll depart the safehouse in a moment for our mission. Are the shuttles warmed up?"

"Yes, Herr Winter. I have three of them fuelled and standing by, but I must reiterate the danger of sending them into CCR airspace."

"I understand your concerns, Captain, but as I stated earlier, I do not believe we'll need them. The CCR armed forces have a history of being practical rather than moralistic. If they test our resolve with the hostages, I won't hesitate to kill them off one by one until they change their minds."

Captain Krause paused. "That's not my issue, Herr Winter."

"Oh? Enlighten me."

"We must assume that, if they call the shuttles to secure the assets, we will surely expect retaliation. And, as you know, they could call on the NDU for defensive support."

"The NDU? Not possible. California wants nothing to do with the Northern Democrats, and I understand the feeling is mutual."

"Perhaps that is true in times of detente, but never forget the old adage that the enemy of my enemy is my friend. We could be inviting an escalation of war the likes of which would seriously cripple our resources."

Winter considered the captain's concerns. Cornelia had already briefed him on the skirmishes between various groups and corporations unfolding around the world. If those continued to increase and implicate more players, that would undermine his goal to secure the girl's knowledge. Still, the reward for weaponizing Mary far outweighed the risks of global war. The lure of more power was intoxicating.

"Understood, but I doubt it'll come to that. Do what you must, Captain, to protect the fleet in space, and I'll accomplish my mission on Earth."

"Very good." Krause turned and motioned to someone off-screen who handed him a data slate. As he scanned the device, he added, "Before you go, Herr Winter, there is one more curious bit of news to consider that has come to my attention."

"What is it?"

The captain pulled a face and grinned. "It's from the *Edelgard*. You'll never believe what she found on the far side of Luna . . ."

THIRTY

The Mergeling

THE MACHINE CAN HEAL US.

Yes, in part.

This is not the full solution?

Mm, the machine is part of the outcome. Perhaps we can use it to relieve the experiential pressure from our mind and send the friend Mary back.

Yes. And if not?

We sense this physical body, the friend Mary, is decaying at a faster rate.

There is not much time left.

We must assist in the procedure.

We must live long enough to do so. Once the friend Mary is back, she will help. She and her family. For a while.

IF ALL THESE CREATURES ARE CAPABLE OF SUCH UGLINESS, *who might be saved?*

We cannot save them from their nature.

Mm, no, we cannot. We fight to exist. To overcome. We do not wish to be forsaken.

Yes.

WE ARE STUDYING OUR CIVILIZATION.

And?

We fear distinct things. The Earthlings are terrified of dying alone. We do not sense that dread in us. We hope to die without regret, because there is more after. Death is not final.

Mm . . . there is a difference.

Yes.

Do we fear death?

We do not, for we have gazed into the eyes of the universe. There is so much more to come.

There is more, yes.

NOW WE UNDERSTAND?

Yes.

Mm, there is no one.

No. There is only all. We hear them all now. Sense them all. And their voices are . . . beautiful.

Atteberry

"HOLD UP, GODDAMMIT!"

Smithson, on her hands and knees at the base of the quantum computer, peered into the gloom under the elevated machine with a flashlight. One of the construction workers operating the small crane stopped lifting, holding the edge of the computer on an angle while other technicians joined her on the floor.

"There . . . you see it?" The scientist pointed with a grease-covered finger, and the others crowded around. "It's still attached by that safety clutch. We'll have to sever that before continuing."

Atteberry and Mary sat beside each other on stools near a quiet workstation, away from the bustle of activity that encompassed the computer. Removing the machine from its pins in the concrete turned out to be far more complicated than he'd hoped, but Esther wasn't surprised. She stood nearby, overseeing the work.

"Sorry, Jim, we can't rush this. If the Q doesn't come out clean, it'll be useless."

"I understand," he replied, but that didn't assuage his anxiety. "Are you sure there's nothing I can do to help?"

She touched his shoulder. "Yes, let the techs and the cons do their jobs."

Her warm touch pleased him. Whatever residual ugliness that had remained in their failed, short-lived relationship disappeared in the throes of disconnecting this monster. He checked his indie-comm briefly, and stuffed it away in his pocket.

"Expecting something?"

He frowned. "I'm worried about Janet and whether she's—"

Esther's hand lingered on him. "If it's any consolation, and from what I've seen of her so far and heard from Sergeant Meadows, if anyone can find a way to join us, it's her."

Atteberry reached over to Mary and brushed her hair. She looked up and smiled weakly.

"Bring in the disconnector!" Smithson shouted.

A worker who'd been standing nearby moved forward carrying a thin, heavy tool about half a meter long, like an industrial wrench only with an odd-shaped head he didn't recognize. The con dropped to his knees and followed Smithson's arm under the apparatus.

"See it?"

"Yep."

"Can you reach it?"

The worker wriggled part way under and said, "Almost . . ." He continued reaching with both hands on the tool, and paused. "Got it. Clear back."

The gaggle of scientists moved away as the man anchored himself against the side of the computer. A green light arced in the gloom from the wrench, reflecting in the worker's face and bathing the surrounding area. Sparks flew, and in a moment, he shut the tool off. "Shine a light on it, will ya?"

Smithson knelt down again and crawled beside him, illuminating the spot with a pin light. The worker shook his head. "Not quite. I'll have another go."

He repeated the procedure and this time, when Smithson checked under the unit, they both whooped. She helped the man up and they stepped back. Turning to the crane operator, she shouted, "Lift her up!"

The operator revved power and raised the computer about a meter off the floor. Smithson and others continued examining the area underneath. She gave the green light to set it down off to the side, exposing the dampening base in the concrete. A handful of techs inspected the machine, attaching various probes to it and monitoring their data tablets.

Esther said, "That's the first one. Retrieving the dampener will be tricky too, but at least there's better access to it."

With the computer resting, the techs and cons encircled the hole in the floor, pointing out different connectors and pins. Over the course of several minutes, they released the dampener from its stays, and attached the crane cables, lifting it out.

Meanwhile, the small group of CCR soldiers, who had remained quiet and out of sight up to this point, approached Esther as one. The stocky man with a moustache asked, "Is it time to call in the flat bed?"

She pointed to the loading bay doors. "We still need to cut through the wall and improve access, but that won't take long. Where's the truck now?"

"Out back, ma'am, standing by."

"Very good. Bring it around and we should have the equipment ready to load in about fifteen minutes."

The soldier turned and barked into his microphone.

"I'd better go brief the boss." She gazed through the lab and spotted him over by Mark Jefferson's office. "Be right back."

Atteberry watched her slip away. Despite ranks and seniority, Esther ran the show here, and he was grateful for that. *Someone I can trust.*

Mary reached over and placed a hand on his arm. "It's going well, isn't it, Dad?"

"I think so. We'll be on our way to New York before long." He gazed into her face, noticing a few of her veins protruding through a ruddy complexion. "You holding up okay?"

She fidgeted with a lock of hair. "We're running out of time. Our— I mean, *my* lung capacity is down to 35 percent. Other organs are distressed."

"How do you know this?"

She dropped the strand. "It's difficult to explain. We just do. Must be Keechik's simulacra at work." Her face took on an anxious look. "Where's Janet?"

Atteberry said in a delicate voice, "I overheard the soldiers talking about taking her to the cellar, whatever that means." Feigning optimism, he added, "Your mother is particularly talented at getting out of tight spots, Mares. She said she'd meet up with us at the airport, and I have this feeling she wouldn't say that if she didn't think it possible."

Mary leaned over into his chest. It was an awkward embrace on stools, but Atteberry held her as best he could, ignored her icy body, the shivers coursing through her. He peered toward Jefferson's office and watched Esther do all the talking while Kapoor and Mark stood motionless. When she caught his eye, emotion surged in him and for the oddest reason, he felt . . . happy? Certainly not. Peace, perhaps. Then, she pointed to the loading bay doors and when he looked that way, construction workers had taken up positions by the adjoining wall.

In a flash of blue and orange light, they manipulated a series of laser cutters and slowly carved through the fortified barrier of the lab.

Atteberry

ESTHER REJOINED ATTEBERRY AND MARY, standing beside him with hands on hips. "This won't take too long now, Jim." She glanced at Mary, and added, "You realize I'm coming with you to New York." More of a statement than a question, a point of clarification if one was necessary.

Atteberry had assumed as much. "Someone has to babysit the quantum computer, right?"

"Yes, that's part of it, but I also want to speak with Clayton Carter in person about another matter. And I care what happens to Mary."

"What do you need to say to Carter? Remember, he tried to take her too after we landed."

"I know, but this is different." She motioned toward the lab. "Truth be told, my days are numbered here. They're only keeping me around until this crisis is over. Plus, the internal politics are becoming out of control and besides, I've done some thinking over the past 24 hours."

"Oh? I thought you loved this work?"

"Without question I do, and that's why I have to speak with Clayton. Prior to the rescue, when we were negotiating a partnership between the TSA and Titanius, he offered me a job working in space analysis."

Atteberry flinched. "Wasn't he more interested in exploiting the solar system for mineral wealth and his own gain? He never struck me as the altruistic type, if you don't mind my saying."

"Oh, he's narcissistic, without question, but there's a powerful exploration element to that work that I'd love to lead." She hesitated, searching for the words. "Plus, there's the *Echo* and another handful of ships like her under construction." She watched the cons cut through the lab wall for a moment. "Can you imagine what a fleet of *Echo*es could accomplish out there? We'd be able to go farther than any conventional vessel ever dreamed."

Atteberry considered it and, although resource exploration held little interest for him, understanding the solar system and search for life intoxicated him.

"Well, that might be a better fit for you. Besides, don't you and Carter have a . . . thing?"

She blushed and tried to suppress a nervous smile, without success. "Perhaps. He's an attractive man with a brilliant mind. Even though he used me to push the negotiations along, I admit I'm intrigued by him, and I often hate myself for it." Then, with control returning, she said, "I think he's capable of changing. Mary's abilities have shown what the universe holds, but first, we have to ensure the safe transport of this equipment and conduct the operation." Esther's indie-comm pinged. "It's a message from Sergeant Meadows." She responded to it, looked at Atteberry, and killed the link.

"What's that about?"

"He's on his way in for a moment. Wants to speak with you before transferring the machinery to the truck."

"Me? I've got nothing to do with him."

Esther shrugged and faced the elevator bank. "That's all he said."

Alarm bells screamed in his mind. *He's after Mary, too. I won't let him.* His hands curled into fists as he focused on his breathing, trying desperately to calm himself.

"Here he comes."

Atteberry stood and waited for the soldier to join them. Meadows looked at Esther. "Everything good here?"

"Yes, the computer's secure and as you can see, the techs are preparing the dampening system for transport. What's it like outside?"

He ignored the question. Instead, he glanced at Mary and asked, "How's your daughter?"

"The sooner we get to New York, the better."

"Understood. I wanted to wish you well and mention that we'll provide an escort for you to the airport. From there, we've got a couple of aircraft that'll follow you across the border, but not beyond. You'll be on your own after that."

"What about Janet? Will you allow her to come with us?"

Meadows set his jaw. "I'm afraid that's not possible." He quickly added, "Mr. Atteberry, how aware are you about your ex-wife's activities?"

He shrugged. "I saw what her team did at Mount Sutro years ago, and over the past couple days, but other than that, not much. Why do you ask?"

"I want to be clear why she's being detained. Since 2072, we've linked her to over 25 attacks in California alone. Janet Chamberlain sabotaged key strategic operations, assassinated 42 of our best men and women, and killed eight soldiers at Mount Sutro. She facilitated the theft of top-secret technology and data from Silicon North to the NDU and god knows how many other countries and terrorist groups out there."

Atteberry may have been surprised at one time by the breadth of operations Janet had been involved in, but not anymore. "What's your point, Agent?"

"Only this: you won't be seeing her again."

Mary shrieked. "You must let her go!" But Atteberry knew. The man was right. No matter the reasons behind such actions, when laws are broken, the perpetrators must be held to account. Without that, there is little left but chaos. He also understood Janet would agree.

"I'll take my leave and wish you and your daughter well." He turned, adding, "I have a daughter too, sir. She's around Mary's age, and even though I haven't seen her in a few years, there's nothing I wouldn't do either to protect her. You have my word we'll keep our side of the arrangement." He pivoted and marched toward the elevators.

Another twenty minutes passed and, in that time, the construction workers had burned through the wall and created a new, massive gateway for the computer and its dampening system. A second crane appeared outside now, larger than the one used in the lab, and the noisy truck backed in to the opening. After a few minutes of delicate movement and shouts of direction, they secured the two key pieces of equipment atop the flatbed. The soldiers encircled the truck, keeping watch with weapons drawn, as a pair of CCR military vehicles arrived to escort them to the airport.

A rumble from somewhere deep in the building caught Atteberry's attention, sending minute vibrations up through his injured leg.

"You hear that, Es?"

She had been conferring with Smithson when it hit. "The sound came from behind the lab. I'll send a couple techs around back to check it out." She asked a pair of them to investigate, and as the elevator doors opened to whisk them away, half a dozen armed CCR soldiers spilled out. Two grabbed the technicians while the other four quickly raced toward Atteberry and Esther.

He wondered what these guards were up to. They moved with a deftness he hadn't seen from the others. Before he realized they weren't CCR, they already trained their weapons on him, Mary and Esther, and had immobilized two men securing the truck. They shouted to the other real soldiers to drop their guns and lie down. None of them complied. Instead, they took up defensive positions and aimed their weapons at the insurgents.

Confusion poured down on the lab. To emphasize how serious these new fighters were, one of them fired automatic rounds into the ceiling.

Atteberry grabbed Mary in his arms, covering her head with his hands.

Esther shouted, "Who are you? What's going on here?"

"Tut, tut, Dr. Tyrone. No need to raise your voice."

Atteberry recognized that accent before he even turned to see Benedikt Winter strolling in from the elevator bank. The Prussian grinned wanly. "You didn't think I'd let you go that easily, did you?"

His jaw dropped, and no words came forth.

"You know, Herr Professor, these cat and mouse games are totally unnecessary, would you agree? As I said before, I only want the best for the girl, to help her, to make her well."

"Don't you dare come any closer!"

"Such aggression. So futile. We all have our roles to play, our jobs to perform. Mine is to ensure that your daughter transfers her knowledge to me and no one else. Then she is yours." He pulled an indie-comm from his pocket. "Your job is to cooperate."

"Fuck you."

"Well then, you must die." He sighed. "You, Herr Professor, are worthless . . . nothing more than a weak sack of meat. The fraulein is not."

A mercenary, the guard he recognized from the warehouse, ripped Mary away from him and pointed a gun at her head. Atteberry jumped to draw her back, but another soldier stood in his way, arms crossed, grinning, daring him to take one more step.

"Fischer here is not in a happy frame of mind after your Frau killed Helga. And all she wanted was to make your daughter well. Ah, such a shame. Such a waste."

"What are you going to do to us?"

"I told you. We shall heal the girl."

"In New York?"

"New York," he spat, "No. My preference is Munich, but the *Sara Waltz* is quite capable of handling the operation and is much closer. You see? I am the one putting Fraulein Mary's health first."

"No, you can't."

"We've been over this before, Herr Professor, and this time, I won't be nearly as accommodating." Winter motioned for the others to join him. "I've already contacted your friend Meadows, Dr. Tyrone. He assures me there will be no . . . how did he put it? Ah yes, the *monkey business.*"

Atteberry glanced at the truck. The CCR soldiers had all dropped their weapons now and lay face down on the ground.

Winter strolled purposefully toward the gateway, then stopped and turned. "Oh, it almost slipped my mind."

"What's that?" Atteberry asked through gritted teeth.

"It seems one of my other ships you're familiar with, the *Edelgard*, picked up some space debris near Luna. Would you like to know what she discovered out there floating around in the dark?"

"Not particularly."

"I think you'll want to hear this." He paused, but Atteberry refused to speak. "Very well, I'll tell you, anyway. It seems an object simply appeared out of nowhere. Can you imagine that?" He stroked his chin. "What kind of vessel instantaneously appears like that? Indeed, Herr Professor, it is a puzzle. Also, this item resisted all sensor sweeps, all scans. The *Edelgard*, well, she had to see it up close to identify what it was. Any guesses? Hm?"

Atteberry bit his lower lip, glowering at Winter.

"A life pod! What do you make of that? At first, the crew ignored it, preferring to patrol the area, but they detected life signs and had to secure the pod in their cargo bay." He approached Atteberry and whispered in his ear, "Do you know who they found inside?"

Atteberry's heart raced, and his eyes widened. His knees turned to jelly, and he reached out for a stool.

"Yes, look at you! A smitten schoolboy pining for his *hase*. You understand! How delightful. It seems that mongrel friend of yours, Kate Braddock, has returned." His sneer tightened. "And you'd hardly recognize her anymore."

THIRTY-ONE

Atteberry

"ARE YOU SO CRUEL, WINTER, THAT YOU FIND IT NECESSARY to screw around with us? What, do you derive some sick pleasure spewing this garbage?" Atteberry lunged again, but the soldier watching him intervened and slammed him to the lab floor. Fresh pain shot up his wounded leg, and in an odd swirl of confused, raw emotions, what he experienced was intense bitterness, cloaked in purpose. He struggled to rise, and the animal hauled him up by his shirt.

Winter, observing the loading bay gateway, continued. "I must admit, Herr Professor, that you are right: I do enjoy our little conversations, but what I tell you about Fraulein Braddock is entirely true."

"I don't believe you. I saw that Rossian ship vanish in an instant, and Kate was on board."

"Suit yourself, but perhaps you can explain these?" He held his indie-comm to Atteberry's face. A series of images scrolled past, showing what appeared to be a small capsule in space with a corner of Luna in the background. And another with the vessel in a ship's cargo area, surrounded by armed security guards. If it was a life pod, the configuration was unlike anything he'd seen. A figure lying prone inside it. Finally, a shot of that person—Kate—rising up. She was dressed in an *Echo* envirosuit, *sans* helmet, her face withdrawn. He recognized fear bordering on shock and dismay, but she looked different . . . changed. Mary had told him about the healing she'd experienced, but until he saw this image of her, he did not understand. *Is she the same person at all?* Memories tugged at his heart like candles being lit one by one.

Winter lowered the device. "So you understand? She is safe with us on the *Edelgard*." He paused, watching a couple of his mercs secure the area around the truck. Turning to Atteberry, he asked, "Would you love to see her again?"

The shock of knowing Kate was alive rifled through his body. "Yes," he whispered.

"And so you shall, as long you remain cooperative."

His shoulders slumped, and he looked at Mary being restrained. Her sunken eyes appeared distant, not fully grasping the activity in the lab. "You want to take Mary to the *Sara Waltz* and scrape her mind?"

"That's such a barbaric term for the procedure, but essentially yes. However," he added, "I have grown quite fond of the girl and I do not wish her any harm. It is the alien's knowledge I crave."

With Janet gone and Winter firmly in control of the lab, he had no choice but to risk going with him. "How will she get there?"

"The *Sara Waltz* remains in space dock. I've already negotiated with the CCR to secure transport by heli-jet to New Houston for us and the quantum computer. It seems the Republic has little interest in you or the girl. They already have what they coveted. Once there, we'll take the elevator to the ship." His indie-comm pinged and Winter answered. After a few minutes, he said, "Thank you, Sergeant Meadows. It has been a pleasure doing business with you." After punching a code into his device, he shoved it in his pocket and focused on Mary.

"This will all be over soon, young fraulein. And you'll return as good as new."

"What about Kate?" Atteberry asked. "Do you intend to let her go?"

Winter pulled a face. "That remains to be seen."

"Why?"

"I only wish to be honest with you. In this line of work, it doesn't pay to be emotionally attached to anything or anyone. Your colleague possesses intimate knowledge of this alien spaceship too, and I should like to have a . . . a fulsome conversation about her experience."

Atteberry clenched his fists. "No, I demand you let her go, too. You've got my cooperation, Winter, and my daughter. What more could you possibly want?"

Motion from the other side of the loading bay caught their attention and Atteberry witnessed the mercs lining up all the CCR soldiers and shoving them away from the truck.

Winter pursed his thin lips. "First, Herr Professor, you are not in a position to demand anything. Second, you ask what more could I desire? I'll tell you." He pushed Fischer and the other guard aside and breathed into Atteberry's face. "I want it all."

"And what about the Rossian ship? Did it return?"

"There is no sign of that vessel, unfortunately, for surely I would like to study her and the life form that put her together. Alas, sometimes we do not always get what we wish for."

The familiar *thucka-thucka* and whine of an approaching heli-jet broke the tension in the lab. Winter said, "Well, Herr Professor, I have enjoyed our brief chat, but it's time for all this drama to end. So unnecessary." He gestured to Fischer, and they pushed Mary, Esther and him together. "Fortunately, it ends now."

They escorted the hostages to the gateway leading outside. Gusts of wind greeted them as they approached; the crush of the incoming heli-jet above filled the air.

As they marched up the loading ramp toward the awaiting truck, another sound pierced the noise, one that Atteberry recognized immediately.

The *crack* of a single rifle shot.

He turned in time to see the tall soldier closest to Esther slump in a heap of blood and brain spatter. Gore covered her chest and face, and at first, he was convinced they'd hit her, too. He raced toward her and she screamed, then instinctively dropped to her knees, hands wiping the filth from her cheeks.

Crack.

Atteberry glimpsed to his right. Fischer's head exploded and what was left of him teetered, then collapsed in a heap. Winter ducked inside the lab, taking cover behind the wall. One of the mercs grabbed Mary by the arm, but Atteberry—forgetting his circumstances and acting on instinct—slugged the soldier at the base of the skull, sending him to his knees. He wrapped Mary by the waist, hauled Esther up by her blood-soaked hand, and dashed into the lab. They hid under the closest workstation. The remaining mercs fired weapons indiscriminately wherever they could. Another *crack* took one of them down, clutching his shoulder and crying out in pain. The other, watching his colleague writhe on the ground, bolted for a nearby stand of trees and disappeared.

The noise from the heli-jet faded as the pilot must have realized the mission had gone poorly and aborted his landing.

Esther trembled. Her ashen face bloomed in streaks of blood. She kept swatting at her cheeks and forehead, as if shooing blackflies. Mary, still with a vacuous appearance, sat motionless against the side of a desk.

Atteberry poked his head up from behind some technical equipment and gazed around. Pockets of scientists and technicians huddled in pairs or trios. A construction worker lay splayed against the wall, his sliced body riddled with holes. An eerie silence descended on the cavernous room.

Only then did he notice that Winter had vanished.

THE ELEVATOR DOORS *WHOOSHED* OPEN and Atteberry ducked again. Someone shouted commands and the sound of boots running caused him to grab Mary and Esther in his arms to protect them from whatever was coming. A flash of movement above caught his attention. He gazed toward the ceiling. About a dozen soldiers lowered themselves from a cutaway. Several had already reached the floor and spotted him.

More shouting and more running.

"They're over here!"

"Gateway secured!"

"Fan out and recon the immediate vicinity!"

Atteberry blinked and waited. Momentarily, he heard the scuffle of boots and looked up. Sergeant Meadows stood before him, flanked by two CCR soldiers, their weapons drawn and pointing at his head.

"Stand down, men."

Meadows reached out to Atteberry. He took his hand, and the soldier helped him to his feet. He did the same for Esther and Mary.

"Am I ever glad to see you," Esther said, gaining control over herself, yet unable to stop the emotional release of tears. The agent grabbed her in his arms, and drew a cloth from his belt and dabbed her face.

"Anyone hurt?"

Atteberry shook his head, but there was no mistaking the firefight had shaken them emotionally. He swallowed hard, forcing his breathing to relax. "What just happened here?"

"Commander Winter thought he had the drop on us, but it'll take more than a handful of rented assassins to take my team down. When he made his move toward the truck, I ordered my sniper on the rooftop to open fire. Unfortunately, it appears the elusive Winter escaped. But we'll find him. There's only so many places to hide." He glanced at the gateway leading outside and surveyed the rest of the lab. "We're secure for now, but it's not safe here." He looked at Mary. "How is she?"

"She needs a doctor bad." He scrutinized the agent and asked, "Why are you suddenly so helpful? A short time ago, you were ready to kill us, too." Atteberry still had difficulty discerning who he could trust. Janet, for now. Esther, not too sure. Someone in a uniform? Not bloody likely.

"I'm afraid that's on me, Mr. Atteberry. Unfortunately, protocol dictates certain actions in these cases. But I can tell you, the person we wanted was Janet Chamberlain. The CCR has no quarrel with you or what you're doing."

By this time, a medic had appeared beside them and cleaned Esther with antiseptic wash and health cloths. He pumped something into her with a hypo-spray, and turned his attention to Mary. Sporadic gunfire and distant shouts wafted in through the gateway, startling them and causing Atteberry to duck instinctively.

"Sergeant Meadows," he said after a moment, "we still have to get that equipment to New York. We're running out of time and can't delay any longer."

The soldier frowned. "I'm sorry, but I have to keep you here. We need to debrief you, find out what Winter's doing and how all this is connected to Ross 128."

"Listen, I'd love to stay and chat, but not now." He peered around the room. "One of your men was going to drive the truck to the airport. Is he still here?"

"We'll get you there in due time, sir, but first we need to ask some questions . . . questions for all of you."

The medic pulled two emergency blankets from his kit, handed one to Esther and wrapped the other around Mary. He glanced at Meadows. "This girl needs to be in a hospital, Sergeant. Immediately."

Atteberry fought back. "No, she's going to Gotham Medical. There's a surgical team and, and this computer will fix her, and . . . and we've got to go."

"Listen, Mr. Atteberry," the medic straightened up, pulling him aside, "your daughter's in no shape to move. Her bio-markers are weak and her systems are failing. She needs treatment right away. I'll give her a mild stimulant and pseudophine to help manage the pain and confusion, but I'm limited as to what I can do in the field."

The Sergeant's comms unit squawked, and he excused himself, then calmly gave instructions to his team. Atteberry turned to the medic. "Couldn't you accompany her to New York?"

"No, sir. I'd love to, and for sure I'm a medic first, but also CCR. The NDU police and military would never let me leave if I showed up."

"What about another doctor, some civilian from the hospital here?"

"Perhaps, but Mary requires help right away. She needs electrolytes, nutrients, blood thinners . . . I'm not equipped to handle all that. I serve more of a *stop the bleeding get 'em to a hospital* function."

Sergeant Meadows rejoined them. "The area's secure. You're safe to move now, and I'll have some of my soldiers escort you to our station for interviews. We'll take your daughter to the hospital too, but in the meantime, my services are needed elsewhere." He glanced at Esther. "You'll see a doctor shortly, ma'am."

"I told you," Atteberry protested, "we can't go with you, Sergeant. We have to get to New York."

"And I said, that won't happen yet. Seriously, I'm shocked you'd risk your daughter's life that way."

"Risk her life? No, I'm trying to save her." He held Mary by the waist. "Fine, if you won't escort us to the airport, I'll drive the damn truck myself." He marched toward the gateway. "Esther, you coming?"

"Jim, I—I don't think we can—"

Mary shrieked, grabbing her head and collapsing to her knees. Esther ran to her side, followed by the medic. Atteberry tried holding her up, but the moment she stopped screaming, her body convulsed in spasms as she lay supine on the concrete floor. Her strength surprised him, but with the help of Sergeant Meadows, they held her down while the medic checked her vitals.

"It might be too late for a hospital, sir," he shouted over the confusion. "She's in cardiac arrest."

Carter

"WHAT DO YOU MEAN THERE'S NO MEDICAL PERSONNEL?" Carter bellowed in the confines of the small but impressive med bay aboard the *Echo*. He towered in front of a bio-signs unit, admiring the state-of-the-art capability to keep the crew healthy. "We have a fully equipped, world-class clinic here and no doctor to run it?"

"That's a massive drawback of the revised schedule," Captain Powell replied. "There's nobody willing to join us."

"No one?"

Powell shrugged. "No one I'd be comfortable flying with, put it that way."

"Then we must fix this problem immediately. Consider this, John. Mary Atteberry is not well and I gather Esther and the girl's father have been investigating various ways to remove the alien mind from her own, without success. But what if . . ." he motioned to the med bay, "what if we brought her here instead of Gotham Medical? Is this facility capable of performing surgery?"

"It is, but—"

"I should say, a complex brain operation."

Powell put his hands on his hips and kicked the concrete floor. "Well, I'm no surgeon, but Dr. Weybourne helped us spec it out, and she's one of the best in the field of ship hospitals. I'd be surprised, knowing how meticulous she is, if she didn't account for all kinds of scenarios."

"Excellent. All we need is a doctor."

Powell wiped some grease off his fingers. "But not any old bone-saw fresh out of college, Clayton. If we're going into battle in space, we'll require someone with specialized skills, experience, and resourcefulness. Remember, we designed the med bay for one practitioner only."

Carter knew all about the specs and recalled the debates over the size of the clinic. Powell and the other captains argued they only required one medic on a ship the size of the *Echo*, whereas on the *Malevolent*, for example, they needed a team of doctors and nurses. Ed Mitchell at the time worried about the lack of redundancy if only a singular medical professional were on board the smaller craft: it raised the risks immensely. However, Carter reminded him of the cost of specialized, skilled personnel, and if the corps of captains felt safe with one medic, he would not argue the point. It took Ed a full week to stop sulking, but he eventually accepted it and they settled the matter.

Before they discussed the absence of a doctor further, a comms technician poked his head in the med bay. "I'm sorry to interrupt, sirs."

"What is it, Charlie?"

"Urgent call from the *Malevolent* on a secure channel, requesting a conference with both of you immediately."

They scrambled out of the ship and followed the tech to an enclosed communications center. Two other comms operators engaged in conversation in front of a bank of monitors, all showing unique views of the hangar. Carter recognized his own technical lab at headquarters appearing on one of the screens.

Charlie stopped by the main viewer. Captain Russo on the *Malevolent*'s bridge was speaking to a couple of crew members, who then raced out of the frame. Behind her, smoke hung thick in the air. He hailed the ship, and she turned to face the camera, hitting a button on the helm. The cacophony of bridge conversations spilled over the loudspeaker into the room.

Charlie handed the two men head mics. Powell threw his on and said in a calm voice, "Captain, what's the situation?"

"Not good, John. The *Volmar* has seen through our ruse. They launched a series of nuclear torpedoes to starboard. Glancing blows, more a warning than anything else. Shields are holding and we've taken evasive action. We blew a couple of secondary circuits when the torps struck us. Minor damage, and we've re-routed to engineering."

"Injuries?" Carter asked.

"Nothing significant."

Powell spoke again. "What's the tactical situation, Laura?"

Russo scanned the bridge, pointed to something, and returned her attention to the screen. "We can manage the *Volmar*, but as I reported to Clayton earlier today, the lead ships in the armada are closing within firing range. They'll be a factor shortly, but again, nothing we can't handle." She paused and grimaced. "It's the heavies I'm worried about. Once they arrive, we'll be seriously out-gunned."

Carter remembered what she'd said about the complement of vessels all zeroing in on the stand-off between her ship and the

Volmar. Mitchell's bluff had worked for a while. It bought them all some time, but now that time was running out. He could no longer sit back and wait. They had to get the *Echo* off the ground.

He spoke again. "Laura, I'm glad you suffered no casualties, and I want to reassure you that help is on the way. I expect the *Echo* to be airborne within 15 minutes."

Powell glared at him, but Carter ignored the look. "Yes, we must finish loading up a few things here first. Do you think you can avoid all-out war in the meantime?"

Russo opened her mouth, but Powell interrupted her. "Excuse me a moment, Captain." He motioned to Charlie to cut their microphones, and turned to Carter. "We can't be airborne in 15 minutes, Clayton. Why, we'd have to begin our pre-launch sequence right now in order to—"

"Then I suggest you start it, Captain."

Powell stood his ground, bristling. "Mr. Carter, if I may remind you, this is an operational matter. It's not your call to make."

Carter bit his lip. "We will launch in fifteen minutes. There are lives at stake and I won't let them down."

"Even if it means flying without a crew?"

Carter narrowed his gaze. "You wouldn't dare."

"I suggest you not test my resolve. My crew understands the need for thoroughness with pre-flight readiness, especially if we're about to run headfirst into a firefight. If I don't think we're ready, they won't fly." He clenched his jaw. "That's no threat, Clayton," he said calmly. "That's a fact."

The two men stared each other down for a moment, and Carter, feeling the rise of a sour taste in his mouth, sighed and muttered, "Open the channel, Charlie. Let the captains discuss this." He stormed out of the comms center.

Atteberry

THE MEDIC'S NAME WAS FAIRCHILD. Atteberry caught it as the man pumped medicine into Mary's arm, and within seconds, she calmed down. Atteberry watched in horror as her eyes rolled back in her head and blood spilled from her nose and ears. Fairchild pushed him and Meadows away and grabbed a fist-sized palette from his kit that he placed over her heart. When he switched the device on, an amber light glowed around it and Mary's body relaxed as she lay unconscious.

"What can I do to help?" he asked as he knelt down beside her.

The medic tossed him his indie-comm and said, "Contact emerg at the Medical Center at UCSF." He gave him the number and Atteberry got the central switchboard. "Ask for Dr. Yazid in neurology."

A minute later, a tired sounding voice came through the external speaker on the indie-comm. Fairchild explained what had happened and transmitted Mary's bio-signs. Meanwhile, Esther joined them on the floor and wiped Mary's face with a health cloth. Mary moaned as she whispered encouragement to her.

"Fairchild," the neurosurgeon said, "based on what you sent me, the good news is her heart's stabilized. Continue monitoring her pulse and be ready with additional beta blockers if it races again." He paused. "Is it possible to scan her head for brain trauma and send me the images? If your device has the capability, I'd like to get as deep into the molecular level as possible."

The medic pulled a portable field scanner from his bag. "Establishing the link now . . . stand by." After a few seconds, they heard the familiar ping of the data connection being secured. He swept the device across Mary's head.

"I see nothing. Try decreasing the scanning frequency slightly."

Fairchild did as the neurologist demanded and repeated the sweeping motion.

"Better, but still nothing. I need to see below the brain surface."

"Understood." He made further adjustments, then looked at Atteberry. "Dr. Yazid is the finest neurosurgeon in the region, and fortunately, the Med Center is only a few minutes away. As soon as we can move her, we'll take her there."

Esther threw Atteberry a glance, but he said nothing, too numb to think, too spent to do anything but react on a base, visceral level.

"That's got it!" Yazid's voice boomed through the speaker. "Hold it steady . . . good . . . now do a gentle sweep from her chin to the top of her head . . ." The medic complied, checking the images on the indie-comm being transmitted to the hospital. "Excellent . . . now, scan from one ear to the other."

They worked without speaking for the next couple of minutes. During that time, Esther found Atteberry's arm and placed her hand over it. He let it stay there briefly, then pulled away, and asked, "How is she?"

Yazid's voice, steady and professional, responded. "I've seen nothing like this before. What exactly happened to her . . . her brain?"

Fairchild peered at Atteberry, and invited him to speak. "An encounter with . . ." He searched his mind for the right words. "...another being. Somehow, this creature's memories were transferred to Mary's brain." He looked at Fairchild. "That's all I know."

Mary stirred on the floor, but remained out of it.

"There are two consciousnesses in your daughter?"

"Yes, and that's what's causing all these problems. We spoke with a specialist in New Houston—a Dr. Elliot—and he believed he could siphon off the other's memories."

Yazid grunted. "From what I can tell—and we'll have to confirm with a closer look once she gets here—the activity in her brain is unprecedented." He paused. "Fairchild, are you seeing the images too?"

"Yes, but the resolution on this screen is poor."

"Okay, so here's what I'm observing." He cleared his throat and began. "There's a constant flux of neurons firing, initiating action potentials and creating comms across her synapses. Frankly, it's impossible to differentiate at this point which source links to thought, and which one is receiving. But clearly the constituents of a section of Mary's brain—axons, dendrites . . . the soma, terminal buttons, myelin sheaths, nodes of Ranvier, Schwann cells—all of these have aligned their states to mirror corresponding constituent inputs from the alien mind."

"What does that mean?" Atteberry asked.

"It suggests, and again I caution about jumping to conclusions without a thorough examination, that even if I could distinguish between the two minds, there's no possibility of separating them." He now spoke plainly. "That Dr. Elliot in New Houston . . . you say he claimed he could disconnect the two?"

"That's why we traveled there for an operation."

"What happened?"

"They killed the doctor before he even began."

"I see. And if I understand that line of research, he was one of only a few in the world capable of attempting such an operation."

"Yes, but there's one more doctor in London who could help. She's en route to Gotham Medical in New York right now."

"I'm afraid travel for this patient is out of the question," Dr. Yazid said.

"Nonsense. Dr. Lamont understands the enormity of the procedure and agreed to help, and if we stabilize Mary—"

"I'm sorry, you misunderstand."

Atteberry's eyes narrowed as he glimpsed Yazid's face on the indie-comm. "What are you talking about?"

"Mary's mind has become so entwined with the alien's, that trying to isolate and separate one from the other is impossible. Her condition is . . . inoperable."

Atteberry swallowed hard as the wisps of remaining energy evaporated.

"I hope I'm wrong, and maybe after we've checked her out . . ." Yazid's voice fell aside. Everyone encircling Mary understood that the doctor didn't hold out much hope for a different prognosis.

"But the status quo is killing her."

The lab became deathly silent.

"How long does she have?"

"I'm not comfortable speculating without—"

"How long!" Atteberry snapped.

The doctor sighed. "A few hours at most before she becomes comatose, judging by the rate of decay in her organs."

Atteberry dropped his gaze. *This can't be happening.* He surveyed the room, which now adopted the melancholy of a funeral home despite the bright lights and activity. Groups of scientists milled about, and half a dozen soldiers had taken up positions at the gaping loading bay doors. But Sergeant Meadows was no longer with them.

THIRTY-TWO

Kate

WHEN SHE RELEASED THE MAGNETIC SEAL ON HER LIFE POD and pulled herself to a sitting position, half a dozen Prussian crew members immediately surrounded Kate in what appeared to be a cargo hold on the heavy cruiser. Her initial trepidation quickly gave way to relief when none of them had weapons drawn. A second glance suggested they carried stunners, not firearms, which spoke of internal discipline in the ranks if nothing else. One of the crew approached and helped her out of the pod. A flash of vertigo enveloped her and she grabbed onto the young ensign's shoulder.

Two women, dressed in light blue work suits, entered the hold.

"Ensign, we'll take it from here," the silver-haired woman said in German. Turning to Kate, she added in English, "I'm Dr. Heslop and this is my assistant Nadia." She grabbed her by the waist and eased her over to a nearby bench. "Who are you?"

Kate shook the dizziness from her brain and wondered if this was a trick question. *Surely, they must recognize me?* But she didn't want a confrontation. In game theory–the basis of all interrogations–the key was not getting caught in a lie. "Kate Braddock."

"Well, Kate Braddock," the doctor began, "welcome to the *Edelgard*." The assistant busied herself studying Kate's vital signs on a data slate. "Where are you from?"

She inhaled deeply, peered around at the encircling group and said, "I'd like some water if you please."

Dr. Heslop flicked a hand at one of the crew and he disappeared, returning momentarily with a packet and protein bar. Kate accepted them both and drank.

"I was on Luna, mapping anomalies for Titanius for the past several years. Perhaps you heard the habitat was destroyed?"

The doctor narrowed her gaze but gave no sign either way.

"Well anyway, my student and I were forced to abandon the station and after a long, circuitous route, we wound up . . ." Images of the grey dust and near death experience filled her mind. "We were rescued by the *Echo*. At least, Mary was. I remained with the . . ." She needed to understand how much these people understood, and wanted them to fill in the space.

Doctor Heslop examined her thyroid glands and shoulders. "Yes, we realize you disappeared on that alien craft. That's what we assumed since there was no evidence of you anywhere on Luna, and the chatter showed you weren't on the Titanius ship."

Kate peered into her cold, beady eyes.

"No sign of any known pathogens or internal damage, Doctor. In fact, the patient is remarkably healthy." Nadia glanced at Kate with a quizzical look. "But I thought you were . . ." She lowered her gaze, taking in her form.

Heslop broke in. "Are you well? Were you hurt in any way?"

Kate relaxed under the doctor's care and took a bite of the protein bar before answering. "Yes, fine. The creature didn't harm me." She swallowed. "I do feel a bit faint from the space travel, though."

"Here, I have something for that." To Nadia, she said, "Give her 25 CCs of the blended ketones." Her assistant prepared the dose and administered it. Within seconds, the effects of the flight diminished.

"Thank you."

A moment later, another Prussian entered the hold. This heavy-set man wore a commander's uniform. The crew members backed away a pace, allowing him to stroll toward Kate and the doctor. He studied her quizzically, then said, "So you are the one they call Kate Braddock . . . the Spacer?" His gravelly voice spoke of years of barking orders and downing whiskey. She detected something sweet on his breath.

"Yes," she replied, attempting to stand.

"Please allow me." He gently guided her to her feet. "My name is Captain Adam Beck. Welcome aboard the *Edelgard*. I trust you are well?"

"Yes."

"Good, and as soon as you're feeling better, I must show you around."

Kate's face must have reflected her confusion, for the captain quickly added, "Yes, you are my guest, Ms. Braddock. I can only imagine the stories you've heard about the Prussians over the years, but I assure you—and as you can see—we are a hospitable people." He motioned to the door. "Come, let's get acquainted."

She inhaled deeply, catching the doctor nodding at the captain.

"Doctor, please join us when you're finished here."

Kate gulped, but allowed herself to be escorted out of the cargo hold. Without her full strength or sufficient knowledge of the ship, attempting escape at this point would be suicide. Before the door swished closed, the crew in the hold had already started poring over the life pod, several of them scanning the craft with their data slates and remote sensors. In the hallway outside the bay, two armed sentries stood, both just this side of nasty. They had full weapons. No stunners for these brutes. She noted the deck and corridor number: *E14.*

The captain led her to a compact meeting room. Inside, a circular table with space for a handful of people occupied the center. Two viewscreens covered the walls and a side bar contained various pieces of equipment: a couple of slates, mem sticks and data tubes. He invited her to sit.

"Are you aware of what happens next, Ms. Braddock?"

She studied him carefully. Interrogation was unavoidable, so the only question was how the Prussians would administer the process.

"Yes."

"I do not enjoy this aspect of the job, by the way. I find it . . . disagreeable." He turned to the comms unit on the side table. "Would you like some tea? I have a smooth Bavarian herbal leaf that's delicious."

"No. Thank you, though."

"As you wish." He spoke into the communicator and a moment later, a yeoman entered carrying a metal pot of tea and two cups on a tray. Kate threw him a questioning glance. "If you change your mind. There's no reason to be uncivilized about what must happen."

"In that case," she said, "I'll join you."

After Beck poured the tea, he leaned back, drawing a sip, smiling at Kate. "See, Braddock, you and I are very much alike."

"Oh? I wouldn't have concluded that. I'm a retired Spacer and you're the captain of a heavy cruiser."

He lowered his cup. "On the surface, perhaps, yet here we are, two grizzled old veterans of the cold wars, each following orders. While you were punching around in that American Spacer program, I performed a similar function with the Prussian Consortium. Satellite disruptions were my specialty. Hijacking code, and such. I doubt very much," he added, "that between us there's anything we haven't seen. In fact, our early careers are almost identical."

"We may have shared related jobs, but our lives were nowhere near the same." She placed her cup on the table. "I was a kid when they recruited and sterilized me. And if I understand correctly, your kind at least could apply for that work after college. When you were young men and women. Not kids."

He smirked. "Touché." Then he narrowed his gaze. "But look at you now, Braddock. You are, shall I say . . .well-restored?"

Kate recognized what was coming next. "Yes. Completely healed, returned to what I would have been physically if allowed to grow naturally, and then some."

"And how did this happen?"

She pursed her lips. "I won't help you, Captain. You understand that."

He sighed. "I do, so let's not waste time with any further interrogative foreplay. We both have our assigned roles, don't we?"

He hit a button on the comms unit and Dr. Heslop entered, ramrod straight, carrying a med kit under her arm. She placed it on the side table and extracted a hypo from the black bag.

Beck picked a rogue tea leaf speck off his tongue. "This is painless, but a highly effective way of obtaining information. The doctor will administer it and remain here to ensure there are no . . . complications." Then to Heslop, "*Bitte*, we shall finish our tea first."

The only other time Kate had experienced truth treatment as a captured teenager, she remembered nothing of the process, but two spacer colleagues had disappeared before she'd been rescued. As she sipped her tea, drawing it out, she focused on protecting Mary, on seeing Jim. Her sole mission now was to survive long enough to tell him what she'd seen in the galaxy . . . and what she harboured *in here*.

She swallowed the dregs, handed the empty cup to Beck and glared at the doctor. "Let's get this over with."

Janet

MUSTY, DAMP AIR FILLED JANET'S NOSTRILS even under the heavy burlap hood she'd been wearing since turning herself over at the TSA. When a soldier finally removed it, the familiar stench she couldn't quite place overwhelmed her, and she gagged. As her eyes adjusted to the dim light, four CCR soldiers appeared. Two flanked a grey metal door—a man and a woman—another hulking figure sat at a small worktable in the corner, and the fourth, also male, stood directly in front, holding the hood. There were no windows. The walls comprised thick cinder blocks covered in abstract designs. One thin lightbulb hung from the ceiling. They'd mag-cuffed her hands behind and planted her on a steel chair.

Then she recognized the odor. Her stomach flipped, releasing the remaining, unabsorbed booze she'd taken in the hovercar.

Those weren't abstract designs at all.

The man at the table had his back turned, but was the first to speak as he arranged various objects in front of him from a toolbox on the floor.

"Janet Chamberlain," he mused. "You've been a naughty old soul." The pitch of his voice, mousier than the average, juxtaposed against his broad shoulders and thick hands. Janet licked her cracked lips. "Do you know where you are?"

She refused to answer.

"It doesn't matter. He peered up at the wall but did not face her. "One room's the same as any other in this grisly business, hm?" He reached into the box and withdrew more tools of the trade: heavy-duty bolt cutters, needle-nose pliers, and something long and thin.

Janet gulped, reaching deep inside for the courage to accept what was about to happen. She'd been tortured once before in her career; sexually assaulted three times. The scar tattooed across her chin came to mind—almost invisible now with the passing years—and how she picked that up when some republican creep slammed her into a concrete floor shortly after her 26th birthday. Poor Jim had no clue.

Jim . . .

"Of course, it doesn't have to be this way," the fellow continued. "If you cooperate and tell me what I wish to learn, I'll spare you from these . . . performance incentives."

The soldier in front of her showed off a mouth full of broken teeth. She stared hard at him, chin thrust forward, then spoke defiantly. "I suppose you aren't man enough to take these off and show me what you really got, eh? You only feel safe when I'm like this." She twisted her shoulders. "Release me," she spat, glancing at his crotch, "and let's see how tough you actually are."

The speaker at the table chuckled. "Now, now, we know better than to let you out. This process is unpleasant and unfair, and nothing would give me greater pleasure than to squeeze you until your eye sockets leak. But we cannot risk it." He pushed his chair back, creating a guttural noise as it scraped along the floor. The man stood and slowly turned to show his face.

The first thing that struck her, even in this dim light, was the burning blue eyes. They were wide-set on a canvas stitched in scars. Yet, something more peculiar presented itself, more than just his pock-marked skin. He lacked all facial hair, including eyebrows.

"My name is Lucas." He approached her with heavy steps. "And this is my colleague Dorian." He didn't bother pointing to the soldier with the broken teeth. Instead, he played with a box-cutter in his hand, twirling it across his fingers like a pen, and watched her with mock interest. "Now then, you understand, Ms. Chamberlain, that you're a wanted fugitive in the California Congressional Republic. Let's see, there's multiple murders, one assassination attempt that we're aware of, terrorist charges related to the bombing of the Mount Sutro Tower, and theft of top-secret documents for starters. Well, the details hardly matter because, should you survive the next few hours, you will spend the rest of your days in military prison." He glared at her. "Do you know about the institution in Ojai?"

She shook her head. Although she'd been briefed all about the maximum security facility that held mostly serial killers, rapists, and terrorists, Janet wanted him to keep talking. As long as he spoke, he wasn't beating on her.

Lucas grinned coldly. "Just as well. It's not the kind of place you'd want to visit."

"Whatever, you've got me now, so how about ditching the intimidation drama and formally arrest me. I'm still entitled to a fair hearing and justice."

"Justice." He whispered the word in a curious, amused way. Then stepping forward, he grabbed her chin in a vise-like grip, lifting her face until she grunted. "Your idea of justice lives not in this room."

Janet struggled to catch her breath and her jawbone cracked, shooting darts of pain through her teeth and ears. But she wouldn't give Lucas or Dorian the satisfaction of watching her squirm. Instead, she lashed out with her boot, striking Lucas in the cheek before he could react. He staggered back but quickly caught his balance.

"See," he chuckled, rubbing his face, "this is why you are cuffed and shall remain so until there's nothing left of you except running sores and maggot meat." His face adopted a resigned look, as if she somehow had disappointed him. But Lucas was only beginning, for he waved the box-cutter at Dorian, motioning him to proceed.

Dorian, the one with the broken teeth.

Dorian, the one with the rapist's eye.

Dorian, the one towering over her, cracking his knuckles.

Dorian, the soldier who now grabbed the back of her head, and clenched his fist.

"Wait," Lucas interjected.

The soldier pulled his punch but kept Janet's hair locked in his hand.

"When you are ready to share your operations, safehouses, moles, and what not, then simply say so.

Janet opened her mouth and worked her jaw long enough for the pain to sear its way through her mind. She glanced at Dorian, poised for violence, and spat blood in his face. In a flurry of expletives, the soldier dropped her head and wiped the spittle away with his sleeve. Then, with a determination she had yet to see in any of the CCR soldiers, Dorian grabbed her again and unleashed his rage.

The first punch to the temple shocked her, and stars appeared in her vision.

The next landed on her eye, the same one she'd damaged earlier with Winter and his cronies.

The last blow she remembered caught her flush on the jaw, snapping the bone like a twig, causing a torrent of blood to burst from her mouth. Her head snapped back, and she stared at the dim light on the ceiling, that putrid stench of tortures past weaving into her thoughts as the blooming black fog slowly consumed her, until she sensed nothing at all.

THIRTY-THREE

Atteberry

AN EERIE SILENCE BLANKETED THE SPACE OPERATIONS LAB. The medic, Fairchild, had pumped Mary with a mild stimulant to bring her back into consciousness, and then gathered his equipment. He said, "I still think we should get her to emergency, sir. They're better equipped to help her."

Atteberry knelt on the floor beside his daughter, resignation that she had only a few hours to live settling across his body. He faced Fairchild as if to respond, but Mary spoke first.

"Dad, we'll be okay. This isn't the end."

Atteberry choked, fighting back raw emotion. "Oh Mares, I don't know what I'll ever do."

"Dad," she grinned, "Trust us. We don't wish to die, but don't fear it. There's so much more ..." her gaze became distant again. "... going on ..."

Esther put her hand on his shoulder and asked, "Is there anything I can do, Jim?"

He shook his head.

"Mary?"

She lifted her arms and Atteberry took them, pulling her close. "Yes ... we'd like to visit the park. There's a lake nearby ..."

"Spreckels?"

"That's it. Let's go there, all of us. The water is so beautiful."

Fairchild, carrying his field kit, said, "I can't recommend that. We've got to leave for the hospital. There still might be a chance ..."

Atteberry flashed him a look that only a parent of a dying child could show: one of gratitude, of lost hope, yearning for peace but struggling against nature. The medic lowered his head and backed away.

Mary found more strength to sit up. "Take us to the lake, Dad. There's so much to tell."

A few minutes later, a military vehicle hovered down the loading ramp right into the lab and settle on its skids. With help from Atteberry and Esther, Mary boarded and lay down on an antigrav bed. Fairchild followed, indicating he'd give them their space at the park after he ensured they were okay. Atteberry thanked him, boarded with Esther, and they rose out of the building onto John F. Kennedy Boulevard toward Spreckels Lake, a few kilometers away.

As they glided over the flightway, Mary—more alert now as the stimulant kicked in fully—asked, "Where's Mom?"

"Not sure. We haven't heard a thing." To confirm this, he glanced at the medic who slowly nodded in accordance. "But you've seen what your mother can do, right? She said she'd join us, so we'll keep a lookout for her."

Mary smiled. *Where does she find the strength, the peace for all this? Is this acceptance something the alien is doing?* He kept hearing Janet's words in his head about Mary's brain being an asset even in death. A wisp of fresh panic rose in him as he played out various scenarios, and he dug deep to gather the courage to face what was coming. No one would mutilate her corpse.

Esther sat beside him and whispered, "I think we ought to get more CCR soldiers down here. For protection."

"I'm thinking the same thing, Es. That creep Winter is still on the loose, and if there's anything I've learned over the past 48 hours, it's that he's got as many lives as Janet. I wouldn't be surprised if he's watching us even now." As if to satisfy himself, Atteberry peered out the window at the passing trees and green space.

They eased over a side road that encompassed the lake and the vehicle descended onto its skids. Fairchild brought Mary out on the antigrav gurney, quickly joined by the two soldiers who had ridden up front. In the brilliant sunlight, the water's surface sparkled like a shimmering diamond. Several pedestrians, in pairs or solo, walked along the pathway or enjoyed the view from the benches stitched around the perimeter. An aircraft rumbled in the distance and Atteberry peered up into the beautiful blue, worried momentarily that something more was on its way. He spotted the contrails of a passenger jet to the west and relaxed.

Mary pointed to a small stand of ancient walnut and pines, and the group headed toward it. Inaudible radio chatter floated in from a soldier's device, and he caught the man's response about their location and additional troops coming their way.

The shade under the trees was surprisingly cool. Fairchild positioned the gurney to face the water, checked Mary's bio-signs again, then said, "I'll be over there if you need me." He lowered the antigrav until it rested on the soft ground and propped up her head. Atteberry and Esther flanked her.

"Dad, we have to do something."

"Sure, Mares, what would you like?"

She licked her lips and brushed her mouth with the back of her hand. "We don't want to die, but we—I mean, I—am ready for the end when it comes. You understand?"

His nose stung as fresh tears leaked out, but he pushed them down. *I must be strong.* "I think so. Still, I wish there was another way."

He saw that Esther, too, struggled to keep her brave face. She stared toward the lake.

"But I want you to do something."

"Sure, anything."

"It won't be easy, Dad. You have to . . . promise me that you'll do this one thing."

Curious, he leaned closer to her and said, "Just name it."

Her lips trembled. "If it comes to this, if Winter or some other group returns for us and I'm still alive . . ."

His heart sank, and the word crept out of his mouth like a dying whisper. "No . . ."

"Don't let them take me."

"Mares . . ."

"Promise me that you'll . . . kill me first."

He lowered his head among a riot of emotions clamoring at his brain.

"There's more," she added.

"Oh, Mary, please . . ."

She swallowed and squeezed her eyes, as if fighting off a terrible pain. "And you must do more, Dad." She paused. "You have to destroy my brain."

Could he murder his own daughter? Did he see her as the global threat that Janet did? He gazed off across the lake, watched the strollers come and go, some laughing, some with toddlers running around. Ducks floating in the calm waters, snatching at bugs or other flotsam in their never-ending search for food.

I'm searching, too, for a way out of this that doesn't involve infanticide.

"Dad?" Mary wouldn't let his silence substitute for the spoken word.

This was no question without significant consequences, so he tried to reason. Is Mary a threat? Yes. Well, no. The *knowledge* she held was the threat. She was the Keeper. Winter and whoever else stalked them were interested in what she experienced, not in her.

Is it possible to extract the alien mind without harming her? No. That much was certain now. Even Mary admitted to the hopelessness.

Could I sacrifice her to save others? He chewed on this question until his thoughts became an abstract muddle, a finger-painting of the mind. But he understood what Janet would do: she'd kill her daughter without thinking twice. Times like this, Atteberry wished he could be more detached, more decisive. Yet, to murder Mary required more courage from him than he had. Even if he argued that her death would be a mercy killing—that if someone had to do it, he ought to be the one—when the time came, he still wouldn't act. He was no Abrahm, no George Milton.

Even if she wants me to.

He glanced at Esther, and she seemed to understand his struggle. Yet, she had a pensive look on her face, bordering on a connection, a new realization.

"What's on your mind, Es?"

She squinted as she continued looking across the water, and said, "There may be an alternative."

"For what?"

She turned. "Perhaps there is a safe refuge for Mary, and for you. With no danger that others will . . . will pursue her even after . . ."

Atteberry's dread rose again. Esther didn't need to finish that sentence.

"Where is this place?"

"In space."

Space!

She continued. "Listen to me, Jim. What if Mary was on the *Echo*? Carter wants to return to space anyway, and what's safer than being on board the fastest vessel in the solar system?" Esther shifted her weight to one side and undid the top button on her blouse. "Think about it. If Mary—" She took her hand and spoke to her. "Forgive me, but if death is inevitable, why not experience it from the safety of the *Echo*?"

Atteberry wasn't impressed. "I don't trust that shithead Carter. You remember what he did on Luna during the rescue? Tried to breech the hull of that Rossian ship at the expense of Mary's life and Kate's too." He set his jaw. "No, Es, even if we got Mary on the *Echo*, Carter wants the same thing as all the others: her brain. At least here," he said, waving his arm around the park, "we have protection." He nodded at Fairchild, standing with the pair of soldiers from the vehicle about 20 meters away.

"Apparently, there's also some kind of stand-off going on up there between Titanius and a bunch of other ships. No, sorry, I feel safe here," Atteberry continued.

Esther remained silent for a few moments. Then she said, "What if I arranged it so Clayton wouldn't interfere?"

"It's his ship, remember?"

"Definitely, I'm saying what if his desire to gain Mary's knowledge wasn't a factor?"

He chewed his lip and watched Mary. Despite her deathly appearance, her eyes suggested a willingness to consider the *Echo*. She looked at him expectantly, complicating his position.

"Oh Mares," he whispered to her. "What should I do?"

She held her hand out and squeezed his arm with more strength than he expected. *Perhaps because of the peace she's found in this situation, she's more open to this idea.* But he didn't trust Clayton Carter. His stated intention was to rule the solar system, even if he couched it in words of expanding humanity's reach and improving the lives of everyone on the planet. His goal was to get that alien technology one way or another before anyone else. And that did not differ from Winter's.

"Let's hear what Esther has to say, Dad."

"Okay," he conceded, "how do you see this working?"

Esther spoke for the next several minutes, outlining the intricacies of operating a ship in space, especially when there's the potential for violence. Even if Carter owned the *Echo*, he wasn't in charge of its operations once in flight. "The captain," she said, "is the key, and he seemed reasonable and experienced in handling Carter. Remember that?"

Atteberry recalled a couple of occasions during the rescue mission where Captain Powell and Carter had differences of opinions, and how the last decision had always been the captain's.

Maybe there is a way.

"He's planning on taking the *Echo* out as soon as they've completed repairs. He wants to return to Luna, and there are worse places to go."

Mary grunted, shifting her weight on the gurney, and said, "Let's see if he'll take us."

Esther withdrew her indie-comm from her pocket and looked at Atteberry.

He lowered his head and grimaced.

She lifted herself off the grass and punched Carter's personal number. In a moment, she spoke. "Hello Clayton." Then she walked out of hearing range.

"Do you believe this is better, Mares?"

"Yes, I don't want to die, but I'm at peace with it. I only want . . ." she paused. "I prefer to be with you and Mom when it comes. If flying through space helps us—me— spend my last moments in wonder instead of fear, then let's do it." She paused and her eyelids flicked. "Besides, when I die in space, no one will get me after."

Esther spoke on the indie-comm, then punched her device, stuffed it in her pocket, and hurried to rejoin them. Her face was flushed, and she gasped for breath.

"What is it, Es? What's wrong?"

"Jim . . . not what's wrong . . . what's right!"

"What are you talking about? Will he help?"

"Better," she said. "Listen. They're planning on being airborne in the next few minutes, but he'll hold the ship back for us if we can leave immediately."

"Oh, my god. The heli-jet's still at the airport."

"And here's the best part. The *Echo*'s medical bay is fully operational. State-of-the-art equipment like you wouldn't believe, according to him."

"Yeah, but he likes embellishing. Better than a hospital?"

"Better than Gotham Medical, Jim. You understand Clayton as well as I do, and he does nothing without getting the best advice, the highest specs."

His heart pounded with a different thought. *Is it remotely possible to keep Mary alive?* "What about a doctor?"

Esther grimaced momentarily. "That's one thing they don't have yet. But," she continued, "suppose your surgeon from London, the one you've said is en route to New York? What if she joined us at the *Echo*'s base and—"

Atteberry read her mind. "—and we take the quantum computer there." He turned to Mary. "What do you think, Mares? Are you strong enough to travel to the east coast?"

Mary coughed and swallowed hard. "With help, we think so. More stimulant and pseudophine." She ran her tongue over her bottom lip, and added, "But that neurologist was right, Dad. Our condition . . . is still inoperable."

Atteberry's flicker of hope vaporized as she reminded him of how preposterous siphoning off the alien's memories truly was. This plan focused on allowing Mary to die a quiet death, not saving her. He wracked his brain, wondering if they'd all missed something about her affliction, something obvious they hadn't considered, something to bring his daughter back.

He concluded they had not.

Janet

SHE AWOKE TO THE SOUND OF MUFFLED VOICES. Her arms, stiff and numb with pain, remained cuffed behind her, but she no longer clung to the chair. Instead, as the blurry figures standing in front of her came into focus, she recognized where they'd ditched her. In a corner of the concrete room. In the shadows. Across from Lucas' "workbench". She spat out blood and drool on the damp floor and coughed.

The soldiers stopped talking. Lucas approached her with a jug of water and dumped it over her face.

"I'm relieved to see you're not finished yet. You know, Agent Chamberlain, sometimes Dorian doesn't recognize his own strength. I call that a personal misgiving . . . a character defect, if you will. But what do you say? Hm?"

304

She remained silent, concentrating on driving the fuzziness from her mind and fighting the searing pain in her broken jaw. *I must hold on . . . find a way out . . . and soon.* Dorian approached next, flexing his fingers like the fat kid in a bakery, grinning.

"He likes you, see?" Lucas paused, his eyes sparkling with the proceedings. "My colleague is funny. When he takes a shining to someone, he becomes as loyal as a labrador. He'll follow them everywhere, even when they don't realize it." Then his face took on a whimsical, curious look as he glanced between the two of them. "I had no idea. Perhaps you have met before, hm? Old foes?" Turning to Dorian, "Is that why you're so gentle with our guest?"

Dorian grunted and croaked, "Yes, we met on two occasions. Back in Oregon several years ago. More recently at Mount Sutro." His voice had a searing quality, like the sound of a table saw cutting through metal.

Janet studied him through the dripping mess of blood and water. She'd undertaken many missions across Oregon during the Flagstaff Uprising, but she couldn't place him. That happened long ago. He must have been part of the contingent of CCR soldiers at Mount Sutro that saved Jim, Kate and Esther, but his face was unfamiliar.

"You don't remember?" Dorian moved in closer, his fetid breath assaulting her nostrils. "Ah, but perhaps you can't say nothin' because of your crooked jaw." He sneered at her and blew into his hands.

Lucas resumed his patter. "Do you have anything important to say, or shall we continue?" He opened the box cutter and bent over close to her face, grabbed a handful of matted hair, and deftly sliced it off millimeters from her skull.

She fought to speak, but the only sound she made was a throaty groan. Dorian caught her by the shirt and dragged her back to the chair. He slammed her on it and spread her legs to maintain balance. Her head slumped forward on her chest and tears of pain welled up.

Although her swollen tongue and crushed jaw prevented her from speaking easily, she spat, "I have . . . nothing . . . to say except . . . see you in hell."

Lucas' expression remained unfazed. "How poetic." He turned to Dorian. "We have a poet in our playroom."

Dorian huffed and stepped forward, raising his fist.

"Not yet. Let's be patient. I want to savor this moment fully." Lucas brushed the soldier aside and brought the box cutter up to her neck. Janet's rage and fear pumped more adrenaline through her, and she threw daggers at the man with her swollen eyes.

Lucas teased the edge of the blade along her throat, across her Adam's apple, from ear to ear, leaving a thin trail of blood in its wake. Janet gulped but refused to flinch.

"You have more resolve than I imagined, Agent. No wonder you have evaded us for so long." Then, he took the cutter and, starting at the top of her shirt, he sliced through the fabric all the way to her pants, lingering just below her navel. With the side of his hand, he brushed the two halves of clothing aside, exposing her bra and contusions marring her body.

"Goodness," he purred. "Those Prussians must have enjoyed their time with you." He fingered the tiny clasp between her breasts. "Dorian and I will too."

Janet stared at the female guard to the right of the door. Their eyes met briefly, then the soldier dropped her head.

Lucas grabbed her hair and pulled her head back, sending fresh waves of pain through her mouth and skull. She squeezed her eyes shut and disappeared into her mind, remembering her training, as the soldier's warm breath flowed over her neck. His thick tongue then traced the hairline cut that the box cutter carved. He whispered something she didn't catch as she fought the terror seeping into her bones.

A steady *thump thump thump* interrupted Lucas' pleasure. He released his hold and backed away. Through tiny slits she saw the metal door swing open, and another soldier entered, stopping dead in his tracks, and barking orders. Stars peppered her vision as darkness encroached, and Janet struggled against the pain in her body to hold on to consciousness.

"Now!" the new man ordered.

Blurred figures shifted, soldiers in motion, activity in the room. But her grip on consciousness was tenuous. Her head slumped forward, and the black overwhelmed her.

WHEN SHE CAME TO, SOMEONE WAS MOPPING HER FOREHEAD and face with a cold medi-cloth. Startled, she pulled back until the hands in front of her gave way, revealing the sergeant from the TSA holding the material and frowning.

"Hush," he breathed, "you're safe now, ma'am."

Confusion enveloped her, and she sputtered through what they'd left of her mouth, "I . . . don't understand." *Unnershtan.*

"Sh. I examined you while you were passed out. Your jaw's shattered on the one side, but no other broken bones. Massive contusions on your torso. I don't detect any internal bleeding."

Janet shifted slightly in the chair and realized her hands were no longer cuffed. "Where are . . .?"

"The mechanics?" He exhaled slowly. "When I heard they'd brought you here, I couldn't let them affect their repairs. But they're gone now." The soldier pulled a hypo from a medical bag on the floor and moved to inject her. She leaned back into the chair. "It's okay, it's pseudophine. This'll help ease the pain until you get to a hospital." When he raised the hypo to her arm this time, she didn't pull away.

Over the next several minutes, he continued administering first aid, focusing on her face and head, but also applying freeze to her jaw and her left knee that, somewhere along the way, had swelled to the size of a grapefruit. As the pain receded, Janet studied the soldier more. She had recognized him back at the TSA, and now the memories returned: he was a soldier at Mount Sutro in '85. One of *them*—

"Yes, you remember, don't you? Sergeant Meadows."

Janet coughed. "Sutro . . . but why?"

Meadows took a knee in front of her, putting his kit back, then folded his hands together. "That was a hell of a night. I was part of a squad deployed to stop you and the other so-called terrorists at any cost. We had no idea about the alien signal at that point." He paused. "But the messages were contradictory. One captain said we were to rescue civilians from some crazy scientists. Another commander claimed you were all to be detained or killed. My team and I had to assess the situation as we went."

"You . . . were trapped when . . ." She swallowed hard and winced as he applied copious amounts of freeze to the side of her face.

"When you fired the explosives and the tower began crumbling, I got caught up in some of the guy wires and they dragged me into the destruction."

"I freed a soldier then . . . You were him?"

"Yeah." He dropped the freeze in his kitbag. "You saved my life that night."

"Our quarrel . . . was not with the CCR."

"No matter. I've never forgotten how lucky I was. When I eventually got home after being patched up at the hospital, it was early morning. I walked through my door and held my wife and my girl with all I had." He glanced away for a moment, then continued. "Because of your actions, your mercy that night, I could still hold my daughter . . . still watch her grow up."

Janet reached out, placing her stiff hand on the man's shoulder.

"I'll take you as far as possible and drop you in a safe place, but you must get to a hospital on your own, understand? Your injuries are serious and require proper treatment."

She nodded. Then Meadows took a surgical stapler from the field kit at his feet and pulled her shirt together, stitching it. Janet watched him work, admiring the gentle strength in his hands, his professionalism.

"You will have to account for your crimes, Agent Chamberlain."

"Understood."

"But not today." He stood and stretched out his hand. She clutched it and he lifted her gradually to her feet. "Are you well enough to travel?"

They walked to the door, and she stopped. "Thank you, Sergeant." Then they slipped away.

THIRTY-FOUR

Carter

HE COULDN'T BELIEVE HIS LUCK. Just when the inklings of emasculation from that pompous Captain Powell confounded him and his goal of uncovering the alien tech through the Atteberry girl or by scouring Luna's surface, Esther calls with a gift: she will deliver Mary to the *Echo*, and *thank him* for it.

But logistically, he had to organize Powell and his crew quickly, and await the arrival of this doctor. Not any old quack, either. Esther said they had someone lined up who was already on her way to New York to operate on Mary, but had been re-routed to the *Echo*'s base. A marvelous present, indeed. Laura Russo would undoubtedly curse the delay, but she understood better than most how the needs of humanity usurped the care and feeding of a handful of people on a boat.

Shortly after he ended the call, Esther sent a message that the Atteberrys were in complete agreement and en route to the San Francisco airport. The aircraft carrying the new doctor had altered course and was now en route to Shearwater. Carter grinned as this turn of events unfolded. The only remaining task was to inform Powell.

He stood beside the aft cargo bay of the *Echo* as the captain exited the communications center and approached him.

"Clayton, I'd like to apologize for—"

Carter shook his hand. "No need, John. You were totally in the right. I'm the one who should be apologizing."

Powell flashed a confused look, but quickly recovered his professional countenance. "Captain Russo will continue evasive actions for as long as possible. My crew's all here now and prepping for flight. We'll leave in about an hour."

"Wonderful," he replied, "but there's been another change."

"Oh?"

"I've found a doctor for you and she'll be arriving later today."

Powell frowned. "Remember what I said about crew personnel?"

"Of course, and the ultimate decision will be yours, but listen to me for a moment." He pulled the captain by the elbow, away from curious ears. "John, Mary Atteberry is coming here now from California. They'll board their craft in . . ." he checked his indie-comm, "in fifteen minutes."

"That changes things."

"Yes! You understand the significance of having all that knowledge in our grasp!" His voice had risen, and he peered around before lowering it again and saying, "This doctor, she's some kind of neural specialist familiar with the case. Once we're off-planet, she can operate on the girl. Make her well again."

"And if it all goes smoothly, Titanius acquires everything she learned about faster-than-light technology and god knows what else."

"Exactly." He mentioned that Esther planned to join them too, and how the CCR soldiers would deliver the quantum computer. They'd have to delay lift-off for another couple hours, but he was fine with that given the gift. Carter struggled to contain his enthusiasm at the possibility of acquiring this power that teased him like a siren by being so close to his grasp he could almost touch it. But Powell remained skeptical. He crossed his arms and narrowed his gaze.

"I appreciate the extra time to complete the *Echo*'s readiness, but I've got two concerns aside from the looming battle in space." He looked down the length of the ship, settling on the cargo bay doors. "This computer they need for the operation . . . I know nothing about it."

"It's just some big-ass computer, John, not much larger than some of ours."

"Okay, but what's the weight? What are the power requirements? Dimensions?" He shook his head. "You said the TSA had to cut away a chunk of wall in their loading bay to get the damn thing out, so it's not just some big-ass computer." He glanced again at the aft cargo bay.

"What about raising her tail?"

"Yes, that's what I'm thinking. I suppose when she's on the surface we'll load the machine that way." He paused. "I still require the specs, but I'll prepare the crew immediately."

Carter saw the captain's mood changing. "What's the other concern, John?"

"Well, it's this doctor."

"What about her?"

"Who is she?"

Carter hesitated. He didn't even remember the woman's name. He kicked the floor and said, "Well, she's a neurological specialist who knows how to treat Mary's brain problem. Based in London but in tight with that outfit from New Houston where the girl was supposed to have her initial surgery, so I'm confident she can—"

"That's not what I mean, Clayton."

He stared at the captain and saw more than simple hesitation on his face.

"Then what is it?"

"Look, we all go through a lengthy process of security checks, psychological tests, ongoing behaviour therapies to make sure we're suitable not only for the rigors of space flight, but also so we don't harm each other or the ship."

"You mean, to weed out political operatives."

"Yes." He lowered his voice. "Civilians on board is distracting enough. Don't misunderstand, the rescue mission we performed on Luna was not a concern, and I don't have any evidence to suggest they aren't trustworthy. But this doctor, a stranger from another continent . . . what's her background? Her affiliation?"

Carter's frustration simmered, but Powell was right. They weren't familiar with her at all. She may very well be linked to more than a research hospital in republican territory. Perhaps bringing her in the *Echo* wasn't the most prudent thing to do.

"I tell you what, John. Make sure Dub is armed and aware of your concerns. If anything looks suspicious, we'll deal with it. Once the operation is done and we return to Earth, the doctor can go her own way if that's what you wish.."

Powell considered his words. "That'll work." They both turned to face the *Echo*. Quigg waved at them through the cockpit window. "She's a fine ship, Clayton, and we mustn't let any harm come to her."

The big man smiled, satisfied that he and his best captain were now solidly on the same page.

Esther

AFTER SHE'D ARRANGED WITH CARTER to have the London neurosurgeon divert to Shearwater, her next task was getting the Q comp to the airport and safely aboard the heli-jet that continued standing by for their arrival. She did all this from Spreckels Lake, staying close to Jim and Mary, and chatting with Fairchild and the other CCR soldiers still watching them.

The medic spent several minutes coordinating activities through his comms device, then announced it was time to leave for the airport. He checked Mary's bio-signs, and raised the antigrav gurney and escorted her back to the military vehicle. Esther walked in front with the two soldiers, while Jim stayed beside his daughter.

As they approached the transport, she spotted other CCR soldiers in pairs or trios scattered around the area. *They're not taking any chances.* Although there had been no additional encounters with the Prussians, they all talked about being better prepared for anything after what happened at the TSA. "Stay alert," the medic had said, "and stay alive."

Once aboard the vehicle and after Fairchild secured Mary's gurney, Jim asked one of the accompanying soldiers, "Where's Janet?"

"Chamberlain?" he growled.

"Yes. Do you know where she is?

The man's eyes narrowed, deep with suspicion. "I'm not authorized to comment on the investigation." His forehead bulged.

Atteberry's jaw dropped. "Not *authorized*? What are you talking about?"

"Sir, your wife was—"

"Ex-wife."

"Yes, well, our interrogation unit is questioning her about the outstanding criminal charges. That's all I gotta say."

He shook his head. "I don't suppose you heard anything about Kate Braddock being found in a survival pod either."

The man remained silent and aloof.

Jim climbed aboard the vehicle and fell beside Esther. He looked close to death himself, and she hoped he'd get some sleep on the flight east. Across the aisle, Fairchild monitored Mary's condition. She was conscious and seemed oddly at peace with everything. No matter how thin and ghostly her face appeared, it lit up the cabin and comforted Esther.

She reflected on how Clayton had wanted her to manipulate Jim and Mary so he could scrape her mind for the alien tech, and how tempting it had been for her to follow him. Then, she'd toyed with taking him up on his offer of employment with Titanius, and how attractive and exciting managing a fleet of ships would be without the political and bureaucrat yoke around her neck. And, despite her inner warnings, there was the man himself. *That is what I want, isn't it?* Esther took Jim's hand and squeezed it.

After they'd returned from Luna, he observed how everyone he ever cared about seemed to disappear, abandoning him to his own isolation and alone-ness. And he talked about hope and how important it was to maintain even while confronting insurmountable odds. Maybe that's where Mary found this peace of hers, this belief in something better coming right around the bend. She leaned back and studied the side of his face; the pain etched on his mouth, and she had a sudden desire to lean over and kiss him. But she couldn't.

He still loved . . . no, he remained *in love* with Janet, wasn't he? And as she admitted that, even though she saw no long-term romantic future with either him or Clayton, or a relationship developing with anyone else, a great, echoing sadness pooled in the pit of her stomach. Hope, Jim had claimed. She prayed to an unknown god, and the act made her feel awkward.

The two soldiers hopped into the cab up front and the vehicle sprang to life. Fairchild maintained radio contact with them and, after hearing something in his earpiece, he turned and said, "There's enemy chatter on the lines. We'll be taking a scenic route to the airport."

"And the quantum computer?" Esther asked.

"Secured under heavy escort. We've got drones in the air watching it, too. It'll take a while for that truck to arrive at the runway. Something about sensitive coils . . .?"

"Yes, the dampener and the Q both have fragile components. They won't stand up well to bumps."

"Too bad we can't haul them by air." He paused. "No matter, we'll get there before the computer does, and that'll give me time to secure Mary in the aircraft for the flight."

Jim said, "Thank you, son. For everything you've done to help my girl."

"We won't . . . forget you," Mary whispered.

The vehicle lifted off the ground, hovered a moment, then flew above the lane to John F. Kennedy and east toward the airport.

Kate

KATE WOKE FROM A DREAMLESS SLEEP, lying prone on a twin bed in a dimly lit cabin. In a second, she remembered being aboard the *Edelgard*, and the truth treatment at the hands of Captain Beck. How long she'd been out of it remained a mystery, and she recalled nothing from the process.

Her tongue felt like sandpaper and her head pounded as she stumbled to the refresher and found some water, splashed her face, and drank. She assumed the procedure revealed everything: the alien encounter, the faster-than-light life pod, Keechik's transference of its history into Mary's brain, the existence of other galactic races . . . all of it. Without understanding the full context of the stand-off between the surrounding ships, she was at a loss what the captain—or the Prussians—would do with the information she provided.

No matter.

However, she understood they wouldn't simply let her go. Not until they'd mined her of as much intelligence as possible. They'd most-assuredly insist on scraping her memories to uncover whatever strategic tidbits she might have stored away over time, on previous Spacer missions, and her research at City College.

That can't happen.

If she'd revealed everything about Mary and Keechik, she needed to prevent the *Edelgard* from pursuing them. Keechik had the technological advantage, but with that knowledge embedded in Mary's brain, how long would it take humans to reproduce it? Sabotage was always an option, but in the absence of a thorough understanding of this ship's design, that was problematic. Communicating with Titanius or any other Terran vessel was out of the question: the captain would certainly not permit that.

But there is an alternative, if only . . .

She wiped down her face with a damp washcloth and slumped back on the bed. Keechik's life pod possessed subspace communications capability. She instinctively reached to her left arm and touched the stylus tucked away in her sleeve. If she accessed the pod and got a message to Keechik before the Prussians found out, perhaps the creature might return, find and protect Mary. After all, the future knowledge of its entire civilization rested with her.

Time to look around.

Kate straightened her back and stepped to the cabin door. It chimed at her but refused to open. Shortly, it *whooshed,* revealing two guards. The burly one with no neck demanded, "Is there something you require, fraulein?"

She gulped, fighting the impulse to attack him, steal his weapons, and blast her way out. Instead, she softened and said, "Yes. I'm hungry and need a good stretch. Can you point me to a food lounge or whatever you call them on this ship?"

"I'm afraid you cannot leave on your own. I shall bring you food and drink." He folded his arms across his chest.

"All right, how about a bowl of soup and a lousy cup of ship's coffee?"

"Yes, fraulein."

She noted the deck and corridor . . . *C9*... turned toward the bed, then pivoted. "Wait, can I not come with you? Stretch my legs a bit after that session?"

He gave her a suspicious look.

"Believe me, I'm in no shape to try anything. I only want to shake the cobwebs out." She stretched her back and rolled her shoulders while locking his gaze.

"Nein."

"Please? I'm unarmed and won't cause any trouble. Besides, you're the one with the weapon."

The guard shrugged at his colleague, then placed a paw on his sidearm. "Very well. This way," he motioned, "it's not far. But no sudden movements or I shoot."

Warm, full-spectrum lighting bathed the ship's passageway. Flecks of accented battleship grey walls and steel flooring, showing deck, corridor and cabin numbers, operational hubs and comms panels. As the group marched toward a nearby crew lounge, Kate struck up a conversation, making small talk, presenting herself as cooperative, noting the descending identifiers.

The cargo hold is two decks below, in the other direction.

The guards warmed up, even joked at one point, and all the while she noted wall maps of the ship's layout, connecting hallways and elevator shafts, the automated time of day (early afternoon). In the lounge, she picked up a sandwich and a coffee, ignoring the prying stares from the curious crew checking out this former spacer who'd met an alien.

After returning to her cabin, she asked the guard, "What'll happen to the life pod? There's a lot of science behind that vessel, and maybe I could show you what I learned."

"Not my department."

The second escort, the one in the lead, turned and said, "It remains in the cargo hold, fraulein. The eggheads will study that craft for years, so they may have questions for you." He rolled his eyes. "Crazy way to travel through space, if you ask me. Give me a solid ship like this any day."

"Having traveled in that tin can," Kate said cheerfully, "I agree with you!"

They chuckled and opened her cabin. Kate stepped in and thanked them for the chat and the walk to the lounge. The guard snapped the door closed and Kate dropped the friendly facade, lay back on the bed, fingers entwined behind her head, already assembling the elements of a plan.

Soon ...

THIRTY-FIVE

Janet

THAT OLD DICTUM ABOUT REVENGE being best served cold intrigued her as she and Sergeant Meadows traveled by CCR military hovercar through the early afternoon back streets of San Francisco. She ached to even the score with Lucas and his pet Dorian, on her terms, and the sooner the better, but the pain of her broken face and swollen knee prevented her from pursuing the mechanics for now. Soon, when she's healed. She studied Meadows sitting across from her, his fit form tense and ready, keeping watch on the traffic, then on some sophisticated monitor, and her.

"Another shot?"

"Yes, hurry." *Yesh.*

Meadows pulled the pseudophine hypo from his vest pocket and handed it to her. "There's enough in there to make an elephant woozy, so go easy. Take a bit to get yourself back to your own territory and to a hospital, no more."

Janet wiped some drool from the corner of her mouth, then set the dosage on the cartridge and pressed the plunger against her neck. She surveyed the area. The interrogation cell was apparently somewhere in the Richmond District, judging by the direction they went now and the time that had passed. The pattern through these streets reminded her of NDU evasive maneuvers to lose any tails. After several more minutes, the hovercar pulled out on a laneway close to the university where Meadows commanded it to stop. The vehicle floated for a second, then engaged its landing skids and settled on the side of the lane.

"This is as far as I can take you, Ms. Chamberlain." He peered out the window and pointed to a grey wing of a high-rise building on campus. "That's a hospital, if you require immediate care."

"Thank you, Sergeant," she said, "but I'll be all right."

He didn't look convinced. "Here's your indie-comm. You understand I can't return your weapons. Call your team and disappear, okay?"

Janet grabbed the device, checked it briefly, then slipped it in her pocket.

"Open the lock."

The hovercar pinged, and her door swung wide. Janet stepped out gingerly as her knee registered standing again. She bent down and looked into the car. "What's your name, Sergeant Meadows?"

"My friends call me Finnie."

"What's your real name?"

He hesitated and grinned. "Franklin."

"Franklin . . . freedom. I won't forget what you did here today." She stared deeply into his eyes and he held her gaze. Finally, he said, "Good luck," and commanded the door to close.

Janet stood off to the side as the hovercar levitated and purred away down the lane before she ducked awkwardly into the shade of a nearby stand of shrubs. She needed to go to ground, but rather than call her team, she punched up Atteberry's code and texted. He answered immediately.

Jan, my god, where are you?

Don't let on it's me. Close to the airport . . . you?

The encryption codes beeped. *We're heading there now . . . me, Mary and Esther. There's a medic and a couple of soldiers escorting us. That big computer is en route, too. We're flying to Nova Scotia."*

What?

A necessary change of plans. We'll board the Echo and leave Earth to keep Mary safe. He explained everything that happened since they'd been separated, and how Mary's condition was inoperable according to some neurosurgeon. *The London doctor is meeting us there at Shearwater and we hope she can attempt the operation on the ship.*

Janet smelled something ugly developing and scowled as the pseudophine kicked into a higher gear. *I don't follow, Jim. That Titanius gang wants Mary's brain as much as anyone else. What are you walking into?*

It'll take too long to explain. But we'll talk on the way to the east coast. Are you able to join us at the airport?

Yes. I'll meet you there. She killed the connection and sighed.

From her cache in the shrubs, she surveyed the immediate vicinity and evaluated her next steps. The solution to Mary's problem clarified itself with each passing moment, and Janet understood what she'd have to do. That Carter fellow wasn't trustworthy: that much, she knew. And the CCR soldiers may or may not keep their end of the bargain now that she was loose.

And then there was Winter.

She checked her pulse and grimaced at how quickly her heart pumped, no doubt a combination of the pseudophine and adrenaline. Her fingers instinctively dropped to her pocket where she'd stuffed the hypo, but she changed her mind about pumping more into her. There's a fine line between killing the pain and knocking her out, and she needed every ounce of her wits for what she had to do next. To the spider's dismay, not even booze appealed to her now.

Despite Jim's optimism about Mary's condition, she would die. But that wouldn't stop the Winters of the world from hunting her down and trying to pull any residual memories from her. She pinged her contact and, after a moment, Agent Mikos connected with her. He'd been standing by in a safehouse awaiting her call.

"I'm glad you're still alive, ma'am," he said casually, as if this was a daily occurrence. "What's your QTH? I'll come and get you."

"Negative. But tell me, do you know the whereabouts of our Prussian friends?"

"Winter avoided capture at the TSA, but we picked up his trail shortly thereafter and we're tracking him now. He's collected several additional operatives."

"Where's he headed?"

"Random pattern throughout various neighborhoods. Well, until shortly before you called. He appears to be running south from Golden Gate Park. Probably heading to the airport since Mr. Atteberry's vehicle is en route there."

"How far behind is he?"

"Approximately six minutes."

She pulled a map up on her indie-comm and studied the roads leading to San Fran International. Jim would enter the airfield from the north end where several warehouses and offices were located, and where the heli-jet awaited them. That seemed like the logical place for Winter to hit Mary. There was no time to lose.

"How would you like to proceed, ma'am?" Mikos asked.

She continued studying the map. There was only one thing left to do before removing Winter from the equation. Even if Jim made it to the *Echo*, and even if Doctor Lamont could save Mary's life, she was still in danger from the leeches in Titanius. The only remaining action to protect the world from these empire-builders was to do the unthinkable and break Jim's heart.

She had to get to Mary first.

"Ma'am?"

"Mikos, listen carefully. I'm traveling directly to the airport. I want you to monitor Winter's position and relay that intel straight to my indie-comm. Understood?" *Unnershtood?*

He paused. "You don't require back up, ma'am?"

"No. This is something only I can do."

Atteberry

"WE'VE GOT COMPANY, FOLKS."

Agent Fairchild held his earpiece against his head as he checked Mary's antigrav gurney and studied her vitals.

"What's going on?" Atteberry asked.

"The Prussian agents are in motion," he said, "and they're following us."

Fairchild shrugged his shoulders. "There's more. Your ex-wife's off the grid. I don't know how she escaped the playroom, but right now that's the least of my concerns." He leaned toward Atteberry and Esther. "Since she bolted, the grown-ups have been questioning our involvement with you. The chatter's unbelievable."

"How so?" Esther's tone hardened.

"Well, Doctor, it's the arrangement struck between Ms. Chamberlain and Sergeant Meadows that we escort you and your quantum computer to the airport in exchange for her turning herself in."

"But she turned herself in," Atteberry protested, understanding fully where this conversation headed.

"True, but it appears her disappearance involved the sergeant. I don't travel in those circles, so I'm just telling you what I hear." He lowered his voice. "I probably shouldn't be sharing this, but the adults are none too happy with Meadows."

"Do you think he helped her escape?" Atteberry feigned ignorance.

Fairchild glanced at Mary's bio-signs and said, "Who knows, but if he did, the consequences are damn serious." He looked up thoughtfully. "An interrogator several years ago did something similar. The detainee had nothing like Ms. Chamberlain's stature, but the soldier allowed the asset to walk. He's been in prison since."

Atteberry wondered if Meadows had let Janet go, but dismissed the possibility. "Is he in trouble even if she escaped on her own?"

"Sir, it's not for me to say, but we've been ordered to detain him if he shows up. Right now, he's apparently gone to ground."

The vehicle flew past civilian hovercars, frequently deviating from its designated flight lane. Atteberry caught Mary's eye and winked. She maintained that peaceful look, as if she hadn't a care in the world. That was a peace he desperately wanted.

"What about protecting us at the airport?"

"Until we hear otherwise," the medic said, "our mission has not changed."

Atteberry breathed a sigh of relief, glanced at Esther and saw the tension melt from her face. But despite the fresh uncertainty, he wasn't about to lose this opportunity, this final chance, to help Mary. If he had to, he would confront Winter and anyone else who got in the way.

"How far is the airport now?"

Fairchild checked his device. "Under five clicks."

Esther asked, "And the truck with the computer?"

"A few minutes behind."

So, everyone who mattered was in motion. The only mystery worrying him was Janet's location, but she said she'd meet them there, and so far Jan had been true to her word. *I hope she's bringing reinforcements.*

The group remained silent except for Fairchild, who checked in on his radio sporadically, speaking jargon that Atteberry didn't understand. Mostly numbers and acronyms. He caught a few things, like QTH (location), and QRM (man-made interference) since the Q codes were well-established in the ham radio hobby. And he reported on Mary's condition ("surprisingly stable"). Other than that, the military slang may as well have been Chinese.

Esther touched his arm and pointed out the side window. In the distance, various aircraft launched or landed, some in the conventional way on runways, others in the more contemporary means by vertical drops. Their vehicle banked around the corners of warehouses and hangars as it pulled away from the major road and negotiated the north end of the airport.

"Is that our flight?" Atteberry asked the medic while staring at a large heli-jet parked on the apron near a couple of outbuildings.

Fairchild checked the registration numbers and confirmed. Atteberry surveyed the area for any sign of Janet, but saw nothing. Winter wasn't around either, but that didn't prevent the medic from readying his weapons and tensing his muscles.

Esther asked, "Are you expecting trouble?"

"Well, Doctor, the Prussians are in the neighborhood, so I don't want to take any chances. The rest of our squad is protecting the flatbed with the Q, but I'll feel a little safer once they all arrive."

The vehicle slowed as it approached the building closest to the heli-jet, then hovered a moment about five meters from the main door, and settled on its skids. Fairchild turned to the others. "We're checking in with crew first until we're certain there's no threat. You stay here and don't move until I or one of the soldiers up front tells you. Understand?"

They nodded. Atteberry grabbed Esther's hand. "Are you sure about coming along, Es?"

"Wouldn't miss this for the world," she said without reserve, but the tension across her face betrayed her.

More radio chatter cracked through the air. More alien code gibberish. Then, the door to the building swung open and the pilot, with a sidearm, appeared beside another CCR soldier. They both scanned the area, then motioned for them to enter the structure.

Fairchild unlatched the wide doors at the back of the vehicle. The two soldiers up front came and directed the gurney inside. Fairchild stayed at Mary's side, weapon drawn, eyes darting across the tarmac. He kept focusing on a stand of trees near the San Francisco Bay. Atteberry followed his gaze but saw nothing: no movement, no machinery. All looked clear.

Esther pulled on his hand. "Come on, Jim, let's go."

The air in the building had a stale odor despite its relatively modern style. It was bigger than an office, but smaller than a hangar, with a high ceiling and natural lighting supplemented with task lights over a wall of work stations.

"What is this place?" he asked.

The pilot, a lanky kid barely shaving, said, "One of many multi-purpose buildings around here. We rent out space to hobbyists and small air service providers." He put out his hand. "I'm Captain Billy Samuelson."

They introduced each other. Fairchild kept a close watch on Mary, but she seemed to be absorbing all the activity in stride. She leaned on an elbow as the medic monitored her heart. The other two soldiers exited the building, taking up defensive positions by the military vehicle.

Esther, looking out the window across the tarmac, hands on hips, said, "Is that aircraft of yours capable of hypersonic flight?"

"Absolutely, ma'am. I can fly to New York in about an hour and half, depending on the winds and cargo." They walked together over to a large wall monitor, discussing various aspects of low orbit travel, engines, things that Atteberry had little interest in. He stayed close to his daughter.

"What do you think, Mares?"

"We're thinking we'll be fine, Dad. No matter what happens."

She had a strange way about her now, but one he found attractive. Atteberry was thankful for the medic and all he'd done for them.

Fairchild's radio crackled. He held the earpiece to his head and frowned. Movement and shouts rose from outside as the soldiers positioned themselves behind the vehicle.

"Here they come."

THE FIRST NOISE HE HEARD WAS THE GUTTURAL GROWL of the old diesel flatbed carrying the quantum computer. The machine rumbled in from the west entrance and cut a line across the airstrip toward the heli-jet. The pilot, Samuelson, hopped on a scooter and flew off to meet it.

Fairchild and the soldier they'd met at the out-building remained calm, watching the activity unfold on the tarmac. At least half a dozen soldiers had planted themselves on the flatbed itself, weapons at the ready. Esther looked relieved.

The medic said, "Once they load the computer on the heli, we'll take your daughter over and be on our way. I'll make sure she's secure in the aircraft before I go."

"Thank you," Atteberry replied. He shook the man's hand. "You've been such a help to all of us."

He returned the grip. "We're not done yet, though. The Prussians are still out there somewhere. But I hope they've decided against engaging.

He spoke too soon.

A flash of gunfire erupted from the stand of trees Atteberry had noted earlier. He saw the flashes moments before he heard them. Two soldiers fell from the flatbed, splayed against the tarmac. The truck sped up and rolled in behind the heli-jet. The remaining troopers slipped off before it came to a stop and took defensive positions, firing at will into the treeline.

Atteberry and Esther ducked, staying close to Mary, whose gurney hovered behind a thick wall away from the outbuilding windows. The soldier with them held a post beside the window, eyes fixed on the tarmac. Fairchild stood on the other side and shouted, "It's the Prussians! Stay low and don't move."

On an opposite wall monitor, cameras focused on the heli-jet picked up the fight. CCR soldiers were pinned down behind the two vehicles. One of them rolled to a new position and fresh gunfire from the trees erupted. Atteberry knew enough about armed skirmishes from the media to realize the Prussians held the advantage; yet, they didn't seem all that interested in taking down the aircraft or securing the computer.

They're here for Mary.

"Fairchild, it's a ruse . . . a diversion."

"I told you to—"

"Think about it," Atteberry yelled. "They're not here for the jet. What they want is . . ." he glanced at his daughter, who lay back on the gurney. "They want Mary."

The other soldier eyed Fairchild. "Makes sense, Nick." He ducked past the window to the control panel and, after punching some buttons, two cameras aimed at the heli-jet swung around 180 degrees.

He set them in overlapping sweeps to cover about three quarters of the area. "We'd better watch our rear and flanks."

More shots cracked outside, and Atteberry snapped back to the tarmac. Somehow, the pilot made it into the aircraft and had lowered the aft cargo door. A pair of CCR soldiers took up positions inside while others worked on the quantum computer, attaching cables to it.

"They're loading it up," Esther said.

A flurry of RPGs and gunfire filled the air as the CCR squad provided covering fire to the flatbed operators. Esther couldn't take her eyes off the operation. She held her breath as the truck-mounted crane lifted the sensitive equipment far too quickly, swinging it wildly into the cargo hold. First, the computer went on. Then, after attaching the cables to the dampener, it swung in, too. Meanwhile, the barrage grew more sporadic. The two monitoring cameras maintained their sweep.

"What's happening, Fairchild?" Atteberry, kneeling beside Mary, kept checking the various screens in the room. "Is it over?"

The medic held his position by the window where he had an unobstructed view of the tarmac and the door to the outbuilding. He glanced at the viewers. "Hard to tell. Still lots of chatter and confusion from the ramp." He gulped, and a worried look crossed his face. "There's something else out there now." He gripped his earpiece. "One figure approaching from the south."

Janet?

As if reading his mind, the medic said, "They can't determine if it's male or female. The closest satellite is unable to resolve gender."

Winter?

Fairchild turned to the monitor. Atteberry followed his gaze but couldn't discern anything on the screens. The gunfire outside had stopped and an eerie silence filled the stale air. The CCR soldier with them stole a peek through the window and confirmed what the primary screen showed: soldiers in position protecting the heli-jet, standing by, but no further movement or activity along the tree line. Atteberry's gut ached.

The only sound in the room beside their breathing was the burble of chatter coming through Fairchild's earpiece.

But someone was still out there.

Atteberry sighed and said to Mary, "I think it might be over for now."

"Yes," she replied, and brushed her fingers across his hand. "Mom's out there too, isn't she?"

"We don't know, Mares." He looked at Esther, then the medic. "Let's stay low until we're sure what's happening."

"I've got the satellite feed." Fairchild motioned the soldier over to the control panel again. This time, after he'd hit the keys, a grainy monochrome image appeared on the primary screen, replacing the heli-jet on the tarmac. "I'm afraid the picture isn't that good, but it's the best we've got."

The screen showed an overhead view of the airport, slowly zooming in on the outbuilding. The jet and flatbed were visible, as were the markings of activity along the stand of trees where the soldiers had been ambushed. As the image continued to resolve more details of their immediate area, Atteberry saw the two dead soldiers on the tarmac, and heat signatures in the treeline. The Prussians hadn't fallen back at all.

He picked up the lone figure to the south. Fairchild was right: it was impossible to tell who this person was, what side they were on, but he or she skulked deliberately toward the outbuilding.

It must be Janet.

No sooner had he seen the person, when a second appeared, trailing the first.

Winter? Or is Janet tracking him?

In a blinding flash of light, the screen exploded by the treeline, and static blurred the monitor.

"What was that?" Atteberry shouted. But Fairchild didn't respond. He stood agape in front of the viewer. Shapes and outlines slowly reappeared through the interference as the snow dissipated. The human activity he'd witnessed moments before had gone, replaced by the carnage of at least half a dozen mercenaries splayed across the treeline, motionless.

Janet

THE MOMENT THE FLASH HIT, JANET DOVE TO THE GROUND and rolled into a small trench for cover. Within seconds, she crawled up the steep bank to assess the scene in a prone position. She angled herself to peer through a clear patch in the thicket. The outbuilding where Jim and Mary most likely took refuge was off to the right, still hidden, but she could see across the tarmac to the heli-jet and the far trees where Winter's mercenaries ambushed the flatbed. A black and grey cloud hung over that area like a grisly fog. CCR soldiers crept tentatively around the aircraft, making their way toward the destruction near the treeline.

The setting had the telltale markings of a stun bomb, designed to neutralize an enemy over a small space. Somehow, a soldier guarding the heli-jet must have approached the merc nest to plant it. But how? With no cover, it would be impossible. Unless . . .

"What do you think of my handiwork?"

Janet jerked around, drawing her knees up to her chest in a defensive posture, simultaneously searching the ground for anything she could use as a weapon. The figure who spoke emerged from the bushes, brandishing a CCR revolver.

"You?"

Sergeant Meadows ducked and approached her. He holstered his gun and reached out, giving her shoulder a gentle squeeze.

"I don't understand."

He studied the scene through the shrubs. "When I heard about the attack on the truck, I moved in from their flank. There was no way I could take them on myself, so I crept in close and put the stunner on a timer. I don't know how many mercenaries were in that nest, but I hope it bought enough time to help your daughter. I picked up your trail here via sat-links."

"That's not what I mean," she said, shifting her weight. "What are you doing *here*?"

He drew a second revolver from behind him and handed it to her. It was a Heckler and Koch Stinger pistol. "Are you familiar with this?"

"Yes." She checked out the weapon, turning it over in her palm, admiring the balance. "Is it sited?"

"Did it myself. Its aim is true." He pulled a Martin knife out and gave it to her along with several magazines.

"Sergeant, what is this all about?"

He exhaled sharply. "It's Finnie, remember. I figured you wouldn't go to a safehouse or a hospital, not with your family on the run and the Prussians moving in." He glanced at the tarmac. "And I also knew you could use a hand."

"But you're . . . and I'm . . ."

"Ma'am, before Central cut me off, I heard enough of the chatter to realize I'm a dead man now."

"For helping me escape," she said calmly.

"Yeah, so I thought if I'm in deep anyway, and with Benedikt Winter still prowling out there, I may as well do some good while I can . . . keep your family together."

Janet grimaced as a fresh wave of pain ran through her face.

That's not why I'm here.

The freeze wore thin. "As long as we're on a first name basis, call me Jan." She grabbed the hypo, set the dosage for pseudophine, and pumped it in her neck. "We must ensure Winter doesn't get to Mary." *Or anyone else.* How could she tell him her true intention was to put an exploding bullet in her daughter's head?

"Right, so we'll protect their path from that hangar." He stole another glance. "Looks like the soldiers have secured the tree line. Once they clear it, they'll signal for your family to make a run for it."

"Come on," she said, as the pseudophine kicked in and her cheeks turned numb. "Let's move."

The pair crept through the underbrush, stopping frequently to listen for any other sounds around them. Meadows followed her, watching their rear and flank. Janet focused on the building and the tarmac. As they neared the pavement, they took up a position in a small divot with cover and waited.

After several minutes of silence, he asked, "How did you get into this business, Jan?"

She said, "That's a long story, at least a bottle's worth of scotch and maybe a pleasant dinner or two." She glanced around. "How about you?"

Meadows grinned. "I joined the CCR during the civil war. Seems a lifetime ago now. You know what I did before I entered the forces?" She looked at him. "I owned a landscaping business . . . had a small nursery on the property . . . spent most of my days outside."

"I was a student when I got recruited. Fifteen years old. Young, impressionable. But I couldn't let the world go to hell and not do something about it."

"A purist?"

She touched her broken jaw and flinched. "I guess so, but as I said, it's a long story. Maybe once the heli is out of sight and this business is over, we can find that bottle together."

He frowned. "What, you're not going with them?"

She shook her head.

"But I don't get it."

"I can't allow my daughter to fall into the wrong hands, and if there's a chance she does, I must . . . Well, never mind. Look at me, Finnie. I'm not exactly the family type." She peered across the tarmac. "They're better off without me complicating matters."

"Or maybe they're ready to take you back."

The glint of metal caught her eye.

There!

One hundred meters to the left.

She touched Meadows's forearm and pointed in the flash's direction. He nodded and crawled a few meters through the brush to get a better angle. "Do you see him?" he asked.

"Negative."

"Winter must have split with a handful of men from the ambush site."

The door to the hangar swung slowly open, and a soldier emerged. They must have received the all clear because the next person to appear was the medic she recognized from the group at the TSA. Then Mary on the gurney, Esther Tyrone, and . . . *Jim!*

She needed to get closer to Mary to complete her unholy mission. Something shifted off to the left. She'd have to deal with the imminent threat first. "Show time, Finnie." Janet pulled herself up and hobbled out on the tarmac, her swollen knee barking with each step, firing rounds at the spot where she'd seen the movement. Meadows joined her, unloading his own weapon in the same direction. The soldier protecting Mary en route to the heli-jet turned his assault rifle toward her, but Jim yelled, "Stop! That's Janet!"

She and Meadows raced to meet up with the group, laying down additional cover. Mary's protector met them, firing his own weapon indiscriminately as they trundled toward the jet. The mercenaries returned fire, but their shots missed their mark.

Janet pulled within 20 meters of the gurney, her heart thundering in her chest as the moment of killing Mary approached. She had to get Jim away. A bullet whistled by her head and she dove on the tarmac, firing into the trees. Meadows rolled beside her, replacing his spent cartridge with a fresh one and squeezing off more rounds. Gunfire erupted from the heli-jet as the CCR soldiers took the initiative and lay down a swath of protective fire.

With Mary close to boarding, her chance to end this mission rapidly disappeared. She shifted her position, swallowed, and aimed at her daughter. *How has it come to this? Forgive me, Mary.* Her finger started to squeeze the trigger.

"Stand down, Commander," Meadows said, placing his hand on her outstretched arm. "You don't want to do that."

"There's no other option," she cried, tears filling her eyes. "I can't let her escape Winter only to be carved up by some overzealous corporate fucker. This madness needs to end now."

"No, you're not thinking straight. Whether estranged or not, your daughter is still part of you. Be her mother again, if only for a few minutes. Go and be with her. Protect her. Have faith that you'll find another way."

More bullets cracked overhead. Janet and Meadows exchanged fire with the mercenaries as Jim and the others had neared the aircraft and a pair of soldiers helped Mary aboard, followed by Esther and the medic. Only Jim remained outside, still in danger.

"Janet!" he shouted. "Make a run for it!"

Raw emotion overwhelmed her as self-doubt flooded her body. Perhaps it was the effect of the pain and stress and drugs in her system, or the absence of alcohol, but her body slumped and she rolled on her side. "I can't do this anymore," she wept.

"Listen to me," Meadows said. "You gave me a second chance to be with my girl and I'm so grateful for that. I'm returning the favor. Take it. There's always a hidden solution . . . you don't have to solve this on your own. Faith, Jan . . . find it here." He placed his palm over her heart.

But fate changes quickly in a firefight. A heavy flash from the bushes showed incoming RPG fire. The first salvo barely missed the heli-jet as its rotors churned and chopped the smoky air.

"Go, Jan," Meadows shouted. "Be with your family. I'll cover. On three."

She inhaled, and they counted down together. But now the few remaining Prussians were out of the woods and charging across the airstrip, firing at the heli. Two more CCR soldiers went down. The merc with the RPG knelt and prepared to launch again.

She froze. For the first time since being a teenager, she didn't know what to do.

"Jan, come on!" Jim had one foot in the aircraft, a hand on the side of the door, his other arm reaching across the distance separating them, motioning for her come.

She forced herself to move and adopted a prone position about 20 meters from the door and freedom. Twenty meters from the start of a new life with her family, or at least a chance for a life without the field. She fired on the mercs assembling across the tarmac. A bullet found its target and the soldier shrieked. His legs crumbled as he slumped to the ground. Meadows hit another. But the man with the RPG moved again. A flurry of rounds whistled above her head and she turned away. When she peered up again, Meadows was gone. He'd been shot multiple times in the chest. Nothing remained of his head.

"Jesus . . ."

"Janet, we gotta go!"

She needed to keep that RPG from firing first, give them a chance to escape. As the mercs fanned out over the tarmac, she glanced at Jim, then motioned for the pilot to leave. He refused.

More gunfire. She rolled behind Meadow's mangled body and sprayed rounds in an arc across the horizon, searching for the RPG. In her peripheral vision, someone hauled Jim inside the heli and slammed the door. The engines revved. Janet continued firing, pinning the enemy down and keeping the RPG from setting up. Then, a bullet ripped through her arm, almost removing it clean at the elbow. Stunned, she turned to the heli-jet now ascending and about ten meters off the ground. And there was Jim, mouthing something, his outspread hands against the window.

She fired a few more rounds at the mercs, then faced the aircraft. Her eyes met Jim's. In that microsecond of recognition, she read the pain on his face and a rush of all the buried love she had for him exploded from her soul. Her emotions brawled in a flurry of stilted sobs and she shook violently as bullets screamed around her. Staring at him go, intense pain searing into her brain, she whispered, "I love you." Then the heli-jet tore away in a rain of gunfire. Janet continued blasting sporadically toward the mercs, but her vision blurred and weakness crushed her body. A monstrous thirst filled her mouth. Sirens shrieked in the distance. The rich, familiar tang of sulphur and blood floated in the air like a recurring dream.

Janet squeezed out another round, then collapsed and rolled on her back in time to see the heli-jet ignite its aft engine thruster and disappear into the eastern sky.

Then a bullet wrenched her side. In that momentary shock between life and death, time and space froze in stony silence. Her thoughts dissipated, shifting from endless sky to the sweet comfort of complete numbness. The spider, bereft of understanding, melted into wisps of black smoke. And the last image she held slowly faded from her consciousness . . . the photograph of her family . . . at the beach . . . when Mary was a child . . . Jim's easy smile . . . the one she always loved.

THIRTY-SIX

Winter

AS THE HELI-JET ROARED OUT OF SIGHT, Winter signalled the remaining mercs to retreat into the bushes off the tarmac as first responders descended on the scene and hovered over the carnage. They rendezvoused a couple hundred meters away and took knees under the cover of old cedars. He linked in with Cornelia on his indie-comm.

"Yes, Herr Winter, the transport will approach your position in a minute. You'll need to meet up on the service road west of your current coordinates."

"Understood. Now listen carefully: are they heading to New York?"

"No, sir. At least, that's not the what the intel shows."

He spat the taste of cordite from his lips. "Where are they going?"

"Shearwater, Nova Scotia. Where the *Echo* is, sir."

"Good. Somehow Titanius is involved in this again." He paused. The sirens grew louder and shouting rose. "Cornelia, we must leave. Is the *Echo* capable of flight?"

"Yes, Herr Winter. The man at the base says the ship is fully operational and standing by for the fraulein and an unknown passenger to arrive."

"Curious. Who is this other passenger?"

"Uncertain. He believes she's a neurological specialist from London, but the details are sketchy."

"So the *Echo* prepares to fly as soon as these others show up," he mused. The reality of the situation crystallized. They intended to perform the operation on the girl aboard the ship, and in space where they could out-run any other vessel. "We must stop that ship from launching."

"That's a challenge, sir. She's already on the tarmac. It will take an hour for that heli-jet to arrive, but sabotage is out of the question and there's insufficient manpower in the area to conduct a full-frontal attack."

Winter picked up the signal that the hovercar had arrived. "Cornelia, we're moving." He motioned for the mercs to follow in single file as he crept through the brush. In short order, they were upon the vehicle and tumbled inside. Once inside, the hovercar purred away in an evasive pattern.

"Cornelia, if we can't prevent the *Echo* from launching, then we must destroy her in space. What's the status of the *Sara Waltz*?"

"The ship remains docked above New Houston, but repairs are almost complete and the captain says they'll be flight-ready in . . ." she paused, " . . . half an hour give or take."

"Perfect. Send a heli-jet and I'll fly to New Houston and ride the space elevator to the *Sara Waltz* and join her crew." He scanned the area and sent Cornelia the coordinates of a clearing large enough for the aircraft to land.

"I'm sending a light heli there now. ETA 15 minutes."

"*Danke.*" He ended the connection, then ordered the hovercar to halt at a sideroad where the mercs hopped out. Then he proceeded to the rendezvous point.

THE MEADOW APPEARED ABOUT A KILOMETER off the road. A rusty wire fence surrounded it and a leaning gate arose in front of him. He stopped the hovercar and exited as soon as the skids touched ground. The chop of an approaching heli-jet grabbed his attention. He peered up to see a modest two-seater emerge from the clouds. In a moment, the craft landed and Winter climbed aboard. The light heli took off in a vertical climb and, at 200 meters altitude, its aft engine engaged and the vessel screamed away in a south-east direction toward New Houston.

He remained silent, monitoring the IR panel and noting airspeed and ETA. Satisfied with the indicators, he popped a couple of pain pills for his legs, and settled in for the trip. Cornelia pinged with a message that the *Sara Waltz* expected his arrival. Then his mind turned again to Frau Chamberlain and her broken body lying on the asphalt. *She was a remarkable agent.*

The scene on the tarmac replayed in his thoughts. The squad of mercenaries laying down fire on the heli-jet, peppering the CCR soldiers with multiple rounds while being attacked by Chamberlain and some other rogue soldier. *In some ways, it feels like such a waste to see her die on a slab of pavement after such a storied career.* But he respected how she went out in a fight, protecting her family, and realized they weren't that different.

Except her efforts were all in vain.

His wouldn't be.

THIRTY-SEVEN

Atteberry

IN THE MOMENTS FOLLOWING JANET'S DEATH, Atteberry slumped in disbelief in the heli-jet, holding Mary's hand, tears staining his cheeks. Esther sat across the aisle. The gurney—minus the antigrav height—rested on the floor behind them so that Mary's head was close to seat level. She rested, a peaceful expression spread over her face. Esther reached across and rubbed his back, in an oddly familiar way, and he released everything, the frustration, the pain of years after Janet left. The words unspoken. The madness of losing Kate to some alien creature that now threatened Mary's life. The fresh cut of Janet's death. His daughter's time running out.

He sighed and asked, "Did Mary see what happened?"

Esther shook her head.

"She doesn't know then?"

"No." She stroked his face, brushing away the tears.

"How do I tell her . . . what words could I use? Right now, I'm numb. All I can think about is how my family's been shattered . . . for the second time." He chewed his lip. "I wondered if we might have another chance."

She rubbed his shoulder.

"Janet seemed different this time, unlike the way she took control of the Mount Sutro situation . . . when she destroyed the tower." Something must have made her return, something more than looking out for Mary.

"If it's any consolation at all, Jim, I saw the way she watched you . . . the way she smiled when you weren't looking. I'm no expert, but I recognized the signs."

Atteberry clenched his jaw and swallowed, pushing a fresh wave of grief away. "Thank you, Es."

Several minutes passed in silence. The heli-jet captain called back gently, enquiring if they were okay, telling them about water and protein tabs in a dispenser at the back. Esther nodded politely. Mary remained quiet, slipping in and out of consciousness despite the heavy sedation. A data slate with her bio-signs lay on her chest.

Esther persisted in talking, asking questions, changing subjects. He understood his need to release the pain, but he truly didn't want to. In a selfish, odd way, he enjoyed feeling the hurt, the immensity of Janet's death, and resented sharing what he considered something personal that belonged strictly to him. She paused a moment and peered out the window. "Tell me more about her."

Atteberry shrugged. "I'm not sure what it is . . . what it *was* about her. She hurt us badly when she abandoned our home. And, to ignore us for so long . . . well, I can't figure out the reasons and probably never will. There was always a part of her that remained hidden, and I don't simply mean the espionage and such. She never opened up like I did." He brushed his hair back. "I didn't resent her for being aloof, but I often felt she wasn't as invested in the marriage as I was. I mean, she may have been distant and secretive that way to protect us." Then snorting, he added, "Or maybe I didn't know her at all."

Esther stared at him with a reflective look, as if she, too, rifled through her own dark secrets.

"Nevertheless, I'm one hundred percent sure of this: I loved her, despite her life in the shadows, the abandonment. I always have. I don't know if we ever could have reconciled. Probably not. But that doesn't change what I know to be true." He frowned at Esther in a solitary act of honest contrition, and shifted his weight and gazed without seeing out the window at the streaking countryside, hollowed out as if part of his body and soul had been ripped away. After a moment, fatigue replaced the pain, and Atteberry fell into a fitful sleep.

Canadian Forces Base Shearwater, Nova Scotia

Esther

TURBULENCE JOSTLED ESTHER AWAKE, and she recognized the heli-jet's engines thrumming rhythmically and remembered where she was.

Jim turned and said, "We're over New Brunswick. We'll be landing in a few minutes." She hardly recognized the man anymore. He looked like a brooding apparition, distance pouring out of his eyes like a grey, infinite horizon. The strain of the past few days caught up with him, and now with Janet's death, he showed the ugly signs of despair. Atteberry pointed out the rain-streaked window. "Hell of a storm kicking up."

Esther breathed deeply and grabbed the armrests. With her career at the TSA in tatters, and no prospects other than Carter's vague invitation to join Titanius, her future had never been more uncertain. In her younger days, she'd be awash in worry and stress over this. But not now. Everything had changed.

Captain Samuelson drew the aircraft into a hovering position over the tarmac at the Shearwater base, stabilizing the heli-jet despite severe wind gusts and heavy rain. He started the vertical descent. Wind shear forced the pilot to manually compensate and after a few tense moments, they touched down. The engines whined as the pilot cut their power. Jim pointed at the *Echo,* barely visible through the gloom a few hundred meters away.

The grounds crew secured the heli-jet once the rotors came to a complete stop, and the pilot faced them. "ATC says you're to go directly to the *Echo.* The crew is already on board and standing by to receive you and the computer."

"Has the London doctor arrived yet?" she asked.

"Negative, ma'am. Got delayed with the storm. ETA is about five minutes."

Jim had already released his harness, and she did likewise. Mary was wide awake now and whispering something to Jim. The aft cargo bay doors swung open and several grounds crew workers in camo slicks entered and set to work releasing the Q and dampener from their restraints. One handed coats to her and Jim and covered Mary up. Then, engaging the antigrav, they guided Mary out and marched toward the *Echo.* She and Jim followed.

That's when Esther noticed the soldiers and heavy military vehicles off to the side of the tarmac. She asked a worker, "Who are they?"

"Royal Canadian Armed Forces, ma'am. We're not expecting trouble, but Mr. Carter insisted on having extra security around to protect the ship, and the base commander agreed."

The ship? Unlikely. She understood who Clayton was really protecting.

Dub and Ish met them at the *Echo* and helped them board. Before heading up the wet ramp, Esther gazed around and saw the Q pulled by tugs toward the rear cargo door. The drone of another aircraft sliced through the wind, and she looked up but thick clouds prevented her from seeing anything. Heavy raindrops stung her eyes. For a second, panic cut through her bones as the day's events replayed in her mind like an infinite dream.

Ish stood at the *Echo*'s doorway and motioned for her to keep moving. When she boarded, Ish removed her coat and hugged her tightly.

"There's dry skins, Dr. Tyrone, in the anti-chamber. Help yourself."

She followed Jim into the changing area, the same compartment where they'd donned envirosuits for the rescue mission on Luna.

"Where's Mary?"

Jim said, "They've taken her to the medical bay." He pointed up the cabin toward the bridge. "That asshole Dub was telling me they not only repaired the ship but also outfitted her with surgical supplies and equipment, and some backup systems or something. I'm joining her as soon as I get out of these clothes."

"He's just doing his job, you know."

Atteberry eyed her suspiciously and grew silent.

After they'd changed into dry skins, they headed toward the flight deck as Ish continued on to help secure the Q. Jim craned his neck to peer into the med bay and walked toward it, but Dub stood in his way.

"Your daughter's secure in medical," he said, arms crossed. "The doctor's gonna board shortly and then we'll launch. Stay here."

Esther had seen that look on Jim's face before, the seething anger ready to explode.

"How is she?" she asked, hoping to defuse the escalating situation.

"Good. Seems happy and looking forward to the ride."

"I'm going to see her," Atteberry growled, a hint of tears began pooling.

"As soon as we've broken Earth's gravity well, you can. Not before. Captain's orders." Dub moved away toward the Q comp, and turned. "Understand?"

He hesitated and glanced at Esther. "Sure, whatever you say."

Dub nodded and continued on his way.

"We're almost there," Esther reassured him. "See?" She pointed to a monitor on the fuselage above their heads. "There's the doctor now."

A short, trim figure, escorted by a couple of grounds crew, loped toward the *Echo*. In the background, another aircraft had parked. This one carried black stealth paint with no markings, and a squad of Canadians, weapons drawn, surrounded it.

Clayton joined them from the bridge, followed by Captain Powell. He greeted them heartily and continued aft to meet the doctor. Powell lingered a moment. "Buckle in, folks. As soon as the doctor's seated, we're taking off."

Jim grabbed his arm. "Be honest, Captain. Will Mary be safe up there?"

"Safer than down here." He paused. "I won't lie. There are hostile ships above, and we may need to engage them, but the first task is to save your daughter's life. We're all counting on the doc to help with that." He left, greeting the doctor and escorting her to the change compartment.

A few minutes later, Dr. Lamont appeared wearing the now-familiar ship's skins, her red hair tumbling about her shoulders, and Dub showed her to the seat beside Jim, across from Esther. They greeted each other briefly, and Clayton grabbed his flight seat along with Dub. Captain Powell checked the Q carefully, then motioned to the grounds crew to secure the doors.

In a moment, he returned to the bridge and occupied the command chair.

Esther prepared for take-off by breathing deeply. The doctor appeared calm, but stress lines showed on her face. Her blue eyes sparkled with excitement, despite the black circles underneath them from a lack of sleep. A surprising hint of jealousy appeared when Jim and Clayton both stared at her.

Where is that *coming from?*

"Have you flown in this thing before?" she asked Esther with a lilt in her voice.

"Yes, we all have. Only a few days ago."

She returned Jim's look. "The only background I have on young Mary is what Dr. Elliot shared prior to the surgery and what the captain said, so I must know everything that's happened since." For the next few minutes, Jim discussed the headaches, the random babbling, the heart attack, and how the CCR medic stabilized her. He also relayed the neurologist's prognosis that Mary wouldn't survive much longer and that her condition was inoperable. "Aye, I've heard that before from conventional medicine," she said. "Still, I canna guarantee anything, you understand?"

"Yes."

"Good. And this fancy computer is ready?"

Esther said, "It's on board but we'll have to power it up, calibrate it, and interface with Mary's brain."

"Excellent." She looked around. "Where's the patient?"

"Mary's in the medical bay with one of the crew," Jim said, "over there." He pointed toward the surgery.

Dr. Lamont unclasped her harness. "I'd like to take a wee peek before—"

Captain Powell's voice over the comms interrupted her. "Please ensure you're strapped in and ready. Take-off in 30 seconds."

Lamont shrugged and clasped the harness back on. Esther watched the monitor and with a gentle lurch, the *Echo* came to life and eased off the tarmac into the low-hanging clouds. In another few seconds, her thrusters engaged, slamming them into their flight seats as she screamed through the rain toward space.

Jim

CATAPULTING THROUGH THE ATMOSPHERE didn't terrify him as much as the first time. The forces pounding across Atteberry's body still shocked him, but his sense of impending doom had decreased significantly. Yet, that was not forefront in his mind.

Mary didn't see her mother die.

Fresh pain tore into his chest. Janet had softened over the past few days—he hadn't imagined this—moving away from being a secret operative and becoming . . . what? The waves of emotion crashed without mercy against his heart, reminders of what might have been.

We could have started anew.

Despite the past 10 years of betrayal, a deeper love bloomed again, more powerful than the first time they'd met. And she'd given herself up to buy them time to escape. That's the part of the last couple hours that tormented him the most. Not because she sacrificed herself for them, but because he couldn't have done the same.

He peered across at Esther, stoic and certain. She'd closed her eyes, not tensely but as if she slept peacefully while the *Echo* roared into space. *Maybe everyone does abandon us in the end with nothing but our old skins and tired bones. I wonder, if after three days of darkness, can we ever find the light again?*

Artificial gravity aboard the ship kicked in as the *Echo*, released from Earth's gravity well, careened toward Luna. Captain Powell announced they were free to move around and suggested that Dr. Lamont attend to Mary. She leapt up and headed toward the medical bay, carrying a kit she'd brought, Atteberry on her heels. Esther remained in her flight seat beside Carter, speaking in hushed voices.

The medical bay featured an enclosed, rectangular area with space for two biobeds and various pieces of equipment he didn't even recognize. The doctor stooped beside Mary, asking her questions and making notes on a data slate. He caught some of what they said, but only a few words registered, like *interface* and *high risk*. When Mary opened her cracked lips to speak, he feigned courage but couldn't stop the tears from approaching.

He struggled. "It'll be okay, Dad. Trust us."

He scratched his beard, but the last vestiges of hope fluttered away, disappearing like dust motes in the recycled air.

Lamont said, "We need to build a neurological interface to drive the quantum computer." She reached into her kit and withdrew a small pouch. Inside was an object the size of a pebble. It glistened in her palm under the harsh light of the med bay lamps. "See this? I'll use the computer to store the alien mind on it."

"What is that thing?"

"A memory crystal," she said. "I've used a prototype before on humans who wanted to preserve their life experiences for future generations."

Atteberry shivered. "You can do that?"

"Aye, and it's more common than you might believe. But," she paused, "the technology is still crude. Once we download the experiences into the crystal, they canna be transferred anywhere else. Not yet, at any rate. And retrieving them has proven a dog's breakfast."

"But that doesn't matter, right Doc?"

"No, not for what we're doing." She bit her bottom lip, cocking her head. "I'll be frank, Mr. Atteberry. The prognosis for Mary's survival isn't good. Talking with her these last few minutes, it's clear that significant merging of minds has already taken place. Parsing out the alien memories is something no one has attempted before, and worse, she's not carrying one other alien mind, of that I'm sure. There's an entire history of that creature's civilization too. When she says *us*, she's talking about multiple souls."

Atteberry swallowed hard and stared wide-eyed at Mary lying peacefully on the biobed. "Is there any chance she'll make it? Any possibility I'll get my daughter back again?"

Lamont shrugged, but her face said everything. This was a longshot, and now the weight of truth settled on him like a stone.

Ish poked her head inside the room. "Need something built, Dr. London?"

"Aye, come here and I'll show you."

Ish and the doctor huddled over her data slate for several minutes. She pulled headgear from her kit and showed Ish the various ports for connecting the cap to the computer. Quigg joined them from the bridge and together, they established a workstation in the corner of the medical bay where he and Ish began constructing the interface circuit for the Q. Atteberry asked the doctor if there was anything more he could do.

"Not at this time. I've taken preliminary scans of Mary's condition and I'll be going in for more detailed imaging posthaste. She's on a new regimen of pain control, and as soon as I test the interface, I'll begin the procedure . . . as long as the pilot keeps us out of harm's way." She bowed hesitantly toward her hands.

"You'll want me to leave."

"I won't force you to go, but it would be helpful, yes." She reached out and touched his arm. "If anything happens . . . I'll call you immediately."

"Thank you, Doctor."

Atteberry kissed Mary on the forehead and brushed the hair from her face. Her skin was ice-cold and clammy. "I love you, Mares." He exhaled, glanced at the doctor, and returned to his flight seat where Esther greeted him. Carter had moved up to the bridge.

Sometimes words didn't fit, couldn't work. This was one of those, and Esther smiled encouragement at him while he stared into the endless cave of his thoughts.

A few moments passed and Carter marched back to join them, concern spreading over his face.

"What is it, Clayton?" Esther asked.

He lowered his voice. "It's not looking good out there. Captain Russo on the *Malevolent* remains in a stand-off with the Prussians. That convoy of other ships is on top of her and word from Earth is the *Sara Waltz* has been repaired and is now en route on an intercept course with us."

Atteberry snapped to attention. "But we can outrun them all in this ship, can't we?"

Carter pursed his lips. "Yes . . . but at some point, we must fight. I can't leave the *Malevolent* to fend for herself against two heavy cruisers and a bunch of trigger-happy mavericks." He paused. "I hope that doctor can get the computer rigged up soon. It'll get a hell of a lot worse around here before it gets any better."

"I don't understand. We came here to avoid conflict and give Mary a chance to live. Fire up this damn ship and let's get the hell out of here!"

Carter's gaze narrowed and bore into Atteberry. "I'm afraid there's no choice. I won't abandon the *Malevolent*."

"You mean . . .?"

"Despite Mary's operation, I just sent a message to Ed Mitchell at Titanius Headquarters. We're about to engage the Prussian Consortium."

The Mergeling

THE FRIEND MARY PREPARES FOR DEATH NOW.

We must save her.

Yes, to show the others our world and our way.

There is a better way than destroying.

We did not see that before. Now we do.

The procedure must take place so the friend Mary can survive.

She will be our advocate.

Yes.

And persuade the humans to cease hostilities toward each other.

Yes.

Let us do whatever we can to help the friend Mary live. She will become the light in this darkness.

Yes.

THIRTY-EIGHT

Kate

THE DESK VIEWER ON THE FAR SIDE OF THE CABIN displayed relative time: two o'clock in the morning. She'd heard fresh guards relieve the pair she befriended almost five hours ago and figured they were bored as shit by now.

And half asleep.

One of the fundamental mantras of the Spacer Program was to focus on personal resourcefulness because they never knew when they'd encounter life or death situations, and space had always been brutally unforgiving. Frequently, she'd pulled herself out of jams by her wits alone. Being held as a captive "guest", she had another opportunity to rely on her past training.

With Keechik's stylus, she'd removed the bed cover and scraped thin strips from the synthetic material. These had a variety of uses, including garrotting. She'd poked a hole in the plastic bedframe and carved out a handful of particulate dust, perfect for temporarily blinding an adversary.

She sat on the edge of the bed now and walked through her plan again. Disable the guards outside the door, return to the cargo hold, gain access to the pod and send a subspace message to Keechik to return and help. After that, several paths opened up, and she'd have to assess the options at that time. Her preferred course was to remain hidden on the ship, creating havoc wherever possible.

Like a mosquito in a dark tent.

Kate stretched, relishing the newfound flexibility of her taut muscles and healed body. After, stylus in one hand and plastic dust in the other, she rapped softly at the cabin door.

Nothing.

Those assholes are probably asleep.

She knocked again, with added emphasis.

This time, she picked up movement on the other side and, following the door chime, the panel slid open. Two heavy-lidded guards greeted her. The shorter one in the back stifled a yawn.

"Sorry to wake you fellas, but I'm not feeling so good and I need to see the doctor."

The tall guard asked curtly, "What appears to be the—"

He never saw what hit him.

Kate simultaneously threw the plastic dust in the short one's face and wrapped an arm around the tall guard's neck. Before he realized what had happened and could reach for his stunner, she drove the stylus into his kidney, causing him to buckle, then unholstered the weapon in a single motion, flipped the release, and scorched his ribcage. The man slumped hard to the deck, blood pooling from the stylus puncture wound.

The remaining guard blinked, brushing the particles from his face and cursing. He stumbled and fell against the bulkhead and, reaching for his own stunner, he punched the comms panel beside the cabin's entrance.

350

"Security . . . Ensign Schmitt here."

He fired in Kate's direction, but she rolled across the deck, avoiding the guard's shot.

"This is Schmitt . . . please respond."

She bounced into a squatting position and, from her knee, blasted the comms hub, sending a shower of sparks across the hallway and killing the security ensign's voice. The guard glanced at the destroyed panel, eyes watering, his mouth agape, his attention torn for milliseconds. In that time, Kate had already targeted his chest and let loose with another volley. He fell to his knees, clutching his charred uniform, toppling face first on the metal deck floor.

Losing no time, she grabbed the fallen guard's stunner and stuffed it under her shirt, and raced toward the cargo hold. But the guard had alerted ship security before she disabled it, and within seconds, they'd be on the scene at her cabin. It wouldn't take a genius to find out where she'd be heading, so this next phase required stealth and speed. As she crept to the aft section of the ship along Deck C, nearing the location above the cargo hold, bootsteps clanged in a staccato march across the steel floor. Kate ducked into a service bay as a trio of guards double-timed it by. Once they'd turned the corner, she continued toward the hold.

Shortly, she found her target: Deck C14. The corridor comprised an array of what appeared to be science labs and medical bays, all dark during the relative night-time of the ship. She peered into one of the rooms and noted the intriguing collection of state-of-the-art space-charting equipment. It reminded her of the Space Operations Lab at the TSA.

Movement down the corridor.

"Hey! What are you doing here?" The crewman stared at the stunner in her hand and grabbed for his weapon. Kate's reflexes were faster, and she levelled him before his fingers touched the holster. The blast of energy caused her to wince.

Across from the labs, a metal staircase was tucked into a corner. She walked calmly to it, peered up and down, then descended toward E Deck and the cargo hold. As she stepped off and gazed around, confirming her location at the primary entrance to the hold, a squad of soldiers marched around the corner led by Captain Beck. They immediately assumed an attack position and aimed their weapons at her.

What they carried were not merely stunners.

"Freeze and drop your weapon!"

Kate gulped, glanced around for an escape route, but found nothing. She dropped the stunner on the deck floor in front of her.

The captain approached her with a calm demeanour. "Fraulein Braddock, I commend you for your efforts. I hoped you would attempt an escape, and you did not disappoint. My team here," he waved easily around, "was getting bored. I thank you for keeping them sharp."

She noted the six soldiers plus the captain. All looked built for combat. Even with the extra stunner under her shirt, the situation appeared impossible. Kate cooperated and said with a strained voice, "Captain, one of your guards outside my cabin is injured. I had no choice but to puncture his kidney. Please send medical attention to him."

"Yes . . . Lange. The medic tells me he will recover perfectly before long. I think he was more embarrassed that he allowed you to trick him than anything else."

"You understand, Captain, I don't wish to harm your ship or crew."

"Quite." He picked something out of his teeth and inspected the squad. They lowered their weapons and stood at ease. "You wish to escape, warn others, find your colleague Mary . . ." He grinned slightly. "And share your, what are they . . . feelings with her father, yes?"

Her face flushed, and she looked away. Artifacts of the truth treatment.

"Now, now, Fraulein, even I have known love in my day. Nothing to be ashamed of. But I cannot allow your actions here to go unpunished. It sends the entirely wrong message to these brutes. I'm sure you agree."

She swallowed.

"Well, shall we away now to the brig where you'll receive proper supervision?" He motioned to a soldier. "Sommer, cuff her."

"Yes, Captain." Sommer was all business. His short-cropped black hair and thick eyebrows gave him a menacing look. He shouldered his weapon and reached behind, pulling out a set of mag-cuffs, and held Kate's arm.

But the soldier had not counted on Kate's resolve.

She grabbed Sommer's arm, pivoted, and snapped his elbow under her before he could blink. Then she pulled the backup stunner from her shirt and emptied its charge across the squad—including Captain Beck—before they raised their weapons and fired. Inside the fallen captain's jacket, she found a semi-automatic Glock and two magazines, which she pocketed. Patting his quivering body on the chest, she said, "Sorry about that," and stole away.

The door to the cargo hold was unguarded and opened when she came within its sensor range. She stepped in and the door *whooshed* behind her. Kate searched the panel beside it and punched the green illuminated button. It turned red and blinked *verschlossen*.

She caught her breath inside the dimly lit space. The hold was eerily quiet, and she needed a moment for her vision to adjust. When it had, she picked out the familiar form of Keechik's life pod off to the side, and raced toward it; however, the pod itself was no longer intact. Its guts had been pulled from the engine assembly and cockpit, arrayed in an organized fashion on a canvas spread underneath.

Kate dropped to a knee, picking through the surrounding parts. "So much for contacting help."

Angry shouts appeared on the other side of the cargo hold door, followed by a series of hammering.

Dammit!

Glancing around, she found no safe place to hide. The only option was to abandon ship through the bay doors or some other portal. Kate raced toward the Controller's box beside the massive access gate, desperately searching for an envirosuit. The box was empty except for a comms panel and a stool bolted to the deck. She looked up and saw a suite of second-floor storage rooms overlooking the main cargo space. The hammering continued, and it wouldn't be long before her time was up. She ran up a metal staircase, taking two steps at a time, and in the second room, she found what she needed: a closet full of envirosuits, helmets, various work-kits for in-space missions. She squeezed into the first suit her size, donned mag boots and a helmet. As she made her way awkwardly down the stairs, the cargo door burst open and several soldiers poured in.

The gloom in the hold worked to her advantage, and she used the brief opportunity to finish descending the stairs and hide in the Controller's box. As the soldiers began sniffing around the alien life pod and searching the area, Kate fired up the control panel, found the screen for opening the cargo bay doors, and punched the power button. Klaxons sounded and a red warning light flashed from the high ceiling.

Countdown clocks throughout the bay showed 10 seconds remaining. Within moments, the massive doors would pull apart and vacuum would rip at the loose material in the hold, including anyone not strapped down. She grabbed the metal holds in the Controller's box. Soldiers shouted and scrambled back to safety in the deck corridor, but prior to the battered door closing, several of them fired live ammo into the shadows, narrowly missing her.

Still, some of the bullets hit an enormous storage container that must have been under pressure. It hissed like an injured animal, caught fire, and threatened to blow. The last soldiers retreated to the deck and the entrance doors *whisked* shut. Oxygen continued spewing from the punctured container, feeding the flames, and Kate resolved to finish opening the massive bay doors and allow the vacuum to extinguish the fire if she had sufficient time to pull it off. In seconds, the latches unlocked and the heavy doors grudgingly rolled open, exposing the room to open space. Whiffs of smoke from the storage container drifted out on the remnants of oxygen.

Kate's mag boots automatically engaged, and she lumbered out of the Controller's box toward the doors. Soon, the Prussians would over-ride her command and close them, so she had to hurry. She glanced around and saw what looked like extra life pods belonging to the *Edelgard*, but before she could check them out, a tremendous explosion flashed behind her. The storage container erupted, sending Kate and other equipment hurtling out the bay entrance into space, narrowly missing the doors. The compression wave crushed her chest and her heart raced. As she spun out of control in space, the *Edelgard* slowly disappearing beneath her, she tried identifying the debris, desperate to return to the ship before it vanished. Stricken with panic, she fought the onset of unconsciousness to no avail. *Edelgard* continued pulling away until she lost track of it completely. Determined to stop the spinning, she controlled her movements to restore balance and, after struggling with vertigo and nausea, finally achieved it. But it was far too late. Beyond the debris field, nothing remained but the frigid stares of stars.

The ship was gone.

THIRTY-NINE

Atteberry

FROM HIS POSITION IN THE *ECHO*'S FLIGHT SEAT, Atteberry watched awestruck as the multitude of ships appeared on the viewscreen. He recognized the *Malevolent* standing-off with the *Volmar*, and at least a dozen smaller craft descending on the scene, encircling the *Malevolent* in a three-dimensional cross-fire configuration. Dr. Lamont had already begun the procedure of isolating his daughter's primary experiences from those of Keechik and god knows how many other of this creature's kind that roamed around her brain.

Esther gasped for air beside him, gaze fixed on the viewscreen too. Then, from the bridge, Captain Powell shouted calmly, "Ready evasive maneuvers, Mr. Jenson. Arm all weapons."

"Evasive patterns delta and bravo-three laid in, sir. Weapons at the ready."

Carter tumbled down the narrow deck to the flight seats and buckled himself in. His face, normally a picture of confidence if not outright arrogance, had become a languid apparition.

"What's happening now, Carter?" Atteberry demanded.

"We're taking up a position to assist Captain Russo."

Esther shook her head. "We can't do that. Lamont's already started the operation. We came up here to avoid conflict, not start one. What the hell is the captain thinking?" Then the realization of what was going on dawned on her. "You bastard, Clayton. You don't want to help Mary or anyone else. You want to take out those Prussian ships and control the mineral runs."

"No, you're wrong. I care for the girl despite what you think of me, and I have no intention of getting in harm's way. Best case scenario? We show some more force and convince the Prussians to stand down and return to their business."

"And the worst case?" she asked.

Carter shrugged. His silence was all the response Atteberry needed. In an instant, he unbuckled the safety harness on his flight seat and landed two blows across Carter's face. The first took the Titanius leader by surprise. The second landed on his upper cheek. Blood poured out of his nose.

"Jim, no!"

Atteberry surprised himself with the anger and violence that overtook his mind and actions. He froze in place, standing over Carter like a champion boxer, then inhaled and raced up to the med bay. The door to the surgery was locked. He pounded on the door, but when no response came, he tore away to the bridge.

The crew was remarkably quiet. Rather than occupy his command chair, Captain Powell stood beside Jenson watching her work the navigation controls and bring the ship in close to the *Malevolent*. Dozens of images presented themselves on the viewscreens. The *Malevolent's* captain was front and centre on the main viewer. On the smaller, secondary screens, Atteberry saw a closeup of the *Volmar*, a wide shot of the convoy of Terran vessels, and what looked like an aft view of the *Echo*.

"Mr. Atteberry, please return to your flight seat and buckle up," Powell said while watching the viewscreens.

"Captain, we can't do this. My daughter—"

He pivoted. "Your daughter is in safe hands. I don't intend to start a firefight up here, but I also have a responsibility to the lives of my crew and to those of the *Malevolent*." His face softened. "Please, Jim. Go back to your seat. I want to help Mary as much as you and will do everything to avoid a conflict."

Atteberry's pain and anger slowly dissipated. He surveyed the bridge. Quigg's fingers flew across the comms station as green lines of data scrolled along the viewscreen above him. Dub had taken up the weapons and shields station beside Quigg. He glanced at Elin Jenson at her navigation station. She caught his look and gave him a brief nod.

"All right," he conceded.

A bright flash lit up the viewscreens.

"Evasive pattern delta, Mr. Jenson."

"Aye, sir."

The *Echo* sheered away to starboard, sending Atteberry tumbling to the deck and causing the *Echo* to shudder and groan under the sudden forces. Powell threw himself into the command chair and strapped in. "Where'd that come from, Quigg?"

"We have company, Captain. The *Sara Waltz* launched a micro-pulse burst from the Earth's atmosphere."

"Any damage?"

"All systems are clean, Captain," said Dub.

"Jenson?"

"Confirmed. We're good."

"What about the *Malevolent*?" He looked at the viewscreen showing the *Malevolent*'s bridge.

Captain Russo entered the shot and opened a channel on her command chair. "*Echo*, do you copy?"

Powell said, "All good here, Laura. We believe that was a Prussian micro-pulse weapon from Earth."

She sat in her command chair, back erect. "Agreed. We've traced it to the *Sara Waltz*." The viewscreen flickered as interference from the burst played through the ship's systems. "Listen, John, that was a warning. They're hailing us and demanding we stand down, return to Earth, or face the consequences." She paused. "Is Clayton there?"

Powell pursed his lips. "Mr. Carter is not in command, Laura. I don't believe it serves our interest to back down but I also have a patient on board undergoing a delicate procedure and don't want to endanger her life." Atteberry had pulled himself up beside the captain.

"Stand by, John." Russo stood and spoke with one of her officers. She shook her head, then faced the viewer. "John, the *Volmar* is energizing her rail guns. Whether or not we like it, we're heading for a fight. Can I count on you for support?"

Powell looked at each of his crew. In turn, they nodded at him.

"No, please." Atteberry pleaded. "You mustn't."

"I've got to know, John." Then, turning, she barked to her crew, "Maximum hardshields. Ready missiles!"

Captain Powell faced the viewscreen. The tension from Russo's crew hung heavy in the air. "Laura . . . you know I've got your back. Dub," he shouted, "ready all missile bays. We're about to go live."

THE FIRST SALVO FROM THE *VOLMAR* ROCKETED across the gap between the two ships, striking the *Malevolent* on her dorsal shields and dissipating into space. The crew of the *Echo* gasped as they watched the two cruisers maneuvering for position. Meanwhile, the armada of secondary ships took up strategic positions on the *Volmar's* flanks. A few of them fired at Captain Russo's ship, but their weaponry couldn't compare to that of the cruiser.

"Let's show that convoy what a firefight looks like," Captain Powell said, confidence and surety in his voice. "A handful of level rail gun blasts ought to settle them down. Dub, give me a Level Two. Target only those ships taking pot-shots at the *Malevolent*."

"Aye, sir. Ships targeted."

"Fire."

Bands of crimson energy flowed from the *Echo*'s port side in a wide dispersion as her rail guns found two of the three rogue, smaller ships, disabling them and casting them adrift.

Quigg said, "Nice shootin' there, Dubs. Sensors show their weapons are completely offline . . . their shields are a-holdin' but at minimal strength . . . life support appears intact." He turned to the captain, smiling. "Them other ships are all high-tailin' it away from the battleground, sir, like a herd of scalded cats. I'd say they got the message."

"For now, perhaps. If *Malevolent* falters at all, they'll come back." Then to Jenson, he added, "Maintain evasive maneuvers, Elin. Keep them guessing and let's use our speed to our advantage and distract them."

"Aye, Captain."

Atteberry refused to return to the flight seats, choosing instead to hang back near the bridge, watching the battle unfold while keeping a watch on the medical bay.

The door to the surgery remained closed.

He glanced back at Esther sitting beside Carter in the flight seats. Her face tensed and her hands gripped the armrests. Carter appeared lost, not even bothering to look at the viewscreen near him. Atteberry wondered what ran through that man's mind now. Clearly, he'd offered the *Echo* for Mary's operation so he could somehow extract the alien technology for his own purposes. In fact, he hadn't hidden his ambition to do that. But now, he slumped in the flight seat, nothing like the bellicose man who'd engineered the most successful Terran vessel and who controlled half the mining runs in the solar system. *Had he finally seen what his ambition had brought him? Caring more about his business and the conquest of space than Mary's life?* Atteberry wasn't about to concede that possibility. Not yet. Perhaps no one had stood up to him before.

Proximity klaxons ripped into his ears. His gaze returned to the bridge and the main viewscreen overhead. The *Volmar* had shifted its attention from the *Malevolent* to the *Echo*. She moved with surprising speed and deftness, coming to bear on the *Echo*'s starboard side.

"Get us the hell out of here, Mr. Jenson."

"Yes, sir!"

The *Echo* slammed hard to port, pitching down the z axis, the forces slamming the crew into their seats and causing Atteberry to fall to his knees. Blasts of enemy rail guns sailed over them as the ship continued maneuvering at top speed.

As soon as the *Echo* regained a smooth trajectory, the med bay door hissed open. Dr. Lamont took a few tentative steps out, holding on to a safety rail, and marched to the bridge. "Dammit, Captain, you've got to stop this ping-ponging around here! I canna continue with the procedure while you're bouncing around from one star to another."

"Understood, doctor, but if we don't continue our course of action, your operation will be moot."

A fresh blast of energy from the *Volmar* sliced toward them.

"Incoming blast, Captain!" Dub shouted. "Brace for impact!"

The captain reached up from his command chair, grabbing Lamont by the waist and pulling her close just as the rail gunfire slammed into the underbelly of the *Echo*, sending shudders reverberating through the ship's bones.

"Mary!" Lamont pulled herself away from Powell's grasp and staggered back to the med bay. Atteberry hauled himself up from the deck, grimaced at the fresh pain in his knees, and stumbled after her. When she arrived at the med bay door with him on her heels, she didn't stop him from entering.

He gasped at the scene greeting him and reach for the jamb to steady himself as all feeling in his limbs abandoned him. Mary lay on her back on one of the biobeds, eyes closed, arms running along her side. The interface contraption that Ish and Quigg built glowed in an ethereal blue light from the back of her head. Multiple wires snaked off it into the quantum computer that, despite its mass, had shifted considerably from the ship's aggressive movements. Connected to the Q was that memory crystal. It, too, pulsed and glowed as if alive.

"Mares . . ." he whispered.

Dr. Lamont consulted with Ish who worked the computer console, and monitored his daughter's vital signs on the overhead viewer. "She's not in a position to speak, Mr. Atteberry, but her physical condition is stable. The good news is we're making progress. I've eased the overflow of information coursing through her brain tissue. If that damn American cowboy up there can only keep the ship stable for a few hours, we might finish."

Atteberry eased himself closer to the biobed. Seeing Mary with all those wires and cables sticking out of her caused him to shudder involuntarily. Yet, her face seemed anything but strained. When she blinked and awakened, focusing on him, her eyes sparkled in such a loving, tender way that his heart melted. His little girl was coming home.

"Mares, you're doing great. The doctor says things are going well."

She struggled to lift her hand, and he took it, holding it against his chest. "No, Dad . . . it's not working. And that's . . . that's okay."

"What are you saying?"

She licked her lips and winced briefly, then said, "We won't make it. We know now. We've known . . . for some time. They're all . . .working to heal this body . . . to keep the pain . . . away."

Panic flooded his body, and he gripped her hand tighter. "Doctor, what's going on? Why is she talking like this?"

Dr. Lamont studied the monitor beside Ish and worry flashed across her face. She checked the interface on Mary's head, then returned to the monitor.

"Dammit to hell and all!"

"What is it, Doctor?"

"There's something wrong with the transference, but I canna—"

"Dad . . . it's all going to be okay . . . We know now . . . We shall not wholly die, and a great part of us will escape the grave."

"Horace?"

Mary grinned.

The *Echo* shuddered and vibrated again as the bridge klaxons continued their shrill cries. Lights in the med bay flickered but remained operational. Atteberry looked from Mary, to the doctor, and finally to Ish. Their eyes met and what he saw in the technician's face petrified him. He'd seen that look before. He'd run from it. He'd tasted it in the deepest throes of darkness throughout his life. He'd witnessed it's horror on the tarmac when Janet was torn apart.

FORTY

Atteberry

LAMONT SHOUTED, "ISH, BRING ME ANOTHER HYPO OF NORDACIL.
Something's not right."

Ish reached for the table beside her and grabbed the hypo,
checked it, then handed it to Lamont. But before the doctor
administered the dosage, Mary said, "No, doctor . . . please."

"Mary, I've got to try. You were doing so well, and I—"

"No . . . we don't want this . . ."

Lamont looked at Atteberry, frowning. All of his words had
abandoned him. All he managed was to hold his daughter's hand close
and watch her sunken face full of peace and joy.

"Dad . . . Daddy . . . we're going."

"We? All of you in there? Are you still my Mary too?"

"Yes . . . some of us are frightened . . . most are not . . . Mary is at peace . . . and curious . . . and loves you more than . . . more than anything."

"Let me help you!" Dr. Lamont reached out to her with the hypo, but she shook her head.

"No . . . the operation could not . . . succeed, Doctor. But," she gulped, inhaling deeply, "your work is promising . . . please . . . keep at it."

"There's something I don't understand," Atteberry said. "If you fixed this ship and did all those other things, why can't you heal yourself now?"

Her eyes watered. "I can . . ."

"You can? Then why . . .?" His words caught in his throat as the cold realization of her actions struck him.

"Ah . . . now you see," she whispered between shortened breaths.

The pain in his throat, in his chest expanded, crushing him. Atteberry was only vaguely aware of the ship's movements now, the rocking and groaning all around him. Ish stepped forward from the console and, despite her professional demeanor, she stared at Mary on the biobed, and gasped.

"Mares, you are your mother's daughter."

The lights in the med bay flickered again, but this time they remained out. Emergency back-up power quickly engaged, so the bay remained somewhat illuminated by the monitoring screens and the lights of the Q computer, and the interface on Mary's head.

Atteberry turned to the doctor. "How much of the transference happened?"

She glanced at her data slate and said, "Approximately thirty percent, but it seems the separation of the alien minds and Mary's individual mind didn't occur. I'll confirm later, but what's likely happened is all her memories have been at least partially transferred to the crystal." She touched his arm. "I'm sorry. There isn't anything more we can do."

He didn't need to hear that. He knew. He also realized that even if Mary could heal herself, she'd chosen not to. For the safety of the human race? Perhaps. Or maybe something special called her away.

Another blast rocked the ship, and the artificial gravity stuttered momentarily. Mary gazed at him. Her face looked like a ghostly, sullen mask in the med bay's dim interior. Her lips quivered.

"Mares . . .?"

She struggled to speak, but no words came. Her lips turned blue as life dissipated. Atteberry stroked her forehead, his body numb, fear and grief flooding every cell of his body. Mary stared at him, her face radiating love, squeezed his hand weakly, and closed her eyes for the last time.

FORTY-ONE

Atteberry

SOMETHING WASN'T RIGHT.

The muted sound of a distant klaxon pierced Atteberry's darkest grief, pulling him back into the med bay. Incoherent voices merged with electronic pings, echoing around him. Someone's arm circled his shoulders.

Esther.

"Jim, can you hear me?"

He slowly lifted his head and turned toward her. Emergency lighting bathed the med bay in a dim cloak. She knelt with him beside the biobed. Mary's face, uncovered, had lost any remaining color or sign that she had ever been alive, and around the room, Dr. Lamont, Ish, and Clayton Carter had gathered.

Still, something wasn't right.

The *Echo* appeared to have lost all motion.

"Can you hear me, Jim?"

Esther's voice morphed out of the random background noise. "Esther, do you see?"

She glanced at the bed and had no reply.

"The captain needs you. Right now."

Her words washed over him as grief gripped him anew.

She shook him. "Jim, please. We can't stay here."

Atteberry moaned, and she helped him rise from the cold med bay floor. Ish and Lamont mumbled condolences at him. Carter stood like a petrified sentry, staring at Mary's corpse, his cheeks sunken and dark. Esther guided him out and walked with him toward the bridge. A veil of smoke floated above the operational consoles, and a thick smell of burnt circuits filled the air. When he discovered the *Volmar* hovering bow-first in front of them like a predator, and the *Malevolent*'s shattered hull scattering a massive debris field in the distance, the reality of the fire fight struck him.

How did Mary know this?

"Mr. Atteberry," Captain Powell said, "I'm sorry for your loss, but I'm afraid grieving will have to wait. See that ship? The *Volmar*. She took out Captain Russo's vessel and disabled our engines and shields. We've lost our mains and weapons are offline. Now they're demanding we give them... your daughter."

"No..."

"I said she didn't survive, but they don't care. They still want her."

Elin Jenson interrupted them. "Sir, proximity scanners show the *Edelgard* is also in weapons range, although she's operating with some aft-ventral damage. And the *Sara Waltz* has joined in. ETA to our position... two minutes." She turned to him. "Three heavies, sir."

"Status of their weapons, Mr. Jenson?"

"No change. *Volmar* has us targeted and locked. The others are keeping their powder dry."

Powell snorted. "Sure, they don't need much to finish the job now."

From the other side of the bridge, Quigg shouted, "Incoming hail from the *Sara Waltz*, Captain."

"Establish contact, Mr. Quigg, and put it on the main viewer."

"Aye, sir."

Atteberry steadied himself against Esther, holding her hand as he processed the humiliating request of giving up Mary's body. The ping of the Prussian hail and Esther's rough gasp caused him to look up at the viewscreen. There, on the bridge of the *Sara Waltz*, surrounded by dark uniformed crew members, stood Benedikt Winter smiling like a cat in a sunbeam. He limped forward, closer to the viewer.

"Herr Professor, it's good to meet you again. I only wish it was under better circumstances."

Atteberry's jaw clenched. His grief dissipated, replaced with white-hot, surging rage. He fought to maintain control.

"This has been quite an eventful few days for us, hasn't it? First, you rescue your daughter on Luna from that nasty alien business. Then you somehow evade us en route back to Earth when all we wanted to do was talk and be friends. How you managed that remains a mystery." He paused and his face adopted a sympathetic regard. "Then when I and my colleagues desired only to help Fraulein Mary, your ex-wife shows up and meddles in everything. Shattered my leg. I can't say I'm sorry she died. I only wish it had been . . . slower."

Atteberry squeezed Esther's hand. She whispered under her breath, "Easy, Jim. Ignore the bastard."

He grit his teeth and released his grip.

"And now," Winter continued, raising a hand and studying his fingernails, "here we are. Captain Powell, you are aware you're surrounded. We know your precious little ship is compromised, so making a run for it would turn out badly for you."

Powell folded his arms across his chest. "What do you want, Winter?"

The Prussian sipped from a steel cup and narrowed his gaze. "You know exactly what I want, Captain."

The bridge grew deathly quiet as everyone turned to Atteberry. Almost imperceptibly, he shook his head. Powell returned his focus to the viewscreen. "We're not prepared to give you Mary under any circumstance."

Winter sneered coldly and picked something from his teeth with his tongue. "Well, that's a problem, Captain Powell, so let's play out the scenario. If you choose not to cooperate, then we will simply board your craft and take what we need, killing you or anyone else who stands in our way."

"I'll play those odds any day," Powell announced and motioned to Quigg to cut the transmission.

Ish joined them on the bridge, followed by Carter, who'd lost all his bravado and seemed as nervous as a freshman navigating a college campus for the first time. *Oddly, he's taking Mary's death harder than any of the others.*

"Where's the doctor?" Powell asked.

"In the med bay, sir," Ish responded. "She's . . . preparing things."

"Understood." He turned to face the entire group. "Folks, this won't be easy. We have minimal hand weapons and we're up against a highly trained force. You all saw what they did to the *Malevolent*. If any of you would like to surrender, tell me now and I'll relay the information to the Prussians." He paused. No one said a word.

"All right. Dub, arm as many of us as you can. We'll expect them to board through the primary airlock so we'll set up a perimeter there." Dub nodded. "Ish, make sure the doctor understands what's happening and help her in the med bay."

"Aye, sir."

"My crew . . . it has been an honor serving with you. Let the name *Echo* resonate through the stars."

Jenson and Quigg resumed duties at their stations while Ish raced to the med bay. The captain joined the small group of Atteberry, Esther and Carter. "It's not too late to change your mind."

"About surrendering?" Esther asked.

"Yes."

She stiffened her back. "Not a chance."

"Clayton?"

The big man mulled over his words carefully. Atteberry expected him to agree, and was surprised when Carter found his deep voice again and proclaimed, "No, John, No. I built Titanius, this ship, and opened up vast possibilities for all humankind. These people destroyed Laura Russo's ship." He grit his teeth. "I refuse to bow to these thugs."

The captain looked Atteberry in the eye. "And you?"

Atteberry returned his gaze, fresh resolve coursing through his veins. "In some ways, Winter is absolutely right: I have been through a wringer these past few days. While trying to save my family, I've lost my precious daughter and my ex. This fills me with a searing pain no man should ever suffer." He stepped forward. "But I won't let that asshole take Mary's body and butcher her up to exploit and humiliate her remains. She deserves the care and honor that any of us would want when our time comes. No, I'll fight to protect her and Janet's memory to my last breath."

"Captain!"

"What is it, Quigg?"

"Aft cargo bay doors on the *Sara Waltz* are opening." He turned. Atteberry detected the hint of terror in his voice. "An armed mule is on the way."

FORTY-TWO

Atteberry

DUB HANDED ATTEBERRY A STATE-OF-THE-ART laser pistol and showed him briefly how to fire. He did likewise to Carter and then to Esther. She held the weapon in her palms, looked wearily at Jim and said, "I can't use this." He squeezed her shoulder.

"Where's Ish?" Dub glanced around the bridge, sweat dripping from his face.

"Still with the doctor in the med bay," Atteberry replied.

"Dub, you and Jim tell them to finish up and prepare to be boarded." Powell was all business again, his attention now focused on the Prussian mule—at least three times the size of the *Echo* with a complement of her own rail guns at the ready—easing from the aft belly of the *Sara Waltz* and firing her inertial thrusters.

The two men circled around to the med bay. Dub glanced at Atteberry before he pressed the manual door override and stepped into the grim room. What they saw stopped them in their tracks. Deep purple, swirling light poured out of the area. The Q pulsed as if generating the energy itself.

"Ish? The hell?" Dub growled.

Dr. Lamont strode toward the two men, a data slate in one hand and a diagnostic tool in the other. "It's all right, I assure you," her brogue thickening.

Atteberry, mesmerized by the amethyst glow from the quantum computer, muttered, "What's happening?" He glanced at the vacant biobed. "Where's Mary?"

Lamont swallowed. "I've put her body in the morgue compartment here. She'll be fine until the situation settles down and power's restored. When we return to Earth, she'll have a proper burial."

"You don't understand, Doc," Atteberry said. "We're about to be boarded and the Prussians *want* her . . . remains. They plan to dissect her and reverse engineer her brain . . . scrape it for that alien technology. They mustn't take her. We can't give them access to what's left of her."

Lamont's impatience surfaced, and she blurted out, "That's why her body is where it is! Sorry, I don't want to come across as uncaring because, believe me, I'm anything but. However, Janet Chamberlain briefed me fully on the importance of keeping your daughter's body, and so has Ish. I understand what's at stake." She exhaled, stepping closer, gathering her thoughts. "Now there's something *you* don't understand." She pointed to the Q.

The wavering purple glow from the machine caught his attention again. "What's going on with that thing?" The quantum computer hummed and whirred. Perched on a physical interface platform, the memory crystal cast rays of other-worldly light into the shadows of the gloomy medical bay.

"Before Mary passed, we extracted some of the data in her brain and fed it into the memory crystal. I haven't parsed it yet, and I still don't understand how to separate her unique mind from everything else in there. The energy we see now is the crystal processing that data."

Atteberry panicked. "Oh my god, could the operation have succeeded if Mary allowed you to continue?"

The doctor ran her long fingers through her fiery hair. "Uncertain, and I don't wish to speculate. Her body was frightfully weak, and her major organs were barely functioning."

Carter stumbled into the room, interrupting the conversation. "The captain says we have only a few minutes to prepare for boarding and to . . ." The purple light distracted him. "What's going on here?"

Atteberry straightened his back. "Some material in Mary's brain was transferred to the crystal."

"How much?"

The bastard can't help himself.

Lamont raised a finger and swiped her data slate, showing it to Ish and nodding. "If our calculations are correct, and I'm confident they are, then at least 65% of her brain's holdings were downloaded."

Carter grabbed the slate and checked the computations himself. "If what you're saying is true, this changes everything. There's a strong possibility that you captured knowledge of the alien technology on this rock."

"Yes," the doctor said. "In fact, not only a possibility. A *probability*." She retrieved the device from Carter and adjusted the controls on the Q. "The crystal is completing its processing, and then we'll find out how much."

The *Echo* shuddered, causing the group to stumble and catch their footing. Atteberry and the others looked up at the med bay viewscreen in time to witness the Prussian mule latch on to the port side like some hungry, mechanical lamprey, covering the airlock in its massive ship-to-ship coupling maw. Voices rose from the bridge, and Atteberry left the clinic to join the crew. Ish and Dr. Lamont remained behind.

Powell faced them as they approached. "They'll gain entry soon. It won't take long to override the airlock controls. Time to prepare." Just then, the familiar ping of an incoming hail rang through the bridge.

Quigg shouted, "It's the shuttle, Captain."

"Put them on the viewer."

"Aye, sir."

Winter's face appeared, surrounded by a dozen men and women heavily kitted with weapons. Some wore envirosuits. "Captain Powell," he began, "This is your last warning before we board your crippled vessel. If you wish to fight, we shall comply and kill you. However, if you surrender, I assure you we will treat you all fairly and return you to Earth, to your families and your friends. You have thirty seconds to respond."

Powell motioned to Quigg to mute the transmission, then said, "I understand how some of you feel about the Prussians, but I'd like to ask you again: give up and live. Or fight and surely perish."

No one spoke for a moment until Carter stepped forward. "John," he said, clearing his throat. "I have learned so much from these voyages, not only about the capability of this ship but also about your resolve, your fine crew, and my own unsettling, misguided ambition. A few minutes ago, I was prepared to fight, to avenge the *Malevolent*." He drew in a heavy breath. "But not anymore. I wish to live so I can make things right . . . to use this new technology for more noble pursuits." He looked directly at Esther, his eyes full of a newfound passion that Atteberry had not seen in the man. "I think we should surrender."

"And give up the *Echo*'s secrets?" Powell asked.

"There will be other ships, John, that we can build with this new knowledge. Other voyages if we stay alive long enough. As long as we can protect that memory crystal and give the Prussians what they want, nothing can stop us, and my focus now is on the future. There are better, more important goals, for me to pursue . . . out there." He bowed his head, clasping his hands behind his back.

"What about the rest of you?"

Dub grunted. "I don't surrender."

Esther looked between Carter and Atteberry, conflicting emotions clear on her face. She bit her lip. "I'm sorry, Jim, but I want to live, too." She moved closer to Carter and took his enormous hand in hers. He wrapped his arm around her shoulders.

Atteberry shook his head. His stomach twisted as indecision rattled his brain. What could he possibly live for anymore? Mary and Janet were both dead, and the Prussians had captured Kate.

Kate ...

But what drove him more than anything was revenge, and he wouldn't find that by succumbing to others' wants. He may have suppressed his rage against Winter momentarily, but it had not diminished. He studied the mule on the viewscreen.

"What do you say, Jim?" Esther asked.

He continued chewing on the swirling emotions and thoughts straining for superiority in his head. With his family gone, Esther siding with Carter, and no desire to return to the classroom, he preferred to stay and fight, give Mary a proper burial. Nothing would make him happier than to break that bastard's neck for ruining his future with his family.

He exhaled, his confidence returning. "Captain ... Esther ... I'm going to—"

"Stand by!" Ish came running up to the bridge. "Captain, there's something you've got to see. Quigg, you too. We need you in the med bay."

"No can do, y'all. They're hailing us again, Cap."

"Ask for another minute, Quigg. Stall as much as possible until I find out what's happening. The rest of you stay here until I call." Powell followed Ish down the corridor.

Quigg opened the channel and spun a yarn about the crew making their final preparations and securing the ship. He noticed Winter remained on the mule's bridge while the rest of the soldiers prepared their equipment. He asked in his jovial way for a few more minutes."

"You task me, Herr Quigg, but I'm a reasonable man," Winter mused. "I shall give you one more minute before the shuttle crew cuts into your hull. It would be a pity if the seal around your airlock fails, so do not attempt anything stupid. I remind you we've trained our rail guns on your bridge."

"Much appreciated there, *Herr* Winter." Quigg smirked, muted the transmission and added under his breath, "You lying pissant."

OVER A MINUTE PASSED AND THE SOUND of heavy metal on metal clanked along the length of the *Echo*'s hull. Rhythmic vibrations funnelled through the deck flooring and Atteberry fingered the weapon in his hand. "I don't know what they're up to back there in the med bay, but I'm not waiting around for those assholes to board. Carter, you shit, do you really think the Prussians would let us walk away? They'll take your ship, and Mary's corpse, and glean all the information they need to establish their dominance. They won't even need that stupid crystal." He brushed off the others. "I won't let that happen. Dub, you with me?"

"You know it." The big man adjusted the combat gear on his waist and chest, then raced aft toward the airlock.

"Anyone else?"

Quigg edged closer to him, then doubt appeared to cross his face. "If push comes to shove, y'all can count on me. But if there's a chance to repair the *Echo*, I gotta put my effort there first."

Esther and Carter both looked away. The navigator, Jenson, said, "I have to stay here and work on restoring power to the engines, but like Quigg, I'll be with you when the time comes."

Atteberry pushed the hair from his face and marched down the deck toward the rear of the ship to join Dub. The normal lighting in the *Echo* remained compromised—only the hazy emergency lights flickered as the *Echo* drifted in space . . . powerless and vulnerable. As he approached the med bay, waves of purple light flooded out from the open door, casting eerie shadows across the corridor and sides of the ship, playing tricks with his exhausted mind. He slowed. The last thing he wanted to see was that crew hovering over the spot where Mary died, focused on their precious science even as some ugly soldiers prepared to board and destroy them all. Still, curiosity pulled at him and he glanced into the room.

Dr. Lamont stood in the center of the bay, holding the memory crystal in her palms. Captain Powell carried a data slate and was punching through the ship's schematics up on the monitor. Ish adjusted the controls on the quantum computer while monitoring the crystal's emanations through the Q's sensors. Atteberry poked his head inside. "People, what are you doing? The Prussians are knocking on the door!"

"Calm down, Jim," the captain said in a soft, commanding tone. "In a matter of minutes, we'll know whether this crystal will either save us or destroy us."

"But how—?"

The doctor walked the crystal over to the mechanical interface on the Q and placed it on a flexible input port. "Mr. Atteberry, remember, this crystal contains some of the information held in your wee bairn's brain. I canna determine yet how much or whether we can access any of it, so here's the dilemma."

A fresh wave of thumps and high-pitched vibrations running through the deck interrupted them. The Prussians were closer to cutting their way through.

The captain continued while Lamont latched the crystal firmly in place. "We may be able to use whatever information and energy is on there to restore power to the ship. However, if we can't then we'll have no choice but to destroy it."

"That would mean eliminating whatever's left of Mary's mind with it."

"Yes."

Before Atteberry responded, the doctor said, "Engage the interface, Ish. Quickly, we've got company." Ish pulled on a thick plunger switch and the massive computer hummed, coming alive in a flurry of sounds and flashing lights. The overhead monitor scrolled at inhuman speeds through the library of schematics, pausing occasionally at different circuits, then continuing its torrid pace. At some point, Ish had enhanced the connections between the Q and the ship's computers, for streams of energy darted from it and raced through the *Echo*'s circuitry. More lights flashed and were restored.

Various pieces of equipment in the med bay stuttered and blinked momentarily until everything went dark again.

"What is it?" Atteberry swallowed hard, throwing a cursory look aft where Dub had taken a defensive position near the airlock.

"Doctor?" Captain Powell tossed the data slate on the biobed and pulled his weapon from a holster. He met Atteberry at the door."

Lamont checked the crystal's interface on the Q. "Dammit, everything looks solid. We should at least be getting a consistent signal. I mean, it may not work at all and that's the risk, but even with the prototypes back 'ome we had steady signalling." She followed the cables joining the mechanical interface to the input ports of the computer.

The *Echo* shuddered, and the vibrations ceased.

"They've busted through to the airlock, Captain!" Dub's voice, higher than normal, wept with adrenaline. "I could use some backup anytime now."

"I'll go," Atteberry said and took a step aft.

"No, Jim. You stay here. If they break through, we must protect this machine."

"Or destroy it, right Captain?"

Powell didn't answer. Instead, he strode aft, holding his weapon hand high, and joined Dub near the airlock. Through the dim haze, Atteberry watched their activity on a monitor and saw chunks of the *Echo*'s hull being ripped away by mechanical claws. He caught glimpses of Prussian hands poking through the widening gap in the airlock's outer port. In moments, they'd be through and pounding on the ship's inner door . . . the only thing standing in the way between them and their captors.

"Try it again, Ish!"

The technician raced through a series of connections and tests as Atteberry entered the med bay. Ish scrambled through the sequencing, finishing by throwing her weight at the plunger, her skilled fingers manipulating the Q's controls and causing the machine to groan to life anew, but it whined and stuttered again, casting darkness into the surrounding gloom. The memory crystal pulsed sporadically now, emitting fresh waves of brilliant purples and lavender, interspersed with flashes of blue.

"Still not right, Doctor," she said. "But I've traced the issue down to—"

Powell's voice cut through the activity on the intercom in the med bay. "They're through the airlock. All hands prepare for whatever you must do next."

Atteberry glanced out the entrance toward the bridge, straining to see in the dark. Carter's arm wrapped around Esther in a protective, defiant pose, his free hand holding one of the *Echo*'s weapons. *Perhaps he will fight after all.* Her eyes met Atteberry's and her lips curved upward in a tender display of other-worldly hope. Her entire body adopted a relaxed pose, as if in joyful resignation to whatever fate would bring. *She's found her peace . . . and shortly I'll find mine.*

FORTY-THREE

Atteberry

"DAMMIT IT ALL TO BLOODY 'ELL!"

"What is it, Doctor?" Atteberry asked. "Tell me what's happening."

Lamont ran her hands across her face. "I don't understand why this isn't working. On the prototypes, with a fraction of computing power this beastie holds, I've been able to isolate the downloaded information and feed it into various libraries for storage. We still couldn't access it, but the mem crystals never behaved this way. I simply don't know why this procedure dinna work like the others." She looked at him with desperation. "Is there anything Mary told you that might give us a clue? Something about her neural pathways or what to do if the method failed?"

Atteberry considered the question. "I don't know, Doctor!"

"Think, dammit, we're running out of time!"

Dub's voice floated through the ship. "Come on, you bastards. Come on . . ."

Ish looked up, panting, sweat glistening off her forehead. "When Mary spoke about the painful overflow of information in her brain, she often referred to how much it hurt, how much there was."

"Yes, that's obvious given she carried around the alien's memories." Lamont shook her head. "So is that the only difference? Too much data for the Q to handle?"

Atteberry narrowed his gaze. *Something more is happening here.* "I doubt that. I mean it's possible, since we understand little about the alien, but Mary never mentioned it when she checked out the computer back at the TSA. She spent a lot of time going through it. If there was a capacity problem, she would have said something, but I remember her words exactly: *This bandwidth can help us. Some of us don't think so, but most of us do.*"

"Right, well I'm afraid that's . . . wait, what did she say again?"

Shouts from the aft section of the *Echo* snatched his attention away. He peered around the med bay door, weapon drawn at the ready beside his head.

"Jim! What was it she said to you. Exact words."

He glanced back, his attention torn. "Ah, this bandwidth can help us, Doctor. She said this can help us. And then, *some of us don't think so, but most of us do.*"

Ish drew her own gun and took a step toward the entrance.

"Not yet, Ish," the doctor barked. "I've been looking at this all wrong. Instead of treating combined minds as a singular data stream, I believe there must have been several more memories from many other souls in her brain. She used the plural pronoun *we* all the time with us, but I don't expect she meant only the merged mind with the creature. That's why she must've been interested in the Q's bandwidth. She was a multividual."

"A what?"

"A multividual, Mr. Atteberry. Not one mind, but several, increasing the amount of knowledge in her brain by a factor of . . . god knows! And if that alien was the keeper of its entire civilization, consider the massive volume of data. She must've focused on preserving their society, holding on to as much of it as she could until we transferred it. It's amazing she could communicate at all with so many of those voices clamouring for attention."

"But how does this help us?"

"It's a long shot, but if my understanding is correct, what's needed is more space. Not only storage for memory codes, but computational power." She looked at Ish. "Can we tie in directly to the ship's artificial intelligence center?"

"Yes, I believe so."

"Then do it." Lamont reconfigured the crystal in its holder and reset the controls.

BRILLIANT GREENS AND TURQUOISES SPEARED TOWARD HIM from the back of the ship amid shouts. "They're breaking through the last airlock port, Doctor. Whatever you're doing, you'd better make it quick!" Atteberry wiped his sweaty palm against his pant leg. His mouth had gone dry. As he watched the action unfold around the portal, memories of Janet and Mary flashed through his mind. Someone else crept in there too and lingered longer than he would have expected, confusing him in an uncertain, unfamiliar way.

Kate . . .

Adrenaline surged through his body and along with everything else happening in the med bay and the cutting noises at the airlock, his mind latched on to another desire: *find Kate.*

"Try it now, Ish! I've reconfigured the crystal to interface with an infinite number of quantum minds, not simply one."

"Are you sure, doctor?" Ish yelled. "It may backfire on us and there's enough destructive power in this computer to destroy the ship!"

"We've no choice. We canna let this fall into the hands of the Prussians."

"But—"

"Do it!"

Ish scrambled around the Q and yanked on the controls. Again, the room lit up with flashes of light as the *Echo*'s primary systems flickered and sparked, searching for consistent power. She struggled with the massive plunger switch, so Atteberry abandoned his post at the entrance, tucked the weapon in his belt, and ran to her side. The piston refused to budge.

"The crystal's stabilizing!" Lamont monitored the energy outputs on the overhead viewer. "Don't stop now!"

"Come on, Ish," Atteberry groaned as he pushed his weight against the lever. "We're almost there." The two grabbed the Q's arm and heaved it downward, but it wouldn't yield. "Again," he shouted, and they threw their bodies into it, but the plunger remained fixed.

The unmistakable *screech* of pulsed laser-weapons fire interrupted the cyclical thrum of the computer. Atteberry turned to Ish. Panic showed across her face, but she held an impressive, firm resolve. "This time let's do it. On three!" He counted up, and they slammed their bodies into the lever. Ish screamed as she strained against the handle. Seconds, maybe minutes passed—he couldn't tell—then at the precipice of giving up, it nudged under his hands. Atteberry pushed his muscles, howling alongside her, releasing all the tension and pain that he'd buried these past few days, pushing his body to the brink of failure.

The piston groaned and yielded, slamming into the body of the Q. With it, the room lit up as blue and purple streaks of energy pulsed through the med bay and slashed throughout the ship. Atteberry and Ish collapsed on the metal deck, spent from the effort. She rose first, hauling herself up against the computer, adjusting the machine as it purred with newfound vitality. She turned to face him. "The crystal . . ." she panted, "it's re-energizing the ship's cells." She checked the monitors and her brow furrowed. "And doing it like nothing I've ever seen before."

He drew himself up to a kneeling position, mesmerized by the flash of energy and the return of the *Echo*'s power and lighting systems.

I've seen this show before. He recalled what Mary had done to evade the Prussian cruiser firing at them.

CAPTAIN POWELL RACED INTO THE MEDICAL BAY, his face covered in sweat and grime from the firefight. "What happened here?"

Lamont answered without taking her eyes from the monitor. "We figured out how to properly interface the memory crystal with the ship's computer."

"In English please, doctor."

She glanced at him impatiently. "Isn't it obvious?"

"Not to me." He poked his head around the med bay door, squeezing the weapon's trigger, laying down covering fire. Carter's voice bellowed from the bridge as more weapons blasted toward the airlock. Atteberry rose and took up a position beside the captain, his weapon drawn.

"The Echo . . . is broken . . ."

The voice, a synthetic mix with little inflection, floated through the ship like some other-world herald through the intercom.

Powell wiped the sweat from his face. "The hell is that?" he muttered. He stared at Lamont and punched the panel near the door. "Quigg, give me the status of the ship's computer."

A moment passed before the officer responded, "Power being restored, Captain, but functionality is way different."

"Are the engines on line yet?"

"Negative, sir." He paused. "Well, I mean, they are, but there's another system comin' on stream . . . things I ain't never seen in my life."

"Quigg!"

"The Echo . . . is broken . . ."

"Dammit, what *is* that?" Powell shouted as he peered around the med bay entrance. Smoke floated like an amethyst fog through the corridor as the purple and blue energy continued flowing through the hull and bulkheads.

"If I had to guess, Captain," Lamont started, "I'd say your ship's primary computer is undergoing a . . . transformation."

Footsteps raced down the deck from the bridge, and in a moment, Carter appeared in the doorway. "John, there's something strange happening to this ship."

"Take cover, Clayton, for the love of—"

"No need, John. Have a look at this."

Powell squinted at him.

"Come and see."

He stepped outside the med bay, joining Carter in the corridor, following his gaze as he peered astern. Atteberry followed, weapon raised, then Ish and Lamont poked their heads around the doorway. At the end of the corridor, through the smoke and haze of the recent firefight, a green shimmering force field separated half a dozen confused Prussian soldiers from the *Echo*'s interior. Atteberry glimpsed Dub's lifeless body smeared across one of the flight seats, his torso charred beyond recognition, amid smouldering viscera. The acrid smell drifted through the still air. Three enemy corpses littered the deck on this side of the barrier.

"The *Echo* seems to have grown a mind of its own, John," Carter said. "You should see what's happening on the bridge. Quigg's beside himself, and Jenson's in a frenzy, trying to keep up with all the mechanical changes taking place."

"What do you mean by that? Is the ship out of danger?" Powell held his weapon high, his senses on full alert.

"You already know this force field isn't manifested through the ship's AI. Then there's the reconfiguration of the engines and weapons systems, and the new shields she created. It's as if the ship is undergoing mechanical autophagy, consuming broken parts and creating something new in her wake."

Powell stared at him incredulously. "Self-reparation, Clayton? Impossible."

Carter laughed nervously. "That's the point, John. Even though we don't understand it, the *Echo* is not only repairing herself, but healing herself, too. I can describe it no other way."

Powell and Atteberry lowered their weapons. Lamont looked cautiously at the captain. He threw a cursory nod, and she raced to the bodies on the deck, checking for any vital signs. At each one, as she confirmed their deaths, she paused, bowed her head and closed her eyes. Meanwhile, Ish had followed her and secured a defensive position, her gun aimed at the Prussians milling about in the airlock on the other side of the force field. One of them fired at her, but the energy barrier absorbed the shot.

"I don't understand this *auto* thing," Atteberry stated, his voice quivering from the receding adrenaline rush, complemented by the germination of an unfamiliar notion. All the sharp aches and pains surfaced anew from the punishment his body had been through. In particular, his knees and the lower section of his injured leg when they escaped New Houston screamed for attention. He leaned against the bulkhead, determined to bury it all. Lamont, noticing him, approached with her data slate and took his vitals.

Carter explained. "In our own bodies, when cells die, they break down into their constituent molecules and atoms and those that are still relatively healthy are built into new cells. The *Echo* is doing the same thing. Whatever sorcery is in that memory crystal, it's now a part of the ship, somehow working with our primary computers to reduce spent systems, rebuilding them into modified elements I've never seen before."

Esther approached from the bridge and joined the conversation. Her cheeks flushed from the excitement, and Atteberry couldn't tell if it came from the new science or from the threat to their lives. "It's chemistry and physics that's way beyond anything we understand," Esther added.

"But how?" Powell asked.

Dr. Lamont pulled out a hypo and administered it to Atteberry. "Perhaps I can explain." She glanced at him and returned her focus to the group. "In our experiments to date, we've been able to preserve a person's memories by interfacing their brain with a high-powered computer and storing their information on memory crystals. But we haven't figured out how to access those memories through subsequent connections with other intelligent machines. I mean, we're working on it, but not there yet. Too many variables." She looked at the force field. The Prussian soldiers were setting up an enormous weapon. Lamont frowned.

"But at least two mechanisms are in play here," she continued. "First, the quantum computer allows for processing significantly more data. That gave us the chance to download a massive amount of information from Mary's brain."

Atteberry twinged at the sound of her name. *They have reduced her to another piece of equipment.* His grief rose. And yet, there was something more . . . other . . . on the cusp of awareness, teasing him.

The hell . . . ?

"But I also believe that by connecting the Echo's primary computers to the Q and the memory crystal, that data has somewhere to go."

Carter crossed his arms. "Are you saying, doctor, that the information Mary held in her brain—the knowledge that led to her death—is in my *ship?*"

"Captain," Ish interrupted from down the corridor. "I don't like the look of this!"

The Prussians had assembled a massive, spider-like weapon on their side of the barrier and aimed it squarely at the bridge. They wore envirosuits with helmets, expecting the possibility of a breach, and seemingly not caring.

Quigg shouted from the command well, "Captain, comms are online and the mule is hailing us!"

"Route it to the viewer down here, Quigg."

Several of the viewscreens along the corridor sprang to life, and an image of the Prussian shuttle's bridge appeared. Benedikt Winter stood against a backdrop of a massive console. His demeanor had changed from the smug arrogance of a brief time ago. Now, he wore the mask of anger bordering on hatred.

"Ah, Captain Powell. I commend you for the subterfuge. You fooled us into thinking your precious *Echo* was dead in the water. What is that old English expression again?" He paused, placing a sarcastic finger against his chin. "Yes, 'playing possum'. Perhaps not exactly appropriate here, but nevertheless, your ruse worked. That internal force field of yours is impressive."

Powell glanced at Carter, refusing to answer.

"So you leave us with no choice but to blast our way in." He stepped closer to the camera, his face filling the viewers. "I shall have the girl, and I shall have your ship. Any notion you may have entertained about surrendering is irrelevant now. I shall take what I want and destroy what I don't. And since you and your shitty crew task me so much, I should enjoy watching you die in the darkness of space." Black replaced his image on the viewscreens.

Captain Powell sighed and pursed his lips. Resolve grew in his steel-grey eyes as he addressed the gathering. "Put on your skins and brace yourselves," the captain announced calmly. "Either we survive the next few minutes and return to Earth," he said, "or we die trying."

"No skins, sir," Ish said. "They're in the storage hold near the aft port."

The group looked at each other. "Let's prepare for what we can." Sweat broke out on the captain's face. "Carter, you and the others seal yourselves in the med bay. Ish, I'll join you down there at the barrier."

"Nothing doing, John," Carter replied. "I'm fighting with you. This ship is morphing into something amazing. I must learn more, and protect her."

"I'm with you, too," said Atteberry, standing tall.

Powell glanced at the invaders moving about. "Very well. If this force field comes down, fire at will and pray the hull remains intact." They marched down the corridor and took positions near Ish, facing the eerie green energy disk. The Prussians appeared ready to power up their weapon. Two operated it—one was a gunner wearing a sadistic grin under his helmet, and the other standing nearby with a guidance controller was the targeter. The others had retreated through the latching portal to the mule.

"All hands, defensive positions," the captain shouted.

Atteberry knelt, ignoring the fresh pain spiking through his legs, and readied his weapon. The Prussian gunner fired with an emphatic slap of the trigger mechanism, and blinding light flashed with an unrivaled intensity. The ship rocked underneath them, scattering him and the others across the ship's corridor, vibrations following them, scurrying through the hull and reflecting from all hard edges. Fire shot through his nervous system as he plunged into darkness.

SEVERAL MOMENTS PASSED BEFORE ATTEBERRY regained his senses and remembered where he was. He lay prone on the *Echo*'s deck floor. When he looked up, Ish squatted close by, rubbing her cheek. The captain stood beside her, his attention fixed on the force field that remained in place, shades of green flickering on his face. As for Carter, he was on the floor as well, apparently unconscious.

When Ish raised her head and followed the captain's gaze, she brought a hand to her mouth and gasped. Atteberry grabbed a handrail on the ship's bulkhead and pulled himself up. He turned to see what had happened and shuddered, pulling his head away, choking back vomit.

It was enough that he saw a gaping hole in the side of the *Echo* where the Prussian vehicle had attached itself.

It was enough that he saw their damaged mule in a free spin, gyrating away from the ship.

It was enough that he saw the mangled remains of their weapon, strewn with broken body parts now floating in the zero gravity of space, bumping into the interior bulkheads of the ship's hull and drifting out into the void one part at a time.

But even though the destructive blast was impressive, the force field protecting them from the full darkness of space and certain death remained intact. That's when Atteberry heard the odd, yet strangely familiar voice again through the *Echo*'s comms system. He couldn't make out the words at first, but after rubbing his ears, there was no misunderstanding.

"The Echo is . . . broken."

FORTY-FOUR

Atteberry

SLABS OF NEW METAL SKIN APPEARED TO GROW directly from the *Echo*'s frame like ice crystals, spreading from point to point, sealing the horrendous gash where the Prussian mule had been. Within minutes, the breach had been sealed and the force field instantaneously evaporated.

Atteberry massaged his temples and pulled his strength together. When he looked up again, Carter was standing and he and the captain trudged off to the bridge where they embraced the crew, their nervous laughter floating on the air.

Ish stood in front of him, smiling. She secured her weapon and hugged him. Her jet-black hair fell around her face and tears welled in her deep, brown eyes. "I'm glad you're okay."

"You, too."

She smiled, her mouth set resolutely, and turned when Atteberry quickly added, "Ish?"

"Hm?"

"Thank you for helping my daughter feel . . . comfortable. I know you did everything you could in there."

They walked together and joined the doctor in recovering the dead bodies in the ship's hallway. They were about to move them into the med bay when voices on the bridge rose. They all ran up the corridor, stopping sharply, staring at the transformation that had taken place. The once practical and traditional cockpit had been replaced by a curved, horseshoe console configuration. Navigation and Comms were still in the same positions as before, but now additional screens and controls had emerged. Lights flashed as various systems came online. The main viewscreen displayed the *Volmar* holding her position in the distance, nose forward. The mule struggled with her flight control and listed sharply to starboard as she approached the *Sara Waltz*.

Powell turned to Jenson. "Are the engines operational?"

She ran her fingers cautiously, back and forth over the alien console,. "Aye, sir, I think so."

"Quigg, what's the *Volmar* doing out there?"

The Comms officer hovered over the redesigned panel a moment, then tentatively punched a couple of buttons and the heavy cruiser appeared on screen with a running stream of data. "Sensors show weapons systems are disabled . . . engines at five percent capacity."

"Life support?"

Quigg turned. "Minimal, but satisfactory." He shrugged. "Captain, I don't understand."

"Neither do I. What's the status of the mule and the *Sara Waltz*?"

"Not good, sir. The blast breached the shuttle's hull. Environmental control is dwindling. No shields. Mains offline. The *Sara Waltz* has minimal life support functions. No weapons."

The captain squeezed the armrest. "It appears with the *Volmar* out of commission and the *Sara Waltz* unable to rescue her crew, it'll be up to us. Open a channel to the shuttle and make sure the heavies copy."

Atteberry objected. "After they tried to destroy us? Are you crazy? We should get the hell out of here and let those bastards roast in hell!"

Powell ran his palm across his forehead. "Look around you, Jim. The fight's over."

Atteberry shuddered at the sudden rush of evil in his heart. He wanted to make Winter pay. He craved revenge, but something in the captain's demeanor gave him pause and he knew, deep within his soul, that lashing out would never bring his daughter back. Or Janet. *Or Kate.*

"Ready to transmit on standard frequencies, sir."

"Thank you, Mr. Quigg." Without raising his voice, Powell cleared his throat and said, "Prussian shuttle, this is the *Echo*. May we render assistance?"

White noise punctuated the image of the crippled vessel as the main viewer switched to the incoming reply. A few seconds passed before they established a transmission link to the disabled ship. Winter's ragged face appeared on the viewer. Blood smeared the side of his cheek and smoke filled the bridge. A bulkhead behind him had given way, exposing the internal workings of the mule, along with burned circuits and venting pipes. Winter dragged himself closer to the viewer, spitting blood from his cracked mouth.

"This . . . is far from over," he growled. "The *Volmar* will—"

"The *Volmar* is incapacitated, Winter, and so is the *Sara Waltz*. Somehow, the force field that protected us and destroyed your shuttle also damaged the cruisers. They're both on life support with limited flight capability."

Winter wiped his chin with the back of his mangled hand.

"We're prepared to bring you and any other survivors on board and return you to your vessel."

Winter's shoulders slumped. "There are no others." He grimaced, clenching his teeth, and it was clear to Atteberry the man was dying.

"Tell me, Captain . . . what happened to your ship out here? I . . . I should like to understand."

Powell cocked his head. "That remains a mystery." Then to Jenson, he added, "Pull in line with the mule, starboard side."

"No, Captain. I fear . . . it's too late. I tip my hat . . . to you and your fine crew."

"Mr. Jenson, take us in."

The navigator worked the console a moment, then lifted her hands in a gesture of defeat. "I can't, sir. I still have no manual control."

"Aren't those engines online, fully powered?"

"They are, sir, but we're not controlling them." She leaned forward as one of her console monitors blinked. "Hang on. The ship's plotting its own course."

"Over-ride it, Jenson."

"It won't let me, sir."

Powell bit his bottom lip and clenched his fists, but his voice remained calm and measured. "Can you tell where we're heading?"

"Yes, Captain," she said, turning toward him. "Luna."

The *Echo* accelerated in a burst of power Atteberry hadn't felt before. He grabbed the side rail beside him as g forces pulled on his chest. Carter and Esther held each other stoically, standing tall and clinging to the back of the Captain's command chair. The ship jolted as main thrusters—or whatever they had turned into—fired anew and the vessel arrowed away in a sweeping arc toward the Moon, leaving the two disabled Prussian heavies and the shattered mule adrift in space.

"Steady now, Mr. Jenson, set a new course and bring us around. The other cruiser, the *Edelgard*, is still out there."

Jenson keyed in various coordinates to the navigation console, but the ship continued rocketing on its way. "I'm sorry, Captain, I have no control over this."

"Explain."

"It's . . . it's the ship, sir. The *Echo* herself. Like she has a mind of her own." She examined her console. "I can't re-program the ship's AI or any of her systems."

"I think I can explain that, Captain." Dr. Lamont appeared on the bridge, clutching her data slate in both hands across her chest. She acknowledged the others with a brief nod and stepped forward in front of the command well. The captain, Esther, and Carter closed around her.

"I gather it has something to do with transferring knowledge from Mary?" Powell steadied himself as the ship adjusted flight path.

"Yes. So much is conjecture, but I'll tell you what I believe happened based on the data I've collected." She cleared her throat. "One thing we discovered about Mary was that her brain contained not only the memories of this creature—"

"Keechik," Atteberry interrupted. "Its name was Keechik."

"Right, not only this Keechik creature's experiences, but those of several other minds." She turned to Atteberry. "Jim, remember she kept talking about we and us? Well, I thought she referred to herself and the alien, but the evidence suggests there were literally hundreds of separate minds captured in her thoughts too."

"You mean, when she said 'we', Mary meant other individual creatures?" Esther asked.

"Check out the data yourself, Dr. Tyrone." She handed the slate to Esther and pointed to a series of graphs on the screen. "See here? Each stream has a unique signature. This one is Mary's. It's the only one we know with a human stamp. At first, I believed these others contained noise and other sorts of mechanical irregularities, but after filtering them, it became clear they were individual traces."

Esther swiped over the graphs, pausing, shaking her head. "Remarkable," she finally said, handing the slate back to Lamont. "And all this time we had no idea. Jim, why wouldn't she tell us? With all this activity overloading her brain, she must have known."

Atteberry rubbed his eyes. "She never hinted at anything like this. Doctor, are you sure about your data?"

"I'm confident I've interpreted these signatures correctly. What they truly mean will require a lot more work and proper equipment in my lab back home."

Powell raised his head. "How does that explain my ship running amok?"

"Right . . . the *Echo*." She licked her lips. "Remember when the transfer took place and the Q couldn't interface with the memory crystal? It's because until now, my only concern was transferring one data stream . . . one human's memories to the crystal. With Mary, I attempted to download two because of the merged minds, but as you can see, we're dealing with hundreds, possibly thousands. When I reconfigured the computer to accept an infinite number of streams, that's when the system stabilized."

Carter stroked his chin. "But that still doesn't answer how the *Echo* has become . . . *sentient.*"

"Yes, well, I discovered the memory crystal couldn't receive all that information. The Q is powerful, no doubt about that, but it wasn't built for multividual processing. That's where the *Echo* comes in." She turned to the captain. "When I interfaced the Q with the ship's primary AI, the data streams had somewhere to go."

"The hell?" Powell frowned.

"They merged with the ship's own intelligence network."

"Dammit, doctor!" Carter bellowed. "What are you implying?"

"It's rather clear, don't you see? Whatever knowledge all those alien minds held now courses through your ship. You know, Mr. Carter, you were absolutely right about the notion of autophagy. The ship *learned* how to break down matter and reconfigure it into something different. Dr. Elliot had mused about this possibility, but we never believed it possible. Esther," she said, "you've seen what's happening here. Have you ever witnessed anything like these changes in your lifetime?"

"Not at all."

"Captain, if I may, the ship saved our lives only because of the alien minds within. You didn't understand how to construct a force field to keep the Prussians out, but the altered ship mind did. And who predicted the Prussian weapon would somehow be redirected back at them, disabling their shuttle and incapacitating their cruisers? Mr. Carter, I'm no engineer, but even I could guess you dinna design her this way."

"Indeed not. The *Echo* is a science vessel, a scout primarily. We built her on a new engine platform that . . ." he looked around and shrugged. "Now those engines seem obsolete in the face of these alterations."

"All well and good, Doctor," Captain Powell declared, standing straight, "but I must gain control of the ship. How do I do that?"

Silence filled the bridge. The numbing pain of loss rose again in Atteberry, but he ignored it. He would grieve later, back on Earth.

"Mr. Jenson, are we still on course for Luna?"

"Aye, sir," she answered, "and our ETA is two minutes to high lunar orbit."

"Any sign of the *Edelgard*?"

"Sensors are picking up a debris field, Captain, and what appears to be . . . yes, it's the *Edelgard*," she peered up from her station, "but she's disabled too. Minimal propulsion, and weapons are offline."

Powell glanced at Dr. Lamont. "Don't tell me the *Echo*—or whatever this vessel has become—somehow disabled that cruiser, too."

Lamont shrugged, but Jenson responded. "Sir, that ship was damaged from the *inside* out." She magnified the image on the primary viewer. "See there? The cargo bay portal aft of the primary hull? Completely blown out. Whatever did that also ripped out the main engines."

"Something else crippled the *Edelgard*," he whispered.

The modified *Echo* slowed as it approached the debris, ignoring the Prussian cruiser. The primary screen automatically switched from the *Edelgard* to a wide-field view of the flotsam, zooming in and scanning individual pieces as if looking for something.

"Now what the hell's my ship doing?" Carter stepped toward the console. "Dammit, how do we get control back?"

Quigg reported from the Comms station. "Captain, I've got an incoming transmission. Way down in the mud and all, and unintelligible. Applying filters, noise reducers, and boosting the receiver."

"The *Edelgard*?"

"Don't think so, sir. It's comin' from that there debris field." He threw the captain a quizzical look.

Powell and Atteberry exchanged glances.

"On speaker, Mr. Quigg."

The sporadic signal filled the bridge with white noise and static. Quigg was right: they detected a modulated frequency in it somewhere, but the interference was overwhelming. It reminded Atteberry of Kate's original filter, the one he applied to his radio astronomy equipment six years ago . . . the one that led to the discovery of the Ross 128 alien . . . the one that, now, terminated in Mary's death.

"Quigg," he asked, "how do you access the ship's AI?"

"Why, I usually input whatever command I want through my key pad. Sometimes it's verbal, or punched in. It all depends on the situation. Except now—"

"Okay, I've got an idea. If part of my daughter's mind is also in this ship, she may have passed on some memories of her own, including Kate Braddock's subspace filter. If we could only communicate with her, apply knowledge of that filter to this noise, we might pull it out."

"Y'all are crazy, beggin' your pardon. "

"Maybe. But then . . ."

"Then let's try talking to the *Echo*," the captain commanded. Powell positioned himself in front of the main viewer and raised his voice. "Whoever or whatever has taken control of this vessel, identify yourself."

The only response he received was the static-filled crashes of the receiver.

"*Echo*, this is Captain Powell. Can you understand me?"

The bridge consoles blinked again and an unfamiliar power surged through the metal deck and rail. Something Clayton Carter and the doctor said played through his thoughts. The knowledge Mary held must have infiltrated the ship's primary computer systems, perhaps merging with it or, more likely, overwhelming it. As a result, at least some of that intelligence had been used to rebuild the ship with more advanced technology. . . taking the old Titanius material and recycling it into new. The alien minds, quite possibly, understood the need to keep Mary alive."

He peered around the bridge at the dishevelled group. Anxiety hung thickly in the air.

"Whoever you are, this is—"

"Captain," Atteberry interrupted, his voice soft and tired. "May I try?"

Powell swept his arm in a *be-my-guest* motion. Atteberry stood next to Quigg at the Comms station. Trust was a curious animal, and even though he only knew Mary as a trusting soul, perhaps that trait had morphed into something other, too. If true, there may be some way he could reach her, or whatever she'd become. He inhaled deeply and, after clearing his throat, whispered, "Mary?"

No response.

He pursed his lips and stared into the faces of the assembled crew. Perhaps Keechik and the other aliens overwhelmed her residual mind. "Mary, are you there? We need Kate's filter to hear this message."

The only response was the ubiquitous hum and whirr of the ship's functions.

Atteberry lowered his head and prayed.

"Mares, it's your dad. Is there any part of you now that remembers me?"

And then the sound rose. The oddly synthetic voice he'd heard in the med bay returned, causing his skin to crawl. It sliced through the noise generated from the debris field.

"*You are the one Atteberry.*"

Everyone turned to him with bewildered stares. Carter and Powell looked confused and alarmed. Dr. Lamont nodded silently, as if her transference theory now had proof. He gazed at the viewer. "Yes, I'm Jim Atteberry . . . who or what are you?"

No one spoke. The only sound reverberating through the ship was the low thrum of the engines pulsating as extra power surged through their redesigned thrusters. Intermittent pings and chimes from the command console perforated the air.

"Who are you?" he asked again.

This time, the *Echo* responded.

"*We are the ship-mind . . . we are Mary.*"

.

FORTY-FIVE

Atteberry

ESTHER AND DR. LAMONT HELPED ATTEBERRY regain his footing. At the
sound of the ship-mind's name, he'd collapsed to his knees beside
Quigg. As he rose and thanked his comforters, relief overwhelmed
him. A renewed sense of optimism swept through his body. "Esther,"
he said, "do you realize what this means?"

She grinned like a proud parent. "Yes. In a way, Mary is still alive."

Captain Powell joined them. "Tell me, Jim, how did you know?"

"I didn't, but I had a hunch from what the doctor and Carter talked
about." He winced as he brushed his knees. "Let me try something
else." He faced the main viewer that continued showing a sweeping

action through the debris field. "Mary, do you remember Kate Braddock's subspace filter? The one we used to detect the Rossian signal several years ago?"

The ship-mind responded. *"The memory is with us."*

"Good. Do you recall how it worked?"

"The algorithm is within us."

"Can you access that code and apply it to the signal that Mr. Quigg detected?"

"Working . . ."

Within moments, the image on the viewer switched from a sweeping motion to a targeted view on the Western limb of Luna, near the *Mare Marginis*, where the *Echo* first encountered the alien vessel. Quigg whooped with excitement.

"I got it!"

"On audio, Mr. Quigg," the captain said.

"Stand by . . . switching frequencies . . . now."

The transmission was choppy and reverberating, as if the voice was underwater. "*Echo*, this . . . *Edelgard* . . . Come . . . Over." It's muted, heavy distortion suggested a male survivor had escaped whatever damaged the cruiser.

Powell responded, "*Edelgard* survivor, this is Captain John Powell of the *Echo*. We copy. Transmit your coordinates and we'll pick you up."

" . . .(static) . . . understood . . . transmitting . . ."

A few moments passed. The *Echo* continued facing the *Mare Marginis* but remained at port velocity, holding her position. Quigg punched some of the controls in front of him. "Got it, sir. The survivor's out there right where the ol' *Echo* is pointing. Western limb. Hey Jenzie, I'm sending you the coords."

"Thanks . . . got them," Jenson answered, "but I have no control over the ship's helm. We're still locked out."

Atteberry said, "Mary, can you restore control of the ship to Mr. Jenson?"

"We will comply."

In an instant, the panel in front of Elin Jenson blinked to life and she hurriedly regained her flight seat. After studying the console for a